MW00466775

Maybe she had used poor judgment, but it was for a good cause...

He practically had righteous indignation billowing out of his ears now, and while its companion was anger, that was at least something she could work with. Better than the cold stone wall he'd presented her at first.

"Okay, you're right. I absolutely showed poor judgment. But let me explain. Just look at it from my point of view, Dante. It was an easy five-hundred dollars from Vince, another hundred from the crowd, a sure win, and only thirty seconds of—" She bit off her words and gulped when the muscle in his jaw tightened and his eyes, already angry, darkened to black ice. "Look, it's not like I cheated on you, or like it will ever happen again." Maybe she'd screwed up, but he could at least show a willingness to straighten things out, couldn't he? She was making an effort to apologize here. "I made a mistake, and I'm truly sorry. I won't do anything like that again." She implored him with her eyes. "Will you please forgive me? *Please.*"

He glanced away, and when he looked back at her the stone wall had reassembled itself. "I apologize for not being clear before. We're done now, Brenna."

Brenna huffed out a long breath and threw her hands up. "Fine. We'll talk more after you get home tonight."

"No, we won't. You don't understand. When I said we're done, I meant—" He cut himself off. His eyes stared into hers and the cold hardness gave way to regret and then to resolve. "This relationship is over, Brenna."

His words washed over her in an icy wave of realization. Her insides shriveled, and it was a moment before she found air.

"You—you're breaking up with me over this? This stupid, *stupid* challenge and the idiotic thing I did to win?" The burn of unshed tears crept into Brenna's throat. Nausea swirled again and she swallowed it back.

Full understanding settled over her, and her hand shook

when she clutched his arm. "Dante, please don't do this."

"You basically sold yourself for five hundred dollars to someone you know I detest, someone whose single goal in life is to hurt me any way he can, and you did it just to win a contest." He softened his tone. "I'm sorry, but we're not coming back from this."

She hates to lose…

Competitive barista Brenna Kinkaid loves a challenge, and she'll do whatever it takes to win, especially when it comes to her nemesis, Dante Caravicci. But when forced to team up to save their best friends' wedding, Brenna recognizes that Dante might just be her ultimate win.

He plays to win…

Restaurateur Dante Caravicci won't quit anything until he can claim success. He's bided his time, but he's used to taking big risks and surviving, so he figures he's got nothing to lose by playing for Brenna.

Hearts at risk…

These two fall fast, and it looks like a win-win—until a competition pits them head-to-head and one of them goes way too far. A nudge from an improbable source may be the only way these two competitors will ever admit that the only way to win is to lose their hearts.

KUDOS for *Love to Win*

In *Love to Win* by Lisa Ricard Claro, we are reunited with the Kinkaid and Walker families and also with Dante Caravicci, the gorgeous hunk who lives next door to Brenna Kinkaid and constantly annoys her. Brenna is waiting for Mr. Right to come along, the man who her late brother Jack said he gave her number to. But Jack has been dead for five years now, and the man hasn't called. And then when a man does come along who claims to be the blind date Jack set up for her, Brenna is disappointed that it isn't Dante. But things are not as they seem, and the blind date turns into a disaster. But then Brenna and Dante team up to save their best friends' wedding, and the two decide that maybe there is something there, after all—until a competition puts them at odds with each other and threatens to destroy what they had begun to build. This was my favorite book in the series. I have always had a thing for Dante and thought he was such a great character. The story is well written and shows how things can go from bad to worse when two stubborn people are involved. A heartwarming, heartbreaking story that will have you laughing, weeping, and sighing. ~ *Taylor Jones, Reviewer*

Love to Win by Lisa Claro is the third installment in the *Fireflies* series, and Claro doesn't disappoint. Our heroine Brenna is an independent, self-confident, and stubborn young woman. She hates to admit she's wrong, but she's left with little choice when she discovers how wrong she has been about our hero Dante Caravicci. Dante has had the hots for Brenna since he first laid eyes on her just after her brother Jack's death five years earlier. But he got off on the wrong foot with her from the beginning. Now as she gets to know him, she discovers that most of her first impressions about him were wrong. Brenna has been waiting for five years for a man her brother wanted to set her up with to call her. Then when he finally appears, Brenna is upset that the man isn't Dante. But when she goes out with the man, she finds out that she has been betrayed and the date disintegrate into a nightmare. And it's Dante to the rescue. As Dante's life-long nemesis tries to throw a wrench into Brenna and Dante's budding relationship, the two lovers are forced to make some hard choices. *Love to Win* is a poignant and heartwarming story about a woman who takes competition too far and a man who believes that the only way to win is not to play—a thought-provoking and entertaining read that should appeal to romance fans of all ages. ~ *Regan Murphy, Reviewer*

ACKNOWLEDGEMENTS

My deepest thanks to:

Lauri Wellington, Faith, Arwen, and the rest of the team at Black Opal Books. I appreciate you.

Melissa Stevens at The Illustrated Author for making the last of the "gazebo" covers as gorgeous as the previous two.

Capt. Hayden Hodges with the Georgia Clarke County Sheriff's Office for answering all of my questions pertaining to Georgia law enforcement. I appreciate your expertise and time. Any errors contained herein are solely my own.

My gal pals: Terry Lynn Thomas, partner in wine—er, crime—critiquing, plotting, planning, retreating, goal setting, and nose-to-the-grindstoning—thank you for being there. Special thanks to Rochelle Spurlock and Leslie Hachtel who accepted my frantic last minute read request and knocked themselves out to help me meet deadline on this. Thank you!

Kristan Higgins, author extraordinaire, for your extreme kindness when I was at my lowest and craziest point in this publishing journey. You threw a lifeline of sage advice and understanding. This "bathroom lady" will be forever grateful for your generosity.

Joe Claro, love of my life, who never complains when "Just give me five more minutes!" turns into an hour; who took it upon himself to do extra household chores so I have more time to write; who believes in me, encourages me, and shows me every day what real romance is. Thank you for being mine.

To Cheryl —
Thanks for
your support!!
God bless —
JR Claw

Love

to
WIN

Fireflies ~ Book 3

LISA RICARD CLARO

A Black Opal Books Publication

GENRE: CONTEMPORARY ROMANCE/WOMEN'S FICTION

This is a work of fiction. Names, places, characters and incidents are either the product of the author's imagination or are used fictitiously, and any resemblance to any actual persons, living or dead, businesses, organizations, events or locales is entirely coincidental. All trademarks, service marks, registered trademarks, and registered service marks are the property of their respective owners and are used herein for identification purposes only. The publisher does not have any control over or assume any responsibility for author or third-party websites or their contents.

LOVE TO WIN ~ Fireflies ~ Book 3
Copyright © 2015 by Lisa Ricard Claro
Cover Design by Melissa Stevens
All cover art copyright © 2016
All Rights Reserved
Print ISBN: 978-1-626945-07-4

First Publication: JULY 2016

Published by Black Opal Books **http://www.blackopalbooks.com**

DEDICATION

For Joe, my real-life hero.

Chapter 1

"Take the Dare, take the Dare!"

The chanting of the crowd inside the Lump & Grind coffeehouse blasted through Brenna Kinkaid's head. She blamed it for the rhythmic throbbing at her temples that reinforced her new hatred of Saturdays.

Brenna, owner of the Lump & Grind, stared at the scrubby slip of paper in her left hand on which one of her customers had scribbled: *Truth—are you the one who got Mrs. Feinbacher high on pot brownies in high school?* In her right hand she held a torn scrap of lined yellow paper daring her to *kiss the first man who walks through the door.* Neither owning up to the brownie incident—which she had certainly spearheaded, but *for the love of God, Mrs. F, it's been thirteen years, let it go!*—nor kissing some random redneck stopping into the L&G for a cup of joe, held the slightest appeal.

Damn the mayor of Bright Hills and her Truth or Dare campaign, anyway. So what if it was for a good cause? Brenna thought it was ridiculous, but when every other shop owner in town had agreed to this harebrained idea, what could she do but be a good sport and go along?

The rules of play were simple enough. During the week, customers dropped suggestions into the Truth or Dare jars at their favorite businesses, along with a dollar for the privilege of doing so. Every Saturday, the business owner withdrew one suggestion from each jar and read them aloud. Patrons put money toward their preference, and whichever collected the most was what the owner had to do, resulting in often hilarious results. Last week the Truth had collected more money than the Dare, and Brenna had been forced to admit that her first kiss had taken place behind the Bright Hills Middle School bleachers with a boy named Hugh. Hugh, by happenstance, was seated at a table enjoying a vanilla latte with his boyfriend, Milton, and had regaled the crowd with his version of the kiss, teasing that it was the reason he decided to come out of the closet.

Yet, as ridiculous as this fundraising campaign was, it appeared to be working. Brenna had collected nearly three-hundred dollars in just six weeks, her weekend business had doubled, and the residents of Bright Hills, Georgia, were reaching into their wallets to support the drive toward having their own police department. Bright Hills was growing, and though the Truheart County Sheriff's Department did a good job of patrolling, it was past time that Bright Hills had its own top cop. All the money collected in the Truth or Dare campaign would go toward this cause, and the business that collected the most money by the end of the fundraiser would win a trophy to be put on display in their place of business.

No one expected the collections to fund a police department, but it was a start toward community awareness and involvement.

And, as with everything she did, Brenna intended to win.

"Hold on, hold on. Just give me a minute and let me think about this." Brenna lifted her gaze from her hands to regard her patrons, all of whom had shown up for their Saturday purchase of designer coffee and to watch her squirm. "Unless one of you wants to toss in more money to break the tie, I have to decide which one of these is the least likely to scandalize my mama."

"I believe your mama wants to know if you're responsible for the brownies." The gruff voice belonged to a shrunken crone in purple stretch pants and an orange smock with a row of geese embroidered across the front. Her lips formed an uncompromising line, and she hid what Brenna suspected were disapproving eyes behind a pair of cat-eye sunglasses, embellished with faux gemstones the color of lime Jell-O.

Brenna ignored the woman, much as she had done while suffering through her chemistry class in high school.

"Here's another ten bucks for the Dare jar." A man waved the bill over his head and stepped up to the counter.

Brenna forced a smile when he stuffed the bill into the plastic collection container. One of her regular customers, he sported a bushy beard and John Deere cap snugged over his balding head, and Brenna thought it would be nice if the big lug would look at her eyes instead of her boobs for a change.

"Thanks for your donation, Duke." *Eyes up here, asshole.*

He lowered his voice and leaned toward her. "Maybe I can step out and then step back in again, be the first man to walk through the door." He leaned his apish forearms on the counter and forced his eyes upward for the purpose of giving her a broad wink.

Brenna held her smile, and temper, in check. Beating the hell out of a customer via a verbal tongue lashing would be bad for business, and if there was one thing Brenna protected, it was her business.

She leaned in as he had done and sugared her tone. "I don't think your wife would approve."

Duke blinked and dropped his gaze back to Brenna's chest. "She wouldn't care."

Brenna gritted her teeth.

"I've got another five for the Dare jar." Brenna's childhood friend, Raelynn, who had grown up to be the best hair stylist in the county, stepped up to the counter and moved Duke out of the way with a solid body chuck. She adjusted her pink-tinted bangs with a toss of her head. "Moron."

Duke made a show of adjusting his cap before he shuffled away to wait for Brenna to make good on her Dare.

"You ever think about playing hockey?" Brenna asked.

Raelynn grinned. "How many more Saturdays do you have to do this?"

"Through the end of July." Brenna waved at the crowd to quiet them down and raised her voice to be heard. "There is no longer a tie. The Dare jar collected the most, unless anyone wants to put fifteen dollars into the Truth jar to tie it up again, or twenty to beat it." She raised her brows at Mrs. Feinbacher who deepened her disapproving frown and clutched her patent leather purse close to her chest. Brenna sighed. "No? That's it then. I guess I'm kissing the next yahoo that walks in." The crowd clapped and whistled, and Brenna lowered her voice and said to Raelynn, "Honest to god, honey, this every Saturday morning Truth or Dare thing is getting old fast. And you should see some of the suggestions I have to throw away. What's wrong with all these people that they come out and actually pay good money for this?"

"Bubba-Jo's has a big crowd, too, and Dante's Bistro is packed right now, thanks to this Truth or Dare thing." Raelynn's dimples popped out when she smiled. "Last week Dante's Dare won, and he had to prank call the mayor. Omigod, it was hilarious. He called her private number, put on a Northern accent, and pretended to be a Boston detective trying to solve a murder." Raelynn laughed, a boisterous sound that traveled above the chatter of the Lump & Grind crowd. "He really played it up."

Brenna frowned. Raelynn, like everyone else in this town, thought the owner of Dante's Bistro was all that and a bowl of Ben & Jerry's. Why, she couldn't understand, because she thought he was as annoying as an eye tic. "What did he pull out of the jar this week?"

"No idea. I ran over here when I saw Mrs. Feinbacher coming in." She cast a glance at the old lady and looked back at Brenna when Mrs. Feinbacher wagged a finger at her. "She's scary. And she has a memory like an elephant."

The bell on the L&G door jingled and the crowd whooped and clapped. Brenna looked past Raelynn to see who had come in, and her chest constricted. Of all the men in Bright Hills, why did *he* have to be the first one to step through her door?

"Speak of the devil." Raelynn fanned her face and gave Brenna a look. "As Dares go, you could do a whole lot worse than kissing Dante Caravicci."

The man in question glanced around at the noisy crowd. It was apparent that their delight was aimed at him, and he played it up and gave them a bow worthy of a royal court.

"Hey, Caravicci, the Dare won. You have to kiss Brenna!" someone called out.

Dante straightened and shot a bemused look over the collection of people, then modified his expression into a comical leer. "Reaaally?" He wriggled his brows and twisted an imaginary mustache. The group went wild, clapping and whooping.

Brenna rolled her eyes. *Why, oh, why, oh why?* But she wanted to win this thing, and winning meant playing along and having every possible person in this town on her side, so she brightened her expression, came around the counter, and put her hands on her hips. Vamping it up for the best Mae West impression she could muster, she flashed her dark-lashed dusky blues at Dante. "Is that a pistol in your pocket, or are you just happy to see me?"

Dante dropped his head back and laughed along with Brenna's customers. The infectious humor seeped into her, and she found herself laughing with them, feeling both ridiculous and pleased that her supporters were getting such a kick out of her goofy role play. This would translate into a bigger crowd next Saturday, and Brenna would never complain about more people coming into her little place to order their designer brew.

"Well, c'mon." She wriggled her fingers in a *come here*

gesture. "The Dare is that I have to kiss the first man who walked in, and that's you. Let's get this over with."

Dante stepped up to Brenna and smiled down at her. "I'm taking Cal to lunch to keep him busy before the wedding. I just dropped by to see if you need any help."

"Thanks, no. You just keep Caleb out of our hair. He's not allowed to see Maddie before the ceremony."

"I know. Maddie already gave me my marching orders."

"You gonna kiss her, or what?" someone hollered.

"Keep your pants on," Dante said over his shoulder and, a moment later, he grabbed Brenna and swung her into an unexpected dip.

Brenna gasped and clutched his shirt while the Lump & Grind exploded with approval. Wide-eyed, she watched his face lower toward hers, and panic whooshed through her. She didn't want to kiss Dante Caravicci. She especially didn't want to suffer through it in front of an audience. Never mind that the man was a special kind of eye candy. He had the whole sexy-Italian-male thing going for him, the bastard—hair and eyes the color of rich espresso, and olive skin that made him look like he'd just enjoyed a few hours at the beach. At the moment, the lower half of his face bore just enough growth of beard to tell her he'd shaved that morning, but too early in the day to keep him smooth for the evening wedding. His Mediterranean heritage, she figured, was to blame for the sexy stubble.

Damn it, she hated giving him a positive critique.

When he was close enough to hear her lowered voice, she said, "Listen to me, Neanderthal. If you stick your tongue in my mouth I'll bite it off. Understand?"

Dante smiled and shook his head. "You have no faith in me at all, Brenna. Relax and enjoy making your customers happy."

"Don't you dare—"

"I would never," he assured her in a silky voice that sounded a lot to her ears like a promise that, *Oh, yes, he absolutely would.*

Dante touched his mouth to Brenna's, a mere hint of a kiss, a feathery whisper. She clutched his shirt tighter and braced herself for what she expected to follow. And how would she handle it?

Make the decision now whether you'll let the jackass have his kiss and please the crowd, or follow through on the threat to make him bleed.

Kissing Dante Caravicci was not something Brenna had fantasized about. *Much.*

She didn't like the man, whom the Fates had decreed would live next door to her, and then made them neighbors again with their downtown businesses located on opposite ends of the same block like a pair of mismatched bookends. A perfect metaphor, she'd often thought, for their relationship. They'd been at odds right from the start, and no matter how good looking he was, or how his lips moved over hers now with a skillful pressure that raced tingles across her skin, he was still the jackass Neanderthal who irritated her beyond reason just by breathing.

Breathing. Hers faltered when he captured her lower lip between his and increased the pressure, drawing it in ever so slightly for one, two, three seconds before releasing her mouth altogether. He executed one more tender brush of his lips against hers and, a moment later, she was upright again, shaky, and surprised that he'd not pressed his advantage.

Smiling down at her, he took her hand in his. Following his lead, and to the delight of her customers, they took a flourishing bow.

"Encore, encore!" someone yelled.

Everyone laughed, and then that became the chant. Brenna wagged her finger at the crowd, included a negative shake of her head, and moved back behind the counter.

"Sorry, y'all, but Truth or Dare is over for this week. Be sure to drop in suggestions for next Saturday."

Dante rested his arms on the counter. "So you're all set, then? You don't need anything from me?"

Just the sight of you walking away, she thought, but her

mama had raised her better than to say something rude like that, especially since the man was being so pleasant. She allowed more agreeable words to claw their way past the sarcasm. "No, but thank you for asking."

"You sure? Stuff for the cake? Something else for the reception?" He leaned closer and flashed her a sexy grin. "Or I could kiss you again, but do it up right this time."

Though the mischievous gleam in his eyes softened his deliberate leer, her kind view of him fled. "And there you go, reminding me why I think you're a jerk. No, I don't need anything. Tell Cal I said hello, and I guess I'm stuck seeing you later." *So much for manners.*

Dante left her, his laughter trailing behind him, and with the Truth or Dare challenge satisfied for the week, the bulk of the L&G crowd dispersed. Brenna took her place at the register and smiled at the customer who stepped up to place an order.

Brenna whirled with a startled yelp when someone touched her shoulder from behind.

"Sorry." The young woman's silver labret flashed like a diamond against the chestnut hue of her skin. "I know you have to get out of here for the wedding, and I didn't mean to be so late, but my babysitter's mother was—"

"No big deal. We only just finished the Truth or Dare." Brenna brushed off the remainder of Shaniqua's explanation. "You're here now, that's all that matters. Ed and Stan are on until two, and then Joy and Kaitlyn work till close." Brenna moved out of the way so Shaniqua could take over the register. "I appreciate you working on a Saturday. You're a gem. I owe you."

Shaniqua waved her away. "Yeah, yeah. Get out of here. Tell Caleb and Maddie I said congratulations. They sure got a beautiful day for an outdoor wedding."

It was just after one o'clock. Brenna still had a ton of stuff to do before the ceremony at six, and she had promised Maddie she'd arrive at the house to set up the cake no later than three. She should have had the good sense to give herself the whole day off, but she intended to win the Truth or Dare challenge, and disappointing people, even for one Saturday, was not the way to ensure victory.

She eased her Audi from the parking space and folded back the roof with the touch of a button, unconcerned with the battering her hair would take from the wind. On a day like today, with the beaming sun drawing into the air every nuance of the pungent aromas inherent to the north Georgia mountains, Brenna couldn't imagine shutting herself inside the car. She would have to later, after she'd dressed for the wedding, but not now.

If God wanted to advertise for the glory of June, she thought, He'd look no farther than this little slice of heaven.

The drive from Bright Hills' quaint downtown to Brenna's townhouse was a ten minute breeze. She zipped into her driveway and exited the car in a series of fluid moves designed for speed. She glanced toward the cluster of townhomes to her left, noted the empty driveway next door, and jogged into her house.

Dante was probably already on his way to collect Caleb for their man lunch and to keep Cal occupied before the ceremony. She supposed they'd do whatever men did to entertain themselves before one of them took the Big Scary Plunge. Drink beer and watch baseball. Play poker. Whatever. God only knew why men did anything, and Brenna didn't want to know, especially if Dante was involved.

The big Neanderthal.

She detoured through her kitchen to grab a bottle of water from the fridge, texted Maddie to tell her she'd arrive as close to three as possible, and headed for the shower. An hour later, hair and makeup completed, she stood in front of the full-length mirror in her bedroom clad in a lacy bra and panties set, her dark brows pinched.

"Oh. My. God." She turned sideways to inspect her body profile and groaned.

She knew that since taking ownership of the Lump & Grind she had gained a *wee bit* of extra weight. Who wouldn't, spending twelve hours a day in a place like that? A steady diet of creamy lattes and sugary cinnamon buns accompanied by a dearth of green vegetables would do that to any woman. But, oh, honey, until this very moment, she hadn't realized just how generous her caloric intake had been.

"How did I let this happen?" She hissed the words aloud to her mirror image, gulped, and turned sideways once again to regard her bottom and thighs in dismay. Like watching a bad B movie in the middle of a sleepless night, she couldn't stop staring.

'Step away from the mirror, meatball!'

Brenna imagined the snarky voice in her head to sound like her younger brother, Jack. A ridiculous notion, since Jack was dead.

True, Jack's widow, Maddie, had claimed for years that Jack communicated with her, and was convinced he had played matchmaker and was responsible for her romance with Caleb Walker, the man Maddie was marrying later today.

And, also true, Brenna's older brother, Sean, was positive that it was Jack who intervened with sage advice when things between Sean and his now wife, Rebecca—Caleb's sister—went South earlier in the year.

Still, all of that was nonsense. Dead was dead, after all, and wishing someone could offer help and advice from the Great Beyond was a far cry from having them actually do it. Though down in the deepest recesses of her soul, when she was being honest with herself, she believed that if anyone could cross the Wide Divide to help his loved ones, it would be Jack.

'Focus on what you can control today,' Jack's voice commanded, *'like something that covers your big, fat—'*

Right.

Brenna strode to her closet. She bypassed the clingy dress she had chosen for today as she had purchased it before her bust and butt had burgeoned to their current unexpected proportions, and opted instead for a cocktail dress with a fitted bodice and silk skirt that flowed like a frothy dream to an inch below her knees. If she could just zip the damn thing, it would be perfect.

She wrestled her curves into a spandex body shaper and stepped into the dress, then drew a deep breath and exhaled to the fullest extent possible, a little technique to deflate her body that she'd learned in college when her Alpha Delta Pi sorority sisters had entered her into the Best Butt on Campus contest, and she'd had to squeeze herself into a pair of jeans meant for someone the size of Thumbelina. She'd lost the contest to an elfin Delta Zeta girl, but survived the wearing-of-the-jeans and added a valuable tool to her arsenal of *Things a Bodacious Girl Needs to Know.*

After battling the zipper into service, Brenna stepped back to the mirror.

Okay, so breathing was constricted, she admitted with a gasp, but the resultant display of boobage was not the least bit tawdry, and the loose skirt skimmed her butt without accentuating a thing, praise the sweet little baby Jesus.

Brenna performed her breathe-deep-and-exhale routine and sat on the edge of the bed to slip into her strappy heels, a marvel of modern design that lifted her height from five-foot-two to a respectable five-foot-seven, made her calves look spectacular, and boosted her confidence level in a way no sensible flats had the power to do. If they pinched in the process, so be it.

In front of the mirror for a final review she smiled, pleased at last with her appearance. Classy and confident, just the way she liked to roll.

A few minutes later she grabbed her purse from the kitchen counter, as well as a tote containing all the tools she would need to construct the three-tiered cake on Maddie and Caleb's dining room table. The three cake layers were in Maddie's fridge waiting for Brenna to put them together. It would be beautiful—glorious, even—and taste like a dream.

Maddie deserved the best and Brenna intended that she have it.

Back in her Audi, she closed the roof and windows, turned on the air, and pointed herself in the direction of Maddie and Caleb's. She glanced at the time on her cell phone, pleased that in spite of her rushed morning she would arrive with ten or fifteen minutes to spare.

She did a double take as a Harley blew past her, going in the opposite direction. It disappeared around the corner.

Twenty minutes later Brenna turned onto the dirt drive that led to Maddie and Caleb's house. Caleb intended to pave the entire half-mile length in the fall, and Brenna applauded his decision. The dirt road, though graded and well maintained, still suffered from potholes and mud in the spring from winter thaws and rain, and Brenna dreaded the teeth-clacking unsteadiness of the ride. Still, it was a pleasant trek through the forest, if one overlooked the uncomfortable jouncing along, and then came the payoff when the old farmhouse Maddie and Caleb called home came into view, a postcard-perfect picture of tranquility set against the breathtaking backdrop of the North Georgia Mountains.

Brenna pressed the brake and stopped to admire the view. Edie, Brenna's mother and a landscaping maven, had helped Maddie with colorful plantings around the yard and a multitude of plants on the wraparound porch, both hanging and standing in large urns. That, along with the improvements Caleb made to the house and barn with his architectural and building expertise, had transformed Maddie's little place into a comfy dream home—assuming what one wished for was an isolated spot in the middle of nowhere. But there was no denying the place was warm, inviting, and beautiful. Very much, Brenna thought, like sweet Maddie herself, and the perfect spot for Maddie and Caleb's intimate and unpretentious wedding.

Before going into the house, Brenna made a circuit of the yard. First she inspected the barn, repurposed for occasional outdoor entertaining. The DJ would set up there and dancing would commence. Maddie's barn cats, five in number, had made themselves scarce and would remain so, Brenna supposed, until the festivities ended. She went next to the wedding tent where two of Dante's catering employees were setting up tables. She paused to chat a moment, satisfied that the Neanderthal's staff had things under control.

The Neanderthal, her neighbor and owner of the popular Caravicci's Pizzeria, as well as the new Dante's Bistro in town, was responsible for the wedding buffet, and Brenna had to admit that when it came to Italian cuisine, the irritating man knew what he was doing. She offered thanks to his two worker bees, help if they needed anything, and headed for the house.

She entered the kitchen by way of the side porch and gave a fleeting thought to the odd construction of the home, positioned in such a way that it did not invite one to enter by the front door. "Coming in through the kitchen is so much friendlier," Maddie had once said, "especially when you're hot and ready for a tall glass of sweet tea."

Brenna's heels clicked on the travertine tile, and she tamped down envy at the size and design of Maddie's kitchen, the result of a renovation last year that had led to today's nuptials. Caleb, the groom, was the carpenter Maddie had hired to do the renovation.

"Maddie's upstairs."

Brenna spun toward the voice. Maddie's mother sat at the kitchen table with her nose pointed at her cell phone and her thumbs scrolling.

"Hi, Phyllis." Brenna waited for a response, sighed when it became apparent none was forthcoming, and marched through the dining room and up the stairs.

Phyllis had flown in three days prior and spent every waking moment texting her Spanish boyfriend, Arnaldo, who, by all accounts, awaited her return to his yacht docked in Miami. At least the woman had cared enough to show up. The same couldn't be said of Maddie's father, who claimed an inability to take the time from his job as a blackjack dealer in Vegas. Maddie had confided to Brenna that she suspected he just didn't want to be in the same room with her mother, no matter the reason.

How, Brenna wondered now, did two such dysfunctional parents manage to raise the grounded and awesome Maddie?

Brenna knocked on the door of the master bedroom, but let herself into the room without awaiting a response. Maddie stood staring through the window, dressed in ratty cutoffs and a stretchy tee, but her hair and makeup were done, and she turned and greeted Brenna with a wide smile.

"I knew you'd get here. You're never late for anything."

Brenna hugged her friend and grinned. "You have no idea what I went through to be on time."

"Have you set up the cake?"

"I wanted to see you first. How are you holding up? Nerves get to you yet?"

Maddie shook her head. "I'm not nervous. Just excited."

"Your hair looks fantastic," Brenna said. "And who did your makeup?"

"Is it too much? I thought it might be too much. You're right, I should probably—"

"I didn't say it was too much, now did I? I asked who did it for you." Brenna held Maddie by the shoulders and gave her a once over. "You look perfect, honey. Beautiful and perfect."

"Oh." Maddie sighed. "Oh. My mother did it. It feels like a lot of goop."

Brenna smiled, pleased to learn Phyllis had done something worthwhile. "Well, two thumbs up. You look gorgeous."

Maddie's phone buzzed on the dresser and she dove for it, read her text, smiled, and tapped a reply. "Caleb," she said, her face luminous. "He's ready for the honeymoon to start."

"No doubt," Brenna said. "Listen, honey, I better go and take care of that cake before it gets any later." She tilted her head to the slamming of the screen door from the kitchen, and then the sound of multiple voices talking and laughing carried up the stairs.

"Sounds like all the parents are here," Maddie said. "And TJ," she amended, when Grandpa Boone's deep voice boomed, "Keep those damn dogs outside, and make sure they don't tear anything up."

Brenna shook her head. "Why aren't the dogs at Sean and Rebecca's?"

"I want them here." Maddie's cheeks grew pink. "I know it sounds silly, but Pirate and Belle are part of the family, too."

Brenna shrugged. "It's your wedding." She strode to the door and laid her hand on the knob. "Mothers incoming." She opened the door and waited. A moment later Brenna's mother, Edie, along with Caleb's mother, Sada, appeared at the top of the stairs. "The bride is in here, ladies."

"You look lovely," Edie said to Brenna, "but what happened to your new dress?"

"I'd rather not discuss it, Mama." Brenna patted her butt and accompanied the gesture with a meaningful arch of her brows.

"Ah." Edie nodded and kissed Brenna's cheek. "You're built like the Kinkaid women, my darling. All tits and ass."

"Mama!" Brenna's eyes flew wide, her surprise followed by immediate laughter.

"Be grateful," Sada said. "The rest of us would love to have your hourglass shape. Look at poor Rebecca, five months pregnant with twins and she barely fills out a B cup."

"Sean doesn't seem to mind." Maddie's observation brought chuckles all around.

"Those two." Sada shook her head and made a lame attempt to look disgusted, but her lips curled with amusement in spite of her words. "Like a pair of randy teenagers all the time. That daughter of mine has no decorum where your son is concerned, Edie."

"I know." Edie's smile blossomed. "Isn't it grand? They're so happy together. And twins!" She clapped her hands, giddy. "We're having twins!"

All eyes turned to Maddie, and Brenna smirked. "You're next in line to produce adorable offspring. I hope you and Cal don't plan on waiting too long to procreate."

"Oh, sweet Lord," Maddie said. "Let's just get through the wedding ceremony, okay? I can't worry about babies today."

"On that note, I'll leave you ladies." Brenna blew kisses across the room. "I've got a cake to make glorious."

∽∾∽

"You sure you're not nervous?" Dante asked Maddie's husband-to-be before taking a bite out of a slice of pepperoni pizza.

"I'm not nervous." Caleb ripped open a sugar packet, dumped it into a tall glass, and stirred the beverage with a straw. "What makes you think I'm nervous?"

Dante grinned. "Because you just put sugar in my Coke."

Caleb's eyes widened and he stared at the glass. He released the straw and ran his hands over his face. "Okay, maybe a little nervous." He grabbed his phone and shot off a text, snatched it up when it buzzed a few seconds later.

"Maddie? What's she say?"

"Nothing I can repeat to you." Cal smiled and relaxed back into the booth. "Her crazy mother taught her how to sext. I never know what to expect when Maddie texts me now. Yesterday she sent me a picture of—you know what? Never mind."

Dante laughed and shook his head. "Lucky bastard."

Cal grinned and tugged a slice of pizza from the tray. "How are things going with the Bistro?"

"Fantastic. We've been busy as hell since we opened. I knew I'd pull people in for dinner, but it turns out the bar is where I'm making my money."

"I'm not surprised. The only other bar is that place outside of town with the sawdust on the floors. What's it called?"

"Boot & Spur Tavern."

"That's right, the Boot & Spur. Not exactly the same crowd as your place."

"Christ, I hope not. Boot & Spur is a popular spot, though. I go sit at their bar sometimes just to get a handle on their clientele and how they manage things. They have line dancing on Wednesdays, a live band on Friday and Saturday nights. And their wings aren't half bad." Dante shrugged his shoulders and grabbed another slice, munched on a wayward piece of pepperoni. "I'm noticing a lot of bar business at my place after five, mostly suits stopping by for a drink on their way home. That's what I didn't expect. I figured on a lot of couples for dinner, especially on the weekends, but the barstools are full almost every night, right up till close."

"Your bar manager might have something to do with that."

"Ah, yes, the fair Roxanne." Dante's smiled widened. "I poached her from Chez Eloise. They had her working the hostess stand." He rolled his eyes. "The woman attended a bartending school in Atlanta and her resume includes the Buckhead Ritz. I'm lucky to have her."

"How are you handling both restaurants? Must be tough to keep so many balls in the air."

"It is, but help is on the way. Trina is moving from North Carolina to manage the Pizzeria so I can focus on the Bistro."

Cal sat up from his slouch and leaned on the table, his eyes gone wide. "Are you out of your mind?"

"What's wrong with Trina? I thought you liked her."

"I do. That isn't the point." Cal shook his head, blew out an exasperated laugh, slumped back in the booth, and regarded Dante with a bemused smile. "How is that even going to work?"

"It's a business arrangement."

"Does Trina know that?"

"Of course." Dante gave Cal a look. "She doesn't want to get back together any more than I do. It'll be fine. We've been apart longer than we were together, and we're friends. Anyway, she's looking for work, and I can use the help. And she's a top notch restaurant manager. Works her ass off."

"And, if I recall, a very nice ass it is."

"On that we agree." Dante caught the attention of the harried waitress and motioned for her to bring the check. He looked around the dining room with a critical eye. "This place isn't bad, but it won't last. The pizza is run-of-the-mill, too much sauce, not enough cheese. Too expensive. Cleanliness, I'd rate maybe a five. Their kitchen is probably full of salmonella."

"Well, that's just great. Why did we come here if it sucks?"

"Scoping out the competition," Dante said. "I do it all the time."

"Well, I better not leave here with food poisoning. My wedding night plans do not include time in the ER."

"You'll be fine. I wouldn't dare get you sick today. Maddie would kill me." Dante picked up his Coke and caught himself before taking a drink, remembering that Cal had dumped sugar in it. He set it down and reached for the water glass instead. "So," he began, hoping he sounded nonchalant, "is Brenna bringing a plus-one to the wedding?"

"Beats me," Cal said. "You want me to find out for you, Romeo?"

Dante motioned to the waitress again. "She hates me."

"The waitress? Nah. She's just busy."

"Not the waitress. Brenna. She—" Dante snapped his mouth shut when Caleb's grin broke free. "You're a dick." Dante fired a balled up napkin at his friend's face.

Cal caught the missile and tossed it on the table, laughing. "Why do you play games with her? You two are ridiculous, always competing over which one of you is better at everything."

"If it weren't for those stupid competitions, I'd get no action out of Brenna at all. I just told you, she hates me, and I can't figure out why."

"Have you ever asked her?"

"She gives me some crap about my garage light waking her up in the middle of the night, and she hates it when the neighbors come over and start a party in the yard on Friday nights. Not that there will be any more impromptu parties. I don't have much downtime, not with both restaurants going full bore."

"What's with the light? What light?"

"When I'm working on restoring a car, sometimes I work in the wee hours. You know, if I can't sleep."

"And the light wakes her up?"

"So she says." Dante fiddled with the discarded wrap from his straw, began tying it in knots. "But I don't see how it's possible. And the other thing she says is that I ignore the neighborhood covenants."

"Well, do you?"

Dante shrugged. "So what if I do? No one cares but Brenna."

Cal stared at Dante. "Are you in middle school, or what? You think sticking her pigtails in the inkwell will earn you play points? Stop deliberately annoying the woman, for Christ's sake."

"I'm nice to her. Even when we have our silly competitions, I go out of my way to be nice. But she treats me like a piece of gum on the bottom of her shoe. If I could just figure out why—really why, I mean. Because her reasons are just so much bullshit."

"I think the problem is that she's the only woman you've ever wanted that didn't drop at your feet." Cal pointed at Dante with his straw. "You're used to winning. Maybe Brenna's unwinnable. She's your Kobayashi Maru."

Dante dropped his head back and laughed. "Seriously? You're quoting Star Trek now?"

"Why not, when it fits?"

"You're just saying that to throw down a challenge. I don't believe in an unwinnable scenario, and you know it."

Cal shrugged. "So, stop mooning after Brenna and either give it up or make a move. How long has it been? Four years? Five?"

Five, Dante thought. Five long and frustrating years since the first time he laid eyes on Brenna Kinkaid.

Dante would remember the moment forever. He'd been in his driveway, working on a beauty of a machine he'd picked up for peanuts from some old guy's barn over in Dahlonega. The man had died, and the wife didn't care what she had, just wanted it gone—a '63 Corvair Monza Spyder convertible. Dante's head had been crammed under the hood for half an hour, and when he looked up, there she was, standing in the driveway next door wearing heeled boots and a red dress that molded to her substantial curves like honey on bread.

Dumbstruck, he'd watched her shake her river of black hair over her shoulders, and he held his breath when she strode toward him with the confident swagger of a runway model.

"Brenna Kinkaid," she'd said, and held out her hand to shake. "I'm your new neighbor."

Blue. Her eyes were blue. Bluer than blue. Purple-blue. Was that even a color? It must be, because that's what her eyes were. A man could drown in those eyes, never come up for air again, and die happy.

He shut his mouth, when he realized it was hanging open, and dropped his eyes to the sparkling necklace at her throat. A Celtic cross accentuated with diamonds, or something that looked like diamonds. What the hell did he know about gemstones?

Whatever, it was as eye-catching as the woman who wore it, and its intricate design, he noted with a shock of surprise, bore a close resemblance to the tattoo over his heart.

He wondered if a man had given it to her—husband, boyfriend? God, he hoped not.

"My eyes are up here, Neanderthal. Are you a mute?"

"Am I—what? Oh, sorry." Dante reached out to shake her hand then pulled back at the last minute, holding his hands palms up. "Grease."

Sweet mother of God, she was gorgeous.

What did she say her name was again?

"Your name is Grease?"

"What? No. Caravicci. Dante." He laughed at himself and shook his head. He'd never been so flummoxed in his life. He knew he was acting like an idiot but had somehow been rendered powerless to stop. "Please let me start over. Dante Caravicci, and I'm covered in grease, so you probably don't want me to touch you."

"Why are you working on your car in the driveway like this? It's on blocks. I thought that was against the covenants."

"The what?"

"The neighborhood covenants. No junk cars in view of the street. Page four, paragraph six."

"Are you serious, right now?" Dante laughed.

She didn't laugh back. "I didn't spend 200K on a townhouse just to have a junkyard next door."

Dante bristled. "Junkyard? This baby is a '63 Corvair, lady. She may not look like much now, but when I'm through—"

"Please move it into your garage where it can't be seen," she said, her tone prim. "Page four, paragraph six."

Rendered mute for a second time, Dante stared at her, his jaw slack. No one had ever complained about his hobby before. He kept the vehicle covered when he wasn't working on it. It didn't constitute an eyesore. What was the big deal?

"Why do gorgeous women always fill their tanks with gallons of Batshit Crazy?"

Those beautiful eyes narrowed and darkened like a midnight storm. When she spoke again it was through gritted teeth. "And why am I stuck next door to a man with the manners of a Neanderthal?"

She'd turned and stalked away and, even through the red haze of annoyance, he'd had to admire her swaying ass.

Maybe he was a Neanderthal after all.

The waitress dropped the check on the table, and Dante snapped back to the present. She gave him an apologetic smile. "I'm so sorry you had to wait. I promise we'll do better next time." She flashed another smile and ran off.

"No, I've got it," Dante said when Cal dug into his pocket. "It was your last meal as a single man. The least I can do is pay for it." He dropped fifty dollars on the table and stood to leave.

"Hey, that's more than double the bill. Don't you want your change?"

"Nah." Dante glanced at the waitress, now juggling a platter of pizza in one hand and a tray of drinks in the other. He regarded her with sympathy and shook his head. "Poor kid. She's been the only server on the floor the whole time we've been here. She earned the tip."

The two men walked out to the parking lot and climbed into a 1976 Pontiac Trans Am, a vehicle Dante had restored to damn near perfect.

"You ready to head back to the house?" Dante asked.

"I guess." Cal wiped his hands on his denim-clad thighs. "I'm not supposed to see Maddie before the ceremony, but I don't know how to avoid it. She insisted on getting married at home, and we both live there." He shook his head and shrugged. "I'm going to end up getting in trouble for something I can't do anything about."

"That's the curse of belonging to the Man Club." Dante backed out of the parking space and regarded his friend. "We're always in trouble for something."

Chapter 2

Brenna squeezed back tears and smiled at Maddie who stood before a cheval glass biting her lip and smoothing the front of her lacy dress.

"It's too pink." Maddie's brows drew into a frown over eyes the color of cinnamon. "I should have gone with the blue."

"It isn't too pink." Brenna pushed from the boudoir chair in which she sat to step up behind Maddie. She laid her hands on the other woman's shoulders and their gazes connected in the mirror. "It's champagne with a hint of pink, and it's romantic and perfect. It makes your complexion look all warm and rosy—like you just had wild monkey sex."

Maddie gasped and whirled to face Brenna, her dark eyes wide and her jaw dropped to its limits.

Brenna laughed and embraced her horrified friend. "Stop fretting. You're beyond gorgeous, honey, and Caleb is going to melt when he sees you. I promise."

The women parted but joined their hands. More tears welled in Brenna's eyes. She blinked to banish the makeup-ruining bastards, but one escaped onto her cheek. She released one of Maddie's hands just long enough to wipe away the tear. "God, I hate weddings," she said, and made Maddie laugh.

"At least this one is small, without all the fanfare. Not like last time." Maddie's wide smile faded to bittersweet.

"No," Brenna said, "not like last time."

The two women regarded each other with shimmering eyes.

"Do you think Jack will be at the wedding?"

Maddie's soft-spoken question drew Brenna's smile, as any mention of her dead brother invariably did. "Oh, honey, he wouldn't miss this for the world. He's going to want to see his matchmaking skills in action."

Maddie's full-wattage smile returned and she nodded. "I think so, too."

A quick rap on the door preceded its opening. "Hey, is this a private party?"

"We're just blubbering." Brenna released one of Maddie's hands and reached out toward her other sister-in-law, Rebecca, married to Brenna's older brother, Sean. Rebecca took Brenna's hand, and the three women came together for a quick hug.

"Your belly's in the way," Brenna complained with good nature.

"All the time." Rebecca smiled and rubbed her rounded abdomen. "The Little Boogers are already making me have to pee all the time, and I still have four months to go."

"You're beautiful," Maddie said. "Glowing."

"I was going to say the same thing about you." Rebecca stepped back to get a better view. "The color on that dress is gorgeous, and you were right to go with the tea-length. It's all flowy and romantic, and perfect. And your hair looks freaking amazing." She admired Maddie's dark hair, woven into a wavy chignon. "Those little rhinestone things will sparkle like those fireflies you love to watch."

"See." Brenna nudged Maddie with her shoulder. "I told you."

Maddie grinned and then spun herself around, laughing, much to the delighted amusement of her companions. "Sweet Lord, I'm so happy!"

"All thanks to Jack." Rebecca's smile dissolved the moment the words left her mouth. "Oh, geez. I'm sorry. That was probably the wrong thing to say."

"No. It was the perfect thing to say." Maddie beamed. "Honest."

"You're late to the party on that topic. We've already gone there," Brenna said.

"We think Jack will be at the wedding," Maddie added, "since he's the one who got me and Caleb together."

"He got me and Sean together, too," Rebecca said.

Brenna glanced at Rebecca's belly. "You and Sean didn't need much help."

Rebecca laughed and rubbed her abdomen. "Well, Jack got us *back* together." She smiled at Maddie and cut a sly glance at Brenna. "I wonder who Jack has chosen for you?"

Brenna waved her hand and shook her head. "I'm not in the marriage market."

"Neither was I," Maddie and Rebecca said at the same time. "Jinx," they parroted each other again and laughed.

"You better prepare yourself, Brenna. Jack may be operating from the Great Beyond, but his matchmaking skills have been spot on so far." Rebecca pushed an errant curl from her face. She'd twisted her red hair into something resembling a French twist, but the escape of corkscrew strands proved her hairclip, though elegant and fashionable, wasn't doing its job.

Brenna grabbed a couple of hairpins from the top of Maddie's dresser and motioned for Rebecca to turn around, which the other woman did without question.

"She's right, Brenna. Gear up, because there's a man in your future whether you like it or not," Maddie said. "Jack will make it happen."

"You two should know by now that I don't ever do anything unless I want to."

Brenna captured Rebecca's twisty fly-aways and used the hairpins to tuck them into place.

"True enough, you know," Rebecca said. "Jack will fix

you up, whether you like it or not. *Ouch!*"

Brenna winced along with Rebecca. "Sorry, honey. I didn't mean to pull." She patted Rebecca's shoulders and stepped back. "There. All fixed."

"Thanks," Rebecca said, without looking in the mirror to see Brenna's handiwork. Brenna both admired and envied Rebecca's lack of vanity and her ability to look lovely in spite of it. Half the time the woman didn't even bother with makeup, though today she had, and looked gorgeous and happy, her green eyes sparkling.

Brenna sighed and pushed her own hair—"Black as the crown of a chickadee's head," her grandmother used to say, as if being compared to a bird was a compliment—over her shoulders where it fell sleek as glass. She dropped into the cushy chair she had abandoned earlier, crossed her legs, and adjusted the skirt of her silk dress over her knees.

"I've got enough problems just making the Lump & Grind profitable right now. Greta keeps threatening to retire, and no one bakes those cinnamon buns like she does—not even me—and damned if she doesn't know it. Two of my best after-schoolers are leaving for college in August, I don't know if I'm going to be approved for the loan I need to expand the L&G, and between that damn Neanderthal opening his Bistro right at the end of the block, and the new Starbucks opening up next to the high school, my evening business has dropped. Anyway, I know all of the men in this little town, and the best ones are already taken. And since I won't settle for anything less than I'm aiming for, I believe I'm destined for spinsterhood."

Rebecca and Maddie exchanged a look.

"Yes, yes, I know. Spinsterhood is hard to believe because I'm so fabulous." Brenna lifted her chin with the back of her hand and fluttered her lashes. "That's why I can't settle for just anyone."

"The ego." Rebecca rolled her eyes and crossed her arms over her baby belly. "Just what kind of guy are you aiming for, anyway? And quit being goofy. I'm seriously curious."

Brenna plucked imaginary lint from the fitted bodice of her dress. Doing so afforded her the opportunity to lower her gaze and bought her a few seconds with which to form a response that her friends would accept without additional comment. What kind of man was she aiming for? The impossible-to-find kind.

"C'mon," Rebecca said. "We're waiting."

Brenna looked out the window. From her perch in the interior of the room there was nothing to see but the wide expanse of azure sky and the lushness of the North Georgia mountains. She stood, smoothed her dress, and sauntered to the casement where she looked out over the back of Maddie's property, acres of open field that edged into deep forest. Caleb had built a play land extraordinaire for his son— *No, not just* his *son, because TJ belongs to Maddie now, too*—that resembled nothing short of a pioneer outpost in spite of the swings and slides and sandboxes. Caleb had used his architectural knowhow to design it all to complement the environment, and his carpentry skills to build it solid and sure. The treehouse alone, accessible by either a rope ladder or by climbing any one of the trio of apple trees against which it was built, would be the envy of any kid worldwide.

Hell, Brenna was almost thirty-one, and *she* thought it was cool.

Brenna closed her eyes and pictured the clearing in the woods, the gazebo where the wedding ceremony would take place, the rushing water of the creek, the flagstone pathways meandering among flowers and bushes bursting with the blooms of young summertime. An oasis in the forest, it appeared at the end of a path through the woods like some Disney princess's wonderland. Brenna wouldn't be surprised if bunnies and fawns gathered around the perimeter of the clearing to experience the joy of the day, like a scene right out of *Snow White*.

This wedding would be perfect. Beautiful and perfect, and Maddie the happiest and loveliest of brides.

You gave her this, Jack. Somehow you gave her all of this when you brought her to Caleb.

Jack. Brenna's brother and Maddie's first husband. Brenna knew it was crazy, but she felt Jack with her now, knew Maddie felt his presence, too. Jack may have been taken from them too soon, but by some miracle of Heaven, he always had their backs.

That's how it felt, anyway.

Brenna turned from the window. "Okay, fine, I'll tell you about the man I'm waiting for." She drew in a deep breath. "Jack picked him out, believe it or not. He wanted to fix me up on a blind date with this guy—one of his clients, he said—but before he could set it up the accident happened, and well, obviously I never met the guy. For all I know, he doesn't even live in Bright Hills anymore."

Rebecca's brows flew up and her mouth dropped into an O. "Are you serious? Jack was fixing you up?"

"So all this time you've been, what, waiting for Jack's client to miraculously land on your doorstep like a special delivery? Sweet Lord, Brenna." Maddie drew Brenna into a hug. "It's been five years. Don't you think it's time to let go of Jack's mystery man and give someone else a chance?"

Brenna stepped back and pointed her finger at Maddie. "You're the pot calling the kettle black. I thought you'd never move on after Jack died. But, thank god, you found Caleb, and you weren't out looking for him. Jack delivered him right to your kitchen door. And you." Her finger poked Rebecca's expanded middle. "Miss Buns-in-the-Oven. Less than a year ago you didn't want a man either, and now look at you—married and preggers. With twins, no less!"

Rebecca's lips curved in a grin. "Don't expect an apology out of me. I never in my life expected to be as happy as I am with Sean."

"Or me with Caleb," Maddie agreed.

Brenna threw her arms up. "My point exactly. Jack took care of you two. So don't give me flak for hoping I'll be the recipient of that same magic. Besides, I've dated here and there. But I've been busy trying to keep the L&G profitable, and that's more than a full time job. It's not that I don't want to find Mr. Right, but I don't have time to waste on Mr. Wrong. Anyway, do you want to give me a hard time, or do you want to hear about this dream man Jack wanted me to meet?"

"Tell us about Jack's mystery man," Maddie said.

"All right, then." Mollified, Brenna paused to put her thoughts in order. "Well, Jack called me about this guy, said he thought he found my dream man. I told Jack I doubted it, because I wanted a guy who's built like Hugh Jackman—sort of a Wolverine without the claws." Brenna frowned, reconsidered, and her lips curled into a slow and wicked grin. "Well, the claws could be fun sometimes," she said, and laughed when her friends rolled their eyes. "Anyway, I ran down my requirements. My dream man has to be handsome, naturally, but smart and capable, too, know his way around the kitchen, and have more than a passing knowledge of how to operate a washer and dryer. He has to like kids and animals, and be patriotic and loyal."

Maddie opened her mouth and started to speak, but Brenna cut her off with a raised hand and continued on with her wish list.

"A great sense of humor is a must. And he has to get me, really get me, understand my snarky humor and the things that make me laugh. Or cry. And he can't get all squirrely when he sees a few tears. He has to know my faults—which we all know are legion—love me anyway, and be faithful.

"In addition to all of that, he must be courageous and heroic—like, run-into-a-burning-building kind of heroic. And yes, what I've detailed is a very tall order. I said all of that to Jack, and when he was done laughing and telling me I'm a piece of work, he told me that as it happened, the guy was a good match." She set her manicured hands on her hips and regarded them with an arched eyebrow. "So you tell me, ladies. Was Jack just teasing? And if he wasn't, then there's some man out there who comes packaged with all of that. I

just can't help wondering if he's really out there somewhere. And I don't want to be tied up with someone else if
Jack does his woo-woo matchmaking from the Great Beyond and manages to…what did you say?…drop him at my
door."

Knuckles rapped on the bedroom door and a male voice
flowed through from the hall. "Excuse me, ladies. Brenna,
you in there?" Rap-rap-rap. "Could use your help with
something."

The Neanderthal.

Brenna groaned. She strode to the door and yanked it
open a crack. She had no patience for this pain-in-the-ass
man. No patience at all. Even if he did know how to kiss.

"What?"

"May I have a private moment, please?"

Brenna glanced back at her friends and pulled a face for
their benefit before stepping into the hall. She closed the
door behind her and crossed her arms over her chest. "Well?
What?"

His dark eyes moved in a slow circuit of her body, ending with a direct gaze into her narrowed Kinkaid blues.
"Wow. You look amazing."

"I know," she said, annoyed when his amused smile created sexy creases in his cheeks and an alluring starburst of
humor lines fanning the edges of his eyes, proof that the
man laughed often and with ease. She cleared her throat.
"What's so important that you had to drag me out here?"

His smiled collapsed. "Right. That. We have a major
problem with the wedding cake."

Brenna frowned as her shoulders tensed. "What kind of
problem? I set the cake up myself an hour ago. It's perfect."

"Not so perfect now. While all the adults were outside,
TJ let the dogs into the house and they—well, they sort of
got into the cake."

Brenna's arms dropped to her sides, her eyes widened,
and she shook her head. "No. No, no, no. How bad is it?"
His grave expression answered her question and she

dropped her face into her hands, still shaking her head. "Can any of it be salvaged?"

"Only if you want to scrape icing off their muzzles."

Brenna whimpered.

"If it's any consolation, they must have enjoyed it because they ate the whole damn thing. There was hardly a mess to clean up at all."

"Two dogs loved the cake I slaved over. Is that your idea of making me feel better?" She caught the inside of her cheek between her teeth and gnawed while she considered options. "Well, hell. I guess we can call around to the local bakeries and see if—"

Dante shook his head. "Already done. Wedding cakes are, as you know, made to order. This late in the day the best we can do is a run-of-the-mill birthday cake. I had another idea, though."

"I can tell by the look on your face that I'm not going to like it."

"Look, I know it was important to you to be the one to make the wedding cake, sort of a gift for Maddie and Cal. But under the circumstances—"

"Will you stop circling and just spit it out?"

"I have an Italian crème cake at the Bistro that I made for a private party for tomorrow night. Three tiers. Not as fancy as your masterpiece, but it'll be a pretty good substitute. And there are some unpacked boxes in the storeroom that have stuff in them—I don't know what, exactly. I haven't had time to go through them, but there's fancy stuff that Chloe bought for some party we booked right after we opened. Maybe we can find some decorations."

Brenna's eyes narrowed. "Decorations? What happened to the cake topper and—" She trailed off when Dante shook his head. "The dogs ate that, too? Are you kidding me?"

"We've got less than two hours before the ceremony. I'm heading over to the Bistro now with Sean. Hopefully, we'll find stuff in the boxes suitable for decorating around a wedding cake."

"Wait a minute. You and Sean? You two won't have the first idea what kind of decorations will satisfy Maddie. You'll come back toting baseball stuff."

"What's wrong with baseball?"

"And that question is exactly why I'm going with you and Sean isn't." Brenna swung around and opened the door a crack. She smiled at Maddie and forced her voice to flow like sweet wine. "Smooth your frown, honey. Everything's fine. Just a small thing the men need help with. A woman's touch, you know? I'll be back in a little while." She winked at Maddie, pulled the door shut, and turned her troubled eyes toward Dante. "Who else knows about the cake?"

"Everyone, now, except Maddie and Rebecca."

"Well, Maddie doesn't need to know. This is one of those things we can all laugh about later. Right now it will just upset her. Where's her mother?"

Dante shrugged and Brenna's dismay increased.

"We'll send Mama and Sada up to help Rebecca keep Maddie occupied." Brenna strode toward the stairs without checking over her shoulder to be sure Dante followed. "Do we need anything special to carry that cake?"

"Everything we need is at the restaurant."

"Of course it is." Brenna blew out a sigh. The man was a capable restaurateur, she had to give him that, though it grated. "Let's get going, then."

Brenna flew down the stairs, in spite of her five-inch heels, and marched into the dining room where the family had congregated to discuss the dogs' complete demolition of the cake.

"Where are those two furry beasts?" She directed her attention to her brother, Sean, as half of the destructive duo—the most disobedient half—belonged to him. Hands on her hips, she surveyed the empty table that a scant hour before had held the beautiful cake she had put her heart and soul into baking and decorating.

"Maddie said the dogs are part of the family and she wanted them here. You can't get mad at me. I only followed orders." Sean shrugged. "Sorry about the cake, though. I saw it before they...uh, you know...got into it. You did a great job. It was really nice."

Nice? Screw nice. The damn thing had been perfect. The three columned tiers had been made beautiful by the painstaking process of working with fondant, which had taken her countless hours to master. The draping and flower cutouts alone had cost her hours of sleep, and all she had to show for it now were the pictures she had snapped on her phone after setting it up.

"Pirate and Belle are outside," Caleb said, referring to the cake-eating canines. He glanced at his son, TJ, the six-year-old culprit who had let the dogs into the house, despite strict orders to the contrary. The boy sat with his legs dangling from a cushioned chair. He'd found a loose thread on the collar of his short-sleeved button-up and twirled the fiber back and forth between his thumb and forefinger in a nonstop motion while his narrow chin quivered beneath his lips.

The boy was such a sweet blending of adorable and miserable that Brenna couldn't bring herself to scold him. Judging from the expressions on the faces of the adults, the poor kid had been chewed out already, and it was clear he felt terrible about what happened. She regarded his downturned lips and watery eyes and gave him a *come here* gesture with her fingers.

He gulped, slid from the chair, and dragged his feet along the carpet as if they weighed fifty pounds each. He stopped when he stood before her and hung his head. She knelt and lifted his chin, meeting his solemn gaze with her own. He blinked and a tear dripped out.

Brenna wiped his cheek with her fingers and smiled. "The only tears allowed today are happy tears, Batman."

TJ threw his arms around her neck in a blast of emotional spontaneity and squeezed with all the might a six-year-old boy is capable of. "I didn't mean to. It was an accident." He buried his tear-stained face in her hair and whispered for her ears alone, "W—what if Miss Maddie won't m—marry us now?"

Brenna's heart broke open and her eyes filled up. "Oh, honey." She wrapped him in a warm hug and pressed a kiss against his head. "Of course, she will." She withdrew from his embrace just enough to look into his eyes, green like his father's, and still shimmering with tears. "There isn't anything you can ever do that will change how much Maddie loves you. More than anything in this whole wide world she wants to marry your daddy and be your mama."

TJ's brows lifted into a hopeful arch. "Really?"

"Really."

He blinked back his remaining tears, wriggled his nose, and sniffled, then brought his arm up, poised to wipe his runny nose. He stopped midway in the act when Dante thrust a paper napkin into his hand. He used the napkin instead of his arm and sniffled again. "I forgot they weren't 'posed to come in. And I didn't know they'd eat the cake."

"Of course you didn't. How could you? Anyway, what kind of crazy dogs eat an entire wedding cake? And how did we get two crazy dogs in the same family?" Brenna poked TJ in the belly and he giggled through his tears. "Bet you won't let them in again."

"No, ma'am. Not today."

Such earnestness, Brenna thought with fondness. She pressed another kiss on the top of his head before standing. She looked at the other adults in the room and shrugged, drained of her annoyance. "It's only a cake, and Maddie's no bridezilla. As long as we have a replacement, it will be fine." She looked at Dante. "You ready to go get us some cake?"

He dug his keys from his pocket. "We have about an hour-and-a-half."

"I thought I was going with you," Sean said.

"Yeah, right." Brenna snorted and gave her brother a look. "This requires female input. Mama, Miss Sada, will you please go up with Maddie? Rebecca's with her, but the photographer will be here soon. We'll be back as soon as we can."

Maddie's soon-to-be mother-in-law, Sada Walker, touched Brenna's mother on the arm. "C'mon, Edie. Let's get upstairs before Maddie figures out something's up."

"Good luck," Sean said to Brenna and Dante on their way through the kitchen to the back porch.

"I'll have another beer in your honor," Brenna's father, Papa Ron, said when she moved past him.

She blinked at his red and orange Hawaiian shirt and shielded her eyes. "Dear god, Daddy, turn that shirt down. Please tell me you're changing into something else before the wedding or pictures."

Papa Ron looked down at his shirt. "What's wrong with this? Maddie said to dress comfortably."

"It's a wedding, not a luau," Brenna said.

"Huh. That's what your mother told me." He turned his eyes toward Dante. "What's your opinion?"

Dante shook his head and held his hands up. "No opinion, sir."

Papa Ron shrugged. "Maddie said comfortable. This is comfortable. And I'll still have another beer in your honor, even though you're giving me sass."

"Me too," said Big Will, Caleb and Rebecca's dad. "Maybe even two."

"You'll certainly stand out in the wedding photos." Brenna went up on her toes to press a kiss against her father's cheek. She repeated the process with Big Will, who bent down so she could reach his face. "Where's Grampa Boone?"

"Rocking on the porch," Big Will said.

"C'mon." Dante nudged her shoulder. "Let's go."

Brenna grabbed her purse from the kitchen table and stepped out to the porch. She smiled at Grandpa Boone— Caleb and Rebecca's grandfather—and wished her own grandparents were still alive. The old man's chin rested on his chest and a quiet snore rumbled through his lips. His impressive white mane ruffled in the breeze.

Dante moved down the steps with Brenna and started toward his car, a fully restored 1976 Pontiac Trans Am. In Starlight Black with gold stripes, it stood out on the grass-spotted gravel drive. Brenna stopped short and stared, her heart thumping hard as she gawked at the muscle car.

"I'll drive." She changed direction toward her Audi while she fumbled in her purse for her keys.

"You can't get out. You're trapped between Sean's truck and Big Will's sedan."

Brenna gulped. Damn him, he was right, and she couldn't argue without explaining her irrational fear of muscle cars, a personal paranoia she'd share with Dante Caravicci only after the moon turned to green cheese.

"Fine. But you watch your speed in this thing." She avoided his gaze when he opened the passenger door for her and concentrated on adjusting the flowing skirt of her dress when he slid into the driver's seat.

They drove in silence down the dirt road that led from Maddie and Caleb's house to the rural two-lane highway. Brenna kept her gaze on the trees outside the passenger window, staring but not seeing the dense forest of hardwoods and pines that Maddie loved so much.

Her body trembled with the growling acceleration of the vehicle's engine and she dug her fingernails into the palms of her hands for control. Sweat beaded her upper lip and brow. She forced long inhalations through her nostrils and slow exhalations through parted lips.

It was bad enough that she was stuck riding in this ridiculous show of testosterone—*why do men require a mechanical extension of their penises, anyway?*—but the acute awareness of Dante only added to her discomfort.

He radiated a heat and energy that suffocated her in the cramped interior of the vehicle, even with the windows open.

"Doesn't this thing have air conditioning?"

"You hot?"

"It's June in Georgia," she snapped. "Of course I'm hot. And the wind is blowing my hair all over the place."

He buzzed the windows up and turned on the air, then glanced at her and opened his mouth, as if to say something, but instead returned his attention to the road without a word. His lips twitched with the hint of a grin. She tamped down her curiosity. Better not to ask.

She thought back to the first time she saw him. She'd just signed the mortgage on her townhouse and pulled into the driveway of her home as the owner for the first time, glanced at the driveway next door, and saw his denim-clad backside sticking out, the top half of him buried under the hood of an old car.

Then he stood up, and oh, honey, the Earth tilted. She'd blinked a few times to clear her vision.

The man was all broad shoulders and sinewy muscles, straining the confines of the greasy T-shirt. A fine scar that ran from the outer edge of his cheekbone and curved down to his unshaven jaw saved him from being too pretty, but he owned a pair of bedroom eyes that zeroed in on her like a heat-seeking missile.

Why, just that look alone made her tingly all over.

And then he'd stared at her boobs with a singular fascination that made her wonder if he'd never seen a pair before.

One of these days she'd find a man who was different.

The one that Jack picked out.

The One.

She squeezed her eyes shut and gave herself a mental head slap for thinking like a romantic fool, crossed her arms, and huffed out a breath. "Can't this old thing go any faster?"

"First, this 'old thing' is a classic, and second, you told me to watch my speed, so I'm watching. Make up your mind."

"It's just getting late, that's all."

"Thirty minutes there, ten minutes to grab the stuff, and

thirty minutes back. We've got plenty of time. Relax, Brenna. It'll be fine."

"Don't go getting all caught up in the restaurant when we get there. It's going into the dinner rush, so you know you're going to want to poke your nose into the kitchen's business. Don't. We need to get the cake, look through the boxes, and then leave. Got it?"

"You're bossy as hell, woman, you know that?" His words held more amusement than bite. "My best friend is getting married. I have every intention of being back there on time."

"Fine," she said, and settled into the seat.

Because she had fussed at him about picking up speed, she held her tongue when he hit the gas. He'd never know what it cost her to sit with her mouth shut, knuckles white, each breath an effort as the landscape flew past.

God, oh, god, she hated cars built for speed.

Her heart lurched into her throat when he zipped into a parking space in front of the restaurant. He cut the engine and her fingers rushed to unbuckle the seat belt. She scrambled from the vehicle and resisted an urge to kiss the ground.

"Hey, boss!" A twenty-something girl with an eyebrow ring and purple hair that looked like it had been cut with a hedge mower strode toward them when they came through the door. "Cake's all packed up in the back, just like you asked."

"You're a doll, Gemma," Dante said, never breaking his stride. "How're things going?"

Gemma speed-walked beside him. "Gearing up to be a busy night. Reservations through nine. Bennie's due in any minute."

"Good deal. If you have a problem, call Chloe. She'll be at the wedding, but she offered to take point tonight," Dante said.

The girl nodded, smiled at Brenna, and then rushed off to greet new diners. Brenna followed Dante through the dining room with its intimate booths and tables glowing with romantic candlelight and covered with linen tablecloths the color of rich Bordeaux rather than pedestrian white. On a small platform stood a baby grand piano, awaiting the musician who would play and take requests later in the evening. They passed the bar, a silky column of golden oak polished to a high sheen, and Dante smiled and nodded at the sloe-eyed bartender who dimpled and waved, but didn't interrupt her conversation with the couple sitting at the bar.

Brenna cursed her shoes when they stepped from the carpeted dining room to the tiled floor of the kitchen as spiked heels, no matter how adorable, were not made for safety in a restaurant kitchen.

As if reading her mind, Dante took her arm. "Careful. It can get slippery back here."

Brenna agreed and so allowed his guidance. He maneuvered her past the busy sous chef who chopped and sautéed with practiced speed, waved at the kitchen manager who responded with a surprised, "Hey, boss," and around a corner to a short and narrow hall. At the far end was an exit door which Brenna knew led to the back alley. The Lump & Grind, located at the opposite corner of the block, had a similar rear door, as did all the shops in between. Along the hallway were two closed doors.

They passed the one on the left and stopped at the other, on the right.

Dante opened the door and slid a wooden chair in front of it. "Don't move that," he said, and let go of her arm as they passed through the doorway. He flipped a switch next to the door and the fluorescent overhead bulb buzzed before flooding the room with harsh light. "In here somewhere is where Chloe put those boxes. I'm not sure what's what, so we'll have to poke through them to figure out what we can use, if anything."

"Are they marked?"

"Nope. Sorry."

They began on opposite sides of the small room, peering

into boxes and pushing aside those that contained nothing they might use.

The hum of conversation from the dining room, chatter of the kitchen staff, clinking of tableware, and bursts of intermittent laughter, traveled down the hallway and into the storage room, accompanied by the savory scents of fresh-baked dough, grilled meats, garlic, and other robust foods. Brenna's stomach rumbled in response, reminding her that she had eaten nothing since breakfast.

"Here it is. I found it." Dante glanced her way. "It's a bunch of silk flowers and some other stuff. You want to come take a look?"

Brenna nodded and, on her way past the open door, grabbed the chair Dante had set against it and dragged it with her. She'd been in heels all afternoon and her feet hurt. No harm in sitting down to go through the box.

Dante turned at the sound of the chair scraping along the floor and lunged for the door. "Don't let the door—" *Click.* He blew out a frustrated sigh and stared at her. "I asked you not to move the chair."

"You didn't ask, and you didn't give me a reason. What you gave me was an order, and I don't pay much attention to those, especially from you. What's the big deal, anyway? You afraid if we're alone with the door closed I'll take advantage of you? Rest assured that isn't even a remote possibility."

"The guy who replaced that knob last week installed the wrong kind. Congratulations. You just locked us in." He hefted the box containing the silk flowers and dropped it onto the seat of the chair then pulled his cell phone from his pocket. "Will you *please* look through the box while I get someone to come open the damn door?"

Brenna freed her throbbing feet from the heeled shoes and wriggled her toes. She considered lambasting the Neanderthal for being an ass, but decided he wasn't worth her breath. She presented him with her back, opened the flaps on the box, and began poking through the contents.

"Damn it," he said a few moments later. "Gemma's not answering her cell. Probably can't hear it."

Brenna closed up the box—the silk flowers and pretty votive candles weren't perfect, but they would do—and faced Dante. "Call the main line for the restaurant, genius. Someone has to answer that, don't they?"

The muscle in Dante's jaw twitched. He held the phone in front of him and tapped the speaker button so she could hear that he had dialed prior to her statement and that the phone was already ringing.

"Good evening! Thank you for calling Dante's Bistro in beautiful downtown Bright Hills. Would you like to make a reservation?" Gemma's chipper voice piped through the speaker.

"Hey Gemma, this is Dante." His pleasant tone belied the scowl with which he regarded Brenna. "We're locked in the storeroom. I'd appreciate it if you'd come back here and let us out."

"Sure thing, boss. Give me a few minutes, though, okay? Bennie's not in yet and Annette called off—her kid is still sick—and I'm the only one up front. We've got an early rush going on."

"Take care of the customers first, but hurry up, okay?"

"Be there in a flash."

Dante clicked off the call and shoved the phone into his pocket without taking his gaze off Brenna. He stalked toward her. She bristled and afforded him a stern narrowing of her eyes, but backed up when it became apparent the man wasn't stopping.

She sucked in a breath when her back hit the wall. Dante kept coming and didn't plant his feet until he was close enough that she had to tilt her neck back to see him. Her eyes widened and her stomach lurched when he slapped his hands against the wall on either side of her head. He lowered his face toward hers and stopped just shy of becoming a blur.

"What the hell did I do to make you hate me so much?"

The quiet rumble of Dante's voice held her as captive as his arms and his gaze. "You're condescending and rude and, frankly, it's getting damn old. In the years we've known each other, with only one early exception that I can recall, I've never treated you that way, never with anything but respect. Will you please be so kind as to tell me what I've ever done to earn your derision?" His voice, low and rough, should have annoyed her, should have drawn her anger.

Instead, it burned through her like a shot of Patron.

"In case you're wondering, Brenna," he leaned closer and his warm breath caressed her cheek, "that was a question."

Two realities jammed into the forefront of her brain. First, even while boring into her with anger, the man's dark gaze compelled her to remain engaged. Second, if he didn't back off, she might do something she'd regret, because right this second hating him was buried somewhere between his demanding intensity and her unexpected response to it.

She could hate him and be aroused at the same time, couldn't she? Did that make her a slut, or just female?

Brenna gulped. She licked her lips and searched for words, but they jumbled up now, tangled with her confusion and nerves, lost in her internal melee.

Relief, and something else she didn't care to label as it bore a strong resemblance to disappointment, rippled through her when he pushed away from the wall and dropped his arms to his sides. Brenna swallowed and waited for him to step back.

Dante stared at her for another moment. His gaze dipped to her mouth and back to her eyes. "Ah, what the hell?" he said, took her face in his hands, and captured her mouth with his.

Brenna slapped her hands against his chest with the intent of pushing him back.

It wasn't until the kiss deepened that she became aware her fingers had curled into his shirt, that the rapid beat of his heart and the heat from his skin engaged her hands through the smooth cotton, and that she wasn't pushing him away at all.

Not even a smidgen.

The man's mouth was magical. It must be, because she couldn't stop pulling him closer, had no desire to end this kiss. God, oh, god, his lips were hard and soft at the same time, hot and insistent, and when he set her mouth free to spread all that delicious heat to her jaw and then along the column of her throat, she slid her arms around him and arched to allow him greater access.

You'll regret this later, warned the sensible half of her brain.

But you're loving it now! declared the other half, the one that, at the moment, screamed the loudest.

Brenna formed no words of protest when he stroked down her ribcage toward her hips. His hands, as charmed as his mouth, gripped her and drew her against him, and when that magical mouth returned to claim hers, her brain stopped offering any words of advice at all.

She lifted to her tiptoes, held on tight, and dove in.

Chapter 3

Dante would never know what the hell possessed him.

One minute he was so pissed off at her snotty attitude he wanted to throttle that elegant neck of hers, and the next he was kissing her brains out.

He expected at any second to feel the sting of her hand across his face because really, it was no less than he deserved, treating Brenna Kinkaid, of all women, like an easy lay.

Except she didn't slap him. She didn't push him away. She didn't howl in outrage.

She exploded in his arms, opened her mouth for his kiss, and clutched him to her as if she was drowning and he was her single source of air.

He should have known she'd surprise him, because Brenna never did the expected thing. That was, after all, one of the reasons he was crazy about her.

He had to stop this, had to stop it right now, because the longer it went on, the worse the end result would be. The second this ended, he'd be persona non grata again, and she'd hate him more after than she had before.

One second more, just one, and he'd stop. That would be the smart thing to do. Except the moment she lifted to her toes and fitted her lush curves against him, every rational thought and drop of blood drained from his head and rushed to parts south.

She was soft, so damn soft, in all the right places, and her mouth was like honey and burning hot and, Jesus, *demanding*, and she smelled sweet and clean, like some expensive girly soap.

Dante breathed her in, drank his fill of her, and gave back with the urgency Brenna demanded. It wasn't enough, this momentary madness, but it might be all he'd ever get.

One more second, just one more—

"Hey, boss! Sorry it took so long but we had a—whoa!" Gemma's voice burst through the doorway and Dante and Brenna flew apart. "Oh, geez. Sorry. I'm so sorry. I'll just come back in a few—"

"No!" Dante and Brenna said in unison.

Dante grabbed the door and held it open wide, pushed a box against it with his foot. Gemma's eyes, still wide with surprise, darted from Dante to Brenna and back to Dante, and he gave the girl a look that had her biting her lip to still nervous laughter.

He grabbed the box containing the silk flowers and candles while Brenna slipped her heels on, and then the three of them walked down the short hallway and through the kitchen in silence, Brenna focusing on her feet with an ostensible effort not to slip on the tile. Gemma detoured to the walk-in freezer and grabbed the bag that held the boxed cake layers, frosting, and things Dante would need to stack the tiers.

"I hope I can rely on your discretion," Brenna said to Gemma when they reached the car.

Gemma blinked in confusion. "Huh?"

"She means keep your mouth shut," Dante said, but his growl lost its power when Brenna leaned toward Gemma and smiled. "He's awfully cranky for someone who just got kissed from here to Sunday, isn't he?" Then she laid her hand on the younger woman's arm and said in a hushed tone, "I know it's juicy gossip, but I'd be so grateful if you'd keep it to yourself."

Gemma's head bounced up and down like it had a spring attached.

"Oh, no, ma'am, Ms. Kinkaid. I won't say a word. Not a word. To anyone." She looked at Dante. "Honest, boss. Not a word. Uh-uh. Not a thing." She bit her lip to hide the grin that wouldn't be contained. "Quiet as a mouse. That's me."

The second Brenna climbed into the car, Gemma looked at Dante over the top of the vehicle, flashed a bright smile, gave him two enthusiastic thumbs up, and loped back into the restaurant. He sighed and closed his eyes. Everyone in the kitchen would know in about five seconds flat. Gemma was a sweet kid, and hardworking, but when it came to holding confidences, she scored a zero. He'd have better luck keeping that kiss a secret if he posted it on the Internet.

Once back in the car, Dante drove in silence, expecting Brenna to rip him a new one. Instead, she plucked at her silky skirt, smoothed it over her knees, then plucked at it again, all the while staring out the passenger window. After several moments, and in a cool voice that made him think of old Southern gentility, sweet tea, and the scent of magnolia blossoms, she said, "Well, I think we can agree that was quite unexpected."

Dante glanced at her the same moment she glanced at him, and he grinned when her cheeks flooded red and she looked away.

"I hope you're not waiting for an apology."

"No. And I'd be lying if I said I've never been curious," she said, surprising him. She crossed her arms in front of her and stared straight ahead. "But what happened was…well, it was…an anomaly. Just the result of a long and stress-filled day. An emotional day—an emotional week, come to that. Anyway, that's all it was. It didn't mean anything, and it won't ever be repeated." In his peripheral vision Dante saw her turn her face towards him. "I'd appreciate it if you'd not say anything about it to anyone."

Dante sighed. After all this time, the woman knew him not at all. "I don't kiss and tell, Brenna."

She nodded and cleared her throat, the sound loud in the interior of the car. "You know, of course, that it will never happen again."

"Right. Because you didn't enjoy it."

"Don't be sarcastic. I won't try to lie. It's obvious I was as into it as you were." She blew out a little laugh. "As much as I hate to compliment you, you certainly know what you're doing, I'll give you that. The truth is, I don't want to be involved with you that way, Dante." *Ouch. A direct hit.* "I'm willing to try and be friends, though." *And a double blow.*

Dante nodded but said nothing. Her words cut deep and he wasn't sure why. It wasn't as though her aversion to him was new. He'd always known she disliked him, thought him to be an idiot. He just didn't know what he'd done to earn that opinion from her. And wasn't that the very question that had started this whole thing?

But she had surprised him again with her maturity and honesty in the aftermath of...what had she called it?...the anomaly, foregoing the snarky comments he expected and was used to receiving from her. Her tone and manner was candid and respectful, so he responded in kind.

"Okay. Friends, then."

Brenna's lips parted as though she meant to say something else, but instead they curved in a quiet smile. When he looked at her again, she was staring straight ahead, arms crossed, her hands balled into fists. Her breathing was steady and controlled. He'd noticed her stiff body language on the way to the Bistro and attributed it to her discomfort with being stuck alone with him, but now he wasn't so sure. She looked rattled, and he didn't think it had anything to do with their recent "anomaly."

"You okay?"

"What?" She cleared her throat and nodded. "Yes, of course. I'm just—hey, what's going on up ahead? Oh, my god." She covered her mouth with her hand.

Dante hit the brakes and brought the car to a stop. This

stretch of rural highway was a winding two-lane road that saw easy traffic on most days, but the jackknifed tractor trailer in front of them had blocked the road and caused the beginnings of a bottleneck that wouldn't clear anytime soon.

"This is the same spot Maddie was run off the road last year," Brenna said. She rubbed her arms with her hands and shivered.

Dante climbed from the car and removed his sunglasses to get a better view. A chill ran over him when he saw what other people stood staring at. A white two-door car was pinned under the trailer on the driver's side.

"Where's all that smoke coming from?" Brenna said.

Dante leaned into the vehicle and tossed his sunglasses onto the driver's seat. "There's a car trapped under the trailer. I think the smoke is coming from the engine, but it's tough to see. I'm sure someone has already called nine-one-one, but it won't hurt to do it again. And call Maddie. We're going to be late."

"Wait! Dante, what are you—"

Dante ignored Brenna's frantic voice and took off at a dead run. He pushed past the small group of onlookers and sprinted toward a heavyset man wielding a fire extinguisher. The man's effort to kill the growing flames, now consuming the engine compartment of the trapped vehicle, made no dent in the fire's fury.

"There's a woman in there!" the man yelled to Dante. "The doors are stuck and I can't get the fire out!" He tossed the empty fire extinguisher to the ground in disgust. "She was driving too fast, skidded toward me. I tried to avoid her, but—" He threw his arms up and shook his head.

Dante's attempt to open the damaged driver door failed, and he ran around to the passenger door, but it, too, was immovable despite his efforts.

Dante's heart pounded as his adrenaline pumped, and he bit down on frustration. The thick smoke inside the car hindered visibility. He peered inside but was unable to tell if the woman in the driver's seat was dead or alive.

"Give me the extinguisher," Dante called to the man, and caught it over the hood of the demolished car. Using the fire extinguisher like a battering ram he slammed the base of it with his full might against the center of the passenger window. Glass shattered.

Smoke billowed from the opening and Dante stepped back, coughing. He reached inside and unlocked the door, but it remained fixed. More than brute strength would be required to open it, but there was no time to figure it out.

He ripped off his dress shirt. Buttons flew and bounced unnoticed on the pavement. His T-shirt came next, and he wrapped it around his head, covering his nose and mouth. Drawing a deep breath, he pushed his body into the vehicle through the window, an act that proved no easy feat. His size may have worked to his benefit on the football field in his college days, but it was a detriment now.

The driver turned her head when he touched her arm. Not a woman, just a kid. Sixteen if she was a day. Blood trickled from her nose. Her eyes shimmered with tears and fear.

೧೨೮೩

Brenna clicked off the nine-one-one call and stood with the rest of the crowd watching the nightmare scene unfold. Half of those around her had their cell phones up and recording, the other half stood in rapt silence, some covering their gaping mouths with their hands.

Dante busted the window with the fire extinguisher and the crowd gasped as one when smoke billowed out.

"Why's he taking his shirt off?" someone said, and the crowd gasped again when he dove headfirst through the window and disappeared into the vehicle with some effort.

"Oh, my god," a woman said. "Is he crazy? Now he'll die, too."

Brenna hugged herself to quell the shaking, but her limbs betrayed her.

Hot, it was hot, standing there on the blacktop with the late afternoon sun bearing down, but she couldn't stop her body from trembling as icy arms of fear wrapped around her. Smoke continued to pour from the window, carried away and dispersed by the mountain breezes, but the acrid scent of it hung like a shroud.

She held her breath as the seconds ticked past.

The crowd cried out when fingers of flame shot high from the engine compartment to burn the air around the vehicle into an undulating wave of shimmering heat.

Brenna squeezed herself tighter, rocked her body as fear for Dante consumed her.

Please, God, please let him be okay. Let him get whoever it is out of there, but please let him be okay. Don't let him die today. Please, please, please. I'll say a million Hail Mary's. I'll go to confession and mass every week. I'll—do anything. Just let him be okay.

Sirens punched a hole in the air. A minute later, uniformed men hit the ground running.

≈≈≈

"To protect you." Dante's voice came muffled but audible through the cotton fabric. He wrapped his dress shirt around the girl's nose and mouth while he made a quick assessment of his options.

Getting her out wouldn't be easy. Her legs remained trapped beneath the crushed dashboard. Smoke and heat rolled into the enclosed space from the engine compartment.

He released the driver's seat belt. "I need to see if the seat will go back."

She squeezed her eyes shut and tears trickled out.

He reached between the girl's knees and under the driver's seat, and grasped the adjustment lever. His hands, slick

from heat and sweat, slid over the narrow bar. His position-
ing and leverage ability was awkward, so he shifted himself
to gain maximum strength. He prayed his way through the
motions, feared her legs would be hurt by the dashboard
when he forced the seat back.

Dante buried the thought and focused on his mission—
the immediate extrication of the girl from the vehicle.

Heat blasted his bare torso. His eyes and throat burned.
His lungs ached.

He ignored his discomfort and gave the lever a mighty
heave. Praise god, the seat slid back and the girl's legs went
with it, gashed and bleeding, but free of the dash.

Relief pumped through Dante. Now to get her out of the
vehicle.

Sweat dripped down his forehead and into his eyes. He
wiped it away with his forearm, coughed, and wished for
fresh air.

Flames licked from behind the dashboard, sneaking into
the passenger compartment. The firewall was breached. The
interior of the car would flare up in a hurry.

"I'll pull her over the console and lift her up," Dante
called to the man on the outside, "but I'll need your help to
get her out."

The man spat chaw juice on the blacktop, hiked up his
jeans, and hollered, "Help just got here. We got more hands
out here now."

"Any chance of opening the door?" Dante asked.

A familiar face appeared in the window, eyes dark and
serious beneath the brim of a Truheart County Sheriff's
deputy hat. "Give us a minute. We're going to pry it open,"
said the deputy Dante recognized as one of Rebecca's old
flames, Nate Humphrey.

"We don't have a minute." Dante's raspy voice evaporated against the sound of the door being forced open by
crowbars and multiple strong hands. "Ready?" he said to the
girl.

She responded with a weak nod.

Dante hauled her up and over the center console, repositioned himself, and heaved her again. A moment later,
hands were there to help, and together Dante, Nate, and another deputy lifted the girl from the burning vehicle.

Nate carried her away with hurried strides. Dante stumbled from the smoke and yanked the T-shirt off his face,
alternating between coughing and sucking in great gulps of
fresh air. Behind him, the interior of the car burst into
flames.

❧❧❧

Dante appeared through the smoky haze, striding from
the fireball like some movie action hero, all dirt-smudged
and grimy, his bare torso glistening with sweat and blood.
Relief at the sight of him gushed through Brenna and weakened her knees. She gasped and sucked in air, unaware until
that moment that she'd been holding her breath.

She forced her feet into motion as an antidote to her
wobbling legs. Tears of relief welled, and she blinked them
back. That damned Neanderthal had scared her witless, doing what he did, and she'd like nothing better than to give
him a solid whack upside the head. Or kiss him till he
begged for mercy.

She gulped and buried the thought.

She rubbed her arms and blew out a breath, worked to
steady her emotions. She'd worry about analyzing them later. For now, she needed to update Caleb and Maddie, and
make sure the favorite 'adopted' son and brother of the
Kinkaid/Walker clan was as unscathed as he appeared to be.

❧❧❧

Dante wiped the sweat and smoky grime from his face
and chest with the T-shirt, and loped over to where Nate had
laid the girl on the ground to await the EMTs.

"How you doing?" he asked the kid, dropping to a squat next to Nate.

She forced a little smile and managed a thumb's up. "Thanks." The word was a whisper through her lips.

Dante smiled and nodded. He took her hand. "What's your name, sweetheart?"

"Morgan."

"Well, Morgan, you scared the crap out of me. Try not to do that again, okay?"

The corners of her lips tilted upward again and she closed her eyes.

Dante squeezed her hand before releasing it. He stood up and nodded to Nate then looked around him as if noting his surroundings for the first time.

Brenna appeared from the crowd of people gathered to watch the car burn. She bulled her way through and ran toward him on those skinny-heeled shoes. He hoped she didn't take a header on the pavement.

The arrival of more emergency vehicles stopped her progress. County deputies materialized to push back the crowd and Brenna was caught up in the sweep. Dante saw her mouth moving and her arms gesticulating, and almost felt sorry for the cop on the receiving end.

Fire trucks and ambulances arrived, followed by more county deputies and several Georgia State Troopers.

What a mess.

Nate moved out of the way when the EMTs ran over to help Morgan. He said something to the girl and then walked to Dante. "You need to let the EMTs check you out."

"Maddie and Caleb's wedding is today. I don't have time."

"Don't be an idiot. You inhaled a lot of smoke, and you're bleeding. You might need stitches for that."

Dante glanced down. Sure as hell, there was an angry gash just blow his ribs. Probably got it climbing through the window. Damn. It hadn't hurt until Nate pointed it out. Dante pressed the dirty T-shirt against the wound. "They can put a butterfly on it. It'll be fine. I really have to get out of here."

Nate pushed his hat up and squinted his eyes toward the crowd. "Hey, is that Brenna Kinkaid?"

"She was riding with me when we came on the accident."

Brenna continued to run her mouth and wave her arms at the cop who turned in a circle, threw his hands up, and let her pass.

I know just how you feel, pal, Dante thought and watched her stride toward him. The cop watched her too, as did Nate and every other man in view of her. Dante couldn't blame them. She was something to behold, black hair blowing in the mountain breeze, striding on those mile-high heels, her silky skirt swirling around her legs. The woman was a work of art.

"Well, hello, Nate. I thought I recognized you." Brenna went on her tiptoes and drew Nate into a quick hug. "You arrived in the nick of time."

"Wouldn't have been in time at all, if Dante hadn't already done the heavy lifting."

"You need to go to the hospital," she said to Dante.

"I'm not—"

"I already talked to Caleb. They want you to get checked out."

"I'm fine."

"Your voice sounds like you ate gravel for lunch. And you're bleeding." Her gaze swooped over his torso to the bloody T-shirt he held balled up against his abdomen, and back up to his face again without pause. "For once, don't be an idiot."

"I'm not going to the hospital."

Nate looked from Dante to Brenna and back to Dante again much as Gemma had done earlier, shook his head, and motioned to one of the EMTs. "Over here. This is the guy who saved the girl. He's injured."

"I'm not injured, I'm just—"

"Let's check you out? All righty?" The paramedic, a perky twenty-something female with cornflower eyes and a reddish-brown ponytail, gave Dante a bright smile and settled a lightweight blanket over his bare shoulders. "You can argue, but I've got bottled water and I bet you could use a drink right now."

Dante blinked. "You're bribing me with water?"

"Is it working?"

"Yes, actually, it is. Water would be great, thanks." To Brenna he said, "How late are we for the wedding?"

"We're not. They're waiting for us. Go get fixed up. I'll call Cal again and fill him in."

Dante nodded. He walked with the bouncy paramedic to the back of the ambulance and thought of other days, a lifetime ago, when fire and smoke had been frequent occurrences, had obscured his vision and burned his throat, torn his lungs apart.

And sand. So much damn sand.

He blinked. His sore lids scratched over his eyes, gritty, and he rubbed them with the heels of his hands to clear out the sand.

No, not sand. Smoke. Just smoke.

Weariness settled over him but somehow his adrenaline still flowed. He sighed, resigned.

There would be no sleep tonight.

c∽c∽

Brenna clicked off a call with Caleb and found a place to stand where she could wait for Dante without being in the way of the paramedics and other emergency workers. She looked toward the spot where Dante had abandoned her and the car, and behind his muscle machine a line of vehicles trailed now like mismatched pearls on a string, disappearing around a curve. Maybe the State Patrol already had an officer farther down the road, directing traffic to turn around.

God knew no one would get through this mess for hours.

Fire trucks from three counties had shown up to douse the fire, and the demolished car sat smoldering now like a dragon breathing its last.

Brenna turned her eyes to Dante, settled her gaze on him from the safety of her sheltered spot. He answered questions and gave a statement to one of the state patrol officers, and, after the cop left, he sat at the back of the ambulance, laughing and joking with the cute paramedic who seemed to be taking more time than necessary to clean his wound and apply a dressing.

Not that Brenna could blame her.

Dante's smiles and laughter were quick and contagious. That was one of his redeeming qualities. He didn't just smile with his mouth, but with his whole face, with his eyes. That drew people in, was one of the reasons he was so successful with his restaurants, to Brenna's way of thinking. Everyone liked him and wanted to be his friend. Well, everyone but her.

Some habits were hard to break.

She watched him flirt with the paramedic, smiled in spite of herself when the woman became flustered and tripped over a response to one of Dante's questions.

Things came easy to him. Way too easy.

Damned Neanderthal. Had he ever had to work hard, really hard, for anything, ever?

She admired his build—nothing wrong with giving appreciation where it was due and, *oh, honey, it was due.* She couldn't help but notice. It wasn't her fault he was sitting there half naked with his broad shoulders and washboard abs on full display. To allow the paramedic easier access to his wound he moved his arms behind him and leaned back, resting his weight on his hands. His biceps responded with a toned display of sinewy strength.

Best not to focus on that.

Brenna frowned. How in the hell did he own and operate two—*two!*—Italian restaurants and maintain a body like that? He cooked all the time and worked the kitchen in both his places. He even *baked*! Didn't he taste test, for god's sake? Didn't he ever eat what he cooked? And if he did, how did he keep from weighing a thousand pounds?

It looked like the wound care marathon was coming to an end, so Brenna strode over to the ambulance and gave the pony-tailed paramedic a smile.

"He's all yours," she said to Brenna. "Take good care of him, all righty? He's stubborn. Wouldn't take oxygen, won't go to the hospital. Be sure he sees his own doctor to-morrow. Get his breathing checked out and the wound looked at. Probably needs stitches, but like I said, he won't go to the hospital. Stubborn."

"See?" Brenna turned to Dante with a sweet smile. "I'm not the only one who thinks you're a pain in the ass."

"I'm not missing the wedding." He stood up and gave her a look that dared her to argue.

"Well, you can't go looking like that." Brenna dropped her gaze to the tattoo on his chest. She blinked and stared.

"What?" He looked down at the white bandage under his ribs. "Am I bleeding again?"

"No. It's—it's nothing." She lifted her eyes to his face. "We have to turn around and go back through town anyway, so we may as well run by the neighborhood so you can shower and change."

"The wedding—"

"I talked to Caleb a few minutes ago. He said they won't start the ceremony until we get there, and to take as long as we need. Everyone's already drinking, and he said Maddie wanted to wait until the fireflies come out anyway," Brenna said. "It's fine if we stop. Really."

"I thought Cal wasn't allowed to see Maddie until the ceremony?"

"That ship sailed about half an hour ago. By the sounds of it, they're partying up a storm while they wait. Music is playing, dogs are barking, people are laughing. The cere-mony will be the cherry on top, I guess." Brenna shrugged.

"No one's upset. It isn't going exactly the way we planned, but as long as the bride and groom are happy, does it really matter?"

"I guess not." Dante sighed and glanced around. "How can we even get out of this mess?"

"The state patrol is letting people turn around." Nate stepped up beside Brenna and nodded toward Dante's bandage. "You didn't need stitches?"

"He's stubborn," Brenna said, and Dante shrugged.

"I'll walk you to your car and make sure you get turned around without a hassle," Nate said. "You earned the right to go home."

"Thanks, man. We appreciate it," Dante said to Nate. He fell into step with Brenna and Nate as they walked back to the Trans Am.

"You want me to drive?" Brenna asked. "I will, if you need some time to chill."

Dante shook his head but his lips curved in a lopsided smile. "So I'll have plenty of time to think about all the ways that extraction might have gone horribly wrong? No thanks. I appreciate the offer, though."

They said goodbye to Nate and, with him controlling traffic, turned the car around with ease. Brenna stared out the passenger window at the blur of hardwoods and pines, saw without noticing the blankets of kudzu covering whole acres of trees, and pondered Dante's atypical silence. Under normal circumstances, he was the chattiest man in the world, a characteristic she claimed drove her crazy. In truth, she envied his ability to draw people, strangers or not, into conversation. Sequestered now in a bubble of quiet, he still managed to emit a vibrant energy that held her on edge.

Unable to handle the silence she faced him and blurted, "That was amazing, you know. What you did, the way you rescued that girl. Everyone else was just standing around, but you got her out." Not to mention that he had also scared the hell out of her, had made her stomach coil and her heart lurch in sheer terror.

And she'd cut out her own tongue before she'd ever say those words out loud, especially to him. It was difficult enough to admit to herself that they were true. She couldn't think about it. Just couldn't. Not right now.

Dante shrugged, but kept his focus on the road. "My training kicked in, that's all. And I didn't get her out alone. I had plenty of help. I'm just glad the kid's okay. The truck driver said she was flying in that little car of hers. She swerved into his lane and he jackknifed trying to avoid her."

"It's scary, how fast everything can change." Brenna's voice wavered. "Every accident I see or hear about, I think of Jack. One second he was driving along, and the next, he was—he was gone. In that moment, life changed for all of us who loved him." She cleared her throat and blinked back tears for about the hundredth time that day. "There are parents, maybe siblings, who won't have to feel what my family felt when Jack died. They still have their girl tonight, because of you, Dante. That's no small thing."

His lips curved and he threw her a sideways glance. "So does this mean you'll lay another hot kiss on me? Maybe let me cop a feel? I'm pretty sure I've earned it for putting my ass in the line of fire, so to speak."

She bristled. "I'm trying to compliment you, you big—"

She bit off her words when the outer edges of his eyes crinkled and dipped downward in that sweet way they had, and the realization that he was joking punched the wind out of her. He'd derailed her emotional roller coaster by being a jerk—which, of course, made him not a jerk at all.

So annoying.

She liked him better when she could stay mad at him.

She forced herself to relax. "You're such a Neanderthal," she said, but a laugh followed her words, and when he glanced her way again they shared a smile.

Twenty minutes later, Dante parked in the driveway of his townhouse and cut the engine. "You're welcome to come in. It'll take me about ten minutes to shower and change."

Brenna glanced at her own residence next door and shrugged. "What do you have to drink in there?"

"Beer and milk. Cheap wine. And Coke, maybe. But not diet," he added, reading her mind.

"I'll take my chances with the wine," she said and slid from the car.

They met around the front of the Trans Am. Brenna followed Dante up the short walkway to his front door, eager to get inside, sit down, and give her feet a rest from the heels. She considered going home to choose a different pair of shoes, but opted to suffer instead. Uncomfortable these might be, but they made her legs look fantastic, and that bought them an extra few hours of wear time.

And if people were looking at her legs, maybe they wouldn't notice the extra fifteen pounds on her butt.

Dante lifted his key to the lock, but the door swung wide, opened by a man with a sardonic smile and eyes as dark as Dante's. "Welcome home, cousin," the stranger said.

"Jesus, Vince. How'd you get in?" Dante scowled. He pushed past his home invader and held the door open for Brenna.

"Key. I had one made the last time I was here." Vince glanced at Brenna and his brows lifted. "Well, hello, Beautiful." His smile widened to show straight teeth, white against his olive skin.

Brenna stared at Dante's guest. He was handsome and devilish with "bad boy" written all over him.

He looked like Dante Caravicci gone wrong.

Chapter 4

Brenna held out her hand to shake Vince's. "Brenna Kinkaid."

"Vince Caravicci." He lifted her hand and kissed the back of it in a show of gallantry.

"Jesus," Dante muttered, and rolled his eyes. He pushed the door shut and led the way down the short hall that opened into a generous living space. The base of the stairs and a hallway led off to the right, with the kitchen on the left. A breakfast bar, empty with the exception of a wicker basket full of what appeared to be mail and takeout menus, separated the kitchen from the living room.

Brenna looked around the townhouse, curious about how the Neanderthal lived. Although tidy, his space was utilitarian and pedestrian, though she gauged his leather furniture to be pricey stuff. There was a sofa and loveseat arrangement, but no pillows or throws to make it homey, blinds but no curtains, clean paint, and no artwork. Speakers and a massive TV took up one whole wall, and the video game controllers sitting out on the sofa table won an amused smile from her. Men and their toys.

At least the place wasn't littered with beer cans crushed in the shape of his forehead. A definite plus.

Upstairs were two bedrooms and a bathroom, she knew, as this floor plan mirrored her own, with the master bedroom located on the main level at the far end of the hall, past a powder room and laundry room.

If the townhouse looked less than lived in, it was no surprise. Dante was, after all, a bachelor who passed the majority of his time elsewhere. With two restaurants to operate, the man spent little time at home.

Not that she'd paid any attention to his schedule, of course.

"Where's your bike?" Dante said as he stepped into the kitchen.

"In the garage." Vince shrugged and rested his arms on the breakfast bar. "I figured if I parked where you could see it, you'd call and tell me to get the hell out."

Dante snorted and regarded his cousin with a stony gaze. "You can stay for a few days, but don't get comfortable." He yanked open the pantry door and grabbed a bottle of red wine. "It's a cheap cabernet, but it's all I have right now. You good with this?" he said to Brenna and, at her nod, took a wineglass from the cabinet nearest the refrigerator— the same location where she kept glasses in her own kitchen, she noted—and poured.

"Thanks." She stepped next to Vince, reached over the bar to take the glass, sipped, and nodded her approval, ignoring the tension that crackled between the two men. "Not bad for cheap stuff," she said, hoping to lighten the mood.

"What happened to you?" Vince pointed his chin in the direction of Dante's bare and bandaged torso.

"Nothing serious." Dante looked at Brenna. "I'll be back in a few." His eyes turned back to Vince. "Behave yourself."

Vince's lips curled upward but the smile didn't reach his eyes. Dante scowled and disappeared down the hallway.

"Sorry for that," Vince said after Brenna settled herself on the sofa. "Me and Dante are like brothers, you know? We don't always get along."

Brenna sipped her wine and moved to the edge of the cushion to set the glass on the sofa table. She picked up a hardback book, Laura Hillenbrand's *Unbroken,* identified the bookmark as a torn page from a Caravicci's Pizzeria takeout menu, and noticed for the first time an amber bottle on the floor next to the sofa.

She pictured Dante sprawled out to read, sipping his beer and passing the time. Somehow that image was contradictory to the workaholic she assumed him to be.

"I guess the last time you saw each other you were at odds?" Brenna's Southern upbringing forced her to offer her full attention to Vince, when her preference would be to wander around and investigate Dante's living space. Not in a nosy way, of course. That would be impolite.

"We, uh, see things differently, I guess you could say." Vince eased in at the other end of the sofa, linked his hands behind his head, and stretched his denim-clad legs out in front of him, crossed at the ankles. His leather harness boots appeared too new to be comfortable. His hair, the same espresso color as Dante's, hung long enough to wear in a ponytail should he be so inclined, and diamonds winked from both earlobes.

"Well, that's how it goes with family sometimes." Brenna smiled and returned the book to the table, picked up the wineglass to sip.

"So, you and Dante have that vibe going on. Are you two serious?"

Brenna choked on her wine. Vince sat up and scooted over to take the glass from her hands. He set it on the table and thumped her back.

"I'm fine, thanks," she choked out, waving him away. "Really. I'm fine."

"I take it I'm off base about you and him." Vince held his place next to her, and smiled. This time he engaged her eyes, and Brenna saw again the similarity to his cousin.

"Yes. You're very off base. We're neighbors—I live in the next unit over—and Dante is a close family friend, so we see each other at family get-togethers. That's as far as it goes."

"Well." Vince's eyes stayed trained on hers, a wealth of meaning in his gaze. "Ain't that handy to know."

In the next second, a black and white tuxedo tom the size of a Zeppelin landed with a thud on the sofa table. The cat stumbled over its own feet, plowed into Brenna's wineglass, howled, and took a mighty leap off the table. The glass tumbled over. Red wine splashed onto Brenna's dress like blood spatter. She gasped and jumped up, but the damage was done. The wineglass lay on its side in a puddle, and the spilled wine dripped to the floor, staining the carpet with a circle of red.

"Damn it, Pavarotti." Vince stood and turned to watch the cat run off down the hall. He shook his head. "I'm sorry. That damned cat. He's so destructive. Did you know my cousin had that idiot cat flown here all the way from Afghanistan? I don't know how Dante puts up with him."

"He flew him from where?"

"And look. Damned cat ruined your dress."

"Lucky for me I live right next door. Tell Dante I'll be back as quick as I can."

Brenna strode across Dante's driveway, slipped off her shoes so the ice pick heels wouldn't sink in the soft border of fescue that separated their townhomes, traipsed through the grass, and jogged to her front door.

A few minutes later she stood staring at her closet as she had earlier in the day, and stomped her foot in a fit of fury over the déjà vu moment.

Fifteen pounds didn't sound like much, but when it collected in two places—boobs and butt—it made squeezing into clothes that much harder. And she'd be damned if she'd go spend money on a bigger size. She'd join a gym, go on a diet, lose the weight.

None of which solved her problem right that second, which was, as it had been earlier, what to wear to Maddie's wedding?

She yanked a pair of stretchy capris pants off the hanger—not dressy, but not ball-park casual either. Kind of gorgeous, actually, in a teal fabric that looked like linen and stretched like spandex—stretched being the operative word, praise the little baby Jesus. She'd bought them in town at the Blueberry Boutique, just a few doors down from the Lump & Grind, and had paid a pretty penny for them, and the matching sweater and tank.

She tugged herself out of the dress, wriggled free of the constricting body shaper and—*gasp!*—normal breathing resumed once again.

Standing in front of the mirror, she praised the inventor of stretch fabrics. No, this wasn't what she wanted to wear to her best friend's wedding, and no, she wasn't happy that she had limited her choices by packing on the pounds.

On the upside, she looked adorable, and she'd been able to trade in the heels for a pair of strappy wedges that showed off her pedicure.

The doorbell rang and she flew down the stairs to yank the door open. Dante stood on the other side, his thick hair damp and curling from his shower. He'd traded his nice khakis for a pair of black Levi's, and his dress shirt for a blue polo.

"Looks like we both went for comfort this time around," Brenna said, turning to lock the door. "You ready?"

"Let's get this show on the road."

༄༅༄

Brenna sniffled and dabbed at her eyes with a tissue, smiling through the happy tears.

Maddie looked radiant, standing in the arched opening of the gazebo with her hands in Caleb's, gazing into his eyes as if all the answers to the universe were there for her to discover. From the moment she had appeared from the pathway in the woods with her arm linked in Papa Ron's, who gave her away—wearing his signature luau attire, because Maddie insisted—Caleb's attention never wavered.

He stared at her like she was Aphrodite rising from the sea.

Brenna thought her mother, Edie, had outdone herself with the decorations. Over the opening of the gazebo, where now stood the bride and groom, Edie had created an archway garland thick with mountain laurel, Queen Anne's Lace, and rosebay rhododendron, and continued the theme around the gazebo archways. She had wanted to add swags of pale pink and white organza, but Maddie declined, saying she wanted to keep the wedding as simple as possible.

And in its simplicity, Brenna believed it to be both beautiful and grand.

There were no dewy-eyed fawns and bunnies sighing and swaying at the perimeter of the gathering as she had teased Maddie there might be, but the place held enchantment nonetheless. Candles and torchlight glowed in the deepening twilight, and fireflies dotted the air like faeries come to give their blessing. And if mosquitos joined in to feast on the blood of the guests, and chirping cicadas drowned the words of the minister, still, it was pure magic.

Everyone clapped and cheered when Caleb kissed Maddie for the first time as her husband, and then the bride and groom, with their faces glowing, faced their intimate group of friends and loved ones. TJ, sitting with Caleb's parents, jumped from his seat and bounded to them. He threw his arms around Maddie's legs in a spasm of love, and when she bent to hug him he looked up at her with his earnest face shining and said, "Can I call you Mama now?"

The little boy's question, posed with innocence and radiant joy, caused a wave of collective quiet over the gathering. Maddie's eyes welled, and one blink sent her tears over the brink and pouring onto her cheeks. She lifted TJ into her arms with more strength than her small frame suggested her capable of, and held him in a tight embrace. "There isn't anything I want more."

"Well, ya don't hafta cry about it," he said, his voice muffled against her shoulder.

Everyone laughed. Caleb, his cheeks as wet as his new

wife's, lifted TJ from Maddie's arms and whispered something to the boy that had him first nodding and smiling, and then squirming to get down. "C'mon, Pirate! C'mon Belle!" He raced off through the woods toward the house, with both dogs in hot pursuit. At Maddie's questioning look, Caleb grinned. "I told him he can have all the cannoli he wants."

Brenna laughed with everyone else and wiped her eyes. She waited her turn to hug the bride and groom and then moved away to allow others the same opportunity.

Rebecca came up beside her and slid her arm through Brenna's, and together they began the walk down the wooded path to the house.

"So, the gossip mill has been churning out some pretty good stuff this afternoon," Rebecca said. "You going to make me beg for details, or are you just going to be nice and share?"

"I don't know what you're talking about." Brenna sidestepped an overhanging branch and Rebecca ducked under it.

"Oh, come on. Have a heart." Rebecca looked over her shoulder and lowered her voice. "Don't tell Sean, but I've had a crush on Dante since I was fifteen. So I need to know if he kisses as great as I always figured."

Brenna rolled her eyes. "You think I'm going to fall for that? You look at Dante like a brother."

"Well, sure. *Now* I do. But back in the day? I remember the first time Caleb brought him home from college for a holiday. Me and my BFF, Bindy-Sue, followed him around for three days, just to gaze at the glory that was Dante. That's when he started calling me 'Twizzler.' Every time he said it I'd swoon, like being nicknamed after a red, skinny candy is a good thing." Rebecca laughed. "I figured out pretty quick he was as much of a pain in the ass as Caleb, always teasing and being impossible. But he did ignite my schoolgirl fantasies there for a while."

"Yeah, well, I don't think Sean is too worried."

Rebecca grinned. "He's not. Nowadays Sean's the only

one who ignites my female fantasies—my very grown-up woman fantasies. Every. Single. One."

"Ew. Ick. You always say stuff like that just to gross me out."

"Uh-huh. And if you tell me about kissing Dante, I'll cut you a break. Details, Brenna."

"Oh, fine." Brenna huffed out a breath and considered her words, not sure where to begin. "Well, it was weird."

"He kisses weird? You have no idea how disappointing that is."

"No, the kissing part wasn't weird. Well, I mean, it was, but not the kissing, just the—oh, hell. I don't know how to explain it." She sighed and dragged Rebecca a few steps off the path for the sake of privacy. Brenna slapped a mosquito off her arm, then her leg, and lowered her voice. "Okay, here it is. The truth and nothing but. It was flipping amazing, all right? Over-the-moon fantastic. Mystical. Magical." She lifted her hands and wriggled her fingers. "It's like he sprinkled me with Lust Dust or something." She glanced over Rebecca's shoulder, smiled at the minister as he passed, and turned her finger wriggling into a pleasant wave.

Rebecca regarded her with a bemused smile. "Lust Dust? That's a new one."

"One minute he was furious with me, and the next minute he was kissing me like there's no tomorrow. Went from zero to sixty in a flash. He took me completely by surprise, and instead of pushing him away I—well, I kissed him back." Her face heated with embarrassment and she was glad for the growing darkness. "The truth is, I couldn't seem to stop myself. He was so—it was so…so…"

"Hot."

"Well, yes. It was that. But I think the word I want is 'unexpected.'"

"And passionate. Crazy sexy."

"Yes, and yes." Brenna narrowed her eyes. "You're not asking me how it was, you're telling me."

"Just repeating what I heard. Chloe called the restaurant to check on how the dinner rush was going, and to let the staff know their boss is a freaking superhero who rescues people from burning cars, and she talked to the kitchen manager who told her what Gemma told him. So of course Chloe had to talk to Gemma personally to hear the details first hand. Gemma told Chloe if she'd opened that door two minutes later you guys would've been naked and doing the big nasty right there on the storeroom floor."

"That's a big, fat lie," Brenna said, and Rebecca gave her a look. Brenna widened her eyes. "It is a lie. We certainly were not on the floor." Rebecca lifted her brows and smirked, and Brenna dug deep to find her dignity. It was a stretch. "He had me against the wall, actually."

Rebecca fanned her face. "So. Freaking. Hot. You know, the first time Sean and I had sex we were in his office. He pushed me against the door and—"

Brenna slapped her hands over her ears and squeezed her eyes shut. "Oh, my god, honey, will you *stop!*"

Rebecca's boisterous laugh echoed through the trees. "Sorry, sorry. I love doing that to you."

Brenna opened her eyes one at a time and scowled at her sister-in-law, whose mirth had yet to be contained. She stood chuckling and rubbing her baby belly.

"Who else did she tell?" Brenna asked.

"Just Maddie. And our mothers. But only because they have super-maternal Spidey senses and knew something big was in the works."

"Well, thanks for the 'head's up,' at least. When my mother starts hinting for information I'll be ahead of the game for knowing."

"Hey, you two." The voice came from Chloe, a friend of Brenna's through Maddie, and who also happened to be Dante's employee and right hand. She stopped when she reached them. "Am I interrupting?"

Rebecca flashed a smile. "Can you guess what we're talking about?"

Brenna closed her eyes and groaned.

"Oh, relax." Rebecca poked Brenna with her elbow. "You're among friends. Besides, she already heard it from Gemma, remember?"

"So, yeah," Chloe stepped closer and lowered her voice. "Gemma said you two were going at it pretty hot and heavy. How was it?"

"I am not going to kiss and tell," Brenna said, and when Rebecca's brows lifted she added, "Any more than I already have. I'm done talking about this."

"She said, and I quote, 'over-the-moon fantastic.' Not, of course, that we ever had a doubt," Rebecca said, nudging Chloe who stood there grinning like a fool.

"He's my boss, and the nearest thing I have to a big brother, so I'll never find out first hand. I've sure always wondered, though. I mean, it'd be hard not to, because—" Chloe licked the tip of her index finger, tapped it in the air, and made a sizzling sound through her teeth.

"Oh, my god." Brenna covered her face with her hands and laughed. "Look, it was just a kiss, and nothing is going to come of it. We've agreed to try and be friends. That's it. Now, if the two of you are done, I'd like to go back to the house now. I haven't eaten all day, and I'm starving."

Though dinner and the reception were well underway when Dante and Brenna had first returned to the house, the festivities resumed after the ceremony. Most had visited the bar Dante's caterers provided before the vows were spoken, and they hit it again upon their return to the house from the gazebo. Even Grampa Boone had finished off countless shots of bourbon and didn't look as if he was ready to call it quits. He got things started by coaxing Rebecca into a dance, and others soon followed.

Brenna wasn't sure when Dante had found the time to set up the cake, but when she asked if he needed help he told her he had it covered.

When the bride and groom cut the first slice, she had to admit he'd put it together well, making good use of the silk flowers and votive candles they'd found in the box in the Bistro storeroom. The cake wasn't as fancy as Brenna's masterpiece, but it was lovely just the same, and delicious. She wanted to believe it didn't taste as good as hers would have, but thanks to the damn furry beasties, she'd never know.

The clock struck twelve, and Maddie and Caleb disappeared into the house to change their clothes. They'd be staying at a bed & breakfast in Helen tonight, and then driving to the Atlanta airport in the morning. Brenna promised Maddie she'd take charge of putting the house and yard back in order, and she intended to devote her day tomorrow to doing just that.

"Sweetheart, have you seen TJ?" Edie asked Brenna. "I can't find him, and I'm sure Caleb and Maddie want to say goodbye to him before they go."

"I can't believe the little guy's still awake," Brenna said. "Are you sure he didn't crash on the couch or something?"

Edie shook her head. "Rebecca said he was with Dante. Maybe if you find Dante, you'll find TJ." The older woman's lips curved in a meaningful smile.

Brenna held her arms out to Edie. "Hug, please, Mama."

Edie moved into Brenna's embrace, and chuckled when Brenna whispered in her ear, "Don't you dare start playing matchmaker. Do you hear me? Please don't do it."

"Scale of one to ten," Edie whispered back.

"Off the charts. Now stop. You're killing me. It was just a kiss, Mama. It didn't mean anything. Okay? No matchmaking, now. Promise me."

Edie sighed. "Oh, fine." She smoothed Brenna's hair behind her shoulders, and pressed her cool cheek against Brenna's. "I'll stay out of it. But only because I think if you've rated him that high, then it's clear the man doesn't need any help."

Brenna wandered around looking for TJ, but the little guy had gone MIA. She flagged down Sada. She was the boy's grandmother, so maybe she knew where he'd gone.

"Why, yes, dear." Sada smiled. "TJ is with Dante. Last I saw them they were walking across the field to the treehouse."

Brenna narrowed her eyes and stared at Sada, suspecting the woman was in cahoots with Edie to play matchmaker, but Sada regarded her with a bland smile, so there was no telling. Brenna didn't trust either of them.

Not for the first time that evening Brenna was glad she'd traded her dress for the capris and her high heels for wedges. Walking through the tall grass toward the treehouse, with the dissolving reception at her back and the moon lighting her way, she watched her step and prayed there were no snakes or other creepy-crawlers lying in wait to send her running. She wished she'd had the foresight to bring a flashlight. She paused once to admire the glow of fireflies dotting the field and hoped that they all found their mates.

She reached the treehouse unscathed and made a go at climbing up the rope ladder. She took her time with it, eager to keep her balance and not end up stuck, or worse, in a heap on the ground.

Her head cleared the top of the ladder. The door stood ajar, and she peeked inside TJ's hideaway. Moonlight slanted through a window on the far right wall, affording her a limited view of the interior. Dante sat on the floor against the back wall near the corner, his face turned toward the window opening to his left, and bathed in moonlight. There was no glass in the window, she saw, just wooden shutters that were opened to allow the pale light to stream through. TJ sat in Dante's lap facing the window, snuggled against the man's shoulder and chest, and drawing the heavy breaths of one in a sound sleep.

Brenna shifted, and Dante turned his head at the sound.

"It's just me," she said, unsure whether he could see her face. "Caleb and Maddie are leaving soon. Figured TJ would want to say goodbye."

"Okay," Dante said, but didn't move. He looked at TJ

and smoothed his hand over the little boy's head. "He knocked out about ten seconds after we got up here. Little dude has had a big day."

Brenna crawled into the treehouse and sat against the wall opposite Dante in a mirror image of his location, though she had no room to stretch out her legs as he was doing.

As he had a child restricting his movements, she drew her legs into a crisscross and relaxed against the wall. She looked around and wished she had more light. "I have to come back in the daylight." She kept her voice quiet so as not to wake TJ. "I was looking at this place earlier and thinking how cool it is."

"It really is. It's too dark to see, but there's a table and chairs in the other corner. He wanted a pirate theme, so Maddie found him a bunch of stuff—a pirate bean bag chair, a sleeping bag. Cal built him a treasure chest, so the little dude has somewhere to stow his booty."

"Very cool, indeed." Brenna returned his smile and, uncomfortable beneath his perusal, looked out the window. "It's beautiful from up here. Look at the mountains in the moonlight. Even the fireflies are still glowing." She glanced back at Dante to find his dark eyes focused on her. She cleared her throat. "Everyone knows about the storeroom. Gemma did everything but take out a billboard."

"It'll blow over soon enough."

Brenna nodded and searched her brain for a change of subject. "Earlier, when we talked about the way you saved that girl, you said your training kicked in. What did you mean by that? What training?"

Dante shrugged and looked away. "I was in the army for a while."

"The army? You? Mr. Break-All-the-Rules Caravicci?"

"That's right."

"What did you do in the army?"

"Army stuff."

"Army stuff," Brenna repeated, and shook her head.

Men. "Vince said you had your cat flown here from Afghanistan. I thought I misheard at the time he said it, but if it's true, that must be quite a story."

"I'm sorry Pavarotti ruined your dress. He's clumsy as hell. For a while I thought it was because he's cross-eyed, but it turns out he's just lacking in the usual cat graces. He's like a bull in a china shop."

So much for old army stories, Brenna thought, but her curiosity peaked. Maybe he'd been dishonorably discharged or something and was too embarrassed to talk about it. Whatever. She made a mental note to ask Rebecca, who was sure to know something.

"It's fine. To be honest, I was happy for a reason to change out of the dress and heels. Neither was very comfortable."

"Why wear them, then?"

"Because I'm a woman," she said, amused by his confusion. "We females often sacrifice comfort for beauty."

"Why would you do that?"

Brenna's soft laugh filled the space again, and she shook her head. "You own the wrong chromosomes. You'll never understand."

"In any event, I'm sorry your dress was ruined. I'll pay to have it cleaned for you."

"Thanks, but unnecessary. Like I said, your clumsy cat did me a favor."

TJ shifted and grabbed hold of the opening of Dante's shirt and tugged it down when he shifted his position. Brenna saw the flash of dark ink.

"Why do you have a tattoo of a Celtic cross?" she blurted.

Dante disengaged TJ's hand from his shirt and looked up to meet Brenna's gaze. "What's with the game of twenty questions? Most of the time you don't say 'boo' to me."

"Maybe I'm just trying to be nice. We agreed to be friends, remember?"

"Yeah, right," Dante said. She gave him a look that

could melt steel and he sighed. "My grandmother was Scottish. There was a necklace that was in the family forever, a Celtic cross. She wanted me to have it, but my aunt got hold of it and gave it to—gave it to another family member. After I joined the army, Gran thought I needed the cross to keep me safe, so—" He shrugged. "—I got the tat to make her happy. Now it's your turn. Where did you get your Celtic cross, and why don't you ever wear it?"

Brenna straightened up from her slouch to regard him with surprise. "How do you know about my cross?"

"You were wearing it the first time we met, the day I called you bat-shit crazy." His lips curved and his face became fully engaged, his eyes bright in the moonlight. "Can't believe you don't remember that."

"Oh, I remember," she said, and lost the effort not to return his smile. "That didn't win you any points, you know."

Dante's soft laugh rumbled from his chest. "I'm aware."

"So you noticed my cross."

"Yes. The diamonds flashed when you moved, and it caught my eye. I couldn't stop staring at it because it was so similar to my tat. There are a lot of Celtic crosses out there, but the placement of the diamonds on yours is almost identical to the rivets on mine. It surprised me. I wanted a closer look, but thought it would be rude to ask. And then you called me a Neanderthal, so—"

"My cross. You were staring at my cross." She held his gaze for a moment and then looked outside, dismayed and embarrassed by her nasty assumption on the day they met that he had been ogling her boobs. She took a moment to collect her thoughts before turning her face back to Dante. "It seems our Gaelic grandmothers thought alike. Mine gave me the necklace on my twenty-first birthday. I stopped wearing it a few years ago because the clasp weakened and I was afraid of losing it."

"You should have it fixed. It's a beautiful piece."

Brenna nodded, but didn't trust herself to speak.

"We better get the little dude back to his parents," Dante

said. "Do you need help climbing down?"

"No, thanks. I'm sure I can manage it. Can I help with TJ?"

"Nah. I've got it covered. Be careful getting down from here."

Brenna eased herself from the treehouse. She took care to find her footing and balance on the wobbling rope ladder. She glanced up to see Dante shift TJ's slack body around with gentle care, resting the boy's cheek against his shoulder. TJ moved, but didn't awaken.

"Hey, little dude." Dante rubbed TJ's back until the boy stirred. "Hold tight to me, okay? We're climbing down out of your treehouse now."

"Uncle Dante?" TJ's sleepy voice was muffled against Dante's shoulder. "Could I have quarters for the racing game?"

"You bet."

"Mm-kay." TJ curled his fingers into Dante's shirt, though his eyes remained closed and he didn't lift his head. His words slurred when he said, "Love you, Uncle Dante."

"Love you, too, little dude, all the way to the moon and back." Dante smoothed his hand over the little boy's head. "Hold tight now. I'll be in big trouble with your parents if I drop you on your head."

Brenna's lips curved when TJ giggled, then she sighed, and prayed not to slip and land in a heap on the ground.

॰৩৫৩

"You sure you don't need help with all this?" Edie asked an hour later, motioning toward the kitchen sink and counters, towering with the detritus of the day's celebration. "I'll be happy to stay."

"I'm not doing anything tonight, Mama. It's too late. I'm heading home soon. I'll be back tomorrow morning to clean up and feed Maddie's cats."

"Dante's taking care of the leftover cake right now, so you don't have to worry about that. Did you taste that Italian crème? Oh, my goodness, it was melt-in-your-mouth delicious. That man certainly knows his way around a kitchen, doesn't he? He'll make a great husband someday," Edie said.

"You know, I've always thought that, too." Sada gave Brenna a meaningful look. "He's a talented chef and baker, you know. And he coaches kids' sports over at the community center."

"He volunteered at the food bank a few times, too," Edie said.

"He brought cupcakes for Maddie's kindergarten class for their end-of-year-party." Sada gave Brenna an owlish nod. "He decorated them to look like zoo animals. Can you imagine? Maddie said the kids loved them."

"Well, of course, he loves children," Edie said with a flip of her hand. "He'll make a wonderful father someday."

"Oh, he certainly will. A *wonderful* father!" Sada nodded in enthusiastic agreement.

"And he's *so* handsome." Edie emitted a dreamy sigh. "Bless his heart."

Brenna rolled her eyes. "Yep, he's a catch all right. Why, I bet he can get wine stains out of silk, and he probably knows what fuchsia is."

"You know," Edie said, nodding, "I bet you're right."

"That was sarcasm, Mama." Brenna strode across the kitchen and poked her head into the dining room. "Excuse me, Dante?"

Dante sealed the lid on a plastic container housing what little was left of the cake and glanced up, licking frosting off his fingers. "Yeah?"

"Fuchsia. Do you know what it is?"

He drew his brows together. "Of course. Don't you?"

"Humor me."

"Fuchsia. Uh, it's some kind of Asian decorating thing, isn't it?"

"That would be feng shui." Brenna smirked and turned back to the mothers. "Sorry, but he has no clue what fuchsia is, which makes him less than perfect. But thank you so much, ladies, for your valuable input. I'm sure everyone's favorite Italian chef will be happy to know you stand solidly on Team Dante. Maybe you could get T-shirts made, just to show your support."

Edie scowled. "Are you being sassy, young lady?"

Brenna took Edie's face in her hands and stared her down. "Stop matchmaking." She turned her gaze and a pointed finger to Sada who had the good graces to look abashed. "You, too. Both of you, and I mean it. Stop."

"Stop what?" Dante bypassed the ladies and slid the cake into the freezer.

"Mama and Sada are trying to—"

"Nothing, nothing," Edie waved her hand and laughed. "It's nothing." She gave Brenna a look. "Nothing at all."

Dante glanced at Sada, whose lips curved in a vague smile. "Lovely wedding, wasn't it?" she said and scurried out to the porch.

Dante turned his gaze to Brenna, who rolled her eyes and shook her head.

"We were just talking about how wonderful your cake was. It was so fortunate that you had it available." Edie sidled toward the door. "Best wedding cake I've ever had, in fact. Perfection."

"Well, thanks a lot, Mama." Brenna put her hands on her hips. "I thought you liked mine best, the one I made for Sean and Rebecca."

Edie blanched. "Oh, yes, well, that was delicious. And I'm sure the one you made for Maddie and Caleb was good, too. It's too bad we never got the chance to taste it."

"But Dante's was better," Brenna said, her tone too sweet.

"Did I say better?" Edie opened the door. "I don't think I said better, dear." She was gone in a flash with the screen door slapping shut behind her.

"Well, I like that," Brenna said. "My own mother likes your cake better."

Dante regarded her with amusement. "Not everything has to be a competition between us, does it? What difference does it make which of us bakes the better cake?"

"Or sautés the better shrimp?" Brenna said, remembering Dante's shrimp dish from Thanksgiving that she, Rebecca, and Maddie had all deemed to be almost better than sex. Not that she'd tell Dante that. She blew out a tired sigh. "I'm sick of losing to you in the food department. I try so hard to be creative, and you whip something up at the last minute that takes home the gold."

"Is it really that big a deal?" He raised his brows.

Brenna stared at him a moment and made him laugh when she said, "Bet your ass! I hate coming in second on anything, especially to you. And say what you will—" She poked his chest with her finger for emphasis. "—but you're just as competitive as I am." He moved back a step and she poked him again. "You don't like to lose at anything either." One more poke. "You always do whatever you have to do to win."

Dante's eyes narrowed, but his lips curved. He stepped forward against the press of her finger, forcing her to step back—once, twice, thrice—and she sucked in a breath when her hips bumped against the counter. She reached behind her to grab the edge of the countertop, and her eyes widened when Dante rested his hands on either side of hers, hemming her in as he had done in the storeroom.

Brenna's heart sped to triple speed. Dante leaned down and she parted her lips, in spite of herself, when his mouth stopped a mere breath away from hers, so close she swore she felt the radiating heat. A second passed, and another. His gaze dipped to her mouth. Brenna licked her lips and her eyes fluttered shut in anticipation, and then the stubble darkening his jaw tickled the skin of her cheek with the barest touch, and his warm breath against her ear made her shiver when he whispered, "You're right. I'll do whatever I

have to do to win. You'd do well to remember that, sweetheart."

He pressed his lips against the tender skin just below her
earlobe and made her shiver again, then stepped back.
Brenna stared at him, her mind whirling.

"It's late. I'll follow you home when you're ready to go,
make sure you get there safe," he said. "And relax, I don't
expect to be invited in. I know you just want to be friends."

Brenna still gripped the edges of the counter, her eyes
wide and lips parted in surprise when he disappeared out to
the porch.

∽∾∽

True to his word, Dante followed her home and did no
more than wave and call a quiet, "Goodnight," from his
driveway as he watched her go through her front door. Her
last view of him was of his arms resting on the roof of the
Trans Am above the driver's door, his lips curved in a gentle smile. Once inside her townhouse she heard his engine
rev, and she peeked through her window to see him driving
away. Though where he might be going at nearly two in the
morning was something she'd rather not consider.

Exhausted, Brenna fell into bed, expecting sleep to find
her in minutes. Instead, she tossed and turned, making a
tangle of her bed sheets and knocking her duvet to the floor.

Hot. The room was too hot. That was the problem.

She rolled out of bed and stomped to the wall switch to
turn on the overhead fan, visited the bathroom sink for a
quick drink of water, traded her cotton pajama bottoms for a
pair of baby-doll sleep shorts, and flopped back onto her
mattress with a huff. The whirring blades above her stirred
the air and cooled her skin but did nothing to ease the racing
of her mind.

That kiss. That damned, stupid kiss.

That damned, stupid, flipping *fantastic* kiss.

Brenna grabbed her extra pillow, curled up with it, hugged it to her, and redoubled her efforts to sleep.

The harder she tried, the more awake she became.

Damned Neanderthal.

She tossed the pillow aside and rolled to her back, staring into the dark. She focused on the gentle and rhythmic click-click-click of the ceiling fan, and gave up forcing sleep. Her brain had too much to catalog, too many new details to put into order.

Dante Caravicci was not the man she had thought he was. She had judged him based on an incorrect assumption all those years ago and had allowed that assumption to color her opinion of everything pertaining to him from that point forward.

The man had not been staring at her boobs like an ill-mannered redneck. He had been scrutinizing her necklace.

Good grief.

She covered her eyes with her arm and blew out a self-deprecating laugh.

How would life be different now if she had known that truth five years ago? If he had simply looked at her and said, "Great necklace. Looks like my tattoo," would things have been different? Would that have sparked a conversation about their grandmothers and Celtic crosses? Would they have dated, maybe once or twice, and parted ways as friends?

Maybe not parted at all, the little voice that sounded like Jack whispered. She tamped it down.

Her opinion of Dante had been simple and superficial.

And wrong.

God, she hated that.

Until today, she hadn't known that he was the kind of man who would get a tattoo to ease an old lady's mind, who would fly a nutty cat halfway around the world to care for it, a man who would put his own life in grave danger to save that of a stranger.

He was, in fact, exactly the kind of man Jack might have

intended to introduce to his sister through a blind date, if only fate hadn't intervened.

Brenna swallowed hard.

Except Dante wasn't that man. He couldn't be. Dante never knew Jack. Had he? No, he certainly would have mentioned it at some point in the last five years.

The truth was that she might never know who Jack had wanted her to meet. And she'd wasted a whole lot of blessed time wishing the mystery man would appear.

"Stupid," she whispered into the dark and curled up with her pillow again.

What the hell was wrong with her? Here she was, a grown woman of thirty, wishing like a little girl for an impossible dream. Well, it was time to grow up. Past time.

She had her family, her friends, and her business. She was a smart and capable woman. She didn't need a man in her life to make her whole. Hadn't she already proven that?

Dante's face swam in her mind and she held onto the image. She'd been judgmental where he was concerned, and stubborn. It wasn't the first time she'd recognized this trait in herself and she didn't like it. Not one little bit.

She sat up, punched her pillow into shape, and snuggled in for a final go at sleep, with all she'd learned of Dante still weighing on her mind.

As she drifted, she replayed the scene in the storeroom. It clouded over until she stood again in Maddie's kitchen with Dante's warm lips pressed beneath her ear. His words followed her into sleep.

So—no newsflash—the man liked to win, hated to lose. Well, by god, so did she. In fact, there was only one thing Brenna Kinkaid hated more than losing.

She hated being wrong.

Chapter 5

Dante yawned while he poured food and fresh water into bowls for Maddie's cats. The oldest of the barn cats, Horace, had trotted behind him into the barn and sat waiting for food with his tail and ears twitching. The other four cats were nowhere to be seen, and Dante assumed they were curled up somewhere snoozing off the last of the night's darkness.

He yawned again as he walked from the barn to the house. Once inside he started a fresh pot of coffee brewing in the kitchen and wandered through the house, double-checking each room to be sure he hadn't missed anything requiring clean up. By the time he returned to the kitchen the coffee was ready for consumption and the air hung full with its rich aroma. He filled a mug and returned outside to watch the sunrise.

The virgin day brought with it a cool stillness that Dante enjoyed. He leaned against the barn to face the field behind the house and the mountains that stood in the distance beyond the forest abutting the property. As darkness eased to light, the mountains turned from black to purple, to varying shades of dusky blue. Bird chatter filled the air, and the morning mist created a hazy patina across the landscape. Dante remained still as a group of deer appeared through the light fog. They ran on nimble legs, slowing about midway across the open field. They nosed the ground and came up chewing.

From somewhere in the woods a branch cracked and fell to the ground, the crash echoing through the hills. The deer raised their heads, still as stone until the largest of the does bolted away. The remaining four raced into the forest behind her.

The sun peeked over the mountains and dissipated the mist in a glory of pink and gold. Dante's eyes burned, but he kept them open until the brightness brought tears, and then he squeezed them shut, the relief as pleasurable as it was painful.

He yearned for sleep.

It had been months since he'd suffered a bout of insomnia, a plague that had visited him off and on since childhood, worsening for a time after his return from Afghanistan, and then improving after he opened the Pizzeria. He'd known yesterday, after the rescue of the young girl, that sleep would elude him. At least he had put the nighttime hours to good use.

After dropping Brenna off, he'd returned to Caleb and Maddie's to clean up the remains of the celebration. His catering crew had dismantled the tent and returned everything to the Bistro hours ago, but out from under Maddie's watchful eye the kitchen had been neglected. The pileup of stuff in the sink and on the counters had reminded Dante of the way Cal's kitchen had looked pre-Maddie, and he'd marveled at the changes in his best friend's life in the short span of a year.

Last year at this time, Caleb was only Maddie's carpenter, the guy she had hired to remodel the kitchen.

Dante remembered Caleb insisting there was nothing going on with his client, that he didn't know her well enough to have an opinion. And he remembered telling Caleb that with the right woman, a second was long enough, and he'd meant it. One second, and a man could lose his heart. Or his mind and his good sense with it, Dante amended, when

Brenna's face floated into his brain. Brenna Kinkaid. Beautiful, stubborn, difficult Brenna.

Their relationship had shifted yesterday in a big way. He wasn't sure what that meant yet, but he appreciated no longer sitting at neutral. If nothing came of that kiss, even if it was never to be repeated, it had jumpstarted a change that pushed them out of the ditch they'd been in for so long and onto the open road. And damn, but it felt good to finally have his foot on the gas pedal, even if he didn't know where he was going.

Dante pushed away from the barn. Time to go home and try to get a few hours of shuteye before swinging by the Pizzeria, and then on to the Bistro.

He unplugged the coffee maker, poured the remaining brew into his mug, and locked up on his way out. He was halfway home when he remembered he had to bake another Italian Crème cake to replace the one he had offered up yesterday for Maddie and Caleb's reception. Weary, he drove past the turnoff to his townhome and aimed the Trans Am toward the Bistro.

ঙ৯ঙ৯

Brenna stood in Maddie's kitchen with her hands on her hips and turned full circle. The stainless steel sink, full of dishes and glasses last night, shone empty and bright. The countertops had been cleared of litter and scrubbed clean. The barstools at the center island were pushed in, and someone had watered Maddie's philodendron. The shutters on the bay window were closed, and the kitchen table was free of clutter.

Emitting a little hum, Brenna strode through the dining room and into the living room, then through the rest of the house. Spotless. Even in the office, the cherry wood of Jack's old desk, refurbished by Caleb, gleamed beneath the overhead light, and the surface lay empty except for a closed laptop and faux Tiffany desk lamp. The framed photos on the credenza behind the desk constituted a mix of the Walker and Kinkaid clans, with pictures of TJ taking up the lion's share of space.

Typical mother, Brenna thought with a smile and trailed her fingertips over the frames, pausing to admire a few. She recognized one of herself with Sean and Jack when they were all in their twenties. She had the same photo on a bookcase in her living room and had seen it on Sean's credenza in his law office. She picked it up and touched the glass protecting the photo, wished she could step into the picture to relive that moment with Jack one more time.

"You did good," she said aloud to Jack's smiling face. "They're on their honeymoon right now. But I guess you probably know that."

The silence grew heavy and maudlin. She blinked back an unexpected rush of tears and returned the photo to its place next to a picture of her parents.

She pushed through the screen door and down the porch stairs toward the barn, stopping to pet Horace, the most wizened of Maddie's barn cats. She stepped past him and into the barn, not surprised to find fresh water and full food dishes. Whoever had cleaned up the house would also have taken care of the cats. She returned to the kitchen and grabbed her cell phone.

"Well, hey, Mama," she said when Edie answered her call. "Thanks for cleaning up at Maddie's. How early did you and Daddy get out here anyway?"

"What in heaven's name are you talking about, child? Ron, stop it now," Edie said, and though she dropped her voice to a whisper Brenna heard her say, "Keep your hands to yourself while I'm on the phone. Five minutes and I'm all yours." Shuffling, muffled laughter, and then, "What's that about cleaning, honey?"

Brenna shut her eyes shut and tried to unstick the mental image of her parents that popped into her brain. "I just got to Maddie's house. The place is clean as a whistle."

"It wasn't me. I'm still in my PJs. Sean and Rebecca must have taken care of it for you."

"I guess. They planned to help me, but I didn't expect them to show up this early. I'll swing by their house on my way to the L&G to say thanks. Go spend time with Daddy." *Ick.*

"Okay!" Edie sounded a little too cheerful. *Double ick.* "Fried chicken and smashed taters for dinner, if you're interested."

"I can't. I'm keeping the L&G open later on Sundays now that Dante's got the Bistro open till ten. Even Bubba-Jo's is staying open later. That damned Neanderthal screwed up Sundays for everyone."

"Bless his heart. He's a hard worker, that one. You could do worse."

Oh, for pity's sake. "Kiss Daddy for me. I'll talk to you later."

When Brenna arrived at Sean and Rebecca's two-story house, she took the time to admire the landscaping Edie had done. The front of the house was alive with blooms and colorful shrubs, and the arbor leading into the backyard stood heavy with a yellow blossomed climbing vine. Ferns hung in baskets on the shade of the porch and swung every so often in the gentle morning breeze.

Belle and Pirate announced Brenna's arrival before she reached the porch stairs. Rebecca opened the door and greeted Brenna with a smile. Behind her, Sean held the dogs' collars. Both animals whined and strained to pull free and welcome the new visitor.

"Hurry up and get in here," her brother told her. "Belle's not very well-behaved with Pirate around."

"Belle's not well-behaved ever," Brenna said, but she stepped into the foyer so Rebecca could close the door. Sean released the dogs and Brenna bent to give the beasties an appropriate hello when they rushed her. Belle, a ninety-pound Lab/Golden Retriever mix, dropped to her back and pawed the air, begging for an immediate belly rub, and Pirate danced on his three legs, ears back, tail wagging. "Who's a bad pair of dogs, huh? Who's so rotten they ought to be thrown out in the trash? Who is it? Is it you? Is it?" Brenna cooed and the tails wagged on. She grinned at her brother and sister-in-law. "I've forgiven them for the cake. They redeemed themselves by behaving after the ceremony."

"They really were good dogs," Rebecca said. "I mean, you know, except for the cake."

"I'm surprised neither one of them got sick, eating all that sugar," Brenna said, still rubbing bellies.

Sean laughed. "They both have a cast iron stomach. Nothing fazes either of these two."

"You want some coffee? I can brew fresh," Rebecca said over her shoulder as they walked down the hall toward the kitchen.

"No thanks. I'm on my way in to the L&G."

"I thought you took this morning off. Aren't we supposed to help you clean over at Maddie and Cal's?" Rebecca slid two stools out from under the breakfast bar and sat on one. Brenna sat in the other and dropped her purse on the counter.

"I thought the two of you already took care of that. I came by to say thanks."

"It wasn't us," Sean said. "I fixed my pregnant wife breakfast in bed this morning."

"Well, somebody cleaned over there," Brenna said.

Rebecca's kitten, Amelia, appeared. She sauntered across the kitchen floor like queen of all she surveyed. Brenna wriggled her fingers to entice the petite feline into jumping onto her lap. Amelia preferred to bat at Belle's tail instead. Belle sat down next to Sean and whined. Thus thwarted, Amelia turned her attention to Pirate who suffered her attentions with a hanging head and stoic acceptance.

"Mom and Dad?"

"No. I already called Mama." Brenna turned her eyes to Rebecca. "Sada and Big Will?"

"Nope. Mom and Dad have TJ, and they planned to let him sleep in and then take him to the Pizzeria for lunch. Dante promised him a bunch of tokens for the racing game."

Brenna frowned. "That leaves Grampa Boone, who we know didn't go over there to clean, or Phyllis."

Rebecca snorted out a laugh. "Right. Like Maddie's mother would trade her Louboutins and Armani ensemble for Levi's and a dust rag. Anyway, she had an early flight out of Hartsfield this morning."

"Okay, so not Phyllis either." Brenna shrugged. "It was the shoemaker's elves, then. The place was spotless when I got there this morning. Not a thing out of place. And now that I think of it, the place smelled like coffee, too. Who do you suppose?"

"Someone who knows where the spare key is hidden," said Rebecca. "If I were you I'd quit worrying about it. Whoever did it let us all off the hook."

"I guess, but I'd sure like to know who to thank."

"Hey, as long as you're here," Sean said, "I'd like to run something by you. Rebecca and I were mentioning to Mom and Dad that we need a bigger place—"

"Because of the Little Boogers." Rebecca patted her belly.

"Right." Sean's face lit up and he flashed a smile. "And Mom and Dad have been talking about downsizing. They've actually gone out looking at condos. Rebecca and I talked about it, and, well, would it bother you if we bought the house?"

Stunned, Brenna stared at Sean. "Mind? No, of course not. I think that'd be fantastic. It's a great house, and it will be perfect for you. I'm just surprised. Mom and Dad want to downsize? Seriously?"

"We were surprised too, but they talked about it last night. They've even had a realtor come and give them an estimate so they'd have some idea what they could get for the place. Rebecca suggested that we should buy it, and the more I've thought about it, well…" He shrugged. "Why not? We made a lot of great memories in that house. I hate the thought of it belonging to strangers. I just didn't want to buy it out from under you if you had some idea of wanting to live there yourself someday."

Brenna dimpled. "Aw. Look at you being all big brother-ly and sweet. Rebecca must be wearing off on you."

"You're a pain in the ass," he said, his tone bland.

Brenna laughed. "You'd think there was something wrong if I wasn't."

つかつ

Dante stopped at the red light at the corner of Bright and Main and stared at the crowd of people taking up real estate in front of his restaurant.

"What the hell?"

His gaze roved the parked vans with their side panel logos announcing their affiliations—Fox News Atlanta, CNN, Channel 2, Channel 13, and a few more he couldn't see from his car. He narrowed his eyes at the dark-haired woman talking to a nerdy-looking guy with a camera perched on his shoulder. The guy said something and she laughed, lifted a microphone, and stepped up to the entrance of the Bistro. She glanced at the door and then stepped once to her left, making the Dante's Bistro logo her companion. Comprehension rolled through him like an ominous tide.

"Ah, shit."

The light flashed from red to green. Dante passed the circus in front of the Bistro, slowed at the alley behind the building where he normally turned in to park. No reporters back here as far as he could see.

But did he really want to go into the restaurant and be trapped inside with the media vultures hanging around waiting for the doors to open?

Probably best to deal with it and move on. Once they

figured out he had no intention of giving them an interview they'd leave him alone. He hoped.

He'd asked everyone at the scene of the accident yesterday to keep his name out of their reports. "Can't you just call me a good Samaritan?" he'd begged, but apparently someone had blabbed.

Annoyed, he parked and let himself into the restaurant from the back alley, careful to lock the door again behind him. He checked the time, knew he had about two hours before the assistant kitchen manager and staff would arrive to begin prep for the lunch crowd. Time enough to take care of the cake for the private party tonight and do some paperwork.

Dante put in his earbuds, turned up the Foo Fighters, and got to work. By the time he punched *save* on his inventory spreadsheet his staff began to arrive. Chloe was the first to appear in his office doorway, excitement flushing her cheeks.

"Hey, boss! Did you see the crowd out front?"

Dante tugged the earbuds from his ears and frowned. "Yeah, I saw them. Just ignore them and get to work."

Chloe's laugh filled the room. She slid through the doorway of the small office and dropped her hobo purse on the floor, then leaned against the wall opposite Dante's desk. The office—or box, as Dante referred to it—had room enough for the desk and chair, a sofa where he crashed on occasion, a filing cabinet, and air. *And sometimes, not enough air.*

"What?" he said when she continued to regard him with a silly grin.

"You're a hero! Seize the day! Go out front and greet your adoring public!"

"It must be a slow week for news." His growl affected her enthusiasm not in the least.

"I don't know what you're complaining about. This'll be great for business. Make sure you mention the Pizzeria, too."

"I'm not mentioning anything," he said. "I want them to go away."

"Well, they're not going to." She crossed her arms over her chest. "They're going to interview the whole staff as they come in, you know." She straightened her posture, made a fist, and held it up to her mouth like a microphone. When she spoke, she lowered her voice to a sexy drawl. "So how long have you worked for Dante Caravicci, Ms. McCabe? And how does it feel to be in the employ of a brave—and smoking hot—ex-army ranger? Did you have any idea before yesterday's daring rescue that he was a superhero?"

Dante narrowed his eyes. "Knock it off. It isn't funny. Those people are going to tank business today."

Chloe threw her arms up. "Are you kidding? We're going to be the most popular place in town. If I had known there'd be reporters hanging around, I would've gotten up early to color my roots."

That teased a quick smile out of him. Chloe's auburn roots often crept from her scalp for several inches before she bothered dyeing them to match the rest of her hair, a tarry black she got from a bottle. He rather liked the red, which he thought to be a good match to the cute splotch of freckles that tumbled over the bridge of her nose and onto her cheeks.

"Seriously, boss. This is great for business. You should milk it."

"I don't want to milk it. I just want them to clear the front of the restaurant so people can get in. They're hogging valuable parking space."

"Trust me, no one will care. The church services are letting out and people are walking over to see what the ruckus is about. You're going to be Bright Hills' most famous son."

Dante sighed. Both a Baptist and Methodist church sat right up the street, and he couldn't argue that drawing in the after-sermon crowd would be good for business. Still, he

didn't want to be in the spotlight, didn't want to be inter-
viewed.

"Look—" He leaned forward and rested his arms on the
desk. "All I did was pull the girl out of the driver's seat. I
couldn't have gotten her out of the car without help. If I
hadn't been there, someone else would've stepped up." He
pushed the chair back and stood. "They're trying to make a
big deal out of something that just isn't."

Chloe stared at him and huffed out an exasperated
breath. "I bet the girl you rescued would disagree with you."

"Hey, boss?" One of the sous chefs poked his head
through the doorway and, unable to contain his smile, said,
"You got a crowd out front waiting on you. You're famous,
man! We're gonna be slammed today!"

Dante pinched the bridge of his nose. "Yep. Let's get to
work."

⋐⋑⋐⋑

Brenna tapped the Audi's directional at the end of Dogwood, Sean and Rebecca's street, intending to turn right, but
a line of traffic idled on Main. She shifted in her seat to see
what held up progress, but saw nothing beyond the light at
Bright Street. As the cars inched past, she waited for someone to let her in. A prune-faced woman Brenna recognized
as Mrs. Feinbacher stared straight ahead, hands clutching
the steering wheel of her boat of a Buick. She ignored
Brenna's turn signal and inched past her. The next vehicle, a
guy in a muddy Suburban, gave her space to pull out, and
she waved her thanks as she turned in front of him. She expected to see the remnants of a motor vehicle accident when
she reached the intersection, but no, the slow-down was due
to rubberneckers gawking at a gathering of news vans and
people in front of Dante's Bistro. It took a moment for her
brain to register the reason for the commotion.

"What a mess," she said under her breath and drove past

the hubbub at the restaurant as Dante had, turning down the
alley behind the row of storefronts. She parked and let herself into the Lump & Grind, her ears picking up the excited
chatter emanating from the front. The overflow from the
Bistro had made its way to her coffee bar, and, when she
stepped from the back through the small kitchen and into
the front of the house area, her jaw dropped. Every table
and chair was occupied and there was a line of people waiting to order.

"Why you gaping, boss lady?" Greta, the genius behind
the cinnamon buns that had made the Lump & Grind famous—pre-Brenna's ownership, back when it was still The
Coffee Mug—regarded Brenna with delight. Her eyebrows
formed a thick and wiry line of battleship gray over dark
eyes that sparked with intelligence. "Never seen a crowd
before?" she cackled and snapped her head toward the teenage girl working the register. "Move faster, *liebchen.
Bewegen sich schneller!*"

The old lady clapped her hands and moved down the line
with greater agility than her support hose and sensible shoes
suggested, looking over the shoulders of her three baristas
and barking orders in German.

Kaitlyn, the young girl at the register, shot a panicked
glance toward Brenna, her amber eyes round and wide.

"She told you to move faster," Brenna said and would
have laughed if the poor girl hadn't look so terrified. She
moved to the register and turned Kaitlyn around by the
shoulders. "Go check the condiment stations, make sure
everything is well-stocked. With this crowd, we'll be running out of creamer in no time." The girl's gaze darted to
Greta, and Brenna sighed. "I'm allowed to take over the
register, honey. I own the place, remember?"

"Yes, ma'am, I know," Kaitlyn said, her voice wobbling
through a forced smile as she wrung her hands. "But Greta
said—"

"I'll clear it with Greta."

The girl's expression remained dubious, but she did as

she was told. Brenna threw herself into customer service mode and greeted the next in line with a wide smile.

"Hey, Beautiful. Looks like you got your hands full."

"Well, hello, Vince. We do indeed. Quite the fuss, isn't it?" She glanced around Vince and waved at Raelynn who stood a few customers back down the line.

"Apparently, my cousin is some kind of he-ro. News caught wind of it, and here they are." Vince shrugged, his expression bored. "Probably ain't as big a deal as they're trying to make it," he said. "But you know Dante. Any old thing he can put in the 'win' column."

"Actually, it is a big deal. He saved a girl's life yesterday, and at great risk to his own," Brenna said, unsure why Vince's words put her hackles up. "I was with him when it happened."

"Were you, now?" His lips curved in a curdled-milk smile. He glanced up at the big board on the wall behind her and nodded to the menu. "I'll try one of them caramel things."

"Caramel macchiato. Okay. You like whipped cream?"

His gaze dropped back to hers and he smirked. "Do we know each other well enough for you to ask me something like that, Beautiful?"

Brenna's neck prickled with unwelcome heat, and when she spoke again it was through clenched teeth. "Whipped cream or not? Yes or no. Hurry up, please. There are people behind you."

"Who the heck is the bad boy with the Fabio hair?" Raelynn asked Brenna when she reached her turn at the counter a few minutes later.

"That's Vince Caravicci, Dante's cousin."

"Looks like he's got a thing for you." Raelynn shot a quick glance at Vince who stood off to the side watching Brenna with blatant interest while he waited for his coffee.

"He's not my type."

"He's sure mine," she said, and her dimples appeared. "Too bad I'm spoken for. Hey," she said as she handed

Brenna money for her order, "Speaking of Dante, did you hear what he did? Saved that girl from a burning car?"

"Yes, I—"

"Did you know he was in the army? He served a bunch of tours in Afghanistan."

Brenna handed Raelynn her change and smiled at the next in line. "Yes, I've heard that."

"I saw it on the news this morning. They even had a picture of him in his dress uniform. Oh. My. God." She leaned toward Brenna, her eyes bright. "So. Hot." She fanned her face and her dimples reappeared. "Did you know he was an army ranger? I didn't know that, as many times as I've been to the Pizzeria, and now the Bistro. Never knew a thing about that, not until I saw it on the news. They said he came home from Afghanistan with a bunch of medals pinned to his chest. He sure did."

Brenna stared at Raelynn as if the woman had sprouted a second nose. "That can't be right." Surely, after five years, she would know if such a thing were true. Someone would have said something. Rebecca would have bragged, even if Dante didn't. "I think you misheard, Raelynn."

Raelynn straightened up and slung her purse over her shoulder. "That's what the news report said. Why else do you think they're making such a big deal out of that rescue? He's not just a Good Samaritan. Dante Caravicci is a bona fide American hero."

⁊><⁊

It was just shy of midnight when Brenna locked the back door of the Lump & Grind and stepped on aching feet toward her Audi. She paused next to her car to glance down the alley. Dante's Trans Am sat in its usual space, but a group of men crowded the back door area. She noted the glow of cigarettes, heard laughter, and a voice said, "He's got to come out sometime. Can't stay in there forever."

Reporters, looking for the hero interview, Brenna thought. Amused, she turned away, put her hand on the driver's door handle, and paused again. It wouldn't cost her anything to help the Neanderthal out.

"Y'all waiting for Dante?" she called, sauntering toward the men.

"Yeah," one of them called back. "You have a way to pry him out of there? We just want a quick interview."

Bathed in the yellow glow of a streetlamp, Brenna stopped when she stood close enough to speak without raising her voice. "I hate to disappoint you fellas, but Dante left a while ago."

A chorus of "What?" resounded, and Brenna just nodded. "Yes, I'm afraid so. He left right after the dinner rush while y'all were interviewing locals out front." She shrugged and smiled. "Can't wait to tell him you hung around out here half the night when he was already long gone."

"Shit," said one of the men. He dropped his cigarette and stepped on it, sighed, and nudged the guy next to him. "I told you we should go wait at his house."

"How the hell did he slip out? We've been out here for hours."

"I didn't say he went out the back," Brenna said. "The man was Special Forces. You really think he can't give the slip to a bunch of nosy reporters?"

The men exchanged dubious glances.

"Feel free to stand here all night long, gentlemen," she said, and her light laugh carried over the short distance. "Hope you have jackets, though. Even though it's June, come three a.m., there's going to be a mountain breeze that'll give you goosebumps." She turned and began walking back to her car. "Nighty-night."

Brenna chuckled to herself as she slid into her car. She'd just done the Neanderthal a solid, and she'd make sure he knew he owed her.

She tossed her purse into the passenger seat and started

the engine, exhausted and happy to be on her way home. When she pulled out of the alley, she glanced toward the Bistro at the other end of the block. There were only two news vans now, but a handful of people still milled about on the sidewalk in front of the restaurant.

Poor Dante. Looks like he's going to be bushwhacked, after all. Oh well. She'd done her part to help him.

She hit the gas, and, yawning, turned on the radio to help her stay awake. She snapped it off a moment later, annoyed.

"Damn commercials," she muttered.

"You know, an MP3 player would solve that problem."

Brenna's scream filled the interior of the vehicle. She slammed her foot on the brake. The car fishtailed and screeched to a halt in the middle of the road. Her head swiveled toward the backseat as Dante's head popped up.

Jaw dropped, eyes wide, Brenna stared at Dante with horrified surprise.

"Hi. I can explain," he said.

"You jackass!" she screamed, shaking with anger and dissipating fear. "You idiot Neanderthal! Were you *trying* to scare me into slamming us into a light post? Are you out of your ever-loving mind? What the *hell* were you thinking, scaring me like that?"

Dante scrubbed his hand through his hair and emitted a frustrated sigh. "I'm sorry. I had to get out of the restaurant. Chloe locked up behind me, but then that group of vultures headed into the alley and I had to think fast." He shrugged. "You shouldn't leave your car unlocked, you know. Anyone could hide in the back seat."

Brenna opened her mouth to lambast him, closed it when fury rendered her speechless, opened it again, sputtered, snapped it shut, and held her tongue.

A car slowed to a stop behind her and the driver honked his horn. She faced forward and hit the gas, sending Dante flying backward.

He slammed into the backseat. "Hey!"

"Buckle up," she snapped.

"Look, I'm sorry," he said. She heard the click of his seatbelt. "I didn't know what else to do."

"A text message or phone call warning me that you were hiding in my backseat would've been nice." She glared at him in the rearview mirror. "You scared the hell out of me with that little stunt." *Idiot man.*

"I don't have your number," he said, "or I would have. And thanks for what you did back there. I know you tried to help me out. I appreciate it."

Brenna glanced at him in the rearview mirror again. She caught his profile in the dim light as he stared out the window, his expression grim. He turned his head and when they passed beneath a streetlight she noted with surprise the exhaustion around his eyes.

Poor guy looked like he hadn't slept in days. She sighed and focused on the road while she wrestled her annoyance under control.

"You're welcome," she said after a few moments and met his weary gaze in the mirror. His lips curved in a lopsided smile, and she shook her head, returning her attention to the road.

Brenna turned into their neighborhood and slowed about a block from the townhouse.

"Reporters," she said, "outside your house."

He huffed out a breath and dropped his head back against the seat. "Damn it."

"Wouldn't it be easier to just give them what they want?" she asked. "Do a quick interview and send them on their way."

"It's never that easy," he said. "They pry. If I just wait a day or so, they'll go away. Something else will come up and this will be forgotten. In the meantime, they'll dig stuff up on their own without my help."

"So you want to wait them out? You sure?"

"Yes. Will you pull into your garage please? I'll wait there until they go away."

Brenna rolled her eyes. "I'm not such an ass that I'm going to make you sleep in the car. You can crash on my so-fa."

Their gazes met in the mirror again and Brenna tingled with an uncomfortable awareness. She suspected Dante read her mind, because a moment later his tired eyes crinkled at the corners and he smiled. "I know, I know. Just friends."

Brenna waited for Dante to disappear behind her, and though she wondered how he managed to fold his six-foot-something frame into the confines of her tiny backseat, she didn't ask. She eyed the reporters and gave a little wave before she pressed the remote button and waited for the garage door to open.

With the location of her garage entry on the side of her townhome rather than toward the street—it faced Dante's garage door as their units were mirror images—she assumed the reporters, camped out at the curb, had no clear view inside her garage despite the row of narrow windows across the door.

The interior car light went on when she opened the driv-er's door and a bell chimed until she removed her keys from the ignition. "Garage door is closed. You're in the clear," she said, wondering what she was thinking bringing the Ne-anderthal into her house for a sleepover.

Nerves on edge, she rolled her shoulders and grabbed her purse. "Well, c'mon in then. We're home."

Chapter 6

Dante trailed Brenna into her residence. The interior garage door led into a mudroom, and another door opened from the mudroom into the front entrance hallway, just like Dante's place. He noted that she'd organized her mudroom with hooks for coats and a rack for boots and shoes, and that she'd added shelving which held boxes marked with things like *Wrapping Paper, Christmas Lights,* and *Notions,* whatever the hell that was. His mudroom looked more like, well, a mudroom. His had hooks, too, where he hung stuff, but muddy boots and shoes came off and ended up in a heap wherever they landed. The rack was a good idea, he supposed. Maybe he'd put one in.

Ah, who the hell was he kidding? No, he wouldn't.

The first thing he noticed on stepping from the mudroom into the front hallway was the scent. His place most often smelled like garlic, tomato sauce, and variations thereof, a side effect of owning two Italian restaurants and testing recipes at home. Brenna's place smelled like…well, he wasn't sure, exactly, something edible and sweet, like vanilla and cinnamon. He sniffed. Cloves? And something else. Something…something *Brenna.*

His memory shot him back to the Bistro storeroom yesterday afternoon, and Maddie and Cal's kitchen last night when he'd pressed his luck by getting closer than ever before for a second time in the same day. He breathed deep and enjoyed the pleasant sensory overload. Damn, but the woman smelled good, and so did her house.

"You hungry?" She toed off her shoes at the base of the stairs and dropped four inches of height in an instant. "Or thirsty? I have wine or—"

"Just water, thanks." He cleared his throat to ease the rasp. "It's late. You don't have to entertain me."

She shook her hair behind her shoulders on her way to the kitchen. "I'm having a glass of wine."

Dante watched the fall of her hair to where it ended at the curve of her waist, stuck his hands in his pockets, and wandered into her living room.

It was weird to be in a place with the same floorplan as his. Like a parallel universe, he thought, where everything was the same, but not.

Brenna's home exuded more personality than his did, but he gave himself a pass for being busy and possessing zero decorating sense. She favored deep jewel tones and wasn't afraid to use them, he noted, as his gaze roved the walls and plush furniture, but he found the splashes of bright color to be warm and somehow cohesive in spite of the variety. Very Brenna, he thought, and then smiled, amused with himself.

He perused the framed photos displayed on one of the bookcases that flanked her television and lifted one of Brenna with Sean and Jack, a photo taken when they were much younger, probably college age, he guessed. It was a great shot, one of those moments that every photographer prays for, with all three of his subjects laughing and unguarded in that split second when the shutter blinks. Gorgeous, with hair like black ice and eyes of midnight blue. Kissed by angels, all three of them.

Brenna stepped up behind him. "That's my favorite photo of the three of us."

"It's a great shot. Do you remember what you were laughing about?"

"No," she said, her voice soft and wistful. "But I wish I did."

"Jack looked a lot like Sean," Dante said.

"He did, yes. Jack was shorter than Sean, and not as big. But they were mistaken for twins sometimes, in spite of that and their age difference."

Brenna handed him a glass filled with ice water. He accepted it and returned the photo to its place on the bookshelf. He paused a moment and picked up a snow globe. Tiny bits of glitter spun and twirled with the movement, dusting the miniature snowman inside. Jack Kinkaid's name and contact information was etched in gold on the side along with the logo and name of the company he'd worked for.

"Jack was an accountant," Brenna said. "I remember when he ordered these to give out to clients at Christmastime. He was worried they were cheesy." She smiled at Dante. "It is kind of cheesy, actually, but also memorable. It's one of those things people leave out just because it's cute."

Dante nodded and set the snow globe back on the shelf. "Do you believe Jack played matchmaker for Maddie and Cal? And Sean and Rebecca, too? They all seem to believe it."

Brenna sipped her wine and shrugged. "If anyone could manage something like that, it would be Jack."

"I heard Maddie say you're next on Jack's list. What do you say to that?"

She stared into her wine for a moment, as if considering something, and then lifted her gaze and held it steady on Dante's. "Actually, Jack already had someone picked out for me. A few days before he died he called and told me he wanted to set me up on a blind date, that he had found my soul mate."

She paused, watched him as if she expected him to comment, then blinked and looked away. "He died before he had a chance to set it up, so...so."

"So you'll never know," Dante finished the thought for her, his voice quiet now as hers had been.

Brenna's hair caught the light when she shrugged. "I guess not. I seem to remember him saying he'd give the guy my phone number, but I don't think he did. If so, there was no follow through." Her expression brightened and she smiled. "In the spirit of being friends, I'm going to tell you something, but you have to promise not to laugh, and you can't tease me with it later. Deal?"

Dante nodded and smiled at her sudden change of mood. "Deal."

She bit her lip and he wasn't sure, but he thought her cheeks grew the slightest bit pink. "I know it's crazy, ridiculous—but I keep waiting for the guy to turn up. My blind date. I can't help but think Jack will make it happen. I know it's stupid in the extreme to—"

"It's not stupid," Dante said. "It's not. There isn't anything wrong with hoping for the right person to come along. Isn't that what we all do? What we all wait for?"

Their eyes met and held. The silence stretched taut and quivered with unexpected heat.

Brenna stepped back. "It's late, and you must be exhausted. I'll get you a blanket and pillow, and be right back."

Dante watched her disappear down the hall. She couldn't get away fast enough, and he reminded himself that as much as he wished things were different between them, she still didn't want him closer than arm's length.

The fact that her behavior over the last two days was contradictory only meant that he should stay farther away than usual.

The last thing he needed was to get tangled up with a woman who had no idea what the hell she really wanted or why she wanted it—or didn't want it, as the case may be. Misery lay at the end of a road like that.

"Here you go." Brenna set a short pile of bedding on the sofa and crossed her arms over her chest like armor. "I don't suppose you know who took care of Maddie and Cal's, do you? I got there this morning and the place had already been cleaned."

"Guilty."

"You must have been there half the night."

"I couldn't sleep, so I figured I'd take care of it. It was no big deal."

"Wait. You were up all night?" Brenna's arms dropped to her sides and she gave him a look. "When was the last time you slept?"

"Friday night."

"So you've been awake for how long now?"

Dante shrugged. "About thirty-eight hours, I suppose, give or take."

"You big idiot." Brenna frowned and shook her head as she moved toward the hallway. She pointed at the sofa. "Lay your Neanderthal ass down and get some sleep. What kind of imbecile stays up for thirty-eight hours straight?"

"The kind with insomnia." His tone was harsher than he intended, so he added, "It's not a new thing. I'm used to it."

Brenna paused in the space where the living room ended and the hallway began, next to the stairs. She stared at him, and he swore he could hear the wheels spinning in that gorgeous head of hers.

Her eyes narrowed. "All the nights over the last few years when you worked in your garage and I complained about the light waking me up—insomnia?"

Dante nodded.

Brenna swallowed hard, and Dante heard the sound from across the room. Her next words came out with slow deliberation. "Because of the war, serving in Afghanistan? Like PTSD?"

Dante smiled a little and shook his head. "I can see why you might think that, but no. My insomnia started when I was a little kid. I've been plagued with it on and off my whole life."

And there go the wheels turning again, he thought, *all*

gears in play. He braced himself for her next insight.

"Earlier you said the reporters would pry. What is it you don't want them to know?"

"Nothing. I just don't want to rehash old news." Dante waited for her Southern hospitality gene to kick in whereby she would accept that asking more questions might be considered rude.

"What old news?"

So much for genetics.

Dante pinched the bridge of his nose. God, but he was tired. He could sleep now, like the dead, he was certain of it, if only she'd stop asking him personal questions and let him lie down on her couch.

"Let it go, Brenna."

"You may as well tell me. I'm going to hear it sooner or later anyway. Is it about the army? Did you get a dishonorable discharge for being a Neanderthal? What?"

"Jesus, you're nosy," he said. "Fine, I'll tell you. But you'll wish you hadn't asked. When I was four-years-old my father murdered my mother. He beat her to death with a brick, and then he killed himself." He paused for her sharp intake of breath. "I'd appreciate it if we could save the rest of my life story for another time."

Brenna held his gaze, her eyes now twin spheres of liquid blue. "I'm sorry. It was rude of me to pry so. I can't imagine how it must have been for you, to grow up with neither of your parents, and under such terrible circumstances."

So, her Southern hospitality gene kicked in after all, he thought, and she even had the good graces to look ashamed of herself for keeping it buried in the first place.

Dante found no pleasure in her discomfort and decided to give her a pass. It was late. They were both tired, after all.

"Don't feel sorry for me," he said, his dark gaze steady on hers. "I don't remember either of them, except for what I've seen in photos. I can't miss what I never had."

Brenna's lips parted as if she would speak, but instead

she just nodded and gave him a quiet smile before she turned and disappeared down the hall.

Dante watched her go and what remained of his energy went with her. His shoulders sagged. He flipped off all the lights, crashed on the sofa, and pressed his nose to the pillow Brenna had left for him. He breathed deep. His last thought before sleep released his exhaustion to the night was of the sweet scent of Brenna's skin.

c∽c∽

In the morning, Brenna showered and dressed before leaving the master bedroom. There was no point in causing an uncomfortable situation by wandering around the house in her PJs, after all. But when she reached the living room it was clear she needn't have fretted over it. The bedding she'd provided to Dante the night before sat in a folded pile in the middle of the sofa. He'd laid a scrap of paper on top of the pillow with a handwritten note that suggested she look in her refrigerator. Bemused, she did just that, and discovered a breakfast plate he'd made for her with fruit from her fridge. He'd sliced a kiwi, a banana, and an apple, and delivered them in a colorful array with a sprinkling of blueberries and brown sugar. He'd dipped three strawberries in chocolate—*where'd he find chocolate?*—and included those in the presentation. He'd covered the plate with clear plastic kitchen wrap and laid a note on top that said only, *thank you*, with a rudimentary caricature drawing of a man she supposed he meant to be himself.

This teased a chuckle out of her, and she thought he better not quit his day job.

When she went to toss the paper in the trash she saw the source of the chocolate: a wadded up Hershey candy bar wrapper. He must have melted the candy to dip her strawberries—and cleaned up after himself, she noted, as there were no dirty dishes in the sink.

Resourceful. She stared at the wrapper a moment then closed the trash bin.

The drawing took up residence on her fridge with the use of a magnet shaped like the University of Georgia bulldog mascot.

Dante had prepared the coffee pot for her as well, so she turned it on to brew and sat at the breakfast bar to eat her fruit plate.

He hadn't really done anything but slice up fruit. Well, okay, the strawberries were a nice touch, and it was a sweet gesture. Maybe he wasn't such a Neanderthal, after all.

And there it was again, that uncomfortable flood of understanding that she had rushed to judgment about Dante, that maybe there was more to the man than she had ever suspected or given him credit for.

She popped the last of the strawberries into her mouth and went upstairs to her office to power up her laptop. Raelynn had said that she'd heard about Dante's past on the news. Nothing a little internet search couldn't dig up, right?

A few minutes later, Brenna sat staring at a photo of Dante Caravicci standing ramrod straight and serious as bad news next to other members of the US Army 75th Ranger Regiment. Raelynn wasn't kidding. The man was flipping hot.

Brenna clicked off the image and sat back in her chair. Dante had been right about not needing to give an interview. He'd said the reporters would dig up information without his input, and they had. She read the report of his mother's death, retold in all the gory details Dante had spared her last night—*no wonder he didn't want to talk to reporters*—and she imagined again the little boy Dante had been, forced to grow up under the shadow of his father's murderous act. But as the journalist pointed out, he excelled first as a student and then served his country with honor as an army ranger, had become a successful restaurateur, and a contributing member of society here in Bright Hills.

Life had thrown raw eggs and lemons into Dante Caravicci's face and the man had made lemon merengue pie.

So much for her long held belief that the almost always cheerful Dante had lived a charmed life wherein all he wished for dropped at his feet with little effort on his part. Stupid. She knew better than to think such a thing about anyone. Why had she allowed herself to lay that mantle on Dante? The truth was, given his childhood, he'd probably worked harder than most to achieve his success.

More proof that she was too judgmental by far. And she had been wrong about him in too many ways to count. Damned if that didn't sting.

In time, Brenna's thoughts shifted from Dante and she began thinking about the day ahead of her. By the time she strode into the Lump & Grind, her mood had turned foul, thanks to a visit with the loan manager at the bank that did not go as she hoped.

The business at the L&G stayed steady, but Brenna knew she had to expand her offerings if she stood a chance of competing with the new places in town that were opening. Bright Hills was growing by leaps and bounds, and that meant the competition for patrons had ramped up. Dante's Bistro, with its fully stocked bar, array of fresh desserts, and a spanking new espresso machine, had put a serious dent in her after-dinner crowd, and the new Starbucks out near the high school had sucked away a lot of business as well. Folks no longer had to detour through downtown for their fix of gourmet brew.

If she planned to keep her doors open in the long term—and both God and the Devil knew she did—she had to offer something more worthy of a trip downtown than specialty coffees and Greta's cinnamon buns, though the cinnamon buns were spectacular. But even that had become a concern as Greta had announced her intention to retire soon, and no one made those sweet treats quite like she did. The woman had been baking them every morning for almost forty years, and damned if she didn't sprinkle magic in every bite.

Brenna rubbed the puckered skin between her eyes and

heard Jack's voice whisper, '*Don't frown. Grandma says your face will get stuck that way.*' She groaned and smoothed her expression.

Forget the cinnamon buns for the moment. Greta's witchy magic over pastry could be dealt with later. For now, she had to figure out how to improve her business without the help of the bank.

She had expanded the menu last year to include sandwiches for breakfast and lunch, but she couldn't offer more without a bigger kitchen, and that wasn't going to happen without a loan.

"Damn it." She tossed her purse into the bottom drawer of her desk and slammed the drawer shut.

"Bad day?" Rebecca poked her head through the doorway and the rest of her followed a moment later. She eased herself into the chair opposite Brenna's desk, dropped her purse on the floor, and rested her hands over her growing belly.

Brenna closed the office door and returned to her seat. She eyed Rebecca's unkempt curls with envy and nodded. "The bank turned down my loan. My business plan isn't detailed enough, they said." She slouched in her seat. "And they're right, damn it. I've got some great ideas, but I have to bring them more into focus."

"Talk to Sean, Brenna. You know he'll loan you the money if you ask."

Brenna shook her head. "No handouts from Sean."

"It would be a loan, not a handout." Rebecca rolled her eyes. "Besides, your brother has more money than the Vatican. The man is an investment genius."

"Yes, he is." Brenna glanced at Rebecca's left hand. "Rich enough to buy you any size diamond ring you want, so why do you only wear a plain gold band?"

Rebecca raised her hand to admire her simple wedding ring. "I don't even wear this one when I'm on site. I switch it out for a silicone wedding band. It's safer. I'm in construction, remember? I don't need some big rock banging into things, or my ring catching on stuff. Besides, I don't care about what Sean can buy me. I only care about Sean."

And that, Brenna thought, *is one of the reasons I love you.*

Rebecca folded her hands over her belly again. "Anyway, don't try to change the subject. Sean would be happy to give you a loan."

"My business, my problem. I want to handle it myself."

"Stubborn. Prideful."

"Self-sufficient. Confident."

The two women stared at each other until Rebecca finally shrugged. "Suit yourself. But if you change your mind, don't be afraid to ask. Sean adores you. You do know that, right?"

Brenna's muscles relaxed when she smiled. "Yes, I do. And maybe I'll talk to him at some point in the future, as a last resort. But please don't say anything to him. He always thinks he has to fix everything."

Rebecca laughed at that. "Typical man. So did you ever figure out who cleaned up over at Maddie and Cal's?"

"It was Dante." Brenna straightened up in her chair and rested her arms on her desk. "Did you know he was an army ranger?"

"Of course. Didn't you?"

"No. Why did you keep something like that a secret?"

"It just never came up. Would it have made a difference?"

"Not the way you mean. But after everything that's happened in the last few days, I am beginning to look at him differently. I'm willing to concede—" *Ouch!* "—that maybe I've been...you know." Brenna shifted in her seat. She drummed her fingers on the desk and sniffed.

Rebecca's smile bloomed and her eyes lit up. "Say it. Please. I won't tell anybody. Not even Sean—okay, that's a big fat lie, I will totally tell Sean. And probably Maddie, when she gets back from her honeymoon, but, c'mon, say it. I just need to hear it with my own ears."

She tilted her head and cupped an ear with her hand.

Brenna huffed out a breath. "Maybe I was—wrong."

Rebecca laughed and clapped her hands. "You just made my whole freaking day. I knew it was a good idea to stop here on my way back to the office."

"Blab if you want. I'll just deny it," Brenna said, but her lips curved and a moment later she laughed with Rebecca. "No one will believe you, anyway."

 handsomehandsome

Brenna drove home at midnight with the top down on her Audi, her hair blowing in glorious disarray, and Imagine Dragons blaring through the speakers. She switched the music off when she reached her neighborhood.

Light from Dante's garage caught her eye. The door was open. A wave of pity rolled through her for his insomnia. *Poor guy*, she thought. But the closer she got to her own garage door she could see Vince sitting just inside Dante's garage in a folding lawn chair. A man she recognized as a neighbor sat in a similar chair beside Vince.

Vince waved to her with the hand that wasn't holding a beer. "Hey, Beautiful. C'mon over and say hello."

Brenna waved back and wondered if it would be rude to drive into her garage and shut the door behind her. She'd been working nonstop since Rebecca left her office, and all she wanted was to curl up and sleep.

'*Yes, it would be rude.*' Jack's laughing voice reverberated in her head. '*You're turning into sour old Aunt Rhoda.*'

"Uncalled for, Jack," she said under her breath, but after she cut the engine and climbed from the car she tugged off her shoes and walked barefoot across the grass toward Dante's garage.

"How about a beer?" Vince hoisted himself from the sagging lawn chair. "Have a sit."

"Thanks, but I'll pass." Brenna smiled and nodded to

Vince's companion. "Hey, Mills. Where's Ellen tonight?"

"Watching some sappy movie with her mother," Mills said. "By the time I get home, she'll be sound asleep in her Barcalounger. What time is it?"

"After midnight," Brenna said.

"Damn. Five o'clock in the a.m. is going to come early. I better be on my way." He tipped his head back and drained the bottle before standing. "Nice to see you, Brenna. Vince, later man." He tossed the empty bottle into a recycle bin near the garage door and disappeared across the lawn.

"Sure you don't want a beer? Or wine?" Vince's mouth formed a warm smile. "The damned cat ain't around to ruin your clothes this time." When Brenna hesitated, he winked and added, "C'mon, now, Beautiful, don't say no. It's just a glass of wine. Have a quick nightcap before you break my heart and walk away."

"You're so full of yourself. Okay, one glass of wine, and then I'm calling it a night."

"You got it," he said and disappeared into the house.

Brenna dropped her shoes next to the lawn chair she eased into. She finger-combed her tangled hair and rolled her head, wincing with every movement. It had been a long day.

Most of the reporters had, as Dante predicted, vamoosed when other more enticing news presented itself—a fire that consumed the home of one of the Atlanta Falcons had sent them scurrying southward—and the few who remained didn't stay longer than mid-afternoon. The customers their presence had encouraged dwindled when the excitement evaporated. Dante's heroism was, after a mere twenty-four hours, considered old news. Still, it had been busier than usual, thanks to the hubbub. Brenna suspected the Bistro had done blazing good business, in light of Dante's new local celebrity, and would continue to do so.

"So tell me," she asked when Vince returned with her wine, "what brought you to Bright Hills? Anything besides Dante?"

"Nah. I had some time to kill, is all." Vince showed her a flash of white teeth. "I pop in every so often just to remind my cousin that he ain't all that. How about you? You have family here?"

"Oh, honey, let me tell you." Brenna blew out a breath and laughed. "This county is lousy with Kinkaids, most of them aunts, uncles, or cousins. My parents live here in Bright Hills, and my brother Sean and his wife, too."

Vince narrowed his eyes and stared into the mid-distance. "Kinkaid. Kinkaid. I want to say I met a guy with the last name Kinkaid when I was here a few years ago." He shifted his gaze back to Brenna. After a moment his expression brightened. "Jack. That was it. Jack Kinkaid."

The sensation of electric current rippled from Brenna's spine to her outer extremities. She set her wineglass on the concrete floor beside her chair and rubbed the goosebumps from her arms. "Jack was my brother."

Vince tilted his head and studied her for a moment, nodded. "Yeah, now that you say that, I can see the resemblance. Nice guy."

"The nicest," Brenna said. "He died in a car crash several years ago."

"Sorry. I didn't know."

Brenna acknowledged his words with a nod. "So how did you know Jack?"

"He was an accountant, I think. Right? I, uh, met him at the Boot & Spur one night. We were, uh—" Vince paused, regarding her with focused interest, as if he were trying to read her mind. "We, uh—" He glanced away. "I—I was there watching a Braves game. Pretty sure he mentioned you, now that I think of it."

"Really?" The tingling sensation revisited her and Brenna suppressed a shiver, but she straightened up and couldn't control her animation. "Do you remember what he said?"

"Yeah, I do." Vince returned his gaze to hers, considering. "Something about a blind date."

Brenna sucked in a breath. "Oh, my god. *You?* You were

my blind date?" Her eyes widened and she couldn't control her surprise. "You have no idea—I've always wondered. Jack told me about—he told me—but then he—he never had the chance to follow through."

Vince stared at her and his lips curved in a slow smile. "Well, well. So your brother Jack wanted to fix us up." He glanced away from her to watch Dante's Trans Am turn into the driveway. "We need to take care of that. When is your first free night, Beautiful?"

Brenna forced a laugh and tamped down her disappointment. "I can't even believe this. Wow." She retrieved her wineglass and took a fortifying gulp. *So not what I expected, Jack, but okay. I'll roll with it.* "I'm actually off Wednesday, so tomorrow night would be great. That way I don't have to watch the clock."

Vince's smile widened. "Then tomorrow night it is. How 'bout I pick you up at seven? Dress for the bike. We'll have a good time, me and you."

"I'm sure of it," Brenna lied, still smiling when Dante stepped into the garage. He glanced from Brenna to Vince, then back to Brenna. She noted the muscles tense and flex in his jaw. Time to go. "Thanks for the wine." She stood and handed her glass to Vince, then scooped her shoes up by the straps.

"You don't have to leave on my account," Dante said when she neared him.

She stopped and tilted her head to look up at him. His dark eyes drew her in, and her chest tightened as bewildering regret for her newfound knowledge rushed through her veins. "Greta's off tomorrow, so I'm opening. I have to be there early to get the cinnamon buns in the oven."

He nodded, but didn't take his gaze off hers, and she couldn't seem to look away. The moment stretched until she said, low, "Thanks for breakfast. The strawberries were a nice touch."

He nodded, and his lips tilted upward in the hint of a smile.

"Vince was my blind date," she blurted.

Dante's smile faded, and the appealing crinkles at the corners of his eyes gave way to hard tension. A sensation of drowning washed over Brenna. Her chest squeezed and began to ache with a miserable tightness.

"What?" The word came through Dante's lips in a harsh breath.

"My blind date." Brenna cleared her throat and forced a laugh. "I told you about that last night, remember? Before Jack died he wanted to fix me up on a blind date. Turns out it was with Vince. Weird coincidence, huh?"

Dante's gaze turned toward his cousin and the warm hue of his eyes transformed to hard onyx as he stared at the other man. "Really."

Brenna laughed again, the sound foreign in her ears. "Crazy, right?"

"What can I say? I'm a lucky guy." Vince put the beer bottle to his lips and drew a long pull. Insolent, was the word that jumped to Brenna's mind. He met Dante's stare with his own, the challenge in his expression unmistakable.

Dante's jaw flexed again, and when he shifted his gaze from Vince to Brenna the vise in her chest squeezed tighter. In his eyes she saw the old Dante, the one who thought she was batshit crazy.

He shook his head and blew out a harsh laugh. "Knock yourselves out, kids," he said and strode inside.

Brenna said goodnight to Vince and forced herself to walk, not run, across the strip of lawn to her own driveway. Heart pounding, she let herself into her house where her shaking legs carried her no farther than the foot of the stairs. She dropped her purse and shoes on the lowest step and sat, still quaking and trying to make sense of her unexpected emotions.

What the hell was wrong with her? She'd found her blind date! The guy Jack wanted her to meet. It had to be. How else could Vince have known? She'd only mentioned it to Dante last night, and judging from the vibes between

Dante and Vince, no way would Dante have shared that with his cousin.

She'd found him. Jack's pick for her.

Awash in surprise and disappointment she whispered into the silence. "What the hell were you thinking, Jack? He's not—he's just not."

Jack had done just what she'd asked of him. He'd put her blind date, the man he'd chosen for her, practically on her doorstep. And after all this time, all this wondering, how could it be that she wanted to throw him back, to tell Jack he was wrong? He had to be wrong. She didn't want it to be Vince.

Stunned, she admitted the truth.

With every piece of her heart, she wanted it to be Dante.

Chapter 7

Brenna removed the motorcycle helmet and shook her hair back over her shoulders. She handed the helmet to Vince and looked up at the signage identifying the establishment.

"It ain't fancy," Vince said, squatting to lock their helmets on the Harley. "But it seemed to fit, since this is where I met your brother."

Brenna nodded, gave him a point for the sentiment, and allowed him to rest his hand at the small of her back and guide her into the Boot & Spur. She blinked to adjust her eyes to the dim lighting and glanced around to reacquaint herself with the place. She'd been here once or twice before for a girls' night out and remembered rounds of margaritas and mojitos, line dancing, and a loud country band. Not a bad place for a cowboy bar, if that's what a girl was after. She'd danced with a few rednecks, had some fun. The place was clean and the service good. Not a bad choice for a casual first date.

A hostess approached them, dressed in tight jeans and a T-shirt with the bar's logo, the two Os inside the word BOOT sporting spurs in the center of each and situated over her boobs in a clear marketing ploy. She led Brenna and Vince to a booth with a good view of the big screen TV hanging over the bar. A moment later, their waitress appeared to tell them about the menu specials. She took their drink order and scurried off.

Brenna perused the menu, but she already knew she'd order light fare. The jeans she'd intended to wear tonight still hung in her closet, too snug to fit over her butt. Like it or not, it was time to start counting calories.

She felt Vince's gaze on her and returned it with a smile. He was handsome, she supposed, if you liked a man with a ponytail and earrings. He carried the bad boy look well. And why she had ever thought he looked like Dante, she didn't know. The men shared coloring and build, but the similarities ended there.

They chatted while waiting for the waitress to return with their drinks. Brenna learned that Vince's father owned a pizzeria in Asheville where both Vince and Dante had worked when they were kids. Vince had taken over the family business when his father passed, and Dante had left North Carolina to "do his own thing." Vince said with a shrug, "He took off and never looked back."

Brenna listened and nodded, asked the appropriate questions, careful not to appear more interested in Dante than Vince. Neutral is what she aimed for and thought she managed it well.

She determined within minutes that Vince knew Jack little if at all and scoured her brain to remember their conversation from the prior night. How had Vince known about the blind date? Still certain Dante wouldn't have told him, she worried that she had given it away somehow, like the hopeful client who offers too much information to a bogus psychic in exchange for the promise of communication from the Great Beyond.

"Why did you lie to me about my brother?" she asked, blindsiding Vince with the hope he would be too surprised to lie.

He stared at her with widened eyes for a brief second, and then his posture relaxed and he curled his lips in an amused smile. "That obvious, huh?"

"How did you know about the blind date?"

Vince shrugged. "I overheard his conversation with someone else."

"Who?"

Brenna held him in her stare, and for one breathtaking moment she believed he had the knowledge to share, but then he shrugged. "Like I said, I only overheard the conversation. I wasn't part of it. Sorry, but I can't help."

"Why did you lie to me last night?"

Vince's eyes crinkled when he laughed and, for a split second, she saw the resemblance to Dante. "You're kidding, right?"

Brenna sighed and shook her head. "You didn't have to lie to me."

"You wouldn't be here with me now if I didn't," he said and, because it was true, Brenna said nothing.

It was a relief, really, to know that Vince had tricked her. She'd get through this date and forget about Jack's matchmaking. She had bigger things to worry about. Besides, she had feelings for Dante that required some exploration.

Or not.

Her unexpected feelings for Dante were probably just emotional fallout from Maddie and Caleb's wedding.

She nursed her margarita while they waited for their dinner. Vince ordered her a second drink without asking if she wanted it, and she sipped it to be polite. The first drink had been strong as hell, enough to fuzz her brain a little, and she had no intention of getting drunk. If he ordered her a third drink it might just end up in his lap.

"Feel like a shot of tequila?" he asked toward the end of their meal. "I'll spring for Patron if you're interested."

"You've read me well. I do enjoy a shot of tequila every now and then, and Patron is my favorite. But I'd rather not do shots tonight, if you don't mind, especially since we have no designated driver." Brenna finished with a smile to take the edge off sounding so prim.

Vince laughed and reached across the table to lay his

hand over hers. "I didn't peg you for such a stickler. Tell
you what, Beautiful. How 'bout we finish our dinner and
share a dessert, and when the band starts playing I'll ask
you again. Maybe you'll be loosened up a little by then."

"Do they have a band here on Tuesday night?" She
withdrew her hand from his and curled her fingers around
the stem of her margarita glass.

"I thought so." Vince shifted in the booth for a better
view of the room. He became still as stone for several seconds and when he spoke again the flat tone of his voice
caught Brenna's attention. "Well, I'll be damned. Look
who's here."

Brenna followed Vince's stare and her breath caught
when she spotted Dante sitting at the bar chatting up the
bartender. A moment later a woman stepped up behind Dante and covered his eyes with her hands, then laughed at
whatever he said, and informed him with good nature that
he was "still an ass." He spun around smiling, stood up, and
held his arms out. The woman flew into them.

Brenna stared. As long as she'd known Dante, she'd
never seen him with a woman, though she knew from gossiping with Rebecca that he dated off and on without becoming entangled with anyone in particular. According to
Rebecca, Dante kept himself at arm's length and single,
claiming he worked so many hours it was easier to fly solo.
Brenna wondered now if Rebecca was wrong, because this
woman behaved as if she had staked a serious claim.

And it figured, didn't it, that she was a little bitty thing?
Short like Brenna, but opposite in every other way. Elfin,
Brenna thought, with her pale blonde hair falling to her
shoulders like a wispy cloud. Fine-boned features in a heart-
shaped face, sweet. Not much boobage, but she had a great
ass that did not require a fifteen pound weight loss to fit into
those size nothing jeans.

Not that Brenna had ever been petite enough for a size
nothing anything.

The woman took Dante's face in her hands and tugged

him toward her for a smacking kiss, which Dante accepted with a smile and then slid his arms around her miniscule waist and lifted her off the floor for another exuberant hug.

Brenna's stomach twisted.

The woman pressed another quick kiss to his lips before sitting down on the barstool next to him and ordering a beer. A moment later her mouth began to move nonstop and her arms gesticulated. Dante appeared able to keep up with the little elf's chatter as he gave her his full and undivided attention.

Brenna swallowed and stared. Her stomach ached. Her throat closed up. Her heart hurt. And she wasn't sure, but she suspected she might be...*jealous*?

It was absurd, of course. Brenna Kinkaid did not get jealous. Ever. Especially not over a man, and certainly not over the Neanderthal, for heaven's sake. Oh, honey, the idea alone was laughable. Ridiculous.

And, double damn it, *true*.

Heat prickled at the back of her neck and she jumped, startled, when Vince waved his hand in front of her face.

"What? Oh, sorry." Brenna forced a little laugh and dragged her gaze from the scene at the bar. "I was just ...uh..."

"You know who that little blonde is?" Vince asked. Brenna swallowed hard and shook her head. Vince paused, drawing out the tension. "That would be Trina Caravicci."

"She's a relative?"

"Oh, you could say that. She's Dante's wife."

His words felled what remained of Brenna's composure like a blow to her solar plexus.

"So—" He leaned toward her, his lips curved with sardonic amusement. "—you ready for that shot of Patron?"

Brenna afforded Dante and the elf another quick look. Then she straightened her spine and met Vince's uncompromising gaze.

"Bet your ass." She finished her margarita with a single toss of her head.

∽∾∽

"What the heck is all that commotion? Hey, wait a minute. Is that your cousin Vince?"

Dante snapped his head toward the direction of Trina's gaze and searched for his cousin amidst a sea of baseball caps, the wearers of which all appeared rowdy and drunk. They formed a half-moon circle around a table with two inhabitants.

Sure as hell, there was Vince, right in the thick of it, and Brenna, too, preparing to toss back a double shot of god-knew-what. They formed the centerpiece of the crowd, though Brenna's groupies were more than triple, if a judgment were to be made by how many stood behind and around her chair.

She downed the shot and slammed the glass on the table, upside down. A cheer went up from her ardent admirers and Brenna acknowledged their adulation with extended arms and seated bow. "She's ahead of you by two!" a guy wearing a Georgia Tech ball cap shouted, followed by laughter and taunts directed at Vince by the rest of the group.

Vince accepted two double shot glasses filled to the brim and quieted the onlookers with raised hands and a plea for silence. "I need to concentrate here," he said over the noise and drew laughter from the crowd.

"There's a contest going on," a waitress said on her way past where Dante and Trina sat staring at what had fast become the Boot & Spur's main event. She paused and rested her tray against her hip. "The guy with the ponytail challenged his date to see who could drink who under the table. I figured he was just an asshole trying to get her drunk, but the lady's holding her own. Believe it or not, he's getting sloppy and she's still talking in straight sentences."

Dante nodded as the pieces fell together. Vince had dangled the carrot of competition in front of Brenna's nose, and if there was one thing that lady couldn't turn down, it was a contest. And didn't he know it. She'd been competing with him for years on every damn thing from cake baking to shrimp sauteeing to—*well, hell.* That hot and heavy *anomaly* in the storeroom was probably just another competition for her, some effort on her part to prove she was the better kisser.

Not that he could argue her mastery at that particular sport.

Striving for first place came to the woman like breathing, but tonight it just might get her hurt. He'd seen her climb on the back of Vince's Harley earlier, though he had no idea they were coming here and would have asked Trina to meet him elsewhere had he known. But he'd be damned if he'd let her get back on the bike with Vince tonight.

Trashed, Vince had abandoned the shot competition and now tugged at Brenna's hands in a sloppy attempt to woo her onto the dance floor. An interesting effort as the band had yet to appear.

"He's really blitzed," Trina said. She turned to face Dante and waited for his attention. "What do you want to do?"

"Vince can't ride tonight. And Brenna lives next door to me. I'll just take them both home." He stood up and rolled his shoulders, prepared for battle. He was about to become very unpopular.

Trina rested her hand on Dante's arm. "Let me take Vince. He won't pick a fight with me, but he will with you. I'll bring him back to my place and—don't look at me like that. Believe me when I tell you that ship has sailed. Anyway, he can crash on the couch. Can you handle Miss All-That by yourself?"

"Her name is Brenna, and she hates me most of the time." Dante scrubbed his hand through his hair. "What the hell? I may as well earn it, I guess."

"You ready?"

"Piece of cake," he said, but felt more like he was entering the Ninth Circle of Hell.

"Well, hey, there, Vincenzo," Trina called out, striding

up to Vince and holding her arms out for a hug. "How's my least favorite ex-cousin-in-law?"

Vince dropped Brenna's hands and favored Trina with a sideways smile before scooping her up for the hug she'd requested. "Damn, you look good, girl," he said, unable to keep his tongue from tripping over itself. "I seen you earlier at the bar." He hugged Trina to his side and turned to face Brenna. "This gorgeous piece of ass is Dante's wife—"

"Ex-wife," Dante said.

"Whatever." Vince waved his free hand, and Trina tightened her grip on him when he swayed. "Beautiful, meet Trina Caravicci. Trina, this is Brenna Kinkaid, another fucking gorgeous piece of—"

Dante's expression darkened and Trina rushed to urge Vince forward. "Let's take a walk outside, Vince. Dante said you have a new Harley. I want to see it."

"I can't just leave—"

Trina turned Vince toward the door. "Sure you can. Brenna doesn't mind, do you, Brenna? No, of course she doesn't."

Dante leaned down to whisper in Trina's ear. "You sure you can handle him?"

"You bet. I'll tuck him into my back seat and he'll be asleep before we leave the parking lot. How about you? You good?"

Dante nodded and glanced at Brenna. She sat with her elbows on the table and her chin resting in her hands. Her eyes, the most amazing shade of sapphire blue, shone dark as midnight in this place, and fathomless, as she regarded his exchange with Trina.

Her silence worried him, given that he was in the process of ruining her date.

Trina maneuvered Vince toward the door. She blew Dante a kiss and called over her shoulder, "I'll see you in the morning, hot stuff!"

Dante watched them go. When they disappeared out the door, he drew a fortifying breath and turned to Brenna. She hadn't moved, but sat watching him, her expression guarded. A couple of the men from Brenna's fan club made a move to vie for occupancy of the chair Vince had vacated, but Dante rerouted them with a look.

He sat and returned Brenna's silent stare. When it became apparent she had nothing to say, he ventured into the deep water on his own. "Sorry about hijacking your date." No comment. Great. He cleared his throat. "It wasn't safe for him to ride the Harley." More silence and the continued dark stare. "Look, I'm sorry. I'll drive you home, okay? Or, if you don't want to ride with me I'll call you a cab and stay with you till it gets here." Crickets. "Jesus, Brenna, it's not the end of the world. Vince will still be—"

"You have a wife."

He closed his mouth mid-sentence and rewired his thought process. "Uh, no. I mean, yes, but not now. Years ago, and only for about five minutes. Trina and I have been divorced longer than we were married. We stayed friends."

"But she moved to Bright Hills to be with you. Just because you wanted her to."

Dante narrowed his gaze. "Don't believe everything that comes out of Vince's mouth."

"So why is she here, if not for you?"

Bemused in the extreme, and a little undone by her focused interest, he said, "She's a qualified restaurant manager. I hired her to manage the Pizzeria so I can give more time to the Bistro. That's it. No ulterior motive."

"She has no boobs, lucky girl." Brenna sniffed, and added with grudging approval, "And she has a very nice ass."

Dante bit back laughter. Brenna Kinkaid was shitfaced drunk.

"Let me pay the bar tab and I'll take you home, okay?"

"Already paid. And I can't go home with you. You're a married man."

"I'm a divorced man, and even if I was married—which I'm not—I could still give you a ride without being inappropriate. You ready to go?"

"Nope," she said, popping the "p."

Dante emitted an exasperated sigh. "Why not? Your date has been torpedoed by alcohol and me, your do-gooding neighbor. The best thing for you is to go home, drink a gallon of water, take two aspirin, and get a good night's sleep."

Brenna shook her head. "Can't."

"Why not?

She leaned forward and crooked her finger in a come-here motion. She stared at Dante until he complied with her unspoken request and met her nose-to-nose in the center of the table. "I had eight shots of...no, six...ten, or maybe...you know what? I don't remember. That's how many shots of Patron I had. And if I stand up all that alcohol will go straight to my head and I'll be snockered."

Dante regarded her with open amusement. "I've got news for you, lady. You're already snockered."

Brenna blinked. "Well, if I am, it's your fault." She leaned back in her chair.

"How is this my fault?"

She pointed to an occupied booth. "We were sitting there. And then the elf showed up so I had some Patron."

Dante stared at her, tried to decipher her meaning, and came up empty. "I have no idea what you're talking about. Grab your purse, and let's go. You want to visit the lady's room before we head out?"

Brenna stood and sat down again an instant later. At Dante's questioning stare she said, "Shouldna stood up."

Dante came around the table and eased Brenna up, amused that her prediction had come true. Sitting down she had maintained reasonable control of her faculties, but the act of standing had somehow created a concentration of her alcohol haze. She swayed like a sailboat at sea with no rudder, and he drew her close to keep her steady and steer her toward the door.

"Whoopsie! My purse!" She yanked free and twirled back toward the table.

Dante spun to grab her, but the dominoes had already

begun to fall. At the moment Brenna stepped toward the table, two of the men sniffing around her collided with one another and bumped into a third who stumbled backward and into a waitress carrying a tray holding a pitcher of beer and six full glasses. The waitress cried out and made an attempt at avoidance, but she was unable to escape the pile-up. The tray tipped, and the pitcher and glasses tumbled, spilling most of the beer on a startled Brenna, who squealed and jumped backward. Dante caught her in time to keep her upright, but not fast enough to move her out of harm's way. Beer splashed the front of her body like an ocean wave.

"Are you okay?" Dante's gaze dropped first to her dripping chin and then downward to where beer trickled from her upper chest and disappeared into her generous cleavage and below the scooped neckline of her shirt. Dry, her top had been somewhat modest. Wet, not so much. He gulped and forced his attention back upward to wait for her response.

She plucked at the soaked front of her shirt and tugged it away from her body. "Well, this isn't good."

"I'm so sorry!" The waitress's eyes rounded in concert with her mouth. "Omigosh. That guy bumped right into me." She looked at the floor around them and her shoulders drooped, but she brightened when a couple of busboys rushed over to help her clean up.

"It's okay, honey," Brenna said with cheer as she snatched up her purse. "Accidents happen. Anyway, I read that beer is good for your hair."

"You know," said the waitress, "I've heard that, too."

Brenna nodded. "And mayo will make your hair soft as anything. The real stuff, not the fat-free crap. And vinegar is great for stripping out a buildup of—"

"Hey, Vidal Sassoon, can we get out of here?" Dante said.

"That sounded a lot like scarcasm. Carcasm." Brenna blinked, considering. She made a popping sound with her mouth. "I think my lips are broke."

Oh, I bet they'd work just fine, Dante thought, wishing he could put them to the test, but he said, "C'mon, say goodbye to your fans, and let's go."

Brenna waved and called goodbye to her drunken admirers. Several of the young men made to approach her, but Dante's expression gave them pause. He braced for a problem, but there was none. They were just looking to party, after all, and, with Brenna under his watchful eye, they turned their attentions to other more available women.

"You should be more careful," Dante told her once they were in the car. "Did you even know any of those guys?"

"Nope!" She popped the 'p' again, and her cheerful tone made him smile, in spite of his concerns. "They were celebrating 'cause one of them just had a baby."

"You mean his wife."

"That's what I said."

"I think you know better than to put yourself in a bad situation, but when you're alone—"

"I wasn't alone. I had a date. At least I did, before the elf showed up." Brenna yawned and rested her head back on the seat. "I don't mind. He wasn't the one, anyway."

"The one for what?"

"No one. Still no one." She sighed and closed her eyes. "I'm not feeling so good."

"Please don't throw up in my car." Silence. "Brenna? Did you hear me?"

"You might wanna pull over." She slapped her hands over her mouth.

"Aw, geez. Hold on, okay? Just—just hold on. Two seconds."

Dante squealed the car to a rough stop on the shoulder of the road and ran around to open the passenger door for Brenna.

"Sorry," she hiccupped, and stumbled from the car. Dante jumped back, but not fast enough to save his shoes from Brenna's gastric deluge. He swallowed back against his own gag reflex and moved in so he could hold her steady while she puked. He scooped her hair back and held it away from her face to keep it from being drenched by anymore foreign substances, and used the hem of his shirt to wipe her mouth when she'd finished.

"That was gross," she said once they were underway again. "And now my mouth tastes icky."

"No more puking," he commanded. "Not till we get home."

Brenna responded with a soft snore. Dante glanced at her and smiled. She lay with her head back and her mouth open. He suspected she'd have drool pooling at the side of her mouth in a few, and considered snapping a picture just to tease her with it later. He thought better of it and decided just to enjoy the moment.

He'd just had his shoes covered in puke by the most beautiful woman he'd ever known, after all. That ought to count for something.

What did it say about him that he could look at her after the events of the last hour and still want her more than his next breath?

And there it was, that little drip of drool from the side of her mouth. Dante grinned like a fool. God, she was cute.

You're pathetic, Caravicci.

Dante sniffed and wrinkled his nose. Between the beer soaking Brenna's clothes and the puke congealing on his shoes, the odor inside the Trans Am was turning ripe. He buzzed the windows down part way and let the evening air flow through the vehicle. Brenna shifted and closed her mouth, and woke up long enough to say, "Ew. I'm icky." She wiped the drool from her chin and closed her eyes again.

After Dante parked in his driveway and cut the engine he gave Brenna a gentle shake. "Hey, sweetheart. We're home." He rubbed her arm. "Brenna."

With a sigh, Dante went around the car and unbuckled his passenger. He stared at her for a moment and considered his options.

Her purse lay on the floor between her feet, and he could rifle through it for her keys, but that seemed rude. And even if he did that, once inside her house he'd have to further invade her privacy to clean her up and put her to bed. And then what?

He'd be on her couch again, because he had no intention of leaving her alone, not in the state she was in.

Multiple shots of Patron. Jesus. What the hell was she thinking?

He scooped up her purse, and then the woman herself, and carried them both into his own home. He toed off his shoes in the mudroom and left them in a heap—they were destined for the trash at his first opportunity—and then delivered Brenna to the master bedroom. He stared down at her while he assessed his options.

She needed a shower, but he figured he'd be in enough trouble as it was come morning and full sobriety, so he opted for the easier road.

"C'mon, sweetheart. Upsy-daisy." He helped her sit and tugged the beer-soaked shirt over her head and off, and replaced it with one of his own cotton tees. He debated leaving her bra on, but it was soaked, too, so he reached under the shirt to unhook it.

"Hey." Her eyes snapped open and she slapped at his hands. "Quit that."

"Then you take it off. It's soaked with beer."

Brenna stared at him while that sank in, and then she complied. She hung the lacy bra on her index finger by one of the straps and held it out to him. Her lips curved in a feline smile.

Dante ran his hand over his face and emitted a muffled laugh. He'd spent an inordinate amount of time in the last five years dreaming of getting her out of her lingerie, but this wasn't how he'd pictured it.

"Uh, thanks." He tossed the wet bra on the floor on top of her shirt. "Jeans next."

"Yeah. In your dreams, Neanderthal." She flopped back

onto the pillows. A moment later the rippling snores began anew.

Uncomfortable in the extreme, Dante unhooked her jeans, zipped them down, and began the process of working them over her hips and tugging them off. Again, not the image that he'd drawn for himself over the years, but then, what was? Nothing ever went as imagined, not in his world, anyway.

The jeans, still damp with beer, clung to her thighs like a second skin. Feeling like a pervert, Dante tried pulling them down while looking elsewhere, but he kept glancing back to check his progress. And damned if she wasn't giving life to a red and black thong the size of a postage stamp.

He snapped his mouth shut and redoubled his efforts to divest her of her denims. In the end they peeled off inside out, and he tossed them on top her other discarded clothes. He allowed himself a quick and appreciative perusal of her bare hips and thighs—the woman was curvy in ways only a heterosexual man could fully appreciate—while he yanked the bedsheets up to her chin.

The beer-stained clothes he tossed into the washing machine on his way to the garage for a bucket to put beside the bed. If she was going to hurl chunks again, he didn't want it landing on his carpet.

Dante passed one more look over the sleeping figure curled up in his bed, and relaxed for a moment against the doorjamb to admire the picture she made. He'd yearned to see her lying there for the longest time, and if he forgot the events that made it possible he might even allow himself to enjoy the moment—her hair, spread out across his pillow like miles of black silk, her dark lashes lying sweet and thick against the curve of her cheek. Her mouth was a work of art, made for kissing.

Miracle of miracles, Brenna Kinkaid, naked in his bed except for a lace-trimmed thong and his T-shirt.

What a beautiful illusion.

Pavarotti bulled his way past Dante's legs and trotted

across the room to the bed. He leapt up, stumbled, paused to stretch as if the mishap were an intended acrobatic move, and then began kneading one of Brenna's legs. He slowed the movements of his paws, yawned, and laid his fluffy body down like the Sphinx along the length of her thigh. His purrs rent the silence.

It was the first time Dante had ever envied the cat.

"Behave." He pointed a warning finger at Pav. The cat afforded him a lazy blink of his eyes. Dante set the door ajar, leaving just enough of an opening for the cat to get out, and went to crash on the couch.

He woke a couple hours later to Pavarotti hissing and bellowing his annoyance with the world at large. Brenna, Dante guessed, had moved in her sleep and disrupted the furry guy. If there was one thing Pav hated, it was being dislodged after he'd gone to sleep. A moment later, Brenna screamed.

Dante ran down the hall and burst into the bedroom to find Brenna sitting up in bed and staring at the cat as if he were an alien entity. Her eyes, wide and disoriented, lifted to Dante. She stared at him, confused, then back at the cat.

She drew the covers up to her chin. "I don't have a cat."

"Relax." Dante stepped into the room. "You're at my place. Did you have a bad dream, or did the cat wake you up?"

"Jack." Her brother's name trembled from her lips, and she wiped her cheeks with her fingers when tears tumbled. "I dreamed about Jack. His accident. It—it was bad."

"Can I get you anything? You want some water?"

She shook her head and slid back down under the sheets.

"Dante?" she asked when he turned to leave. "Will you—will you stay? Just for a little while?"

He hesitated just the barest of seconds. "Yeah, sure."

Dante adjusted a pillow against the headboard and sat with his back against it on top of the covers. Brenna snuggled up against him, and he held his breath while she settled in, afraid to put his hands in the wrong place or otherwise screw up a good thing. All the varying scenarios ran through his mind as to how this situation might work to his favor once she sobered up, but then he looked down at her pale face, at the eyelashes still thick and starry with tears, and his lust gave way to an overpowering urge to protect her from further hurt.

"Sweet dreams, Brenna." He brought her close, pressed a kiss to her forehead, and laid his head back to rest.

∽✺∾

Brenna focused on the sound, an engine of some kind. Close by, but a little muffled. She snuggled deeper into the pillows and worked to shift from the beginning stages of wakefulness back to sleep, but the harder she tried, the more awake she became.

Alternating prickles dug into her thigh—left, right, left right—and the engine grew louder.

She gasped and sat up.

Dante's cat, irked with being dislodged from his place of comfort on her leg, emitted a mournful *mroooow*. He followed it up with a hiss, batted at her with halfhearted effort, and showed her his backside and twitching tail before jumping from the bed. He trotted through the door, left ajar, and disappeared from view.

Brenna drew the covers over her chest and stared at the door as if Attila the Hun and his mighty hordes might blast through at any moment. Hyperaware, she sat unmoving, ears pricking toward the sounds from down the hall.

"Hey, Pav, you ready for breakfast, buddy?"

Dante's voice traveled, though it was clear he'd made an attempt to keep it quiet, and she held her breath, straining to hear more. The cat meowed, loud as a bullhorn, and Dante told him, "Shh. Food's coming."

Kitchen noises—metal on glass, a cabinet opening, closing, water running—set Brenna into motion.

She flung the covers back and gasped at her attire, or lack thereof. A shirt, not her own, covered her with surprising modesty. Though the crew neck slid down to bear one shoulder, the shirt was roomy and long enough to fall below her knees. No bra, she noted with dismay, but her thong was still where it belonged, so that was a good thing, right?

She visited the bathroom and stared at herself in the mirror.

"Oh. My. God."

She grabbed a fistful of hair and watched it fall as she dropped it, whole sections stuck together by some unknown substance. Black splotches and lines covered her cheeks, the detritus of mascara and eye shadow at the wrong end of a lost night. Her eyes dropped to the shirt covering her. Faded to a dusty black, with the word *RANGER* in gold lettering across the chest, it was soft from years of wear and washings. She grabbed the supple cotton in her hands and drew it up to her nose. Whatever had dried in her hair wasn't on the shirt, which smelled like Dante, clean and masculine, with maybe a hint of fresh oregano.

She sniffed again. Probably imagined the oregano.

She used his toothpaste to finger-brush her teeth, then washed her face and poked in the medicine cabinet hoping to find aspirin or something like it. Nothing but guy stuff in there, and she took her time looking at it, feeling only a little bit guilty for snooping. There was nothing earthshattering—Band-Aids, shaving stuff, deodorant, an expired zolpidem prescription, aspirin, and a bottle of mouthwash.

'*Quit stalling,*' Jack's voice said, and she winced at the noise in her head. '*Go face the music.*'

'*I would,*' she thought back to Jack, '*if I had any clue what that was.*'

Unfortunately, the period of time from about her fourth shot of Patron to waking up this morning was a blank. She had no idea how she'd ended up in Dante's bed, or what had transpired while she'd been there.

This was a first. She'd never blacked out before, never

had so much to drink that she couldn't remember what she had done. Even in college she'd kept herself on the right side of a party night. The knowledge that she put herself into this situation both scared and shamed her, and the only thing she was certain of was that she would never do anything like it again.

Which didn't help her right this minute.

Brenna cupped her hands to guzzle water and helped herself to some aspirin from the medicine cabinet. She vacated the bathroom and looked around the bedroom for her clothes with no luck. In the process she noted a decided lack of personal items on Dante's dresser and bedside tables. No family photos, no old army photos, no old wedding photo or—

"The elf!" The words blew through her lips in a shouted whisper and she clapped her hands over her mouth. How could she forget the elf?

Splotches of memory tumbled from whatever over-stuffed mental closet she'd locked them in, and the image of Trina Caravicci laying one on Dante at the bar initiated the return of the prickling heat to the back of Brenna's neck.

She eased herself down on the side of the bed as her memory regurgitated bits and pieces of the previous night. Vince left with Trina, and she had left with Dante. She had a vague image of throwing up on his shoes—she covered her face with her hands and stifled a groan—while the man held her hair out of harm's way with one hand and kept her from face-planting the pavement with his other.

She struggled to remember, to put the random images into order. A clear memory of handing him her bra popped into her mind, then it was nothing but a blank page until the nightmare. It was the same one she'd been having ever since Jack died, killed by a drunk driver wielding his muscle car as a weapon. She pushed the terrifying dream images from her mind.

She remembered now waking up confused, because the bedroom was similar to her own in design, with the same double-tray ceiling and overhead fan, the same bay window and built-in bench—though Dante's was covered with piles of folded laundry and magazines with names like *Hot Rod* and *Car and Driver*, whereas hers displayed fluffy pillows and a stack of romance novels waiting to go back to the library.

She'd been startled by the cat. And then Dante had come in. She'd rested against his thick chest, and the beat of his heart had lulled her like ocean waves, along with the rhythmic motion of his gentle hand smoothing her hair over her head and down her back. He'd made her feel safe again, and she'd gone back to sleep.

Whatever else might have occurred was lost.

Brenna stood and turned toward the door. She drew a steadying breath, caught up her mass of hair and dropped it behind her shoulders, shook it back, and ignored the stiff pieces that felt like they'd been dipped in glue. She couldn't hide in the bedroom forever.

"Okay. Time to do this."

She drew another deep breath, straightened her shoulders, and headed for the kitchen.

Chapter 8

Brenna peeked around the bedroom door and into the hallway. The scent of coffee wafted to her, and a moment later she identified a sizzling sound as bacon on a griddle. She rested a hand on her stomach when it rumbled with hunger and took her time stepping into the hallway.

The best thing she could say about her walk of shame was that no one but herself and Pavarotti was there to witness it. The cat sat blinking his luminous eyes at her from the far end of the hall, sauntered to meet her halfway, and then trotted ahead to precede her steps like a grand marshal.

The hall opened up into the living room, and Brenna walked on silent feet across the carpet toward the kitchen. She paused just short of the tiled floor that was identical to her own and, nervous, curled her toes into the carpet, and cleared her throat to get Dante's attention. He stood barefoot and relaxed at the stove, transferring cooked bacon from the skillet onto a paper towel to drain. Clad in stonewashed denims and a snug gray tee, when he swung his attention away from the bacon to her, she wondered why she'd ever thought the man to be anything but gorgeous. Morning stubble darkened the lower half of his face, always a plus. His dark eyes softened at the sight of her and the sexy ripple of lines appeared when he smiled.

"Hi."

"Hi." She tucked her hair behind her ears and tried to smile. Her lips curved, but embarrassment made it a stiff effort.

"You want some coffee?" He nodded toward the table and chairs at the other end of the kitchen, situated as hers was in front of a wide window. His table and chairs were warm oak, hers were glass and iron. His window had wooden shutters, hers had custom curtains.

She would have to pass him to get to the table and chairs, so she sat at the breakfast bar instead.

Dante slid a steaming mug of coffee in front of her, accompanied by a sugar bowl, a carton of half-and-half, and a spoon. A moment later a plate of scrambled eggs, bacon, and toast followed.

"You want some OJ?" He took a jug of juice from the fridge and poured some into a glass before she could say no.

Brenna stared at the fare in front of her and pressed her hand to her stomach. This was nerve-racking, the not knowing.

"About last night," she said and winced at the cliché.

Dante finished off a glass of orange juice and met her gaze full on. "What about it?"

"Well. That's the problem. I, uh..." She cleared her throat and moved the eggs around on the plate with her fork. "I don't remember, exactly." She squeezed her eyes shut for a couple seconds, praying for clarity, then set the fork down and folded her hands in her lap. She lifted her gaze to Dante's, whose attention had remained on her, and bit her lip. "What did we—I mean, we didn't—did we?"

The lines around his eyes became more pronounced as his smile widened. Brenna knew sure misery. How had she let this happen?

Dante's cell phone rang out from the vicinity of the sofa behind her, and she jumped. Still smiling like the Cheshire Cat, he retrieved his phone, told whoever was on the calling end that he'd be there in a few, then stepped up beside

Brenna. She forced her eyes upward, hated the betraying heat that whooshed into her face when her gaze locked with Dante's.

"I have to go." His gaze shifted to her mouth and then back to her eyes, and the Cheshire Cat smile continued to play at his lips as her face grew hotter. "As fun as it is to watch you squirm, I won't drag it out. The truth is, nothing happened last night. But just so we're clear—" Dante leaned in and Brenna's breath caught as his eyes darkened to black pools and his voice lowered to the equivalent of a leonine purr. "—when I take you to bed, Brenna, it won't be something you'll forget."

Brenna swallowed hard, dug deep for composure against the urge to kiss the man from here to Sunday, and uncovered her sass instead. Her voice carried a blunt edge when she replied, "That is such a typical man thing to say. I expected something more original from you." She sniffed and gave her tone an acerbic drip. "It's a little disappointing to find out that, underneath that cloak of gallantry, you really are just a Neanderthal with too high an opinion of himself."

Dante stepped back and regarded her with amusement before he dropped his head back and laughed. "Nice one. I'm glad you've recovered your attitude. You know, I think I actually like you better when you're snotty like this." He winked at her, grabbed his phone, and started down the hall.

"Hey, Neanderthal. Where are my clothes?"

"Folded up on top of the dryer. I washed everything for you. Well, except the thong. And may I just say, by the way, that's a nice little bit of business, Miss Kinkaid."

Brenna bit back her humiliation and forced a laugh. "You're a jackass."

"You look like heaven in my shirt," he called from the bedroom.

"Glad you think so," she shot back, "because I'm keeping it." And she did.

∽∾∽

Two hours later, Brenna sat in her stylist's chair and met the woman's baby-blue gaze in the mirror.

Raelynn bit her lip and frowned. "Omigosh. You sure about this?" She held Brenna's waist-length locks up and let them flow like an ebony waterfall. "Going so short all at once could be a shock to you. You've had your hair long since you were a kid."

"Well, now, honey, that's kind of the point," Brenna said. "Things have gone sideways lately and I need a major change. Like a mental adjustment, you know?"

"But to cut it all off?" Raelynn shook her head and her messy topknot wobbled. "Your hair is gorgeous. It'll take you years to grow it back."

"Maybe I won't want to grow it back."

"And maybe you'll go into cardiac arrest when you see it all lying on the floor."

"No," Brenna twisted around to look Raelynn in the eye. "Don't toss it on the floor. I'm sending it in to the Wigs 4 Kids charity."

"You're serious about this."

"As a swarm of angry wasps, honey."

Raelynn nodded and her lips curved. Clearly excited, she clapped her hands and did a little dance. "Omigosh, Bren, this is gonna be so awesome. I love doing big style changes like this. Did you really mean it when you said I can cut it any which way I want?"

Brenna nodded. "You've been playing with my hair since we were in high school, and you're the best hairstylist in five counties. I trust you."

"Well, all righty then." Raelynn slapped her hands together. "You won't recognize yourself when I'm done with you."

"That's the plan," Brenna said.

"How about color? Omigosh, you'd kill it as a blonde! With those eyes of yours? We'll do something Nordic, like Elin Nordegren. Remember her? She was married to—"

"No color, just cut. And keep the chair turned around. I

don't want to watch you do it. I might chicken out."

"Okay, well, maybe we'll go blonde next time."

Brenna closed her eyes and listened to Raelynn's chatter. The woman's voice became just so much white noise while she worked, and Brenna's gut clenched with every snip and slice of the scissors. It was too late to second guess her decision now that the process had begun, and she questioned her sanity more than once.

After slipping into her jeans at Dante's she had gone home to shower. Washing her hair was always a chore because of its thickness and length, but today the process dragged on, due to the stickiness from beer and god-knew-what-all-else. Puke, probably, she admitted with disgust, splashed into her hair before Dante went above and beyond the call of duty to keep her tresses out of harm's way.

And what the hell was wrong with her, anyway? What kind of grown woman accepts a shot challenge in a cowboy bar with a guy she barely knows? If Dante hadn't been there, would she have climbed back on that motorcycle with Vince and allowed his drunk butt to drive her home?

It was Maddie and Caleb's wedding that had made her crazy, the emotional stress of planning, of wanting everything to be so perfect for Maddie, and the whole mess with the cake, and the heightened awareness of Jack because, let's face it, even though Jack was gone he was still *there* in so many ways. And that nightmare, that damned nightmare that had ruined her sleep in the months right after Jack died, had come back full force over the last two weeks.

It was always the same.

She rode as a passenger in a car driven by Jack. Outside, it poured, and the wipers made a steady clicking sound as they worked to squeegee the rain from the windshield. Seeing beyond the beam of the headlights cutting into the dark night was impossible. In spite of the dangerous road conditions, she and Jack chatted and laughed, though when Brenna awoke she never remembered what they had talked about. And in spite of the cheerful chatter, the sense of impending doom drew down upon her, dark and cold as the black nighttime surrounding the vehicle.

Then, out of the darkness, came the Mustang, built for speed and flexing its muscles on the dangerous road. It first appeared as headlights in the distance before it veered from its lane. It careened toward her and Jack in slow motion. Jack was always unaware of what headed their way, as if he couldn't see the oncoming headlights, even when it drew close enough to illuminate the interior of their car. In the way of dreams, Brenna's fear coagulated in her throat, and though she struggled to speak a warning, no words would come. She could only watch, helpless, as the muscle car hit them head-on.

Jack was always smiling at her when the collision occurred, and there was nothing she could do, just wait for the crash, for the screaming metal and shattering glass, her hair tangled in her face, blinding her, soaked and dripping with blood, Jack's and her own, and she'd scream and scream and scream, the taste of gore metallic on her tongue.

She opened her eyes and forced herself to breathe.

You're not dreaming now.

After the shower, she'd stared at her dripping locks in the mirror and saw the solution, wondering why she hadn't realized it before. The hair had to go.

Her sensible side told her it was a leap to think cutting her hair would solve the problem. She ignored it and listened to her emotional side instead. No hair, no after-accident blindness, no long tresses soaked with blood. Maybe if she did the deed, her subconscious would get the message.

"You ready to see?" Raelynn's eyes sparkled with excitement. "I have to say, I outdid myself."

Brenna gripped the arms of the chair and nodded. Raelynn turned the chair and watched Brenna's reaction in the mirror.

"You hate it." Raelynn's shoulders drooped and the corners of her mouth turned down like a sad emoji.

Brenna stared at the stranger in the mirror. "I don't hate it." She lifted a tentative hand to touch the back of the stranger's head, and for the first of what would be at least a hundred times that day, she smoothed her fingers over the short crop of hair that stopped at the base of her neck. She flashed a wobbling smile at Raelynn. "It's going to take some getting used to, but I think I like it."

"I knew you'd rock this cut. See how it's all long and tousled in the front?" Raelynn fingered the hair, adjusting the fall of bangs that framed Brenna's eyes. "You can do so much with this. Omigosh, Bren. I have to admit, I'm a flippin' genius."

"Well. You know what I need to do now, don't you?"

Raelynn placed her hands on Brenna's shoulders, met her gaze in the mirror, and smiled. "Girl. You need new shoes!"

❧❧❧

By the time she was through, Brenna had not only found a new pair of shoes, but a little black dress to go with them. She'd stopped by the Blueberry Boutique on her way to the L&G and found the perfect accompaniment to her new 'do. At the time she purchased the shoes, and the dress with it, she hadn't fully formed her plan for the evening. But ideas brewed beneath that short cap of hair, and she had a pretty good notion of how she wanted the night to go.

She strode into the Lump & Grind through the front door and stood back to watch her crew at work. Greta had left at two and Shaniqua was in charge. She stood at the register, explaining to a customer the difference between a latte and espresso. Kaitlyn, on her way from the refrigerator with pitchers of half-and-half, did a double take when she spotted Brenna and stopped in her tracks. Her sudden halt resulted in a collision from behind when Ed, walking close on her heels, slammed into her. Kaitlyn pitched forward and the

containers of half-and-half flew from her hands. Both lost
their lids when they hit the floor. Creamer splashed the cab-
inets beneath the counter and pooled on the tiles. Kaitlyn
squealed and, in her arm-spinning effort to stay upright, she
whacked Ed on the nose. Ed howled and grabbed his of-
fended appendage. Blood spurted. Kaitlyn saw the gushing
red and her eyes rolled back in her head. She crumpled like
an abandoned marionette. Shaniqua spun around in time to
catch Kaitlyn, but her balance was compromised and both
females landed in a heap on the floor. Ed, who slipped in
the spilt cream, joined them.

Brenna scrambled to their aid and, an hour later, she sat
in the ER with Ed on one side and Kaitlyn on the other.
Ed's nose had swollen to the size of a golf ball and his eyes
had already begun their transition to black and blue. He sat
sprawled like a scarecrow in the plastic seat, his head resting back against the wall, ice pack in place.

"I'm sorry. Geez. I'm so sorry. Ed, do you forgive me? I
didn't mean to hit you. I saw Brenna but I wasn't sure it was
her, you know? Because of her hair." Kaitlyn turned her
amber eyes toward Brenna. "Which looks, like, totally awesome, by the way. Just saying." She dimpled and then swiveled back to Ed. "So are you, like, really hurting? It looks
really sore, like, really, really sore. And I'm, like, so, so sorry."

Brenna looked heavenward for divine assistance. The
water-stained ceiling tiles offered no insights. "Kaitlyn,
honey, why don't you rest until your mama gets here, okay?
I know you didn't hit your head or anything, but you did
pass out. It'd probably be best if you stopped talking now."

"Oh. Oh, okay." Kaitlyn mimicked Ed's relaxed pose,
and after a minute lifted her head to look around Brenna.
"Sorry, Ed. I'm so sorry."

Lord, save me from guilt-ridden teenagers.

"I'll be fide," Ed said, breathing through his mouth.
"Doh deed to worry aboud bee. By dose will be as good as
dew in doh tibe."

Brenna bit back a laugh and turned her head away from Ed. Her gaze connected with Kaitlyn's and they shared a moment of silent laughter.

"You may owe him a date to prom," Brenna told the girl after a nurse called Ed from the waiting room.

Kaitlyn lifted her brows and emitted a nervous laugh. "He's nice and all that, but not really my type."

"You know, I wouldn't have thought so either, a few days ago. But you ought to at least take the time to get to know him a little. Did you know he works with the 'Giving You Paws' pet rescue group? That's how I met him. And he's going to UGA in the fall. He wants to be a veterinarian."

"Really? Well that's cool, I guess. He's just not, you know."

"Your type. Right." Brenna nodded. "Did you know he plays in a local rock band on the weekends?"

Kaitlyn perked up. She flipped her dark hair over her shoulders, smiled, and sat up straighter in her seat. "He does?"

"Mm-hm. He's the drummer. Plays bass guitar, too."

"Maybe I could hear him play sometime."

"I bet he'd like that," Brenna said. "Just give him a chance."

"Yeah, but he's really not—"

"Not your type." Brenna sighed. "I know, honey. I've heard that one before. But take my word for it. Sometimes *not my type* turns into *what have I been missing?*"

❧❧❧

Okay, so the day didn't go quite as planned. That didn't mean the night had to be a bust too, did it? Of course not.

Brenna stood in front of her full length mirror and smoothed the new dress over her hips. "It fits like a dream," she said and then puffed out a breath and laughed at herself.

Who the heck was she kidding? It fit like a compression sock. A curve-hugging, body-bragging, boob enhancing, thigh-exposing compression sock. This dress had one job and one job only: grab male attention.

If anyone had told her a week ago that she'd be revving up to make Dante Caravicci drool, she'd have called them a big fat liar. But something had happened over the wedding weekend, something she couldn't explain. And it didn't really matter that she couldn't explain it. All that mattered was that she needed to sort it out.

According to Chloe when Brenna had called the Bistro earlier, Dante had taken the night off.

"He said he had some experimenting to do," Chloe told her. "He's not expected at either the Pizzeria or the Bistro tonight. Maybe you can catch him at home."

So Brenna altered her plans. She owed the man a major apology and an even bigger thank you. She aimed to give him both tonight, in the form of a little something to think about—hence the dress—and a nice bottle of French merlot that had cost her more than the dress and shoes combined.

She sat on the edge of the bed to slip on her new heels, considering the care she'd have to take walking through the grass between the driveways. She grinned, imagining Dante's surprise when he opened his front door.

She stood up. There. Not five-foot-two anymore, but a respectable five-foot seven. She eyed her hair. Wow. It was quite the change.

Well, too late to do anything about it now. Anyway, it was kind of growing on her. She fluffed the bangs and liked the way the cut accentuated her eyes and cheekbones.

Brenna walked to the window and peeked out. Dante's garage was closed but his Trans Am sat in the driveway.

Time to rock and roll.

She stood with the bottle of wine at the edge of her driveway and gave the splotchy grass a once over. Instead of risking the shoes she took the long way around, walking down her driveway and on the street past their mailboxes, then up his driveway straight to his front door. She drew a calming breath, raised her hand, exhaled, and knocked.

After a few moments, the door swung open. Brenna forced a bright smile that froze on her lips a scant second later.

"May I help you?"

Brenna stared at The Elf. In her heels she towered over the tiny woman who, in Brenna's estimation, was too cute to live.

"Hi." Brenna held up the bottle of merlot. "I just wanted to drop this off for Dante."

Trina hollered toward the kitchen. "Hey, hot stuff, you have company!" She tucked her hair behind her ears and the ends curled with angelic wispiness against her delicate jaw-line. "C'mon in." When Brenna stepped into the entryway Trina widened her eyes, a golden hazel that Brenna envied. "Hey, wait a sec. You're Miss All-That from the bar last night. Holy Toledo. You cut off all that gorgeous hair."

Brenna nodded, aware that her smile might crack her cheeks if she wasn't careful. "Guilty." She forced the word through her teeth so The Elf wouldn't think her the speech-less town idiot.

"We were never properly introduced," The Elf said. She held out her hand, smiled, gave Brenna a conspiratorial wink, and said in a loud voice, "I'm Trini Caravicci, *Dante's wife*." And then in a hushed voice, she said, "Okay, wait for it."

"*Ex*-wife!" Dante's voice reverberated from the kitchen. A moment later his head popped around the corner. "Ex, Trina. *Ex*. Will you quit telling people we're still—Oh, hey Brenna. Hold on a minute." He disappeared back into the kitchen.

Trina laughed and her eyes shone with merriment. "I love doing that to him. It drives him crazy."

Dante stepped from the kitchen and strode down the short entry hall, wiping his hands on a utilitarian apron tied around his waist. He shot a narrowed look at Trina. "Go stir the sauce, and stay out of trouble."

"Nice to meet you," Trina said.

"You too." Brenna ran a nervous hand over the back of her head while Trina took her cute little elf-self back to the kitchen.

"So, what can I do for you?" Dante asked. "You want to come in and sit, have some wine? You can test drive my new puttanesca sauce, tell me if you think it's ready for prime time. Nice bangs, by the way. Looks nice."

"Oh, uh, thanks, but no. I'm…uh…" *Dear god, how to explain the little black dress? Think, Brenna, think.* "Um…I'm…um…actually meeting someone in a little while, so I can't stay." *Good, that's good! Totally believable.* She straightened her shoulders. "I just want to deliver this, to say thank you for everything you did for me last night." She handed him the wine and breathed easy, back on steady ground. "You went above and beyond under the circumstances and, well…" Her hand brushed over the back of her head again. "I'm grateful, Dante. Thank you."

"Yeah, sure." He read the label on the bottle and his brows shot up. "Wow. Very nice." He lifted his gaze to hers. "You sure you can't stay? We can—"

"Hey, hot stuff! When do I add the fresh basil leaves?" Trina called from the kitchen.

"Sorry," Dante said to Brenna and turned around to holler back at Trina. "Don't worry about the basil. I'll take care of it when I get back in there."

"Okie-doke. Sorry. Stirring here. Just stirring."

"Keep it on simmer, Treen."

Brenna took Dante's split attention as her opportunity to vamoose. She opened the front door and stepped outside. He watched her from the doorway.

"Really, Brenna, you don't have to go."

Eager to escape, she said, "Yes, really, I do. Like I said, I'm meeting someone, so. Anyway, thanks again, and good luck with your puttanesca sauce."

"Thanks," he said, and she knew the second it registered in his brain that her hair was gone. His smile vanished when his jaw dropped. His eyes widened in what she read to be horrified surprise. Dante said nothing for several weighty seconds as he processed the change.

"Turn around. Show me the back."

Surprised, Brenna obliged without a complaint about his dictatorial tone. When she completed her circle he said, "When I saw you inside I thought you had just cut bangs and pinned it up."

"Nope. I had it all cut off."

"I can see that, now." He stared into her eyes and she shifted, uncomfortable, as the seconds ticked past. "You know, I thought you couldn't possibly be more beautiful than you already were. I was wrong."

Brenna's stomach did an acrobatic tumble. "Thank you. That's a kind thing to say."

"I didn't say it to be kind."

"Hey, hot stuff! That weird vegetable concoction you put in the oven is, like, starting to smoke. Can I take it out, or is it doing what you want it to do?"

Dante dropped his head back and sighed. "Take it out of the oven."

"Okay! Will do!"

Brenna emitted a soft laugh. "You better get back in there before your house burns down." She turned to leave.

"Brenna."

She stopped and looked back at Dante. The intensity of his gaze blasted through her like a lightning bolt, and she gulped when her insides responded to the sizzle. She didn't trust her voice and so waited, as trapped in his stare now as she had been in his embrace just a few days ago.

"You look stunning."

The dress and heels, it seemed, had done their job. She needed to say something like, *Why, thank you, kind sir,* or *Too bad you're all tied up with The Elf,* or *I did this for you, only for you, you big idiot Neanderthal.*

She said none of those things, but regarded him with a steady stare while wondering how he'd managed to render her mute with just three words and a smoldering look.

"Enjoy your date, Brenna. Whoever he is, he's a lucky man."

An hour later, showered clean of makeup and hair styling goop, she lay sprawled on her sofa, clad in a pair of ratty yoga pants and Dante's oversized Ranger shirt. She kept running her fingers through her new 'do, which she'd allowed to air dry—she'd figure out how to style it tomorrow—and flipped through TV channels until she found *Law & Order* reruns. She, Maddie, and Rebecca hadn't had a crime show marathon in a while, and she considered calling Rebecca to come over and watch with her, but decided she'd rather brood alone. She wasn't ready for Rebecca's honest opinion about her hair, especially since, at the moment, it was au naturel and made her look, in her estimation, like a human dandelion.

She called the L&G to check in, then ordered a large hand-tossed Dante's Inferno—minus the serrano peppers—from Caravicci's Pizzeria, and settled back with a pint of Ben and Jerry's Red Velvet Cake ice cream while she waited for the delivery.

Mmm, so good, she thought, scooping up a spoonful of the ice cream big enough to rival the Rock of Gibraltar. The doorbell rang and she jumped. The ice cream dropped off the spoon and landed on the shirt over her boobs with a soft splat. She watched the melting trail as it slid between the girls toward her abdomen, and feeling slothful, she picked it up with her fingers and popped the whole thing into her mouth. No point wasting it. She wiped at the sticky smear with a napkin and made it worse.

Pizza's here, she thought and, still processing the big lump of ice cream in her mouth, called out as best she could, "Hold on a sec!" She hoisted herself from the couch, set the pint of ice cream on the sofa table, wiped her sticky hands on the fabric covering her thighs, and grabbed a twenty dollar bill on her way to the front door.

She yanked the door open with a ready smile, and for the second time that day her expression froze in place.

Chapter 9

H i." Dante gave her a quick once over. She saw him assess the situation and the prickling heat of embarrassment crawled into her face. He grinned. "You look comfy."

"I thought you were the pizza delivery guy."

He held up the Caravicci's Pizzeria box in one hand and the French merlot in the other. "I am the pizza delivery guy. I might even say the ultimate pizza delivery guy, as I own the restaurant. I saw the car when it pulled in, figured your date got canceled."

"My date?" Her eyes widened when Jack's voice reminded her, '*Makeup, heels, little black dress.*' "Oh, right. That." She nodded and a self-conscious laugh bubbled up. "Canceled. Right. Sorry." She waved her hand. "I wasn't…um…you know. I didn't…ah, do you want to come in? Just, you know, put the pizza in the, uh…"

Her train of thought fled when he stepped through the door, close enough that she swore it was the heat from his body making her glow.

'*Glow? Who are you kidding? You're sweating like a boxer in training,*' Jack's voice whispered.

'*Glowing,*' she shot back, '*because a Southern lady never sweats.*'

Dante's eyes narrowed with concern. "You okay?"

Brenna looked up, and up. The man towered over her by about a foot. She needed her high heels to even the playing field a little. He regarded her with steady bemusement through eyes the color of her favorite espresso, and she melted like butter in the sun. "Oh. The...uh..."

His lips curved and his eyes did their adorable crinkling thing. "Kitchen?"

She nodded and gave herself a mental head slap for being a yammering fool. It wasn't like the man was Chris Hemsworth, for god's sake. He was just Dante Caravicci, her Neanderthal neighbor.

Her really *hot* Neanderthal neighbor.

She glanced down at her sloppy outfit and cursed the holey yoga pants and ice cream splattered shirt. Even her fingers were sticky. Should she excuse herself to go wash up and change into something that didn't look like she'd just come home from a middle school sleepover? No. Changing her clothes would afford too much importance to this visit which was, likely, just a case of Dante playing Mr. Nice Guy.

"You keep your wineglasses in the same cupboard as I do," he said when she joined him in the kitchen.

Brenna looked at the pair of empty wineglasses on the counter and the corkscrew next to them. Dante held up the bottle of wine. "I hoped you'd agree to share this with me." He didn't wait for a response, but wielded the corkscrew with practiced ease and poured just the right amount into the glasses.

She washed the stickiness from her hands before taking his offering and sat down at her kitchen table to eat. She flipped the lid on the pizza box and sniffed. "Best pizza in town, right here."

"Ah, yes, the famous Inferno. I see the jalapeños, but it looks like you ordered it without the other key ingredient."

"The serrano peppers?" She lifted a slice and took a bite. "Those things make my eyeballs bleed."

Dante laughed and sat down in the chair opposite hers.

"Yeah, they're hotter than hell." He tasted the wine and nodded. "I don't know what it cost you, but this wine is worth every penny you paid for it."

"Is it classless of me to drink it with pizza?"

"It would be classless if you had ordered from anywhere but Caravicci's. Since the pizza came from my place, I think it's a perfect pairing."

"Have a slice."

"You kidding? I don't eat that stuff," he said, and laughed at her indignant expression. "Just kidding. I eat it all the time, but right now I'm full of pasta puttanesca."

"I take it your new sauce came out well?"

"It needs a little more tweaking, but yeah. Not bad."

"So where's your wife?" Brenna sipped the wine. He was right. Worth every penny.

"Ex-wife." Dante sighed. "*Ex.* Don't let Trina pull you over to the Dark Side."

"If she's your ex, why doesn't she introduce herself that way?"

"Because she's a pain in the ass." At Brenna's lifted brows, he capitulated. "Fine, fine. Here's the short version. We got married after I joined the army. We got divorced less than a year later. We were friends before and stayed friends after. As a friend, she likes to annoy me. That's pretty much it."

"You make it sound simple."

"It is simple."

"Marriage and divorce is never simple. It's life, and life is messy."

Dante shrugged, focused on the design etched into the wineglass, and rubbed it with his thumb. "So what torpedoed your date this time? That's two nights in a row you've run into trouble."

Brenna closed the lid on the pizza box and sipped her wine to buy time while she considered the best answer.

'*A good offense is the best defense*,' Jack's voice reminded her.

She took his advice and leaned forward. "Did you really come here to ask me about my canceled date?"

Dante mirrored her movement. "Do you really care why I got divorced?"

Their gazes locked.

"Then why are you here, Dante?"

She knew the question came off as rude, but his nearness made her blood pump through her veins like molten gold, made her needy, reckless. The pulse in her throat beat hard and steady, and she wondered if he could see it thrumming.

Dante's attention dropped to her mouth and, when he returned his gaze to hers, his eyes were two shades darker. "I want you to explode in my arms again."

The desire to jump into his lap did battle with her need to maintain a little dignity. Burn the kitchen down or put it into a deep freeze? It boiled down to a choice between lust or loftiness, and the longer he looked at her like that, his dark gaze intense and hungry, the more probable it became that lust would win the day.

Why? Why do you want me? Why, when I've been nothing but a bitch to you, judgmental and unfair. And wrong. Why? Is this some game to see which of us wins? The words danced on the tip of her tongue, but then a whisper of fear crept in, an insidious little voice that sounded nothing like Jack and a lot like Brenna herself, that told her maybe it was better not to know, better just to figure out the rules of the game as she went along.

Her cell phone buzzed and vibrated on the table, and she jumped, yanked from her internal debate.

"It's the L&G." She snatched up the offending device and pushed away from the table. Dante owned two restaurants and would understand better than anyone why she had to detour and take the call.

She paced the kitchen floor while she listened and gave instructions to Shaniqua. Dante moved their wine from the kitchen to the couch. He held up her pint of Ben & Jerry's and she nodded when he pointed to the fridge. She'd forgotten the ice cream. It must be soup by now.

Dante returned to the couch to wait and watch *Law &
Order* while she talked Shaniqua through a mechanical is-
sue with the espresso machine.

Brenna clicked off the call and ran her hand over the
back of her head, hyperaware of her lack of hair. She hadn't
realized how often she'd relied on that mop as a shield.
There would be no sitting on that couch and dropping her
chin just so, to let the fall of hair hide her eyes. For the first
time that day she felt naked and vulnerable.

Dante muted the TV and set the remote on the sofa table
when Brenna joined him. She sat down on the opposite end
of the couch and curled her feet under her, doing her best to
appear relaxed and confident. Faking confidence was one of
her best things, and she'd found that, most of the time, the
lie became truth if she kept it up long enough.

"Crisis averted?"

"Dirk was misbehaving. Not a big deal."

"Dirk?"

Brenna sipped her wine and nodded. "The espresso machine. I bought it last year and named it Dirk." She lowered
her voice to a sexy purr. "You know, big, buff, and steaming hot."

Dante dropped his head back and laughed. "Only you,
Brenna. Does Dirk live up to his name?"

"Most of the time, but lately he's become a little temper-
amental." She glanced at his empty wineglass. "You want a
refill?"

"No." He paused, his expression grown contemplative.
"I should go."

Brenna uncurled as Dante delivered his wineglass to the
sink. A flurry of emotions whirled through her as she
stalked toward the kitchen. She heard the water running and
rolled her eyes. The guy was cleaning up after himself. Who
but Dante? And yes, there he was, drying the wineglass now
and setting it back in the cupboard. She'd think his OCD
was adorable if she wasn't so annoyed.

Brenna put her hands on her hips and blurted, "Serious-ly? You're chickening out?"

"Excuse me?"

He faced her but didn't step closer, so she took the initia-tive and ate up the space between them in a few quick strides. She poked him in the chest and tilted her head back to look into his eyes.

"You, you big idiot Neanderthal. It was for you, all right? It was all for you."

Dante stared at her as if she'd just spouted Swahili. "What the hell are you talking about?"

Brenna threw her hands up. "The damn dress, the shoes, the makeup. I didn't have a stupid date. It was for—"

His mouth took hers a scant second before his hands claimed her face. She wrapped her arms around him and held on, the heavy flow of desire throbbing through her in an undulating wave. She rode that wave and met his kiss, beat for pounding beat.

"I seem to be exploding," she said when they came up for air. "Question answered."

Dante looked into her eyes. "I didn't ask a question, Brenna." He brushed her lower lip with his thumb. "I just told you what I want."

She grabbed one of his hands and dragged him to the couch. They dropped to the cushions as a singular unit and resumed their explorations without further pause.

Brenna wrapped herself around him and her pretentions evaporated. Every inch of her body pulsed for him, her need growing with each touch of his lips and hands. His mouth explored her throat, paused to worship at the curve of her neck and shoulder, the spot that had rendered her helpless during their heated encounter in the storeroom. *He remem-bered,* she thought, in a brief burst of clarity that dissipated with the rush of tingling heat over her skin.

Dante moved lower, tasting her through the supple fabric of the shirt.

She gasped at the first sensation of his mouth at her

breast, the moist heat an aphrodisiac that made her arch her back and clutch her hands in his hair.

"Mmmm. You taste like ice cream." He returned his mouth to hers, and again she felt the smile on his lips before he sank into the kiss, and she had to admit, she could lay there with his mouth on hers all night and die happy with it.

"What's wrong?" she asked, breathless, when he rested his forehead against hers, putting an end to all that delicious kissing.

"What are we doing here, Brenna?"

It was her turn to smile. She combed her fingers through his hair and sighed, content and amused. "Pretty sure we're making out on my couch, Dante."

That drew a laugh from him and he drew back to look into her eyes. "Yeah, I have that part figured out."

"So what's the problem?"

The muscle in his jaw flexed when Brenna traced the scar there, and he turned his head just enough to nip at her finger and draw it into his mouth for a quick taste before saying, "You know, a week ago if this had happened, I'd be happy to roll with it, just see where we landed."

Brenna swallowed. "But not now?"

"I don't want to wake up tomorrow morning and find out this was just…what'd you call it before?…an anomaly. I want more from you, Brenna. I want to know that after I leave here tonight, I'll still have the right to be back tomorrow. That you'll want me back tomorrow."

Serious. So serious, those dark eyes. They drew her in and held her captive. If he only knew what he did to her, the power he held. Best that he didn't, especially when she was still surprised and confused by it herself.

Brenna forced lightness into her voice that she didn't feel. "Why, Mr. Caravicci. If I didn't know better, I'd think you were asking me to go steady."

A moment later he smiled, that whole-face smile that made her heart flutter, and Brenna bloomed beneath the warmth of it, smiling back.

"Well, Miss Kinkaid, I guess I am," he said.

She toyed with his hair, soft and full against her fingers, and sighed. "Well, to be honest, I'm probably not doing you any favors by saying yes. You may find this hard to believe, but I'm very high maintenance." She flashed a coquettish sideways look from beneath her lashes that made him grin.

"No, really? You?"

She nodded. "Mm-hm. I'm stubborn, moody, and frequently bitchy. I'm demanding in the extreme, often unreasonable, and more than a little judgmental. You should also be warned that I've recently become aware of a very nasty jealous streak that leads me to make questionable choices about alcohol at cowboy bars."

Dante rubbed her nose with his. "You're persistent, passionate, and driven. You're caring and thoughtful, loyal above and beyond, and would do absolutely anything for the people you love."

Brenna grinned. "Wow, I've really got you snowed. What about the jealous streak?"

"I think I can handle it."

"If I agree to go steady, will you kiss me some more?"

"Count on it."

Brenna gripped his hair and drew him closer. "Then yes," she said against his mouth, and, "Yes," again when his hands, warm and firm, slipped under the hem of her shirt to travel the generous curve of her hips, over her waist, ribs, and higher. "Yes," she said again, breathless this time, and sank into Dante's kiss.

His hands stilled when Brenna's phone buzzed and vibrated on the surface of the sofa table as if it contained an angry bee bent on escape. A second later, his rang out with the theme from the Godfather.

"Oh, seriously? Are you kidding me?" Brenna groaned in frustration.

Dante dropped a quick kiss on her lips and sat up. He tossed her phone to her and then answered his own.

"Hello," they both said at the same time. He sighed and
scrubbed a hand through his hair, and with his gaze locked
on Brenna's he said, "No, don't do anything. Put him at a
table, give him a beer, and I'll be there in about fifteen
minutes. And comp the customer's whole meal—yeah, everyone in his party. And give him a gift card, too. Tell him
I'll be there tomorrow if he wants to talk to me personally,
or he can hang around now and talk to me tonight." He ended the call and dropped the phone back on the table.

"But no one slipped and fell, right?" Brenna said into her
phone. "Okay, then, honey. Thanks for handling it. I'll see
you tomorrow."

"Everything okay?" Dante asked when her phone joined
his on the sofa table.

"Today was the day for spills and accidents. I was at the
ER this afternoon with two of my employees. But yes, everything's fine. Shaniqua just wanted to give me a head's up
that Myrtle got stuck in the *on* position and dumped ice all
over the floor."

"Myrtle?"

"The ice machine."

"Do you name all your appliances?

Brenna flashed him a grin. "So what's up at the Bistro?"

"Not the Bistro, the Pizzeria. My idiot cousin. I'm sorry,
but I have to go. Damn Vince."

"What did he do?"

"Long story. I'll tell you later." His gaze locked on hers.
"There will be a later, right?"

"Well, we *are* going steady."

He grinned, and his eyes shifted upward to the top of her
head.

Brenna wrinkled her nose. "It's sticking up, isn't it."

"Like a rooster, yeah." He chuckled and made an effort
to smooth her unruly 'do.

Undaunted by her traitorous hair, Brenna swung one of
her legs across both of Dante's and shifted her position to
straddle his lap, her knees bent. "Take this with you when

you go, Mr. Caravicci. You know, since we're going steady and all." She took his face in her hands and planted a kiss on him, long, deep, and bursting with promise.

Dante's sigh sounded like ten different kinds of frustrated. "You're killing me right now."

"I know," she said, leaned down for one more touch of his lips against hers, and set him free.

ᥴᥗᥱᥗ

Trina met Dante at the back door of the Pizzeria and let him in, locking the door behind him.

"So tell me again what the hell happened." Dante strode through the kitchen without waiting for Trina to speak up. He nodded hello to the cook and busboy and continued his course toward the front of the restaurant, stopping where the kitchen tiles met the dining room carpet. His eyes searched the dining room for Vince and found him nursing a beer in a booth at the back, focused on his phone. Dante turned to Trina and pinched the bridge of his nose. "Not the shortened abridged version this time. Details."

"Well, I wasn't in the dining room when it happened, Dante. I had just arrived and was in the kitchen. I didn't even know Vince was here until Chloe called me up front to help stop the fight."

"Chloe." Dante stared at Trina, processing. "Why was Chloe here and not at the Bistro?"

Trina shifted from one foot to the other and crossed her arms over her chest. She glanced into the mid-distance and chewed the inside of her mouth for a second before looking back at Dante. "You're gonna be pissed."

"You think?"

Trina winced. "Gloria called off, and Haley was a no call, no show. I didn't want to bug you, have you think I couldn't handle the first thing that cropped up, so I called Chloe to see if she had any suggestions about who might pick up the shift. She offered to come wait tables until I could find someone. Lorelei came in and Chloe went back to the Bistro."

"So who handled the Bistro while Chloe was here running tables?"

"I don't know, but Chloe said she had it covered." Trina pushed her shoulders back and straightened her stance. "Look, hot stuff, we're fine here, and the Bistro is fine. We maybe didn't handle it the way you would have, but we handled it. It was no big deal, just a shift glitch. Now do you want to know about the fight or not?"

Dante forced himself to relax, acknowledged to himself that he was pressuring her about the wrong thing. "Sorry. I do trust you, and I trust Chloe." He glanced back at his cousin who had put his phone down to flirt with Lorelei. "So, the fight."

"Okay, then." Trina tucked her hair behind her ears. "Like I said, I was in the kitchen. Next thing I know there's a crash and Chloe's hollering for me to get my butt out here. We had a whole softball team come in, a party of eighteen or twenty. A couple of the guys were hitting on Chloe but, you know, she's used to it, right? She's a pro, so she's handling it smart, joking around. Apparently, Vince was already here—drunk before he ever showed up. He got involved, and, the next thing, there was a shouting match between Vince and one of the guys. Chloe tried to smooth things over, but Vince threw a punch—"

"Great." Dante pinched the bridge of his nose again. A pulse throbbed in his temple. "Cops?"

"No, no one called the cops. Vince threw a punch, but like I said, he was drunk so he didn't connect. The crash I heard was Vince stumbling against the table. He got pissed off, grabbed it, and upended it. Stuff slid everywhere. Chloe and I got Vince to the booth and made him promise to stay put, then I called you while Chloe took care of the guests. We finished cleaning up the mess right before you got here."

"So it wasn't really a fight, then, just Vince being an asshole."

Trina shrugged. "Yeah, I guess. I mean, it could've turned bad, Dante. Chloe really stepped up, took care of things—better than I could have, if I'm being honest. Vince knows how to get around me, and—"

"Yeah, I remember." Dante regretted the words the second they were out of his mouth. He held up his hands before Trina could respond. "Sorry. I'm sorry. Ancient history." He dropped his head back, stared at the ceiling, and wished himself back on Brenna's couch, cradled again by her soft curves.

"I screwed up big back then, but you know it wasn't what you thought," Trina said, and Dante was surprised at the quick tears that sprang to her eyes, even after all this time.

"I said I was sorry, Treen. My anger is at Vince, not at you. Let it go."

"You're the one who brought it up."

"You and I are fine, we're good. Like I said, my anger is with Vince." Dante stared at his cousin, sitting in the booth in Dante's restaurant, drinking Dante's beer, flirting with Dante's employee, after causing a problem with Dante's guests, and soon he'd be in Dante's car, riding to Dante's house, sleeping in Dante's guest room. *Will I ever be able to live my life without Vince believing he has a right to put his thumbprint on everything that's mine?*

"What are you going to do?" Trina asked.

"Take his sorry ass home, sober him up, and tell him to get the hell out of Bright Hills and leave me alone."

"He'll never leave you alone," Trina said. "He wants to be you."

Dante glanced at Trina and shook his head, his voice resigned. "He doesn't want to be me, sweetheart. He just doesn't want to let me be."

തര

Dante wrestled off Vince's boots and dropped them on the floor, covered the drunken man with a light blanket, shooed Pavarotti from the room, and closed the door on his way out.

Playing nursemaid twice in forty-eight hours had to be some kind of record.

Vince didn't surprise him, and this wasn't the first time in their lives Dante had put the other man to bed to sleep off his liquor. Vince had been drinking to get drunk since their teenage years, and this was just the latest in a lifetime of overindulgence.

Brenna, on the other hand, had over-imbibed for reasons unknown—other than the contest with Vince, who had read her competitive streak like a penny novel. But the last year of participating in the Kinkaid/Walker get-togethers had taught him that the lady never had more than a couple shots or a couple drinks, never let herself get sloppy. Well, except for that one time with Maddie last year, but he wasn't witness to that, and there were special circumstances, as he recalled. The point being, Brenna was no lush.

The same could not be said, however, about Vince.

Dante grabbed a bottle of water from the fridge and took it upstairs to his office where he booted up his laptop and settled in to do some work. He gave brief thought to knocking on Brenna's door, but the time for that was past. He dropped his head back and closed his eyes, imagined her sleeping or stretched out on the couch watching the rest of her crime show marathon. With her new hairdo sticking up in all directions.

He smiled, remembering.

The laptop chimed. Dante brought up his spreadsheet and reached for his paperwork. He had set an item on top of his file folders to act as a paperweight and deter Pavarotti from knocking the documents to the floor. Dante lifted the item now, measured the weight of it in his hands, and ran his thumb across the words labeling the front. He gave it a shake and watched the glitter swirl, and then set it back in its usual spot on top of an old business card next to the desk lamp. He stared at it for a moment, considering, and then tried to focus on his work.

Around one a.m., brain and body humming like a new Mercedes engine, he powered down his laptop and scrounged the kitchen for something to eat. He wished for a slice of the Inferno growing old in a greasy box at Brenna's and settled for a few bites of leftover Chinese takeout while being serenaded by Pav. The cat wound a figure eight around Dante's ankles and sang the song of his feline people.

How in the hell, Dante wondered, could Vince sleep through the caterwauling?

He dumped a can of cat food into a bowl, which stayed Pavarotti's vocal exercises for a few minutes, and prowled the house, picking up after himself and Vince. He folded laundry from the dryer and started a new load in the washer.

At two a.m. his eyes stung and his muscles ached, and he thought he might sleep, but laying down caused heart palpitations, so he did what he'd been avoiding in deference to Brenna. He flipped the garage lights on and, a moment later, the garage door rumbled open to invite in the cool nighttime air. Some quality time with his car never failed to help wind him down.

How the hell could his garage lights keep Brenna awake, anyway? His garage faced hers, and her bedroom window was toward the back of her townhouse, same as his.

There wasn't much required for the Trans Am, which he kept purring like a well-behaved panther, so he gathered cleaning tools and set about polishing the leather interior.

It was time to sell it, buy another old classic to restore and pamper, but he had a fondness for this one and had put off his search for a new project.

"Hey, Neanderthal."

Dante spun his head around, whacking his forehead on the Trans Am's "A" pillar. He barked out a curse and rubbed the rising lump with his hand while he slid from the car. "What are you doing here? It's the middle of the night."

"It's three a.m., to be exact, and you're coming with me."

Dante's head buzzed. "What?"

Brenna grabbed his hand and dragged him along behind her, across the concrete drive and the soft grassy divide between their townhomes. She moved, he thought, like a miniature locomotive, all steam and unstoppable motion.

"Brenna, hold up. What's this all about?" he asked after she dragged him into her house.

"I need you in my bedroom." She marched ahead, not bothering to see if he followed. "Right this instant."

Dante blinked, considered that he might have fallen asleep in the car and be dreaming all this, but it seemed unlikely. Almost as unlikely as Brenna Kinkaid ordering him to her bedroom *right this instant.* Not that he didn't like the sound of that, but—*holy shit.*

He picked up his pace.

"What do you see, Dante?" The sweetness of her tone belied her tapping foot.

"What?" He stepped into the mystery of her bedroom and waited for clarification. Was this a trick question? It sounded like a trick question.

"Look around." She extended her arms like a model on the floor of a new car showroom. "And tell me what you see."

Definitely a trick question.

Dante perused the room. "Uh, well, there's a dresser. There's a bed—looks like a queen—with a lot of...you know...uh...fluffy stuff. And bedside tables." He regarded her with a hopeful expression but she seemed to be waiting for more. "Uh, let's see. You have a window with a bench. I have one too. But yours has more fluffy stuff than mine."

"Right. And you can see everything rather well, can't you?"

Another trick question. Dante regarded her with a cautious narrowing of his eyes. "I guess."

"Do you know why that is?"

"I have a feeling you're going to tell me."

She grabbed his hand and hauled him to the window. "You know why you can see everything? Because the Neanderthal next door has his damn garage door open with the lights on, that's why. Take a look. The light. Shining in my bedroom window like a solar explosion. At three o'clock in the blessed a.m.!"

Dante peered out the window. No way was his garage light—

"Ah, hell. That's not coming from inside the garage. There must be a problem with the position of the spotlight on the outside. It's supposed to be on a motion sensor, but—" He sighed and ran a hand through his hair. "Looks like it's staying on, connected to the garage lights somehow."

"And shining right into my bedroom window. It's like flippin' daylight in here."

Dante sighed and nodded. "That appears to be correct, Miss Kinkaid."

"Yes, Mr. Caravicci, it does, as I've been telling you for some time now." She crossed her arms over her chest and sniffed, vindicated at last.

"If you had invited me into your bedroom sooner, we might have figured this out before now." He wriggled his brows and gave her what he hoped was an inviting smile.

She narrowed her gaze. "When was the last time you slept?"

"It feels like we just had this conversation."

Brenna's expression eased and she shook her head, reaching a hand up to smooth his hair. "You idiot Neanderthal. Get onto my bed and lay down on your belly."

"I—excuse me, what?"

"Go on. Get on my bed." Brenna pointed. "Right now."

Dante blinked. "What are you—Are you—"

Brenna laughed. "You're not getting laid. I'm giving you a massage."

"A what?"

"Wow, your brain is really not synapsing right now." She pushed him toward the bed. "Take your shirt off and lay down. I'm going to help you get to sleep."

"You're kidding, right? If I'm in your bed, the last thing I want to do is—fine, fine," he said, when her expression darkened again. He toed off his shoes, removed his shirt at her direction, and stretched out on her bed, belly down. "Jesus," he said, sinking in, his voice muffled by down pillows. "A little much, don't you think?"

"Be quiet." Brenna straddled his torso. "Close your eyes and go to your Empty Man-Place."

"My what?"

"Your Empty Man-Place."

He groaned when her hands began kneading his shoulders.

"Every man has an Empty Man-Place. It's that place men go when they aren't thinking about anything. You know, when your girlfriend—" She leaned down and whispered in his ear, "—that would be me," and caused a pleasant ripple of sensation along his spine, then straightened and continued working his muscles with her cool hands, "asks you what you're thinking, and you say, 'nothing.' It's true. You really are thinking nothing. You're in your Empty Man-Place, vegging out. But women, now, we're always thinking something. Always." She laughed, a soft sound that poured over Dante like warm honey.

He did his best to follow her quiet voice, but it became a melodic dipping and rising of sound that drifted away until it became so much white noise. Her body, hovering over his, moved with the rhythm of her ministrations, and his muscles answered the demands of her hands, easing, easing, until the white noise grew, a crescendo that overtook him and pushed him over the crest and into the dreamless black.

Dante breathed in. He knew the scent in an instant, breathed deeper, wanted more, and his eyes flew open. He sat up to confirm his whereabouts.

Sunshine streamed through Brenna's bedroom window, bathing everything it touched in a lemony glow. Dante blinked to clear the sleepy haze from his eyes.

Sure as hell, he'd spent the night in Brenna Kinkaid's bed and, damn it, been unconscious the whole time. She hadn't been joking. The woman really had put him to sleep.

He dropped his face back into the downy pillows and inhaled, inviting Brenna's scent to permeate his senses further. Damn, but the woman smelled good.

He listened, straining to hear her moving about, but in the continued silence dozed off again, too warm and comfortable to fully awaken. Brenna's face swam into his mind, her smile, her laugh, her capable hands moving over the tense muscles of his shoulders and back, her voice soothing along with her hands, urging him to sleep. Something about a man thing.

I'll show you a man thing.

The thought made him smirk, and his eyes flew open for a second time.

Jesus, what time was it?

Awareness seeped in and he sat up again, forced himself to sit on the edge of the bed. She had no bedside clock— probably used her cell phone alarm, as he did. And his cell phone was in the garage on the workbench where he'd set it last night. Judging from the bright sunlight, it was at least midmorning, and he was probably late for work.

Dante tugged on his shoes and found his shirt balled up at the foot of the bed where he had tossed it last night. He pulled it on and ventured toward the main part of the townhouse to confirm Brenna's absence, and found a note on the breakfast bar telling him the cupboards were bare except for the leftover pizza, but that she promised to fix him an impressive breakfast the next time he spent the night. She'd ended it with a smiley face blowing a heart, and her drawing skills were akin to his.

But he tucked the note in his back pocket, smiling.

Next time. There would be a next time.

He helped himself to a couple slices of cold pizza, washed them down with the coffee she'd left warming in the pot, and cleaned up the kitchen before letting himself out.

He still didn't know what time it was, but he had a couple things to do before heading to the Bistro, the first of which entailed fixing the damned light. Also, Brenna deserved both an apology for his having ignored her complaints for so long, and a thank you for the massage and first good night's sleep in a while.

He wasn't sure what the apology and thanks would involve, only that he'd make certain it was memorable.

Chapter 10

Brenna lifted her head toward the tap-tap-tap of knuckles on the front window of the Lump & Grind, prepared to tell whoever it was that the place was closed for the evening.

"Hey, that's the guy who owns Dante's Bistro." Shaniqua paused from her end-of-night cleaning. She smiled and waved the washrag she was using to wipe the counters. Dante returned her smile and waved back. Shaniqua sighed. "Mm, mm. That is one fine specimen of a man."

"Yes, well, don't tell him that. His ego is plenty big already," Brenna said, rounding the end of the counter. She strode to the door, wiping her hands on her apron as she went. She opened the door and poked her head outside. "Sorry, we're closed. You'll have to go to the restaurant down at the end of the block. Their coffee can't touch ours, but it's not bad for second best."

"Funny lady." Dante grinned. "I have a surprise for you."

"What kind of surprise? Am I going to like it?"

"I think so." He turned toward the Bistro and waved at three young women walking toward them. Brenna looked around him for a better view, and he said, "You remember Gemma."

"Hi," Gemma waved with enthusiasm and her smile stretched ear to ear.

"The other two are Cissy and Annette." The women smiled and waved. All three wore the Bistro uniform of a white tuxedo shirt, black pants and vest. "They're part of your cleaning crew tonight."

"He's paying us time-and-a-half," Cissy said, and winced when Annette cuffed the back of her head. "What? He is."

"What's this all about, Dante?"

"I told you. I have a surprise for you."

"I don't need you to pay people to clean my place. I'm perfectly capable of—"

"Put your hackles down. The cleaning crew isn't the surprise. Well, they are, but not the main surprise. They're just part of the surprise that allows me to give you the rest of the surprise."

Gemma patted Brenna's shoulder. "You'll really like it, Ms. Kinkaid." She smiled and moved past Brenna into the Lump & Grind with Cissy and Annette following behind her. "Hi," Gemma said to Shaniqua. "We're here to clean. Just tell us what to do."

The bell on the door tinkled when the door closed, leaving Brenna standing alone on the sidewalk with Dante. She watched through the plate glass window while Shaniqua chatted with Dante's crew.

"Okay." Brenna looked up at Dante and smiled, bemused. "I'll play. What's this big surprise?"

"Go get your purse. I'll wait."

"Okay, give me a sec."

Brenna collected her purse, changed from her sensible rubber-soled shoes into her heels, and told Shaniqua, "I'll be back to help you close. And thank you, ladies, for agreeing to help with the work."

"Don't bother coming back." Shaniqua wobbled her head for emphasis and added, "That man is fine—"

"I know, right?" said Annette. She pulled her ponytail

tighter and exchanged a look with Cissy who nodded and mouthed, "So hot!"

Brenna rolled her eyes, though she agreed with their assessment. "Call if you need me. I don't know where he thinks he's taking me at eleven o'clock at night, but I'll have to come back for my car anyway."

"You're just going to the Bistro," Gemma said, pushing hair from her eyes with the back of her hand. "I can't tell you what for—" Her smile flashed. "—just that you're going to like it."

"Let's go," Dante said when Brenna stepped outside.

"Hold on." She dug her keys from her purse and locked the door, nodded to Shaniqua through the window. "Okay, I'm all yours."

"If only that were true."

"We're going steady, honey. Did you forget already? You haven't given me your class ring and letter sweater yet, but it's still official." She patted his arm and gave him a sideways look that made him smile. "So, I'm told we're going to the Bistro. What's at the Bistro?"

"C'mon, and I'll show you."

To her amusement, Dante tucked her hand in the crook of his arm and led her down the sidewalk as if they were on a Sunday promenade. At this time of night, downtown Bright Hills was deserted, empty streets lit by the glow of lampposts, storefronts dim. A cool evening breeze made the short hair at the back of her neck prickle, and a mild shiver rustled through her, though the sensation was not an unpleasant one. She breathed in, enjoyed the scents afforded by the virtue of living in a mountain town—earthy, was how she thought of it, with the scent of pines and hardwoods comingling with the tangy bite of Georgia red clay, all infused with the sweetness permeating the air from countless flowering plants and bushes, along with the odor of concrete drawn into the air by the early summer humidity—and resolved to enjoy whatever it was Dante had planned.

Dante unlocked the Bistro door and ushered Brenna inside. A pianist sat beneath a soft spotlight at the baby grand, his fingers dancing over the keys while the strains of a Scott Joplin tune rang out. He finished with a flourish when he saw Dante and Brenna and, smiling, he began to play again, this time a soft ballad. Chloe came around the bar, smiled at Brenna, and made an elegant gesture with her hands, indicating that the couple should proceed ahead of her.

Brenna gasped her surprise and delight when she spied the intimate table set for two in a quiet corner of the restaurant. While the other tables lay dark, this one glowed with candlelight and a bud vase formed the centerpiece, boasting not the typical single-stemmed rose, but an arranged pair of Stargazer lilies, Brenna's favorite.

So, the man had done his homework.

She sat in the chair Dante slid out for her and regarded him across the small table after he joined her in sitting. He nodded at Chloe, who grinned at Brenna and retreated to the bar.

Brenna watched her go and said to Dante, "It's a little late for—"

"I have it on good authority that you haven't eaten a thing since lunchtime." He reached across the table to take both of her hands in his.

Brenna ignored the tingle that raced over her skin when he laced his warm fingers with hers. "You've been talking to my mother."

"I can't reveal my source," Dante said.

Brenna gave him a look. "Mama must have been ecstatic when you called her. She's been dying to play matchmaker, and now you've opened Pandora's box. She'll be relentless, you know."

Dante smiled. "I'm not worried." He squeezed her hands and released them when Chloe appeared at the table with two glasses of wine.

Brenna sipped and raised her brows. "Nice. So what's the fare for this late night dinner?"

"My source tells me that you have a particular fondness for lobster bisque and crab salad, so I took the liberty of personally preparing those dishes for you. Light enough fare for a midnight meal, I think."

"Your source knows her daughter well." Brenna smiled. "And how did you prepare the salad, Chef Caravicci?"

"A spring mix with bibb, with lightly seasoned lump crab served with a jalapeño-avocado vinaigrette, and a mango-pomegranate chutney on the side."

"Mmmm. That sounds amazing. Dessert?"

"Tiramisu, cannoli, red velvet cake, or all of the above. The tiramisu is my personal favorite, but they're all good."

"Did you make them all yourself?"

"Just the tiramisu."

"Then I'll have that after dinner with a cup of your cappuccino. We'll see how it compares to mine."

Dante shook his head, but his voice held laughter. "Brenna, Brenna. Always competing. Can't you just relax and enjoy your dinner without making comparisons?"

After a moment of consideration, she said, "Not really, no," and made him laugh. "So what is all this?" She indicated their surroundings with an elegant movement of her hands. "It's a lovely gesture, but what prompted it?"

"Well, for one, I owe you an apology. And two, I owe you a thank you. This dinner is intended to serve as both."

"An apology. For the garage light, I presume? It's about time."

"Past time, and I am sorry." Dante paused when Chloe delivered a fresh loaf of bread to the table along with two servings of lobster bisque. After she retreated, he added, "I didn't take your complaint seriously, and I should have. I was wrong."

"Wow, you're laying it on thick," Brenna said.

"Is it working?"

She tasted the soup and held back a moan of satisfaction. *Good god, but the man could cook.* "Yes," she said. "And what's the thank you for?"

"My first really good night's sleep in days. You have magic hands."

Brenna almost choked on the lobster bisque. She had thought the same thing of him the other day, but for different reasons, and was glad for the dim light when heat whooshed into her face. "I'm glad I could help," she managed to say, and rushed to change the subject. "I want to expand the kitchen at the L&G."

Dante stared at her for a moment, processing the change of topic. "What kind of plans do you have?"

"Big ones," she said and laughed. "The truth is, my idea is a little crazy. I know I can make it work, but it won't happen overnight."

"Details. Maybe I can help."

Brenna finished her lobster bisque and then lifted her wineglass to sip, considering how much information she wanted to divulge. In the end, she opted to share it all. He owned and operated two restaurants with success. He'd understand her excitement, as well as her trepidation.

"Last year on vacation, I discovered a great spot down in Florida called LéLu Coffee Lounge on Siesta Key. It's the coolest little place. It's a great casual hangout, terrific coffee and food, but—here's what makes it different—it's a bar, too. They specialize in before and after-dinner coffee drinks and martinis." Brenna set her wineglass down and leaned forward, warming to her subject. "Their logo is 'caffeine and cocktails.' I had the idea that I could do something similar with the L&G. Not cocktails, but beer and wine after hours, in addition to the coffee. With live music. Not anything big, just locals starting out, you know? Like a coffeehouse showcase kind of thing.

"It can easily become a local hangout, the kind of place tourists remember and feel at home when they visit. The kind of place that people remember after they're gone. The L&G isn't big enough now, or even designed for something like that, and there's no space to build out. So I had the idea to build up. I don't even know if it's feasible yet. I have to ask Rebecca or Caleb take a look, and then I'd have to have the landlord approve it.

"So anyway." She paused to sip her wine. "Anyway, it would be the same as always from five a.m. on, right? But then at six p.m. the upstairs would open. People could still come in the evening for a latte or whatever, power up their laptops, but then there'd be the upstairs, with stuff going on. I don't know, I haven't worked it all out yet, but I know it could be something. Maybe not exactly as I've just described it, but something like that. I feel it. And Bright Hills is growing. The L&G can't just stay the same, it has to grow, too."

She leaned back in her seat when Chloe arrived to remove the bowls and deliver their salads. Brenna eyed Dante and bit her lip. He probably thought she was batshit crazy again, turning the L&G into some sort of local dive. She should've just kept her mouth shut, waited until she had done more planning, had developed concrete ideas.

No wonder the bank had turned her down. She hadn't thought it through. Maybe the whole concept was nuts, just wouldn't fly in a little town like this.

Embarrassed by her excited babbling, she forked a piece of crab and focused on her salad, wishing she'd kept her mouth shut.

"Coffee bar by day, coffeehouse by night, expand upward instead of out." Dante's dark eyes regarded her with intensity, to the point she lowered her fork and stared back. "Beer and wine, yeah. I can see that. You'll need a greater food offering, though. Nothing big, nothing fancy. Specialty sandwiches and appetizers would be enough." His eyes lit and he leaned forward. "And specialty coffees, too, Brenna. Cozy coffees, like keoke. Hell, maybe you don't even have to mess with beer and wine. Coffee is your specialty, so play to that. Get your liquor license and create specialty nightcap coffees, with liqueurs—Kahlua, Bailey's, Tia Maria. I'll help you create some signatures for the L&G. We can experiment." He flashed a smile that tightened her up in all the right places and shot heat into her veins. "And the upstairs—it doesn't have to sit empty during the day, sweetheart. You can rent it out for special events, meetings."

Brenna swallowed and felt her lips curving. "So, you don't think I'm batshit crazy?"

"I think you're brilliant," he said, and she knew from his expression that he meant it.

"I love the idea of the nightcap coffees instead of beer and wine. It's perfect." She frowned. "I wish I'd been the one to think of it."

"You would have."

"Now you're just trying to make me feel better. I hate it when you win," she said and couldn't stop herself from smiling. "And that idea is definitely one for the 'win' column."

"Glad to be of service. So what do you think of the salad?"

"Outstanding. Another win," she admitted. The man had hit a homerun tonight. She glanced at the pianist who continued to provide background music for their tête-à- tête—a Norah Jones tune this time—and looked back at her handsome host.

"Good. Maybe I'll add it to the menu." At her questioning look, he explained, "I created it especially for you for tonight. This is the debut." His lips twitched and he added, "It's called the Crabby Brenna Salad. What do you think?"

Brenna laughed, delighted. "That it lives up to its name. How does an army ranger know so much about cooking, anyway? Don't even try to tell me you had time to attend a culinary school. I won't believe you."

"I didn't, but my uncle did. Le Cordon Bleu, no less. He had grand plans to open a fine Italian restaurant, but he enjoyed his booze a little too much. He settled for Stan's Pizzeria. And in between tossing pies and making subs, we talked food. When I showed an interest, he taught me what he knew. I love the chemistry involved in mixing textures

and flavors. He taught me just enough to be dangerous."
Dante grinned. "You ought to taste some of the stuff I con-
coct that *doesn't* turn out."

They discussed random topics over cappuccino and tiramisu, which she admitted tasted amazing and, when their
dinner ended, Brenna expressed her thanks to the pianist
and then to Chloe whose face erupted in a giddy smile behind Dante's back while she gave Brenna two thumbs up.

Brenna followed Dante and staff out through the back of
the restaurant, as they had all parked their vehicles in the
alley. He set the alarm, locked up, and ushered Brenna into
the Trans Am for the short ride to her Audi. He left his car
running, but got out to see her to her vehicle, and drew her
into a kiss before she climbed into her car and buckled up.

"I'll follow you home," he said, and she nodded her
agreement then grabbed the front of his shirt and pulled him
down for another promising kiss.

Why, she wondered during her drive home, giddy and
tapping the steering wheel with her fingers, had she waited
so long to test these waters?

'*Because you're a stubborn, judgmental ass,*' Jack's
voice said.

She pictured her brother's lips curved in a sarcastic grin
and laughed aloud, well pleased with the turn of events now
that she'd taken her stubbornness and judgments about Dante Caravicci and tossed them out the window. She'd seen, in
the last week, the Dante that everyone else knew and loved.
Better late to the party than not at all, she thought.

Brenna liked to win, and tonight there appeared to be
nothing but brass rings for the taking, as far as her eye could
see.

ତ∕৩ତ∕৩

Dante knew he was in for trouble the minute he turned
onto his street behind Brenna's Audi and saw the flashing
lights bathing his driveway in a rhythmic blue glow. A

handful of neighbors stood huddled together on the street in front of his townhome, some in their pajamas and slippers. What the hell had Vince done now?

Dante parked at the curb and strode toward his garage to meet Deputy Nate Humphrey, who had seen him and waved him over.

"Hey, Nate. What's going on?"

"Did you know there was a party here tonight, Dante?"

"I think you already know the answer to that. I've been at the Bistro all night."

Nate sighed and nodded, planted his hands on his hips and glanced at Brenna who had parked in her garage and was tiptoeing barefoot between the yards, carrying her shoes in one hand and her purse in the other. He waited for her arrival before saying anything else, a decision Dante thought was good one as Brenna would have just insisted he repeat himself so she could hear the details first hand.

"Here's the short of it," Nate said. "We got a call from a concerned neighbor about the noise. There were about thirty people here, Dante, all drinking, smoking weed—I caught a whiff, but nothing I can prove—and some were underage, including a couple of fifteen-year-old girls."

Dante ran a hand over his face and pinched the bridge of his nose. A pulse began to throb at his temple and he willed it to stop. "This would be my cousin's doing."

"If Vincent Caravicci is your cousin, then yes." At Dante's terse nod, Nate continued. "He's been arrested and is being booked for disturbing the peace and contributing to the delinquency of minors. I couldn't get him on a marijuana charge, or I would have. He was high and belligerent. My advice is, don't bail him out until tomorrow."

"The girls you found here. Are they okay? They weren't hurt?" Dante asked, unable to mask the horror in his voice, and Brenna stepped beside him and slipped her hand into his.

Her strength seeped into him and he held on, grateful for her show of support.

Teenagers. Little girls, for Christ's sake. What the hell was Vince thinking?

"Just high, as far as I could see. They've been brought into the station and their parents will be called."

"What do I need to do?"

"It's your house, but you can prove you weren't here and had no knowledge of any of this, so I doubt there will be any ramifications for you. But you did have a lot of strangers here tonight, and not exactly the standup kind. Go through the house, make sure nothing was stolen. If you're missing anything, report it."

"Thanks, Nate."

Nate nodded, touched the brim of his hat in deference to Brenna, and strode off.

"He's a nice guy, but I'm glad Rebecca married my brother instead," Brenna said while watching Nate walk to his cruiser. She turned back to Dante and squeezed his hand. "So what now?"

Dante sighed, annoyed and frustrated with Vince and the night's end in general. "You go home and get some sleep. This isn't your problem, Brenna."

"Silly man." Brenna slid her arms around his waist and looked up at him, her tone light. "You keep forgetting that we're going steady."

"I haven't forgotten. I just haven't had a good opportunity to take advantage of it." He brought her close and rested his cheek on the top of her head and breathed in. She smelled flowery and fresh, and he wished he could stand like this for the next hour, with her softness pressed against him and her scent inside him, both somehow providing an antidote to his stress. "This isn't how the rest of tonight was supposed to go."

"Going steady doesn't just mean making out on my couch, you know." She looked into his face again.

"I'm hoping it also means—"

"It doesn't mean that, either. You men are all the same. Your brain goes straight to sex."

He gave her a look. "Yours doesn't?"

Brenna laughed and pinched him hard enough to elicit an, "Ow."

"At the moment, no," she said. "What I'm thinking is that you probably have a mess inside that needs cleaning up, and you could use some help doing it. *That's* where going steady comes in handy. You have a helpmate."

She held her gaze on his, and he thought she had the prettiest eyes he'd ever seen, a marine blue as fathomless as the deepest sea right now, rimmed with lashes thick and dark. He wondered why she bothered with makeup when she was so gorgeous without it—he'd noticed that the other night—but knew she'd laugh at him if he voiced his thought, so he said instead, "That sounds good. I think I might like this going steady stuff."

"C'mon," Brenna said. "Let's go see what Vince left for us."

What Vince left was a kitchen sink piled with dirty dishes and glasses, counters covered with open bags of various brands of chips and snacks, trash strewn throughout the house, bottles and cans containing varying amounts of beer, and an unidentifiable substance, black and sticky, covering a foot-wide area on the carpeted upstairs landing. Three empty pizza boxes lay open on the floor in the living room and were not, Dante noted, from his Pizzeria.

While Brenna began emptying beer into the sink and tossing the empties into a plastic trash bag, Dante went on a hunt for Pavarotti and found the cat hiding under the bed in the master bedroom, his backend pressed as close to the back wall as he could get, hackles up, tail twitching. When Dante peered under the bed, Pavarotti's luminous eyes regarded him with accusation for a scant moment before the cat employed his feline vocals to bellow angry discontent.

"Sorry, pal," Dante said and left the animal to continue its squalling alone.

An hour later, with the dishwasher running and the last of the trash delivered to the garbage can in the garage, Dante dropped onto the sofa next to Brenna. She snuggled up under his arm and yawned, and he caught it like a virus, stretching his jaw in a mighty yawn as well.

"What time do you have to go in tomorrow? Please say you're not opening," Dante said, covering a second yawn with his hand.

"No. Greta likes to open. Been opening that kitchen for forty years." Brenna covered up a yawn and they both laughed when Dante yawned again, too. "Did you know she says she's retiring at the end of the summer?"

"Heard something about it." He turned his head and buried his nose in her short cap of hair. "You always smell so good."

"Mmmm." She pressed her nose against the shirt on his chest and breathed in. "You too."

"Thanks for helping me with the mess."

"Mm-hm." She nodded, curled her legs beneath her, and snuggled closer. A moment later Dante felt her muscles go lax. Her breathing settled into a gentle cadence.

He sighed. Not exactly the evening he'd hoped for.

Dante held her close, amazed at the lightning speed with which things had changed. If last week at this time someone had told him that in seven days Brenna Kinkaid, in all her curvaceous glory, would be wrapped up in his embrace—by her own design, no less—he would have called them delusional, or a liar. But here she was, the woman of his dreams, with her body resting against his and her head and hand pressed against his heart. He closed his eyes and enjoyed the gentle feel of her breasts moving against him in measure to her breathing.

She trusted him. The knowledge welled inside him, the desire to protect her rising strong. He tightened his embrace and she sighed.

Dante didn't think he could sleep, but Brenna's presence acted as a balm. His racing mind focused on her—the scent of her hair, the softness of her body, the pace of her breathing—and when he opened his eyes again it was to urge her to his bed, where they fell together fully clothed into an ocean of dreams.

Their cell phones blared, one after the other, and Dante and Brenna awoke spooned against each other. They parted with reluctance and grabbed for their phones.

"Hello," they said at the same time, and then, "Oops. Sorry, hold on," and traded phones.

"It's Trina," Brenna told him. "Greta," Dante told her, and they each sat up and claimed opposite edges of the bed to take their calls.

"I have to go," Brenna said, when they clicked off their calls. She stood and stretched, stifled a yawn. "Myrtle won't stop making ice and the repair guy is giving Greta heartburn."

Dante nodded. "Trina said someone tried to jimmy the back door at the Pizzeria again. Been happening a few times a month."

"Bright Hills needs its own police department. I hate to admit it, but that stupid Truth or Dare fundraiser is doing a good job of raising community awareness." Brenna paused at the door. "So, I'll see you later?"

Dante stared at her, amazed that Brenna Kinkaid was here with him, in his house, standing at his bedroom door, asking if she would see him later. It didn't even matter that for the third time this week they'd spent the night under the same roof and he still hadn't managed to push past first base.

She was here, and she wanted to see him later.

"I didn't realize an answer to that question would require so much thought." Brenna rested her hands on her hips. "You breaking up with me already?"

Dante met her in the doorway and stroked her cheek once with the back of his hand, still marveling that he could touch her like that without receiving a verbal smack down.

"Actually, I was thinking we should take a couple days off, get away from the restaurants for an overnight. Go somewhere and leave our cell phones behind."

"Where do you want to go?"

Dante shrugged. "I don't care. Anywhere we can be alone and uninterrupted. I want you in my bed, Brenna." He took her hands in his, and his thumbs rubbed her knuckles with a soft circular motion while his eyes held her gaze. "Naked and fully conscious."

He waited for her response. Unease trickled through him as the seconds ticked by and she said not a word.

Chapter 11

An overnight trip with Dante Caravicci.

A week ago today she would have laughed at the idea as absurd. Today, his suggestion was a drug mainlining desire and throbbing need into her veins.

The truth sluiced over her, a warm wash of self-realization.

"I've wasted so much time for us," she said, and, at the question in his eyes, she shook her head and smiled. "Never mind. Yes. We should do just what you said. I even know where we can go. Maddie has some friends in Helen who run a B&B. I think that would be perfect. It's close, so if either of us has a real emergency, we can get back to Bright Hills quickly, but it's far enough away that we can forget about reality for a while. It will be fun, too, wandering around all the shops. I love watching the glassblowers."

Brenna was rewarded with his smile, the one that engaged his whole face and warmed her from the inside out. She benefitted from its full wattage now and acknowledged the quickening deep inside, that duel flash of happiness and desire that Dante had somehow awakened inside her.

The opening and slamming of the front door drew their attention. Heavy footsteps stomped past the kitchen and stairs, and Vince appeared at the end of the hallway, his eyes narrowed and bloodshot, clothing disheveled, and lips arced downward like a hairless Fu Manchu. "Thanks for not bailing me out, asshole."

Dante's jaw tightened. "I'm surprised you're out so soon."

"I called Trina," Vince said and smirked. "Girl never could tell me no."

Brenna watched Dante's hands ball into fists and she readied herself to stop him from charging his cousin, but Dante blew out a slow breath. "What the hell were you thinking, Vince? You had underage girls here, for Christ's sake."

"They said they were eighteen. What the hell was I supposed to do, check their IDs?"

"Stay away from girls half your age, and get your shit out of my goddamned house."

"Whatever." Vince strode to the bathroom off the hallway, pausing just outside the door. His eyes skimmed Brenna. "Hey, Beautiful. See you've decided to slum it." He slid his glance to Dante and his eyes held a challenging glint. "Still settling for my sloppy seconds, I see."

Brenna lunged in front of Dante. She grabbed him with both hands to prevent him from taking Vince's bait. His muscles vibrated with tension beneath her hands. There was a part of her that wanted to let him give Vince what he deserved. But that would feed Vince the drama he craved, so she held Dante in a vise-like grip.

Vince stepped into the bathroom and slammed the door behind him, laughing.

"Sonuvabitch," Dante said through clenched teeth. He pulled free of Brenna and she stepped back, watching yet another facet of Dante reveal itself. How much more was there to this man, she wondered, that she had never taken the time to know?

She'd not witnessed his anger before this moment. Oh, she'd seen him annoyed in the extreme, seen him pushed to the edge of palpable frustration—many times she herself had been the one to lead him there. But she'd never seen this dark fury alive in him, and it was fearsome to behold. He was a big man pulsating with black anger, held in check by what she gauged to be a very thin margin.

"You need to go, Brenna."

"Dante—"

He turned his eyes on her, black pools of glittering onyx. His voice, though quiet and low of timber, brooked no argument. "I said you need to go."

Brenna swallowed, but held her ground. They were just testing the waters of this relationship, and she'd be damned if she'd allow him to think he could ever tell her what to do.

She planted her hands on her hips and her feet in front of him, narrowed her eyes, and stared him down. She wished she had her heels on, because her neck ached from looking up at him. But he got the message.

He dropped his head back, stared at the ceiling for a few seconds, and snorted out a short laugh. "Woman, you are such a pain in the ass," he said, and when he looked at her again, though his lips weren't smiling, his eyes had softened to the warm espresso she'd come to expect whenever he looked at her.

"Walk me to the door." She showed him her back and strolled down the hall toward the front door, not looking over her shoulder to see if he followed. She could be just as bossy as he could, thank you.

She paused at the stairs to coo at Pavarotti, and lifted him from his resting place atop her shoes, surprised by the solid weight of him. He emitted a mournful cry, as if she'd pulled his whiskers or twisted his tail, and she responded by scratching him under the chin and pressing a kiss between his ears. The cat rewarded her with a gentle head butt, rubbed the side of his face against her hand, and began to purr, then settled down to continue his nap on the stairs. Brenna collected her purse and heels and began once again to move toward the door.

She felt Dante behind her and smiled, pleased that he'd humored her without argument.

She was a woman who appreciated small victories. Any victories, come to that.

"Call me later," she said when she reached the front door, turning to face him at last. She gasped when in the next instant he pressed her back against the door and took her mouth with his, a quick branding, fast and hard and deep. He left her breathless when he stepped back. She blinked at him wide-eyed and then smiled. "You've got more surprises than Santa's bag," she said, and not to be outdone, dropped her purse and shoes, went up on her tiptoes, and pulled him to her for another kiss.

She controlled this one and ended it with a strong nip to his lower lip that had him soothing the spot with his tongue when she was through. "Call me." She gifted him with a sultry smile designed to burn through the rest of his anger and, she hoped, any remaining desire he might have to pummel his idiot cousin.

❦❦❦

"You know as well as I do that I ain't going nowhere." Vince popped the top on a beer, rested his hips against the kitchen counter, and drew a long pull. He wiped his mouth with the back of his hand. "I've got to be here for the court date."

"Not my problem." Dante grabbed the beer from Vince's hands and dumped it down the sink. "Get your shit and get out."

"Why're you being an asshole?" Vince threw his hands up. "So I fucked up. Sorry. I won't invite friends over again."

"You don't have friends in Bright Hills. You have strangers you brought into my home without my permission, two of them underage girls."

"I told you, they said they was eighteen." Vince ran his hands through his hair and shook it back out of his face. The diamond earrings winked from his lobes. "You're just pissed off because I had Beautiful before you did. It ain't my fault you dragged your feet tapping that."

Dante held his temper in check. "You didn't *have* her. You lied to her about her brother to get her to go out with you."

"I didn't see you doing anything to stop me."

"Brenna's a smart lady. I knew it wouldn't take her long to figure you out."

Vince stared at Dante, eyes narrowed in thought, and Dante waited for his cousin's comeback. He'd seen that expression on Vince's face before, the fake show of contriteness, the self-deprecating half-smile. He had seen it too many times to count, in fact, enough to know that whatever little Vince gave would only be for the purpose of enabling him to somehow take even more.

"I shouldn't be telling you this, probably," Vince began, and Dante waited for it, wondered what it would be—the give before the grab. "The other night at the Boot & Spur? Beautiful was sleepwalking through dinner with me. She didn't wake up until she saw you at the bar." Vince shrugged. "Turns out she was already yours. She just didn't know it yet."

Dante stepped up to Vince and looked him in the eye, unflinching. "I don't give a damn about the other night. But you better believe that she's mine now."

Vince straightened up as if he might turn the conversation into something more physical, but then looked away and put his hands up in front of him. "All right, all right. I got it. Beautiful belongs to you."

Dante waited. There was more. With Vince, there was always more.

"So, we're cool now, right? I can stay as long as I don't invite anyone over and I keep my hands off your woman."

"No, Vince. You need to get out."

"C'mon, Dante. Don't be an asshole. I said I was sorry."

"Out. Go back to Asheville."

"Fuck you," Vince said. "I'll just find another place to stay. And we both know who won't tell me no."

"Stay away from Trina."

Vince stepped forward, nose to nose with Dante. "Why? She yours, too, now?"

"She doesn't need you messing her life up again."

"You left the door wide open. All I did was walk in."

Dante's jaw tensed and he held himself by a short, straining leash. "Just leave her alone. She pulled her life together in spite of us, and she doesn't need trouble."

"I ain't in the habit of taking orders from you. I aim to see what Trina has to say."

"Brenna's not the only one who has you figured out."

Vince sniffed, and his eyes lit with trouble. "You're so damn sure Beautiful is yours. Sure enough to make a wager?" Dante's eyes narrowed as Vince plowed on. "Five hundred says I'll get a kiss out of her before the end of July. A real one. Mouth to mouth, full on."

"You're an asshole. You have a problem with me, fine. Deal with me. But leave Brenna out of it."

Vince's slow smile pricked open a scab under Dante's skin, and Vince must have recognized the show of blood, because he gave it a tug and ripped it off. "Comes down to it, she ain't no different than Trina. I'll prove it, too. Five hundred, straight into your pocket if you're right and she tells me to blow off. If I win—and I aim to win—you don't pay me nothing, but I get to move back in here until I'm damn good and ready to leave." Vince's smile twisted into a sneer. "So how much do you trust your woman? If she's yours like you say, you'll be five hundred richer in a few weeks."

"Brenna's not a thing to be wagered, asshole."

"One thing I've learned in life, cousin, is there ain't nothing that can't be wagered."

Dante remained rooted in the kitchen after Vince pushed past him. A few minutes later the sound of Vince's heavy footfalls reverberated through the house. The front door opened and closed. Outside, the Harley revved, and Dante waited in the kitchen as the growling of the engine faded away.

Dante blew out a hefty sigh and grabbed up his phone.

"Why in hell did you bail Vince out?" Dante said the minute Trina answered her phone.

"He said you told him to call me, that you were tied up with the cops and couldn't take care of it." Trina sighed, and Dante imagined her tucking her hair behind her ears. "I take it he lied."

"When has Vince ever told the truth about anything?"

"I should've called you to confirm."

"Just a head's up, he's going to be looking for a place to stay."

"Well, it won't be with me. Is he on his way to my apartment? Because I'm not there. I'm at the Pizzeria."

"If he shows up at the Pizzeria, call the cops."

"Dante, seriously? He's still your cousin."

"Did he tell you why he got arrested?"

"Said he was DUI."

"He had a party at my house and the neighbors called the cops. He had underage girls here, Trina."

Silence followed Dante's words, but he heard her heavy breaths through the phone. "Damn him. Well, I appreciate the warning. It's easier to tell him no if I know he's going to ask."

Dante breathed a sigh of relief. "Be sure you do. I'm having my locks changed so he can't get back in here. If he has nowhere to stay, maybe he'll go home to Asheville."

"Maybe. Hold on, one of the wait staff has a question." She covered the phone and Dante heard muffled conversation about the lunch special. "Okay, I'm back."

"Everything okay?"

"Yeah. Listen, I heard through the grapevine you had a romantic dinner at the Bistro last night with Miss All-That. Why you pulling out all the stops on this one?"

"I owed her an apology, as well as a thank you. Dinner

served as both." He put the phone in his other hand and
squatted at the stairs to pet the cat. Pavarotti turned his motor on, and Dante let the cat's enthusiastic purrs and head
butts work on dissipating what remained of his anger. "I'm
swinging by there in about an hour. If anyone needs me,
that's the time. I'll be at the Bistro the rest of the day."

"You never answered me about your dinner with Miss
All-That."

"No, I didn't, but I think it's pretty obvious I'm crazy
about her, isn't it?" He gave Pav one last scratch behind the
ears and stood. "See you in a few."

❧❧❧

Brenna parked in her usual spot behind the Lump &
Grind, but instead of going into her place of business she
trekked the length of the alley to the end of the block. She
gave the rear entrance to Dante's Bistro a cursory glance
and then turned left onto Main Street. She walked a few
doors down to the office identified in gold lettering as *Sean
P. Kinkaid, Attorney at Law.*

"Hi, Mrs. M." Brenna smiled and waved at Sean's office
manager and legal secretary, Myra Manischewitz, who sat
behind a brass nameplate Sean had given her that read *The
Great & Powerful Mrs. M.* The older woman smiled, and
Brenna admired the warm mocha of her skin against the red
hibiscus hue of her tailored suit, and told her so.

"Why, thank you. It's Ann Taylor. And look at your
hair! Oh, my goodness!" Mrs. M. stood and circled Brenna,
her dark eyes focused on Brenna's head. "You know, as
gorgeous as your long hair was, this is better. It really
shows off your eyes, and those cheekbones are to die for."
She planted her hands on her hips and continued her scrutiny. "If you had asked my opinion, I would have begged you
not to cut it off, and I would have been wrong. You look
sensational." Mrs. M's serious expression dissolved when

she looked into Brenna's eyes and smiled wide. "Don't tell your brother I said that. He thinks I'm never wrong about anything."

"That's because you never are."

Sean's voice came from the end of the hallway, and Brenna glanced toward him. She braced for the exuberant greeting she saw coming from Sean's dog, Belle. The animal accompanied him everywhere, even the office, a routine Sean adhered to without apology.

"Well, c'mere, you beastie," Brenna said.

The dog bolted down the hallway and jumped up to plant her big paws on Brenna's shoulders. Her tongue swept across Brenna's cheek. A moment later, Sean strode into the front office to join them, and ordered his ill-mannered dog to sit. Belle complied in a nanosecond, and her tail swooshed across the carpet while she regarded her master with gooey-eyed adoration.

"What's this?" Sean's eyes widened and his lips parted with surprise. "Your hair."

Brenna ran her hand over the back of her head, still a bit in shock when her fingers encountered the bare skin of her neck. She raised her brows. "So, what do you think?"

"I think you look like you got into a fight with a—"

"Don't you dare tease your sister." Mrs. M stopped Sean's big brother commentary with a manicured index finger. "You be sweet. She wants an honest opinion, so don't be a brat."

Sean gave the older woman a look. "You never let me have any fun. Okay, give me a minute to get used to it, will you?" He peered at Brenna much as Mrs. M had done.

Brenna fidgeted under his perusal, finally huffing out a breath and waving him away. "I don't care what you think, so just never mind. I didn't come so you could critique my hair. I need to talk to you about something else, kind of important."

The mischievous glint in Sean's eyes morphed into immediate concern. "Everything okay?"

"Fine, yes. I just need to ask you about something."

"Sure. C'mon down to my office. Mrs. M, hold my calls, okay?"

Sean waited until Brenna stepped into his office before closing the door. He gestured to one of the plush guest chairs in front of his desk and sat down in its twin so that he wasn't facing her over the expanse of his desk. Belle collapsed at his feet and rested her hefty muzzle on his shoe with an expulsion of breath that sounded like a bellows.

"So what's going on?"

Brenna gnawed the inside of her mouth for a moment and then blurted, "How did you know, with Rebecca?"

"Know what?" Sean blinked at her, his expression a study in befuddlement.

"Oh, my god, Sean, you're such a man." She plucked at a thread on her jeans and gnawed her cheek some more. The silence grew while Sean waited for clarification. Brenna folded her hands in her lap and tried Dante's trick of staring up at the ceiling. He looked adorable doing it, but it didn't work for her, so she faced Sean, who continued to watch her in stoic silence. His focused regard set her nerves on edge. She imagined his clients babbled the truth, and nothing but, under the scrutiny of that laser-sharp stare. She forced the words out. "How did you know that you were…you know, that it was the real deal, I mean, and not just…" She shrugged a shoulder. "That it was more than just a physical—oh, c'mon, Sean. You know what I'm asking."

Sean's brows shot up. "Who are we talking about here? Caravicci?" Brenna's cheeks heated and Sean laughed. "Wow. That must have been some kiss. Way to go, Dante."

Brenna huffed out a breath and pushed from the chair, her body hot as fire from the chest up. Belle lifted her head with interest when Brenna strode toward the door. "Never mind. I should have known better than to ask you. I'll talk to your wife."

"No, Brenna, come on." Sean's voice held both insistence and laughter. "C'mon, meatball, come back and sit down." She took her hand off the doorknob when he invoked her childhood nickname. "I'll talk to you about it, and no teasing. I promise."

Brenna retraced her steps and dropped back into the chair. Her lips curved in spite of herself when she looked at him again. "You're a jackass."

Sean smiled and settled back into the chair. "So, how did I know it was the real deal? The answer is, I have no clue. I fell hard for Rebecca the second I saw her, even though I didn't do anything about it for a while."

Brenna nodded. "The Fourth of July picnic last year. I remember. You brought that snotty woman with you. What was her name?"

"Cynthia."

"Right. Cynthia. She was horrid." Brenna rolled her eyes when Sean's lips curved. "It was her amazing rack that held your interest, I know. Kind of ironic, you ending up with Rebecca, because she's flat as a board."

"Rebecca has other winning assets," Sean said, and his smile widened.

Brenna waved his comment away with her hand and gave him a look. "Okay, we're not going there. And I don't need to hear about the two of you having sex in your office, either." She glanced at the door and made a face.

Sean choked out a laugh. "You know about that?"

"You'd be horrified to know the intimate details we women share." Sean's obvious discomfort at that statement eased Brenna's discomposure and she refocused on her subject. "But never mind that. I want to know how you *knew*."

Sean considered and shook his head with a shrug. "I don't really know. My feelings for Rebecca just sort of crept up on me."

"Unexpected?"

"I suppose, yes. No." He narrowed his gaze. "Is this a trick? Are you wearing a wire or something?"

Brenna laughed outright. "You're such an idiot. No, I'm not wearing a wire. I'm seriously curious."

"Because you believe you're in love with Dante?"

Sean's words sobered Brenna up in a flash. She hadn't said the words aloud—*oh, honey, please, no way*—and hadn't thought them either, come to that. She'd skirted around them in her mind with ambiguous phrases like *What if this is it?* and *I think I might have real feelings for him.* But those actual words, *in love with Dante*, no, she hadn't let those cross her mind or her lips. The very notion set her heart to beating faster and clenched her stomach in a painful grip. Those were big words, scary words. Those were no-turning-back words.

"What I'm feeling," Brenna said with care after several quiet moments, "is just so big. It's scary and unexpected." She looked down at her hands, one clenched into a fist on her lap and held into such a knot that her knuckles strained white, the other plucking at the loose thread on her thigh again. "I've never felt this for anyone. It's like I'm being sucked into something that might crush me if I don't stop it." She swallowed and brought her gaze to Sean's. "But at the same time, it's so amazing I don't want it to ever end."

Silence reigned. Belle twitched in her sleep and yipped, and silence resumed.

"Jesus, meatball, you've got it bad," Sean said after a while, his expression serious as the evening news. His tone bore no trace of humor.

"So, is it the real deal? Or am I just—"

"Horny?"

Brenna glared at him. "I'm serious, Sean."

"So am I. It's not always easy to separate love from lust. Why do you think so many people get married and di-vorced? The best advice I can give you is just to roll with it. It's early days yet, right? You two are just getting started. Quit worrying about what it is or isn't, and just enjoy the ride." He smirked. "So to speak."

Brenna laughed. "You're ridiculous."

"I have to say, I'm glad it's Dante. He's a good man, Brenna."

"I know he is. I've always known. I just didn't want to admit it." Her gaze traveled across Sean's desk to his credenza and the framed photos there. "I have that same picture, the one of you, me, and Jack." She returned her attention to Sean. "Did he ever tell you about a blind date he wanted to set up for me?"

"No, he didn't. What about it?"

"Nothing, just that he called me a few days before the accident and told me he'd met my soul mate. He said he'd give the guy my number, if I was game, and we could arrange to meet. Jack died, and I never got a call. I guess he never had a chance to pass my number along." She shrugged. "I've hoped for a long time that the guy would show up, kind of a final gift from Jack. Silly, right?"

"No, I don't think so. Did Jack know Dante?"

Brenna shook her head. "No. Dante would have said something by now. I mentioned the blind date to him and he didn't know anything about it, so. So." She sighed. "I guess I won't benefit from Jack's matchmaking skills the way you and Maddie did."

"Don't sell Jack short. Maybe he'll give you the push you need when the time comes."

She looked back at the photograph. "That's a lovely thought."

"You want to grab some lunch? I know a great little Italian place right at the corner. They tell me the owner is one helluva kisser."

"You're such a jerk," she said, but didn't argue.

"It looks fantastic, by the way. Your hair," Sean said, and he laughed when she dimpled and said, "Oh, honey, I know."

Mrs. M joined them for lunch at the Bistro, and they sat at one of the outside tables so Belle could join them. She curled her bulk into a tight circle at Sean's feet and would remain there, unobtrusive, for the whole of their meal.

The place filled up after they were seated, and Brenna enjoyed watching Dante thrive in his element. She tamped a flare of jealousy when he responded in kind to flirting by several female guests, but noted that he turned the conversation around in a way that made them laugh and then slid from that into talking sports with a group of men at another table. He kept glancing at her and finally made his way over. She hated herself for the flood of pleasure. It was new, this delight in the mere presence of a man. He wielded certain power over her, and she wasn't sure she liked it. But she didn't dislike it either, and that was a fact.

"Welcome," he said to them as a group, but his eyes homed in on Brenna. "You want the crab salad?"

"I didn't see crab salad on the menu," Mrs. M said.

"It's new. I prepare it with bibb and a spring mix, along with seasoned lump crab, served with a jalapeño-avocado vinaigrette, and a side of mango-pomegranate chutney. I call it The Crabby Brenna Salad."

Sean burst out laughing. "Such a romantic bastard you are, Caravicci."

Dante grinned. "It's the Italian blood." He squatted next to Brenna so she wouldn't have to keep looking up at him. "I take it they know we're seeing each other."

"They do now," she said, unable to stop looking at him.

Dante lifted her hand and kissed the back of it before standing, a sweet gesture that flooded Brenna with warmth and caused a quickening in her belly. "She's still waiting for my letter jacket and class ring," he said to Sean. "But I'm pretty sure it's official anyway." One of his wait staff caught his eye and waved him over. Dante smiled at the two ladies who had requested his presence, nodded, and turned back to Brenna. "I'll be here late doing storeroom inventory, so I won't see you tonight. You working tomorrow?"

"Yes. All day. Maddie and Cal get back tomorrow, and Mama's having a get together at the house on Sunday so we can hear all about the honeymoon. Will you be there?"

"I don't know if anyone can cover for me. I'll try."

"Do or do not," she said, her tone and expression solemn. "There is no try."

Dante's face erupted in a smile and he looked at Sean. "The woman quotes Yoda. How can I not be smitten?" He looked back at Brenna. "You're the woman of my dreams, no doubt about it now. Do you know how to handle a light saber, too?"

"That better not be a euphemism," Sean murmured, and Mrs. M kicked him under the table, eliciting a surprised, "Ouch!"

"Crab salads all around?" Dante confirmed their order and passed it along to their waiter before rushing off to chat with the two ladies who had requested a word with him. The blue-hairs tittered their approval of something Dante said, and Brenna recognized them as members of her mother's garden club. They complimented him on the petunia-filled flowerboxes hanging on the wrought iron fence that bordered the patio, and the urns overflowing with blooms. He responded with gracious thanks, and she expected them to be on the phone with Edie gossiping about the décor as a lead in to Dante kissing her hand. Let them gossip. Maybe every woman in town would hear about it and they'd all stop flirting with the man.

Every table was in use and, as soon as one emptied, it became full again a few minutes later. She didn't know there were so many people in Bright Hills. Her eye caught an attractive woman sitting alone in the far corner, her back pressed to the black wrought iron fence surrounding the patio. She looked like Marilyn Monroe with her platinum waves and red lipstick and, Brenna noted, her eyes followed Dante like a turkey vulture tracking potential roadkill. Those blood-red lips curled in a welcoming smile when Dante stopped at her table, and Brenna bit down an unwelcome upsurge of jealousy when he dropped his head back and laughed at something she said before sliding out a chair to sit and chat with her.

He hadn't sat down with anyone else, she noted, not even her. So who was blondie, and why was she so interested in Dante?

The arrival of their salads distracted her, and when she glanced back the woman was gone, as was Dante, who re-appeared moments later in the doorway, nodding to one of his staff before disappearing back into the interior of the restaurant.

"Earth to Brenna. What's got your panties twisted up?" Sean forked a bite of crab salad. "Holy shit, this stuff is fan-tastic." He grimaced the moment the words were out of his mouth. With a frown, he dug around in his pocket and handed Mrs. M a five dollar bill, grumbling, "I was doing so good today, too."

"For the swear jar." Mrs. M held up the money and smiled at Brenna. "He's got a terrible potty mouth, you know."

"I've been trying to clean up my act for a while, but I've doubled down now that we've got babies on the way." Sean took another bite of the salad. "This stuff is really good."

"It is." Brenna sighed and looked around. "My panties aren't twisted up. I was just thinking how good Dante is at all this, and that I wish the L&G was busy like this all the time."

"Rebecca told me you need a loan to expand. How much are you looking at, and do you have a business plan put to-gether yet?"

"Your wife has a big mouth. She wasn't supposed to say anything to you. I do have a business plan, but I need to re-work it."

"After you've got your shi—stuff together," Sean said, his eyes darting to Mrs. M before he continued, "let me have a look at it. If you want some advice ahead of time, I'm right here, you know. I'll help you any way I can."

"I know that, Sean." Brenna squeezed his arm and smiled.

She noted movement in her peripheral vision and turned toward it. Three rough looking young men stood in front of the Bistro. They boasted muscles that screamed *gym rat* and strained the confines of their T-shirts, worn motorcycle boots, and leather vests. Each wore a ponytail and sported multiple tattoos. Brenna's first thought was that they looked like cloned extras from a B movie about biker gangs.

Dante blew through the front door and met them on the sidewalk. "I understand you asked to speak with me. What can I do for you gentlemen?"

"You may not want to do this here," one of the men drawled, sauntering up to Dante, "as we aim to kick your pretty boy ass. Would hate for your blood to stain up these nice Mayberry streets."

Dante glanced from one man to the other, his expression bland. "Seriously? What's this all about? Did Vince put you up to this?"

"You need a lesson, pretty boy."

"I hate to spoil your outing, but I'm in the middle of my lunch rush and don't have time for nonsense right now. So if you boys would run along, I'd sure appreciate it." Dante dismissed them with a look and turned to go back inside the restaurant.

"You're not taking this seriously enough, but you're about to," said one of the men, grabbing Dante's arm.

Dante narrowed his gaze and yanked his arm free. "You do not want to take me on," he said in a tone much like the one he had used on Brenna earlier when he'd been mad at Vince. She imagined his eyes turning to that hard onyx and was happy not be on the receiving end of that cold stare.

"Aw, listen, Hal. Ain't that sweet? He's worried about us," one of them said, and all three of them sniggered.

Dante shook his head. "Okay, but don't say you weren't warned. Let me take off my jacket. I don't want it getting bloody." Dante shrugged out of his jacket and tossed it over the patio fence. He unbuttoned the cuffs of his shirt and began rolling up his sleeves.

"Look at that." The man called Hal nudged the other two. "He's ready to bleed."

Sean set his fork down, as did several other diners, and turned toward the conversation. Brenna sucked in a breath, wondered if she should call nine-one-one, but she couldn't take her eyes off the scene long enough to pick up her phone.

Dante regarded the men with a bored stare. "I'm guessing this has to do with Vince. Do yourselves a favor and leave before you do something you'll regret."

Brenna tapped Sean's arm. "Aren't you going to go help him?"

Sean grinned. "You kidding? He doesn't need it. I'm going to sit back and watch the show."

Chapter 12

It was over so fast Brenna questioned what she saw. The men closed in on Dante, and the one named Hal threw the first punch. Dante's head snapped back from the blow to his cheekbone and Brenna gasped. A second later, Dante slammed his elbow into Hal's nose. The man stumbled back, bellowing in pain. Blood erupted from his nostrils. The second man threw a wild punch and received a quick jab to his solar plexus. He doubled over, dropped to the ground, moaning, and curled up like a shrimp. Dante took a step toward the third man, said "Boo," and sent him running. His heavy footfalls thumped on the sidewalk as he ran away.

Dante retrieved his jacket from the fence and held out a hand to the man gasping for breath on the sidewalk. Dante helped him up and then turned to Hal and said, "Lean your head forward so you don't choke on your own blood, idiot. Your nose isn't broken. The bleeding will stop in a minute."

"How the hell would you know?" the guy said, his voice a miserable wail.

"If I wanted to break your nose, I would have." Dante shook his head. "Typical Vince, sending the Three Stooges." To the man he'd helped up from the ground, he said, "Go around there to the gate and take a seat at the empty table in the corner. Your friend here needs to clean up first, but I'll send him out to you in a minute. And quit whining. I didn't hit you that hard."

"I think you broke a rib, dude," he choked out. "Maybe pierced a lung."

"Go sit your ass down. Call your other friend back and tell him he's getting a comped meal."

Hal perked up in spite of the blood still dripping onto his shirt. "You're giving us free food?"

"Not you. You two assholes are paying for your meals. I'm giving *him* free food because he didn't take a swing at me." Dante buttoned his cuffs and shrugged into his jacket. "I recommend the pasta puttanesca. It's a new sauce. I think you'll like it."

Brenna's lips parted and she, along with everyone else on the patio, observed the goings on with surprised bemusement.

The men exchanged a dubious glance. The one nursing a sore midsection trudged through the patio gate to sit at the rear table as Dante had instructed, and Hal followed Dante into the restaurant, wearing the expression of a five-year-old just punished with a time-out. A few minutes later, Dante's three assailants sipped tall glasses of sweet tea while they waited for their pasta. Hal sat with his head hanging forward and an ice pack pressed to the bridge of his nose. He sported a clean shirt advertising Caravicci's Pizzeria.

"What in the world just happened?" one of the garden club ladies asked to no one in particular, and chuckles erupted from the surrounding tables.

"I'm coming here for lunch every day," someone else said, eliciting more laughter.

Sean smiled at Brenna. "Your man is a badass," he said and held up a finger to stop Mrs. M from commenting. "Badass does not require money in the swear jar. Badass is an appropriate noun in this circumstance."

Mrs. M smiled and patted Sean's arm. "Silly. I was just going to say that Brenna's young man is more than just a badass. He's a *gentleman* badass." She directed her gaze to

Brenna and fanned herself with her napkin. "It was quite titillating, really. Rather sexy."

"Aw, geez." Sean squeezed his eyes shut. "You didn't just say that."

"So true." Brenna nodded at Mrs. M and smiled, pleased with her man. A gentleman badass, indeed.

こうこう

It was ridiculous, Brenna thought, to suffer withdrawals from a man after less than twelve hours.

She locked up the Lump & Grind and glanced with longing down the alley toward the Bistro, giving consideration to making the offer to help with Dante's inventory. But she wouldn't be doing it to help, she'd be doing it to spend time with him. It smacked of neediness, and Brenna wasn't willing to concede that at this point. The man had work to do. She should stay out of his way and let him do it.

Really, she should.

She sat in her car and gnawed the inside of her cheek, considering.

Did her reasons matter so much? Wouldn't it be a kind gesture to offer her help?

Of course it would.

Brenna parked beside Dante's Trans Am and lifted her fist to bang on the Bistro's alley door. She paused, wondered if anyone would hear her through the loud rock music blaring from the interior of the restaurant, and reconsidered. She might look quite the fool standing out here at midnight trying to be heard over the noise.

The door burst open and she jumped back.

"Oh, hey, Brenna." Chloe's grayish-green eyes lit up. "Would you mind holding the door for a minute? I've got a couple boxes to toss in the dumpster."

Brenna mumbled, "Sure thing," and peeked around Chloe, but the hallway was a short stretch of empty. The

music boomed louder now with the door open, a genre
Brenna deemed hard and obnoxious, with wailing guitars
and a screamo frontman. It was a wonder the cacophony
hadn't rendered Dante and his entire staff deaf.

"He's in the storeroom," Chloe said a moment later with
a lack of preamble. "We're in the middle of doing inventory
in there, trying to figure out what we have. A lot of stuff got
shoved in there when we moved in, and we need to get a
handle on it."

"I don't want to interrupt," Brenna said, her face heating.
"I just thought maybe you could use some help."

"We're always up for that." Chloe led Brenna inside.
"Hey, boss, look who showed up to help."

Dante's eyes lit when he saw Brenna, and his lips formed
an immediate smile. "Hello. I didn't expect to see you tonight."

Brenna shrugged and tried to be nonchalant, but giddi-
ness bloomed at the sight of him and her lips curled of their
own accord. "Many hands make light work."

He narrowed his eyes. "That's not Yoda."

"Confucius."

"Whatever. I'm glad you're here," he said.

Ridiculous happiness bubbled inside her. "So what do
you need me to do? I'm ready to work."

And work she did, sorting through boxes, taking notes,
marking checklists, and repacking the boxes. By two a.m.
she sat on the storeroom floor bleary-eyed, and certain Dante had more extra linens and silverware than the Bistro
would ever need. She was more than ready to call it quits
when Dante told his crew they were free to go.

Brenna yawned, rubbed her eyes, and waved goodbye to
the last of the Bistro employees. She dropped onto the sofa
in Dante's office, stretched her legs in front of her, and laid
her head back, relieved by the blessed silence that ensued
after Dante flipped off the music.

"How can you be so awake?" she asked, eyes closed, after Dante joined her.

"Fading fast." He took her hand and held it in his and, when she opened her eyes, his head was back and his eyes were shut, dark lashes resting against his cheeks. Her stomach did a flip and she cursed herself for being so drawn in. She needed some distance, a chance to gain control. She should tell him goodnight and get the heck out of there.

She kissed him instead, pressing her lips to his with gentle pressure. Dante slid his free hand through her hair and held her head in place, deepening the kiss for a few beats before she ended it. She smiled against his mouth, felt him smile back, and kissed him again, a quick touch, before she drew back.

She traced the bruise on his face from the punch he'd taken at lunchtime, and ran her finger along the scar running parallel to his jawline on the other side.

"How'd you get that scar?"

"Vince. We got in a fight and he came at me with a piece of broken glass." He threaded his fingers through her short cap of hair again, and she leaned her head into the pressure of his touch.

"Did you take stitches?"

"Mm-hm. I don't remember how many. My aunt was so pissed."

"No wonder. Her son came at you with a deadly weapon."

Dante snorted out a laugh. "That's not why. She was mad because she had to take me to the ER. We were there forever."

Brenna leaned back to look at him, waited for him to open his eyes.

"What?" he said.

"Did Vince's parents raise you?"

"After my parents died I lived with my grandparents. A few years after my grandfather died, Gran and I moved in with my aunt and uncle—Vince's parents. I guess I was about eight or nine."

"How was that, living with them?" Brenna prompted

when he neglected to offer more details. Why were men so tight-lipped?

"Uncle Stan was okay. He owned the pizza joint in Asheville I told you about, where I worked as a kid. Everything I know about running a restaurant I owe to him. I love what I do, so no complaints."

"Vince worked there too?"

Dante's lips curved in a half smile and he resumed playing with her hair, gliding the short strands through his fingers and watching them fall. "Vince pushed a mop once in a while. He inherited the place when my uncle died, ran it out of business in about six months. What's with all the questions?"

"Can't I just be interested?"

"So what about you? What kind of childhood did you have?"

"You're only asking to be polite. You already know. I had a wonderful childhood. I was loved and indulged, tried everything from ballet to piano lessons. I didn't really know what I wanted to be when I grew up. The only two things I knew for certain were that I wasn't afraid of hard work, and I don't like having other people tell me what to do."

Dante smiled at that. "Not exactly a newsflash."

"I worked at a coffeehouse through high school and college breaks, and I liked the environment, enjoyed being busy all the time, loved the smell of the place, you know?"

"I do know," Dante said.

"When my grandmother passed, she left money to me, Sean, and Jack. I used mine to buy the L&G, and I never looked back. I really love that little place." She covered a yawn with her hand and sat up. "I need to go home and get some sleep. Shaniqua's opening tomorrow, but I need to be in before noon for the stupid Truth or Dare."

Dante took her face in his hands and drew her in for a kiss. Her heart beat faster, and when his sped up beneath her palms, her exhaustion fled. "Come home with me, Brenna," he said, but took her mouth again before she could answer.

It was a miracle, she thought, what the man did to her, the way he managed to shoot her from zero to one-hundred in less than a second. She'd never met anyone else like him, had never been with a man who elicited this kind of reaction from her—and more, she thought, putting her heart into the kiss. So much more. Why had she been stubborn for so long?

"Let's get out of here," he said, but kept on kissing her as if she were a drug he couldn't shake, and she was of the mind that they didn't need to leave, that here, anywhere, would do, as long as she was with him. She looked into his eyes, dark now with desire, and she knew by the heated pulsing of blood through her veins that hers were the same.

His gaze held hers and he read her mind. "Here? You sure?" His fingers traced the bare skin beneath her shirt, toyed with the clasp of her bra.

"I don't need scented candles and rose petals."

"I'd still like to give them to you."

"You, Dante. I only need you," she said, and deep inside she knew a quickening—twin shivers of dread and desire, because those words were true.

Dante unclasped her bra with a practiced deftness which Brenna would, much later, consider with a smidge of ridiculous jealousy. But in the moment she knew only the warm firmness of his hands and mouth, which traversed her body with tender passion and a sure knowledge of the terrain. During their encounters over the last week he had learned and remembered her most sensitive places—the curve of her neck and shoulder, the rise of her breast, the tender inside of her wrist.

The extra weight about which she was so concerned didn't seem to decrease his desire, and she soon forgot to worry about the width of her hips or the circumference of her waist. She knew only Dante, the fire of his skin beneath her hands, the beautiful dance of his muscles as he moved over her.

And much later, when the pounding of their hearts began

to ease and Dante rested his head upon her breasts with a satisfied sigh, she thought of Maddie's fireflies, of how she had once told Maddie that she, Brenna, in spite of intimate relationships, had never glowed for anyone.

Is this what it's like to be a firefly? she wondered, while the fingertips of one hand glided with lazy caresses along the muscles of Dante's back, and she toyed with his soft hair with her other. Was this what Maddie felt for Caleb? What Rebecca felt for Sean? How could anyone feel this much and survive the sheer enormity of it? How could something be so heavy and so light, all at the same time?

Dante pressed a kiss to the inside of her breast. She shivered at the scrape of his stubble against the tender skin, and then he shifted to meet her mouth with his. "You're mine now," he said, the words a sweet whisper against her lips.

She threaded her hands through his messy hair. "And you're mine."

"Brenna." Dante took her face in his hands and held her gaze, but many moments passed before he gave her the words she had already seen in his eyes. "I have always been yours."

So heavy, so light.

espes

The ka-thunking of the back door, followed by voices in conversation, jabbed into Brenna's dreams. Her eyes opened and awareness of her surroundings flooded into her mind.

Sometime during the night she and Dante had reversed positions, and he lay asleep on his back with Brenna sprawled on top of him. She scrambled off of him and tripped over their abandoned shoes and clothes in an effort to reach the office door before someone discovered them. She lunged toward the door and gave it a mighty shove. It closed with a bang. Dante bolted upright, startled and bleary-eyed.

Brenna locked the door and rested back against it for a moment while she got her bearings. The voices paused outside the office door and someone knocked.

"Hey, boss, everything okay in there?"

Brenna identified the voice as Gemma's and stood still as stone while Dante rubbed his eyes and woke up enough to growl out, "Fine. I'll be out in a few."

"Okay," Gemma said, and the conversation with her companion began again as their footsteps and voices disappeared down the short hall to the kitchen.

"That was a close one," Brenna said, her voice almost inaudible.

She found her bra and panties amid the pile of clothes on the floor and donned the lingerie with efficient movements, then pulled on her shirt and wriggled into her jeans while Dante observed her with blatant appreciation from where he lay stretched out on the couch.

"You want to help me sneak out?"

"Your car is still out back. They already know you're in here."

Brenna blinked at him. She hadn't thought of that. He held his arms out to her and she slid into them, content to snuggle for a minute or two while he finished waking up.

"What's on your agenda today?" she asked, feeling dreamy while he toyed with her hair.

"Just work. You?"

"The same. Will I see you later?"

"Count on it."

"What about tomorrow? Think you can make it over to Mama's for the party?"

"I'll be late, but I'll be there." He kissed her hair and buried his nose in it, breathed in. "You always smell so good."

Brenna smiled. "I'll smell better after I shower. And on that note, I should go." She withdrew from his embrace with reluctance and sat down at the end of the couch to put on her shoes. "You're a bad influence on me. I'm probably going to be late to work because of you. And I'm opening the door in a second, so you might want to put your clothes on before your employees get an eyeful."

"Right. Gimme a sec."

Brenna watched Dante tug on his clothes. "How do you own two Italian restaurants and keep yourself in shape?"

Dante zipped his Levi's and shrugged. "I have a good metabolism, I guess."

Brenna eyed his muscled torso before he pulled his T-shirt on, and shook her head. "That's not it. You go to the gym?"

His eyes flicked up to meet her gaze. "Crossfit, usually three or four times a week, and I have weights at home. Why, you thinking of joining a gym?"

"Oh, honey, no. The only time I want to glow is in a sauna, post massage. I've put on a few pounds since opening the L&G, that's all." She shrugged and looked away, uncomfortable with the topic she'd raised. "I need to watch the cinnamon buns." When he didn't answer, she met his gaze again, her neck prickling at his obvious amusement. "What?"

"Brenna, you're perfect. You're built like a—" He cut himself off and shook his head, laughing. "You're perfect. Trust me on this."

"Hm," she said, because she didn't believe him, but arguing would make her sound like she was fishing for compliments, or worse, needy and less than confident. "You ready?"

At his nod, she opened the door. She peered into the hallway, prepared to put on a confident face should she be forced to speak to someone, but the coast was clear.

"Hold up," he said when she grabbed her purse and prepared to bolt. "I'll walk you out."

They stood at her car for a while, saying goodbye, and parted with reluctance when more of Dante's employees began arriving for work.

"Thanks for helping with the, uh, inventory."

"It wasn't as bad as I expected," Brenna said and laughed when he raised his brows. "Oh, you mean *that* inventory. *That* inventory was fan*tastic*. We should take inventory again tonight."

"I'll come over as soon as I get home."

Brenna smiled. "I'll be waiting."

❦❦❦

The fireflies dotted the twilight landscape of the Kinkaid's flourishing front yard with their effervescent glow. Brenna, Maddie, and Rebecca sat on the porch stairs sipping sweet tea and watching the light show. Edie and Sada had gone inside to escape the mosquitos.

The second the front door clicked shut behind the mothers, Maddie said, "I'd like to run something by y'all." She sighed, fidgeted, and adjusted her glasses. "Caleb wants to build me a house."

Maddie's pronouncement was met with a wall of silence, and she rushed to fill the void. "It's not a done deal, or anything, just something we talked about." Her worried eyes turned Brenna's way. "The old house needs so much work, and if we're going to stay there, we'll have to build on. Not that we couldn't. Caleb can build or rebuild anything, but..." She trailed off and bit her lip, searching for the words. "I have an idea about something. Something big."

Brenna swallowed back the sadness that rose within her. She remembered the first time she saw the old farmhouse and the isolated property on which it sat. She'd believed Maddie and Jack were out of their minds for wanting to live so far out of the way, smack in the middle of the woods, and she'd told them as much. But Maddie loved the house and the solitude that came with it, and Jack could never deny her anything. They bought it and moved in right after they married, Maddie and Jack—and that, of course, was probably the whole point. It was no longer Maddie and Jack. It was Maddie and Caleb now.

Brenna kept her tone light when she said, "I don't blame him." She took one of Maddie's hands in her own and smiled. "Cal probably wants to build you a castle, and I think you should let him."

"He does." Maddie squeezed Brenna's hand. "Thank you for understanding." She bit her lip again and her smile bloomed around her nibbling teeth. "Not that I need or want a castle. Anyway, that's not even the best part. There's more. A lot more." She stood and moved into a crisscross sit on the stone pathway at the foot of the steps, looking up at Brenna and Rebecca. Her excitement bubbled over, and she talked with her hands and arms gesticulating.

"Okay, so like I said, Caleb wants to build us a house. He's going to build way at the back of the field. It's like, five or six acres back, something like that. Farther than it looks. And we talked about fencing in the whole field, maybe even getting horses eventually. And *then* we started talking about the wedding, and how great it was, using the barn and a tent for the reception, and the gazebo for the ceremony. It was so perfect, you know?"

Maddie's face lit with excitement and she stood, electrified by her own news. "I want to turn it into an event center, for weddings and stuff like that. A bride and her whole wedding party could use the house before the wedding, to get dressed and stuff. Shoot, they could rent it overnight and *sleep* there if they wanted! That would be so convenient." Her brows shot up. "It could be perfect for the bachelorette party, too. Think about it! The bride and her friends could have, like, a giant sleepover in the house, and then they'd have use of the gazebo in the morning, just to sit and have their coffee. And they can take pictures everywhere outside, in the gazebo clearing—it's so beautiful there now that Edie has landscaped everything—and the creek is right there, too. It'd be perfect. People could book it for weddings, use the whole space just like Caleb and I did.

"I'd never have to worry about repairs or anything, because you and Caleb could handle all of that." She directed the statement to Rebecca and then swung her eyes in Brenna's direction. "You and Dante can provide all the catering, and Sean can handle the legal stuff. Oh, sweet Lord, this could be so great!" She clasped her hands beneath her chin and, looking much like a giddy child, blurted, "So what do you think?"

Brenna and Rebecca exchanged bemused looks.

"You and Cal going to manage it, or will you hire someone?" Rebecca asked.

Maddie nodded, her face a study in excited bliss. "Caleb and I will manage it. It won't be in use all the time, of course, but when it is, we'll be right there on the property the whole time. Close enough to help and keep an eye on things, and far enough back to give people their privacy and maintain our own."

"Will you clear any of the forest to make the space bigger?" Brenna asked, considering the possibilities.

"No." Maddie shook her head. "It would be a place for small, intimate gatherings, the way our wedding was. No big groups."

"Not just weddings, Mads. People could use the property for photo shoots, too, engagement pictures, a weekend retreat." Brenna straightened her posture and rubbed her hands on her thighs, excitement brewing. "Last fall there were four older ladies who came into the L&G. I remember them because they were real characters, all of them. They had on matching T-shirts that said *Silver Surfer Siren's Club*. They come up here to the mountains every year for a girls' weekend. They usually stay at that B&B on Bright Street down past the railroad tracks. Your place would be perfect for people like them."

"You'd still have plenty of privacy, too," Rebecca said, her eyes narrowing while she tapped her chin with her index finger. "We can build you a long drive that goes all the way around the property to the right, and put in an ornamental iron gate." She grinned and raised her brows at Maddie. "Like the Ponderosa."

Maddie laughed. "Nothing so grand, but yes, that's a great idea."

"And you'll need somewhere to talk to potential clients. Maybe we can build a nice reception area onto the front of the house. You never use the front, anyway. You always go into the house through the porch on the kitchen side," Rebecca said.

"The front yard can be used for parking," Brenna said. "You don't even have to pave it. Just make a gravel parking area."

"Oh, sweet Lord. We can really do this, can't we? We can really make this happen." Maddie clapped her hands and giggled like a little girl, her excitement contagious.

The three of them began talking all at once, ideas flowing.

"I have to say, though, Mads, I'm a little worried about you and Caleb, using your honeymoon time to cook up land use and business plans. You did leave time for romance, right?" Brenna gave her friend a meaningful look. "Hmm?"

Maddie's eyes sparkled and her cheeks flushed. "You know we did."

"I still think you should have taken two weeks," Rebecca said.

"Caleb wanted to, but I didn't want to be away from TJ for that long." She glanced at Brenna. "And I still can't believe you cut your hair."

Brenna smoothed the back of her hair with her hand. "It's still a little bit of a shock, but I like it. Saves me a lot of time in the morning."

"I can't lie," Rebecca said, eyeing Brenna's pixie. "I hate you a little right now."

"You can't hate me. You have all those gorgeous red curls," Brenna said.

Rebecca snorted and rolled her eyes. "Yeah, right." She grabbed a curl that had come loose from her messy bun and pulled it straight, let go, and watched it spring back into a spiral. "The kids used to call me Slinky-head."

Maddie sat between Brenna and Rebecca, and patted Rebecca's belly. "I wonder if the twins will inherit the black Kinkaid hair or your red curls?"

Rebecca grinned. "It's kind of like Christmas, waiting for these Little Boogers to be born. Who knows?"

"So." Maddie leaned into Brenna and gave her a long nudge. "Now that I finished dropping my bombshell about the house, what's going on with you and Dante?"

"Something big," Rebecca said. "Have you seen the way she lights up when someone says his name? C'mon, Brenna, dish. Has he kissed you again since the storeroom incident?"

Brenna rubbed at the cool condensate on her glass with the pads of her thumbs and watched the fireflies while she considered her answer. Playing coy was not her intent, but she expected a flurry of questions to follow full disclosure and wasn't ready to answer them yet.

She thought back to last night, and the look on Dante's face when she'd opened her front door to him, made up like they were headed out for a night on the town. She wore mile-high heels, the little black dress, and nothing else. He stepped through the doorway without a word and had her against the wall and naked in under thirty seconds. She closed her eyes and played it back in her mind—the urgent thrill, the delicious need, met and sated with matched desires. They collapsed to the floor after, laughing together at the demise of her dress and his tangled jeans. When he reached for her, still smiling his Dante smile, she melted into his embrace and thought she'd never been happier, or felt safer with anyone, than she did with him in that moment. She straightened her posture when his Trans Am drove up the long Kinkaid drive.

"Speak of the devil," Rebecca said and slid her gaze across Maddie to Brenna. "That look on your face says you've been holding out on us."

"Sweet Lord, look at that. You're glowing," Maddie said.

"Stop it you two," Brenna scolded, but she couldn't contain her smile. She ignored her friends and watched her man pocket his keys, kept her attention on him as he strode across the yard to the walkway.

"Hello, ladies," he said when he neared them.

As they were blocking the way, all three women stood to give him egress into the house.

"Welcome home, Mrs. Walker," he said to Maddie and drew her into a hug. Rebecca was next, and Brenna waited her turn, pleased when he tipped her chin up with his fingers and kissed her hello. "I have a present for you, Miss Kinkaid."

"You do?"

"Mm-hm." He dug around in his pocket and came up with the prize. "I couldn't find the letter jacket. Sorry, but I think it's long gone."

Brenna closed her fingers around his offering and laughed up at him. "You're ridiculous. I can't believe you actually took the time to find this."

"Well, we are going steady, after all," he said, his eyes alight with humor. "Did you have to suffer through a Truth, or was it a Dare today?"

"Truth. So much easier than that terrible experience last week," she said and waited for his smile. He didn't disappoint, and her heart fluttered. She forced a normal tone and said, "Those yahoos wanted to know if I've ever had any plastic surgery."

Rebecca laughed. "You mean they wondered if you've had a boob job."

"I'm sure. I told them no, which is true, of course, but I'm not sure they believed me." Brenna turned her attention to Dante. "What did you have to do today?"

"A Dare this week. I had to sit on top of the piano and sing *That's Amore.*"

"I didn't know you could sing," Maddie said.

Dante grinned. "I can't. It was a performance the general public probably won't ask to have repeated. Collected about a hundred bucks for it, though." His gaze bore into Brenna's. "Chloe counted almost six-seventy today. Unless you can top that, I'm winning."

Brenna shrugged off a prickle across her shoulders. "I don't have that much, but we still have a few weeks to go, so don't get too cocky. You hungry? The men are in the man cave, and as usual, we have more food than we'll ever consume in one sitting."

"Perfect." He dropped another quick kiss on her mouth before starting up the stairs. "Ladies," he said and disappeared into the house.

Rebecca and Maddie stood unspeaking. The nighttime sounds of summer in North Georgia filled the silence. Insects chirped, whirred, and rustled in the trees and bushes as the fireflies sprinkled the deepening twilight with their gentle glow, tiny beacons in the gloaming.

Maddie was the first to break the silence. "I take it you and Dante have had, um, situational developments?"

Rebecca smiled at Maddie's euphemism. "When did you two start sleeping together? And what did he give you?"

Brenna held up Dante's high school class ring. "It's kind of an inside joke, because we're sort of going steady."

"Okay. And you started sleeping together when?" Rebecca pressed. "Is this because of the Lust Dust?"

"The what?" Maddie pushed her glasses up her nose and peered at Brenna. "Lust what?"

Brenna laughed and hugged Maddie. "Oh, honey, you look so scandalized." She exchanged an amused look with Rebecca. "The mosquitos are starting to get to me. Let's go refill our sweet tea and head upstairs. I'll fill you both in."

Ten minutes later, the three women lay sprawled in their usual places on the canopied bed in Brenna's childhood bedroom, Brenna and Maddie with their backs to the headboard, and Rebecca lying on her side across the foot of the bed. Three walls of pale pink were offset by one painted bright fuchsia.

The University of Georgia bulldog mascot figured into

the décor. Boy band posters clung to the walls along with a set of four replications of Monet's Water Lilies series and pennants from Bright Hills High School and UGA. Red fuzzy dice hung from one of the bedposts while an assortment of Mardis Gras beads decorated another.

A mountain of pillows lay on the floor where they had been tossed to make room on the bed, and a Bedazzled princess phone claimed real estate on the bedside table.

"I get a headache in here," Rebecca said, glancing around. "It's like your closet vomited up all the Disney princesses at once."

Brenna laughed. "I wasn't a tomboy like you. I liked my girlie stuff."

"Seems like Dante likes your girlie stuff, too," Rebecca said and earned a gasp and a laugh from Maddie. "So give us details."

"Sean didn't say anything to you?" Brenna asked.

"About what?" Rebecca sat up. "Has he been holding out on me, too?"

"He's a man. It probably never crossed his mind to tell you." Brenna leaned over the side of the bed and grabbed a pillow to hug. "You already knew that my feelings for Dante were changing."

"Right," Rebecca nodded and narrowed her eyes. "So, c'mon, Brenna. Out with it."

"There isn't much to tell that you don't already know or haven't figured out. We're seeing each other and have agreed to keep it exclusive." Brenna paused and the other two women regarded her in rapt silence, waiting for more. Brenna shrugged. "What do you want me to say?"

Maddie pushed her glasses up and stared at Brenna. "Details, Brenna. We want details. How, when, where, what, why."

"And most important," Rebecca said, grinning, "how great was it?"

Brenna looked from Maddie to Rebecca and back to Maddie. What was the point of having best friends if you couldn't spill your guts? So she spilled.

"This is freaking epic," Rebecca said after the last detail had been dished. "You're really in deep."

Brenna sighed and hugged the pillow tighter. "I know. It's kind of terrifying, actually. It happened so fast. It's like riding a big wave, and right now, oh, honey, I'm on top of the world, but there's the big potential for a bad crash. I don't want to crash."

"You're his Kobayashi Maru," Maddie said.

"His what?"

"That's a thing from Star Trek," Rebecca said. "It's an unwinnable scenario. It's this test, and Captain Kirk rigs it so he can win, because he doesn't believe in the unwinnable scenario."

"So what does that mean?" Brenna pressed.

"Well, nothing, really," Maddie said. "Just that Caleb and I were talking about Dante kissing you the day of the wedding, and he told me he had kind of given Dante a push at lunch, told him you were his Kobayashi Maru."

"Oh, okay," Rebecca said. "I get it. So you were like a challenge. Win the unwinnable."

Brenna's head buzzed and her heartbeat slowed to heavy thumps. "Excuse me? What?"

Rebecca and Maddie exchanged a look, and Rebecca rushed to amend her statement. "I didn't mean it the way it sounded, Brenna. I'm sure it's not like that. I only meant—"

"But it makes sense, doesn't it?" The words crawled from Brenna's mouth and stung like fire ants. "All these years he's just been a big pain in the ass, treated *me* like a pain in the ass, and all of a sudden this big push for something more. Caleb challenged him, and he took up the gauntlet." She squeezed her eyes shut, angry with herself for being drawn in with such ease. Humiliation burned. "Damn it. I should've known it was too good to be true. I'm such an idiot."

"Brenna—" Maddie began.

"No, Mads." Brenna returned the pillow back into the

heap with an angry toss and stood up, pacing. "Damn it, he played me. And I let him."

Maddie exchanged a worried glance with Rebecca. "You don't really believe that."

Brenna stopped pacing and blew out a long sigh. "I don't want to believe it."

"Then don't," Rebecca said.

Brenna looked from Rebecca to Maddie and shook her head. "It's not as simple as that," she said and strode from the room.

Chapter 13

Dante knew something was wrong before Brenna ever spoke a word. It showed in her pallor and the firmness of her mouth, and when she said, "Excuse me, gentlemen. Dante, may I have a private word with you please?" there was no mistaking the negative undercurrent.

With the curious stares of the men at his back, he followed her out of Papa Ron's man cave and up the stairs, down the hall, and onto the front porch. Dread filled him with every step. What the hell had happened in the last hour?

Brenna faced him, arms crossed over her chest. Her body vibrated with unnamed emotion, and the only thing he was certain of was that it wasn't good.

"Kobayashi Maru."

Dante stared at her and shrugged off the prickling sensation crawling up the back of his neck. "What about it?"

"Is that what this was all about?"

"What do you mean?"

"We've known each other for how long? Five years?"

"Give or take. So?"

"Why now, Dante? Why did you make a move now?"

"I guess I got tired of waiting." He shrugged. "Does it matter?"

Brenna blinked and looked away into the yard. He

watched her, his brain scrambling for traction on a slippery slope. She was more than upset, he thought, as she fought for emotional control. She was hurt, and he was somehow to blame.

The last thing he wanted was to cause whatever this was to boil over, to become worse than it already was, so he took care with his tone and his words, so that they came through his lips in a gentle flow. "What are you accusing me of, Brenna? Give me a clue, here, sweetheart."

"I'm not accusing." She turned her gaze back on him and his heart broke, seeing those gorgeous eyes, almost purple in this shadowy light, ready to spill tears because of something he might have done. "I'm not accusing. I'm not. I just want the truth." She drew a deep breath and blew it out, a steady stream of decompression, and dammed up the waterworks. "Caleb called me your Kobayashi Maru. The unwinnable scenario. Is this thing with us because of that? This past week, were you only taking on a challenge, just— just to see if you could win?"

He stared at her, and it was many moments before he found his voice. "That's what you've taken away from this past week? That I'm *playing* you? Jesus Christ, Brenna." It was his turn to study the yard, the milky blooms of the magnolia tree, the flower-laden pathway, all awash in purple twilight with the heady scent of gardenias wafting up from somewhere amid Edie's garden cornucopia, and the fireflies beaming here and there. He returned his attention to Brenna, and the questions clouding her eyes burned into him. "That's one hell of an opinion you have of me."

"You haven't denied it," she pointed out, and under his stony regard she sighed, and said, "Look, believe it or not, nothing has to change between us. But I need to know what field we're playing on, Dante. If there's nothing more to this than fun and games, just say so."

He stared at her, rolling her words over in his mind, and with each turn his anger bubbled up. "Let me be sure I understand. You don't give a damn what this is or where it might be going, you just want to be sure you weren't played. Does that about sum it up?"

Brenna returned his stare, and Dante would give a king's ransom to know what was going on behind her stormy eyes. "Your righteous indignation isn't answering the question, Dante. Please just tell me the truth. Are you with me to win some stupid man challenge?"

"I'm not the one who turns everything into a competition."

"Why are you with me, Dante?"

"How can you think that I'd—"

"Why are you with me?"

"Jesus, Brenna."

"Why?"

"Because I'm in love with you." The words tumbled out, and he thought if he had thrown ice water in Brenna's face she couldn't have looked more shocked. He didn't blame her. They'd been together a scant week. Early days in a relationship to start throwing the "L" word around.

He tried to identify the feelings moving through him, whether it was relief at having finally spoken the words he'd known for years to be true, or misery because the truth of those words was a weapon too powerful to put into the hands of a woman who had no clue what she really wanted.

Annoyed with Brenna for baiting him, and with himself for snapping it up like a hungry trout, he stepped around her to sit on the top step of the porch where she had perched earlier with Maddie and Rebecca. He looked out over Edie's flourishing yard and wondered how such a promising evening had gone so wrong.

He could almost see the humor in it, her shock at his revelation—she certainly got more than she bargained for when she dragged him out here to poke at the hornet's nest. Priceless, was the look on her face, and now an end to things before they'd even begun.

He would have been better off lying, better off saying she was right about the challenge. Competitive as she was, she could at least respect that, even if she didn't like being used.

I don't want to be involved with you that way, Dante. She had said those words to him only a week ago, and he supposed he should have taken them to heart, instead of pushing past the perennial stop sign. Still, he'd never be sorry. It had been one helluva ride, even if it had crashed and burned.

Well, she was in for a surprise, because he had no intention of junking this, not without a fight. He had bided his time before, he could do it again. This wasn't over. He was in this race to win, and by god, he'd find a way to finesse the engine and get the damn thing back on the road.

He waited to hear the front door open and close, wanting nothing more than to be left alone for a few minutes before going back inside and having to act like nothing was wrong. Instead, her capris-clad legs appeared next to his shoulders, and when he glanced her way his gaze dropped to her pedicured toes playing peekaboo from the front of her heeled sandals. Her little digits were lined up in perfect succession, and he swallowed a sigh. Even her feet were flawless.

She sat beside him, leaving nary an inch of space between them. She slid her arm through his and rested her head on his shoulder.

Brenna tipped her face up to look at him, and the tears she'd held back earlier slipped from her eyes now. "I do care what this is. I'm so far gone, that even if it had been a stupid man challenge I still would've held on." She swallowed hard. "I love you, too, you big Neanderthal."

"Brenna—"

"Shh." She covered his lips with her fingers. "I'm not just saying it. I think it's been true for a really long time. It's just so big. It was easier to hate you before, because there was no risk in that."

Relieved and elated, but cautious—the woman was mercurial and he wasn't ready to claim total victory yet—he wiped the tears from her cheeks with his thumbs and pressed his lips to her forehead. She sighed and rested her head against him when he drew her close.

From heaven to hell and back to heaven again, he thought. The woman was going to give him whiplash.

But she said she loved him, and he'd be damned if he'd ever let her take it back.

๏๏๏

"And then the Neanderthal says, *I recommend the pasta puttanesca. I think you'll like it.* Next thing we know the rednecks are sitting on the patio ordering lunch, and the guy with the bloody nose is wearing a shirt advertising for the Pizzeria." Brenna hugged Dante from under his arm, and he returned the squeeze. She patted his chest and looked up at him. "Mrs. M called you a 'gentleman badass.' I have to agree."

"Well, bless your heart!" Edie's eyes widened and her hand flattened against her chest. "Why in the world would your cousin arrange for such a thing? What would you have done if they had been more than just cowardly hooligans?"

"Hooligans? I would've just called them assholes." Papa Ron reached into the fridge for a Bud Light. "But my lovely bride makes a good point. What *would* you have done?"

"Probably gotten my ass kicked," Dante admitted. "As to my cousin's motivation, I'm sure he just wanted to cause trouble at my place of business. Not like it's the first time." He shrugged. "As it turns out, two of the guys have worked landscaping in the past, so I hooked them up with a buddy of mine over in Gainesville. He'll background check them first, but he's always looking for people in the summer. The third guy—bloody nose—is just a kid. He's only twenty-three. I hired him to work at the Pizzeria, as long as he stays out of trouble."

Brenna stepped away from Dante to regard him with wide eyes and an open mouth. She planted her hands on her hips, and the movement drew his gaze downward. It was an effort to hide his appreciation for the view, but standing in the Kinkaids' kitchen, with everyone who comprised the Kinkaid/Walker clan in attendance, was not the time or place. He saved himself trouble by taking a swig of his beer.

"Are you out of your mind?" Brenna said.

"What? He's just a kid."

"A kid who took payment to beat you up," she said. "That speaks to character."

"Doesn't mean he won't straighten up with a lucky break. He only did it because he was two months past due on his rent and his roommates threatened to boot him if he didn't pay up. Kid was desperate for money."

"So you gave him a job." Brenna sighed and shook her head. "Dante."

He gave her a look. "What? The kid needed a break. Nothing turned up on a background check, and if he turns out to be a pain in the ass Trina will fire him."

"Who's Trina?" Edie asked.

"She's his ex-wife," Brenna said, beating Dante to the punch, "and the new manager at the Pizzeria."

Sada let out a sigh of obvious relief that Brenna knew who Trina was, and her reaction made Dante smile. Aside from his grandmother, Sada was the only mother he had ever known—she had taken on the role of her own accord after learning of his past—and his affection for her burgeoned now. Sada's gaze met his and she gave him a subtle nod of approval. He returned a wink and made her smile.

"Aside from being very pleasant," Brenna continued, "she's also blonde and adorable in the extreme, and probably wears a size double zero in jeans." Brenna pointed at Dante with a tilt of her chin. "Lucky for me the gentleman badass has changed his type."

"I would've said lucky for me." Dante's eyes focused on Brenna, and she rewarded him with a sexy smile.

"Oh, my god, I think I'm throwing up a little in my mouth right now," Rebecca said with a grin. "You two need to stop being so cute together."

"Or get a room!" Grampa Boone boomed before he stomped across the kitchen to toss his empty in the recycle bin. Laughter followed the old man's pronouncement, and he peered at the group from beneath the brim of his Atlanta Braves cap. "What? Two people look at each other like that and it's time for everyone to go home."

Brenna covered her face with her hands and muttered, "Oh, my god," but her shoulders shook with laughter. Dante dropped his head back to stare at the ceiling for a minute, a better option than meeting the gaze of Papa Ron or Sean, neither of whom appeared to be amused.

"Well. On that note, I think maybe it's time for us to go," Big Will said. He followed it up with a hearty chuckle and slapped Dante on the back.

Sada lifted her purse from the breakfast bar and changed the subject. God bless her. "Are you driving your car in the Fourth of July parade this year, sweetheart?"

Dante hurried to answer. "No. Between the wedding stuff for these two—" He nodded to Cal and Maddie. "—and getting the Bistro on its feet, I opted out. I'm keeping both restaurants open until six."

"What about the L&G? You were closed last year," Maddie said.

"That was a dumb move on my part," Brenna said. "This year I asked for volunteers to work, and I was surprised by how many offered. Of course, it's holiday pay, time-and-a-half, so…" She shrugged. "I'm staying open until midnight. We're only a short walk from the park, so I expect business to be really good. Bubba-Jo's is closing at six like the Bistro, so the L&G will be the closest place open."

Edie pouted. "You won't be with us in the park, then. It's our Second Annual Walker/Kinkaid Fourth of July Bash."

"Sorry, Mama. I'll swing by if I can, but I'm expecting to be slammed all day long. I hope so, anyway."

A few minutes later, after everyone had said their good-byes, Dante stood with Brenna beside her Audi in front of the Kinkaids' house. "After the Bistro closes on the Fourth, I'll come by the L&G to help you out."

"You don't have to do that," Brenna said and waved a last goodbye to Maddie while Caleb strapped the sleeping TJ into their truck's child safety seat. Pirate leapt in after TJ, and the dog's head with its mismatched ears created an odd silhouette after Cal and Maddie climbed into their vehicle and buckled up.

"But I will. Helpmate is part of the job description, remember?" Dante tilted her chin up and leaned down for a kiss. "Your dad is staring at us from the porch. I think I'm getting the evil eye," he murmured against her lips.

Brenna responded with a soft laugh. "Don't you worry about Daddy." She looked over her shoulder and waved then blew Papa Ron a kiss. He nodded and repeated the gesture before Edie grabbed him by the arm and dragged him into the house. The door closed an instant later, and the porch light snapped off.

Such blatant approval by Brenna's mother, Dante thought, was a beautiful thing.

Left alone with his dream woman in the moonlit darkness, Dante whispered, "You want to stay over tonight?" He closed his eyes to enjoy the feel of her lips smiling against his. Her answer was another soft kiss, and he drew her close and breathed her in before releasing her.

"See you at home, Neanderthal," she whispered back in a voice full of promise, and Dante thought he'd never heard sweeter words.

∽✺∽

Brenna held tight to Dante while she waited for their racing hearts to ease into a gentler rhythm. It was tough to tell her own rapid heartbeat from his, and she didn't bother to try, just enjoyed the sweet harmony they made together. His breathing, still ragged in her ear, only made her hold on tighter.

It took her a moment to realize that some of the uneven breathing was her own, and Dante drew back to look at her when a quiet laugh erupted from her throat and her arms fell from him to drop onto the mattress.

"What's funny?" he asked, rubbing her nose with his.

"Not funny," she said and laughed again. "Not funny, just—I'm so blissed out, you know?"

Dante grinned and kissed her. "I do know." He shifted to his back and drew her close. She snuggled up, buried her nose into the inverted arch at the junction of his neck and shoulder, and breathed in. "You smell good, all manly." She kissed the same spot. "You taste good, too. Salty."

"Hm. Salty and manly." He waited a beat. "Uh, thank you, I guess?"

Brenna smiled and nestled in for a good snooze now that her muscles were loose as liquid gold and her heart had slowed to a normal pace. The pitter patter of feet on the bedroom carpet had her bracing for the inevitable furry bombshell that was Pavarotti, and a moment later the cat landed on the bed with a soft thump. A few seconds after that, she and Dante buried their faces against each other to avoid the cat's enthusiastic head butting.

"Okay, Pav, that's enough." Dante lifted the furry body off his chest. Pavarotti howled once, meowed, and then settled himself alongside Dante's torso. Brenna slid her arm across Dante's abdomen to pet the cat.

"Did you really bring Pav home from Afghanistan?"

"Yes."

"How did you find him?" Brenna asked the question, almost holding her breath while waiting for an answer. Dante never talked about his army experience, and when asked a direct question his short responses invited no further discussion.

Long seconds ticked by. His absolute silence led her to wonder if he had fallen asleep, but then his voice came from out of the darkness, quiet but steady.

"My unit was clearing a village and fighting erupted. A

mangy cat—Pav—darted out from an alley. A minute later this little kid—" Dante cleared his throat, but his voice still came through his lips with graveled rawness. "This little kid, about TJ's age, came running out of nowhere, and I mean, right into the middle of everything, bullets flying. He threw himself on top of the cat. Stupid, so stupid. Running into a gun battle to protect a cat. We held our fire immediately, even before the order was shouted, but the insurgents—"

Dante stopped talking. Brenna laced her fingers with his atop his abdomen. She swallowed tears and gave him silence and space.

"If the cat was important enough to that little kid to do what he did, how could I leave the animal? So, I went back for him. Didn't really think I'd find him, figured he'd've bolted, be long gone. But he was still—Pav stayed right there. Where the boy—" He turned his head into her hair and breathed in, and Brenna gave up her tears. She let them fall and pressed a kiss against Dante's tattooed skin, squeezed his hand. "You wouldn't believe it looking at him now, but Pav was all skin and bones, had bald patches. And mean. He hissed and scratched anyone who tried to get close. Except me. It was like he knew that I was the one to take care of him."

"I'm so sorry," she whispered. "I can't imagine—but you did a good thing, Dante. You did a good thing."

"Did I?" he said, his tone weary. "Rescued the cat, couldn't protect the kid."

"You did all that you could do," Brenna said.

As if voicing his agreement, Pavarotti meowed long and loud, snuggled closer to Dante, and turned his motor on.

∽◌∽

The wipers slid back and forth across the windshield, clearing the glass for an instant before the rain again ob-

scured the view, and then—swoosh!—the rubber scrapers pushed the water away for another nanosecond. Beyond the wipers and the rain, the world existed in darkness. The vehicle's headlights illuminated nothing beyond the tarry blacktop, slick and shiny with the wet.

Comfortable inside the car, Brenna noted the slap-slap-slap of the windshield wipers in a peripheral way while she talked and laughed with Jack. Her handsome brother regaled her with some ridiculous story, his eyes, blue like hers, gleaming with strange colors from the glow of the dash.

A pinpoint of light appeared up ahead to play peekaboo with the wipers and rain.

Brenna shrugged off her discomfort and strained to hear Jack's voice, but it faded to background noise. He continued to talk and smile, to laugh, but the rhythmic slapping of the wipers overtook the sound of his voice. The rain thundered against the vehicle and the noise of the wipers grew louder as the light approached.

Brenna's ragged breathing caught in her throat. Fear slithered into her, a sinister potion of preternatural understanding before the flood of despair.

This was going to happen, and she couldn't stop it.

Jack! She tried to call his name. Her voice refused to obey. Her limbs declined to move. Like deadweights attached to her torso, they lay as useless as her vocal cords.

The oncoming light grew brighter.

The windshield wipers slammed against the windshield, pounding now, hammering so hard they became the pulse beating inside Brenna's ears and at the base of her throat, until at last she recognized the beat of it, knew that it was her own heart slamming against her chest. Ka-thump, ka-thump, ka-thump.

The light shifted. The oncoming vehicle veered from its lane. Brenna could see it now. It was a muscle car, a Mustang, its engine designed for maximum power, maximum speed. Coming straight for them.

Brenna turned to look one more time upon the happy face of her brother. She blinked back tears. Jack smiled at her and the inside of the vehicle burst into white light on impact before descending into darkness as metal groaned and screamed—and maybe it wasn't the cars at all, maybe it was Brenna herself making that dreadful sound, because her hair flew into her face, blinded her, as it dripped blood and gore, the taste of death sharp and metallic on her tongue.

And then, in the way of dreams, everything shifted.

Brenna stood beside the wreckage, but night had flipped itself to day, and the world around her shone a dazzling and blinding white.

Snow. So beautiful. She'd always loved the snow.

She looked up, but saw no sky. There were only the fat flakes tumbling down to blanket the blacktop and the deep forest of trees that bordered it. And the tangled metal, that grotesque beast, even it became a beautiful disaster in the fallen snow, a glittering sculpture of white on white.

Brenna took a tentative step forward. Was Jack still in the car? Maybe he was still alive. Maybe she could save him after all.

She spun away from the wreckage when Jack grabbed her hand. Why, he wasn't hurt at all. Not at all!

Laughing and crying both, she seized him into a fierce hug, and when she freed him they were children, reverted to their younger selves.

"C'mon, meatball, let's go," Jack lisped through a mouthful of gleaming orthodontia. He took off running.

"Wait," Brenna called after him. "Jack, wait!" She tossed her long braids over her shoulders and jogged through the snow to catch up with him. Even though she was a couple years older, he was faster, always faster. She bent over to catch her breath, frustrated because her brother soon became a black speck calling to her from out of the sparkling, endless white.

"Let's build a snowman, Brenna!" Jack's voice echoed from the distance. "You've always loved the snow!"

⌘⌘⌘

Brenna gasped and her eyes flew open. Her heartbeat rioted inside her chest, and she squeezed her eyes shut, willing herself back to sleep. Jack was alive in that dream world, alive, and young, and happy. She wanted to see her brother again with a desperation that evolved into a physical ache.

Her heart continued to pound, but the intensity slowed. Beside her, Dante slept on his back, his breathing deep and rhythmic. Pavarotti had moved and now lay curled against her hip, purring like a jumbo jet. He was, without a doubt, the noisiest cat Brenna had ever heard. She stroked his fur, eliciting louder purrs, before she shifted around to snuggle with Dante. The second she moved, the cat hissed his annoyance and repositioned himself at the foot of the bed.

The sound jolted Dante awake with a quick intake of breath, but he relaxed in the instant Brenna moved against him.

"Everything okay?" he murmured, sliding his fingers through her hair with a gentle stroke.

"Yes," she lied, not wanting to wake him up for a dream she didn't want to talk about. She could tell him about it in the morning.

Still mostly asleep, Dante drew her into his arms and touched his lips to her forehead. Brenna closed her eyes and focused on the steady beat of his heart beneath her cheek, the sweet hush of his breathing.

And just like that, it wasn't a lie anymore. Everything was okay, just by being in his arms.

⌘⌘⌘

Brenna slid the manila folder containing the expansion

plans for the L&G under the basket on Dante's breakfast bar. Between the two of them, they had amassed a collection of notes and sketches, financial projections and random ideas. Dante thought she was silly for not scanning everything and keeping an electronic file, but Brenna liked the physical package, liked being able to lay everything out, to see it all at once, jotting notes or questions in the margins without having to go home to get her laptop. There was just something about being able to touch the sheets of paper that made it all more real. She was really going to do this, and soon.

"You need a tablet, or to start bringing your laptop with you." Dante sauntered from the hallway to stand beside her. He pressed a kiss to the top of her head and moved off into the kitchen. "You hungry?"

"No, thanks. I'll grab something at the L&G." She dropped one elbow on the breakfast bar and rested her chin in her hand. "So, I had a weird dream about Jack last night."

"Yeah?" Dante glanced at her and then turned back to scrambling eggs. "Is that what woke you up?"

"It is. I had the same dream I always have—apparently, I cut my hair for nothing, because that part of the dream didn't change—but the ending was different."

Sizzling sounded as the eggs hit the skillet, and Dante turned the heat down on the burner. He dropped two pieces of bread in the toaster, grabbed a silicone spatula to agitate the eggs, and looked back at Brenna. "You want me to beg for details?"

She grinned. "I just wanted to be sure you're paying attention."

He pointed the spatula at her. "I always pay attention," he said and turned back to the eggs.

Brenna admired him from behind, the spread of the cotton T-shirt over his broad shoulders, the movement of his muscles as he tended to his breakfast. "Well?" he said, and she obliged his interest with a detailed description of her dream.

"What do you think it means?" She watched him fork the eggs into his mouth and follow it with a swig of black coffee.

"Why does it have to mean anything?"

Brenna shrugged, and slid off the stool to get more coffee. She refilled her mug, and topped off Dante's with the last of the brew.

"It's just weird, that's all. I mean, why were we little kids? Why all the snow?"

"Maybe your subconscious just took you back to a happier time." He rinsed his plate and put it in the dishwasher, and then leaned against the counter to give her his full attention. "Maybe the dream is changing because you're starting to move on from it."

"Maybe." Brenna sighed and raked her fingers through her hair, smoothing it down with her palms a moment later when she saw Dante's amused grin. He rubbed his hand over her head to mess her hair up again, and she ducked out of the way, laughing. "Stop it. That's not fair. I can't reach the top of your head to mess up yours."

Dante lunged for her, and she avoided him by loping into the living room. He followed, and she ran around to the end of the sofa, moving in the opposite direction when he came after her. Her excitement from the chase bubbled up into giddy laughter as they circled the couch, Dante playing the hunter to her escaping prey.

"C'mon, now." A smile played at the corners of his mouth as he moved toward her with slow deliberation. "You know I'm going to get you."

Brenna shook her head and moved in sync with him, staying well beyond his arm's reach. He edged around the end of the sofa, and she did the same, until they faced each other at the center, Dante standing behind the couch, Brenna in front. He lunged and caught her arm, but she yanked from his grasp with a squeal and wild laughter and took off in the direction of the hallway. Dante was faster. He caught her in his arms and held her against him.

Brenna had no intention of going quietly. She wrestled, and he lost his balance, falling backward over the arm of the sofa, taking Brenna with him. She attempted to scramble off of him, but he held fast, releasing her when, breathless, she dropped her head onto his chest and said, "Okay, okay. You win."

"What's that?" Dante messed up her hair with a few rapid strokes of his hand. "Say it again, I didn't hear you the first time."

"I said you win."

"I *what*? What was that?"

Brenna lifted her head and gave him a look, but he lifted his brows and made a face, and she couldn't contain her laughter. "You're such an idiot Neanderthal." She scrubbed her hand over the top of his head and messed up his hair as he had done to hers. "You win, okay? You win, you win, you win."

Dante grinned and relaxed back into the cushions, stroking her back with his fingers. "Ahh. I love the sound of victory in the morning."

"You're ridiculous," she said, her smile taking all the bite from her words.

Dante's dark eyes softened. Brenna's excitement from their silly chase eased into desire and her body melted against his like warm wax. He lay solid and strong beneath her, and the caress of his hands along her spine shot tingles into her belly. She leaned in to press her lips to his, and fell short of the mark with a sigh when his phone rang out from down the hall.

"How do they *know*?" he said, his tone so beleaguered that Brenna laughed.

She pressed a quick, hard kiss to his lips, and pushed herself off of him. "Go take care of business, mister. I have to run home and shower anyway."

Dante sat up and caught her hand before she could move away. He tugged her down for another kiss, sighed, and lifted himself off the couch to walk her to the door.

"Aren't you going to get your phone?"

"I'll call them back in a minute," he said and drew her to him for another kiss goodbye. They parted with reluctance, and Dante stayed in the doorway to watch her walk the few steps home. "Brenna," he called when she reached the strip of grass between their townhomes. She turned at the sound of his voice. "I love you."

Brenna's heart fluttered and she blew him a kiss. "I love you, too," she said. "Will you come over after work?"

His smile warmed her. "Try and stop me."

"Not in this life," she said, and a renewed sense of surprise at the strength of her emotions for this man, whom she had wasted five good years trying to hate, overcame her.

Why? Why was I so stubborn? she thought, and Jack's voice whispered in her ears, *'It wasn't time. You weren't ready.'*

Startled, her mind flashed back to her dream and the image of young Jack running away and calling, *'You've always loved the snow!'*

A shiver took her. She felt Dante's eyes watching her as she crossed her driveway, and she stopped to wave and blow him another kiss before letting herself into her house. She tamped down the unease caused by Jack's memory and ignored the whisper of his voice insisting that there was something important he wanted her to know.

෴

Dante whistled while he dressed for work. He whistled on his way to work, and he continued whistling while he worked, a circumstance that had the sous chef rolling his eyes and Chloe giving Dante looks every time she came into the kitchen. Dante didn't care. He felt good. More than good. Terrific, actually.

With Brenna in his bed, he'd been sleeping great, with no episodes of insomnia. Best of all, he was in love, didn't have to hide it anymore, and miracle of miracles, the woman loved him back.

Life was on the upswing, and he intended to revel in every moment of it.

"Hey, boss." Chloe poked her head into the Bistro kitchen and waited for Dante to glance her way. "There's a woman here to see you, a Monica Somebody-or-Other. She looks like Marilyn Monroe." Chloe wrinkled her nose. "It's kind of creepy."

"Monica Thounhurst. She sells real estate. Just put her at a two-seater and get her whatever she wants to drink. Tell her I'll be out in a minute."

Chloe nodded and disappeared into the dining room.

"Monica." Dante greeted the woman a few minutes later and sat in the chair opposite her. "What can I do for you?"

"I have a client who would love your townhouse." She held up a manicured hand when he began to protest. "Hold on. I know you aren't ready to sell, but hear me out. The location is *perfect* for these people, the size is just what they want, the layout—literally everything about it is *perfect*, Dante."

"Except that I'm not ready to sell."

"What if I can get you into a house here in town, within walking distance of the Bistro?"

Dante narrowed his eyes. "You talking about Sean and Rebecca Kinkaid's Victorian over on Dogwood ?"

Monica straightened her posture and beamed at him. "Yes! Exactly the one." She reached across the table to pat his arm. "It's perfect for you. *Perfect.* It's bigger than where you are now, and has a fenced yard, big enough for you to build a second garage if you want. Best of all, you can walk to the Bistro in under ten minutes. Think about it, Dante. Just think about it. It's *perfect*, I'm telling you. Just *perfect.*"

Dante glanced away from her toothy smile, framed by lips redder than nature ever intended. When he looked back at her, she continued to regard him through eyes bright with interest, and he mused that her startling resemblance to Marilyn Monroe contained more than a passing hint of *Jaws*. He imagined her circling him, ready to chomp down a couple of property sales.

"Just tell me you'll *think* about it, okay? Because it's a *perfect* scenario, Dante. It really is. Just—"

"Perfect. Yeah, I get it." He shook his head and rewarded her efforts with a smile. "I'll let you know. Give me some time to think about it."

"Well, don't think too long, okay?" She sipped her sweet tea and continued beaming. "What do you recommend for a nice light lunch?"

"Try the Crabby Brenna Salad," he said, standing. "It's new, and the customer feedback is great."

"That's an interesting name for a salad," she said.

Dante grinned. "Named for an interesting lady. I'll put your order in, Monica. Enjoy."

"Hey, boss." Chloe caught Dante on his way back into the kitchen. His smile faded when she said, "I'm sorry, but your cousin Vince is in your office. He followed Gemma in through the back."

"I knew this day was going too well. Thanks for the head's up."

"You got it," she said and strode off toward the hostess stand.

Dante steeled himself before entering his office. He wondered which face Vince would be showing him today.

"Hey," Dante said. "We're going into lunch rush. What do you want?"

"What'd you think of the friends I sent your way?" Vince shifted on the sofa, tucked his hands behind his head, and smirked. "Figured you'd beat the crap out of them, maybe get yourself into some hot water, but you got them jobs instead." He shook his head and snorted out a laugh. "Impossible to prank you. You never stop do-gooding. Always the prince."

"Get off my couch."

Vince stared at him and Dante imagined the other man's internal debate. Vince's nature was to argue, but if he wanted something, he'd comply with Dante's directive.

Vince shrugged and hoisted himself off the couch.

"What do you want Vince?"

"I need some cash. Before you tell me no, just listen. I'm ready to go back to Asheville, but there's some people I owe money to there, and I can't show my face without paying them off. So if you want me to get gone, you're going to have to give me some dough."

"How much do you owe?"

Vince dropped his gaze to the floor and he dug his toe into the carpet and sniffed. "Five hundred."

Dante laughed. "And you think I'm going to give it to you?"

Vince's head snapped up. "Well, I can always ask Trina. She'll pay it, just to watch me walk away."

Dante clenched his teeth and willed the muscle in his jaw to still.

"Look, I can pay it back quick. Swear to god, Dante, I can. But I want to go back home and I can't, not without the money. So you can either help me blow outta here, or you can see my face around town. You pick."

Against his better judgment, Dante said, "Come back in an hour. I'll have your goddamned money. But you leave Bright Hills and you don't come back, Vince. You've worn out your welcome."

Vince nodded. "Okay then. I'll be back in an hour, and then I'll get the hell out of Dodge. Ain't nothing going on in this town anyway." He pushed past Dante and stopped at the door. "How you doing with that Truth or Dare thing? I suppose you're winning."

"Last time I checked."

"What are you ahead by?"

"Why do you care?"

Vince held his hands up. "Cool down, man. I'm just curious to know how far ahead you are. Been here long enough to know it's a big thing in town, keeping people talking."

"I'm ahead by three-hundred dollars at the last official count."

"Well, shit." Vince pursed his lips and nodded, doing a great impression, Dante thought, of being impressed. "Good for you. When does the contest end?"

"This upcoming Saturday." Dante crossed his arms in front of him. "The cash isn't here in the restaurant, Vince. The mayor collected it."

"I ain't looking to steal nothing," Vince said, his expression souring. "I was just curious. Jesus, Dante. I know I ain't your favorite person, but give me a fucking break."

"I did give you a break."

Vince stared at Dante but couldn't maintain his expression of affronted indignation. His eyes hardened and he looked away. Dante's spine tingled a warning. Vince was sure as hell up to something.

"What do you want from me, Vince?"

Vince's eyes moved upward and his dark gaze locked onto Dante's. "Besides that five hundred you're giving me to save my ass and send me on my way? Anything I can get," he said, then turned and walked away.

Chapter 14

Brenna came in through the rear door of the Lump & Grind, stopped by her office to stow her purse, and speed walked through the tiny L&G kitchen—*soon to be expanded, please god*—and into the front of the house where a crowd had gathered to drink designer coffee, nosh pastries, and wait for Brenna to make good on the last Bright Hills Truth or Dare Challenge.

"Hey," Shaniqua said when Brenna stepped up to the counter. "Word is the Bistro is ahead by five-hundred-and-fifty. Dante picked up a Dare for his last challenge." She grinned. "A few weeks ago he had to climb on top of the piano and sing. This week he had to get up there and dance, and word is he turned it into a striptease."

Brenna's eyes widened. "Excuse me?"

Shaniqua nodded, her dark eyes bright. "He turned it up for the ladies and they started throwing bills at him," she said and laughed.

Greta cackled and shook her head. The steel-gray bun into which she twisted her hair held fast as a tightened screw. "Wish I'da had the chance to see *that*. *Schöner mann*, that one. A big, strapping darling, he is. Let me tell you, *liebchen*, when I was younger—"

"What kind of striptease?" Brenna demanded.

"The kind where all the women handed over their hard-earned money to watch him shake his booty and do sexy things with his tie," Shaniqua replied.

"Dear god." Brenna covered her mouth with her hand. She didn't know whether to be irritated at the lengths to which the man went to win the contest, jealous that he'd used his considerable sex appeal on other women, or disappointed that she'd missed the show. All three, she supposed, though she intended to demand a private performance, and the thought mollified her a bit.

"Sorry you missed it, eh?" Greta patted Brenna on the back. "Relax, boss lady. Mrs. Feinbacher put twenty dollars into the Bistro jar, said he only teased them a little. Your man didn't go showing off his great, big, bulging—"

"Oh, honey, *please*," Brenna said, her cheeks heating.

"Ha, ha! I was gonna say his great, big, bulging *muskeln*—muscles." Greta clapped her hands and her laughter escalated. "What'd you think I was talking about? Ha, ha, ha!" The old woman wiped her eyes and strode off toward the kitchen, still hooting with laughter.

Brenna blew out a relieved breath of air, a little ashamed at where her mind had gone.

"The Bistro is winning now, by a couple hundred dollars," Shaniqua said. "We're in second place, so whatever you pull out of the jars today better be good."

Brenna nodded and put forth a show of steely determination, but disappointment dropped like a stone to her belly. She had damn well intended to win this thing, had wanted the silly trophy here at the L&G, not shining behind the bar at Dante's Bistro. Damn the man. Did he have to best her at everything?

Had the disparity in their collected amounts been under a hundred dollars, she might have a chance at meeting it, but a couple hundred? No way would this crowd fork over that kind of money, and it was against the rules for her to pay into her own kitty.

"Quiet down, y'all," Brenna called out to her chatting customers and waited for their attention. "As everyone knows, today is the final day of the first annual Bright Hills Truth or Dare Challenge. All the donations will be used to help hire our very own sheriff."

"I hope they hire someone who looks like Ryan Gosling, and I'll park illegally just so he can give me a ticket!" Raelynn called out, and everyone laughed.

Brenna acknowledged the comment with a smile and got back to business.

"I just learned that Dante's Bistro is ahead by several hundred dollars, so if we want the L&G to win, we have to reach deep, y'all. Remember now, this is for the good of our little town. It's high time the folks in Bright Hills have their own sheriff. Let's make it happen!"

The crowd clapped, and someone shouted, "Hurry up and pick from the jars, Brenna. I've got a soccer game to get to."

"Right." She nodded, and made a show of wriggling her fingers and loosening up before reaching first into the Truth jar, and then into the Dare jar. The bell over the door jangled, and she glanced up to see Vince saunter in. He took a few steps inside, but stayed at the back of the crowd with his arms crossed over his chest. He winked at Brenna, and she afforded him a polite smile.

"Okay, folks. Here we go." She held up the first paper. "Truth: Would you ever date a married man?" Her disappointment doubled. What a silly question. No one would pay good money for an answer to that. She looked over the crowd and saw Duke watching her with a goofy grin on his face. He adjusted his omnipresent John Deere cap and dropped his gaze to her chest. Brenna sighed. In her mind's eye, the trophy grew legs and walked out the door.

"And the Dare: Eat ten of Greta's famous cinnamon buns in less than a minute." *Seriously?* She swallowed an inward groan. Dante got to do a striptease on his piano, which even *she* would pay money to see, and the best her customers could come up with was a redneck contest to see how fast she could gorge on pastries. As Maddie would say, *sweet*

Lord! The cartoon trophy in Brenna's imagination laced up its running shoes and sprinted toward the Bistro.

"So what will it be, folks? Donations for the Truth? Anyone?"

"I've got a big Hamilton for you here, Brenna!" Duke waved a ten dollar bill over his head and pushed his way to the counter, his beer belly leading the way. His hungry gaze dropped to her boobs and she snatched the ten from his fingers.

"Why, Duke, bless your heart, thank you so much," Brenna said with honeyed sweetness. "Anyone else?"

Vince raised his hand and strolled toward the counter.

"Hello, Vince. Are you donating for the Truth or the Dare today?

"Neither one of those that you've pulled out of the jar." He dug into his pocket and came up with five crisp one-hundred dollar bills which he held up before the crowd. "I have a suggestion for a Dare that beats either of those, and if this fine crowd agrees and pitches in, all this money goes to your win."

The sight of serious money quieted all the chattering.

Brenna's shoulders tightened with a warning tingle. "What is it you're suggesting?"

"Well, now, I understand that a few weeks ago you kissed someone for your Dare, and I also understand that it maybe wasn't quite the kiss your admirers here was hoping to see." He waved the hundred dollar bills at the crowd. "Ain't that right?"

"Now that you mention it," Mrs. Feinbacher said, "it was a little tame." She plucked something from her sweater and sniffed.

The tingle across Brenna's shoulders grew stronger, and the rock of disappointment in her belly plopped over with a nauseating thud. She gulped. She didn't like where this was going. She didn't like it at all.

Vince turned his dark gaze on Brenna. "This five hundred pays for this Dare: I get to kiss you—really kiss you,

Beautiful, and you know what I'm talking about." He made eyes at the crowd and garnered a few laughs. "And I get twenty seconds for every hundred dollars in my hand."

Brenna's eyes widened and she stared speechless at Vince. His smile crept upward as a murmur went through the gathering. The buzz of conversation rose to a crescendo as the chatter began. Wallets came out of pockets and purses flew open.

Brenna looked around and wondered how many of the Bright Hills residents whipping out money to pimp out her lips for an L&G win would be doing the same thing tomorrow for the benefit of the collection plate at church.

Bless the sweet little baby Jesus, she thought and shook her head.

"We collected almost another hundred," Shaniqua said a few minutes later. She leaned in and whispered to Brenna, "Look at everyone, Brenna. You have to do it, you know you do. This will give us the win."

Brenna's heart thudded in her chest and her face heated with discomfort as she considered the possible ramifications of kissing Vincent Caravicci for the Truth or Dare Challenge. The pros and cons raced through her mind. There were several pros, including the collection of an additional six hundred big ones for the Bright Hills sheriff's fund and the entertainment of her customers, not to mention the obvious: It would clinch a win for the L&G.

The cartoon trophy stopped short outside the door to Dante's Bistro, turned around, and sprinted back through the door of the L&G, smiling at her and pumping its fist in a show of sure victory.

She didn't want to kiss Vince, hoped she could stand it without gagging. That was the only con as far as she could see. Well, that and Dante's reaction when he found out what she'd done. But he was as competitive as she, always "in it to win it."

And what was it he had said to her in Maddie's kitchen after the wedding? '*I'll do whatever I have to do to win.*

You'd do well to remember that, sweetheart.' Well, Brenna would do whatever she had to do to win, too, and Dante was about to find that his words applied to her also. He couldn't get mad at her for doing what he would do under the same circumstances. And the man had performed a flipping strip-tease this morning, thank you very much, even if he had, by all accounts, kept it G-rated.

Stripteases and kissing? This Truth or Dare Challenge would require serious rules and regulations before she'd participate next year, and she'd say it to the mayor in no uncertain terms.

Vince's eyes glittered and he held out the five hundred dollars. "Well?"

Brenna gnawed the inside of her mouth and did battle with herself while she considered her counteroffer. "Not at twenty seconds per hundred. Knock it to one second and you're on."

Vince gave her look of derision and snorted. "Please. My money needs to buy me something. I ain't settling for less than fifteen."

"I won't agree to more than five."

His face beamed with a satisfied smile and he held out his hand to shake on it. "Five seconds per hundred it is. That's thirty seconds of my mouth on yours, a real kiss, not some half-assed version. You ready to do this, Beautiful?"

Brenna glanced over the jittery crowd and nodded. "Bet your ass."

A shout went up and her customers cheered approval. Cell phones went up to record the event.

Brenna cast a nervous glance at Shaniqua.

"You know this guy, right? He's not some random stranger?" Shaniqua asked, and at Brenna's nod the other woman gave her a thumbs-up. "Then you've got this. It's no big deal. Just a stupid kiss, right? And it's for a good cause. Think of it like a sorority kissing booth. Didn't you tell me you worked one of those at a college fundraiser once?"

"Yes. But that was a long time ago, and—"

"Well, this isn't any different than that. At least you're not in a secluded booth, right?"

The warning tingle across Brenna's shoulders vibrated through her extremities. She shook her hands and arms to loosen up and relax and ignored the miserable burn in her belly.

"Thirty seconds, Shaniqua, and not one nanosecond more," Brenna said.

Shaniqua nodded and set the timer on her cell phone. "Thirty seconds."

Brenna gulped down her trepidation and looked at Vince. "Okay," she said. "Let's get this over with. And don't get funny. If you try to do anything besides kiss me, I get to keep the money and the Dare is off."

"What could I do? There's a dozen of your redneck friends in here that'll beat the shit out of me if I touch you wrong."

Brenna glanced around at her customers. She didn't see too many friends, just a lot of people who had paid good money to watch her do something she knew was stupid.

c∕∂e∕∂

Dante strode down the sidewalk toward the Lump & Grind. Brenna would be in the middle of her last Truth or Dare and he wanted to be there to rub in his win, not in a mean-spirited way, but enough to rile up her customers into upping donations more than they already had. No way the L&G could win, of course.

The Bistro was so far ahead of the other participating businesses that he had already cleared a spot behind the bar for the trophy. Still, it would be nice if Brenna could give a good showing.

He saw the laughing and clapping crowd through the big front window, the raised cell phones, and heard the noise before he opened the door and walked in.

"Hey, Duke," Dante said to the big guy in the John Deere cap. "What's going on?"

"Some guy just paid five hundred bucks to kiss Brenna Kinkaid." He adjusted his cap and shook his head. "Damn sure wish I'd thought of it. Worth every penny, I bet."

Dante blinked at Duke, digesting the other man's words. "Someone paid—I'm sorry, what?"

"See for yourself." Duke turned his bulk sideways to invite Dante's view of the event. "Five hundred bucks, plus another hundred collected from the bunch of us." He indicated the room full of people with a wave of his hand. "Lucky sonofabitch. They been going at it about twenty seconds now, I reckon." He snorted out a laugh and slapped Dante on the back. "You can kiss that trophy goodbye, my friend. That baby is going to be right here at the Lump & Grind. This is better than damn reality TV, right here." Duke guffawed. "Love this Truth or Dare thing."

Dante looked past Duke, around the bobbing heads and recording cell phones, toward the front of the shop. His vision tunneled and a dead weight slammed into his chest.

There was Brenna—*his Brenna*—with Vince's mouth on hers, and the man's hands edging toward her hips.

All the air evaporated from the room and Dante's throat closed up, strangling him. The noisy chatter and catcalls reduced to a peripheral buzz while he watched Vince plunder Brenna's mouth, watched Brenna not pull away. Vince tugged her closer and her palms flattened against his chest. The crowd loved it.

Dante existed in a vacuum for what seemed millennia, and then Shaniqua shouted, "Time!"

Brenna pushed away from Vince like she'd been shot from a cannon, and she wiped her mouth with the back of her hand. Vince stumbled back in the opposite direction from the force of her movement. Someone made a comment about him being too dazed by the gorgeous Brenna to stand up of his own accord, and Vince agreed that those thirty seconds were the best five-hundred bucks he'd ever paid for anything. And then, as if drawn by a magnet, his eyes darted up and his gaze met Dante's across the room. His lips curled into the snide smile Dante hated, the one he'd seen a thousand times before. The one that sneered, *I win.*

"We win!" Shaniqua shouted the words to the crowd and a roar went up in the L&G. Brenna became the object of a group hug by all of her employees, except for Greta, who stood behind the counter grinning and shaking her head. The pretty teenager, Kaitlyn, even hugged Ed, the boy Brenna said worshiped the girl from afar. Ed's face reddened, and he appeared amazed at his own good fortune to find the girl of his dreams squeezing the stuffing out of him.

Don't get too excited about it, kid, Dante thought, forcing himself to breathe. *It won't last past a second.*

Someone in Brenna's group pointed him out to Brenna, and she beamed a happy smile on him, shouting, "The L&G just kicked the Bistro's ass!" Another round of cheers went up from her loyal band of coffee addicts, and two of her male customers lifted her onto the counter to do a happy dance.

Dante watched the celebration while his emotions roiled. He tamped down the misery he couldn't dissolve, left it to simmer while the image of Vince kissing Brenna embedded itself in his brain on a permanent loop. He'd become a master of controlling those undesirable emotions. Life had taught him that cold deliberation won more personal victories than shows of temper ever would. It was the practice of this understanding that had made him a solid army ranger. He reminded himself of this now. Repeated it like a mantra.

"Told you she'd kiss me."

Dante's focus turned from Brenna to Vince. He hadn't seen his cousin sidle up to him. He stared at Vince, at the diamonds flashing from his earlobes, at the sleek ponytail hanging to his shoulder blades, and wondered how two men who grew to maturity in the same household could be so different. Vince turned his head to look at Brenna, a bold perusal, and Dante's anger flared, in spite of his efforts to keep it controlled. He forced himself to breathe with even inhalations, and held his fisted hands at his sides.

"There was no wager, Vince, nothing to be gained. And now you're out the five hundred."

"It was worth every penny just to see the look on your face."

"You need a new hobby." Dante pushed past Vince toward the door, and Vince grabbed his arm.

"Beautiful's hotter than fucking fire and built like a wet dream. No wonder you don't want to share."

Dante's fist smashed into Vince's cheekbone like the hammer of Thor. Those closest to the action gasped and scurried out of the way as Vince flew back onto one of the tables, knocking it to its side and upending a couple of chairs. He slid to the floor and shook his head like a cartoon character seeing stars.

"Stay out of my life." Dante's voice, low and dangerous, sounded loud in the pregnant hush of the coffeehouse.

So much for cold deliberation, he thought.

Pissed off at both Vince and Brenna, and now at himself for taking Vince's bait, he strode from the Lump & Grind without a backward glance.

☙❧☙

Brenna jumped down from the counter and started to go after Dante, then paused at Vince's feet. The woman-in-love part of her ached to go after her man and do some damage control, and it engaged in a furious battle with the businesswoman side of her that said she needed to stay and make sure Vince was okay. The last thing she needed was to be sued for his injuries sustained in her place of business.

Brenna made up her mind and looked from Vince to Shaniqua. "Can you—"

"Yes, go on." She waved Brenna toward the door. "I'll take care of this lunkhead. You go fix things."

The hushed crowd parted for her like the Red Sea.

She pushed through the door of the L&G and sprinted down the sidewalk after Dante. She called to him, but he walked without changing his pace. Was he ignoring her? Maybe he couldn't hear her voice over the rise and fall of Bright Hills' Saturday noise. Car engines idled waiting for the red light at Main and Bright to turn green, and shouts from little league spectators urging their kids to "*get a piece of that ball!*" emanated from the park. She wove through the pedestrian traffic with speed, but took care lest she knock people over in her haste to reach the fast-striding Dante.

"Dante! Will you please wait?"

She grabbed his arm when she caught up to him, and he turned and pulled free at the same time. Breathless, she stared at him, and his expression shot a mountain of sickening dread into her chest and stomach.

He regarded her through shuttered eyes, and the cold blasted from him with more power than the punch he had delivered to Vince.

She swallowed and forced her words through dry lips. "What happened back there?"

He studied her for several seconds, and when he spoke his tone was clipped and distant. "I apologize for the disruption to the L&G, but my cousin deserved what he got, and I guess I've earned an assault charge if he chooses to file one. Don't worry about any liability to your place. This is between me and Vince. By the way, congratulations on your win."

Stunned, Brenna stood rooted when he walked away. Presented with his back, it took several seconds to power her legs into movement.

"Dante, wait. Please." She loped to keep up with him, but he kept walking. "Damn it all, will you wait?" He stopped a few feet short of the Bistro patio but didn't turn around, making it necessary for Brenna to step in front of him to see his face. "Are you mad because I won, or because I kissed your stupid cousin? Or both?"

"It wouldn't matter. The result is the same." He spoke in the same quiet, disaffected voice.

"And what result is that?" Her heart slammed against her chest and brought an ache she'd never in her life experienced before now.

"Maybe we can talk sometime after all of this blows over. It's still pretty raw."

He made a move to go past her, but she blocked his way. Her heart pounded a painful beat, and her chest ached from a cache of building fear. Nausea roiled in her stomach. "Maybe we can talk *sometime? Maybe?* What's going on here Dante? At least tell me which thing to apologize for first."

"There's no apology required or expected."

She sidestepped to block him again. "So, you're pissed off because I found a way to win the Challenge?"

"No. But I don't think it's unreasonable of me to be bothered by the fact that another man just had his tongue in your mouth."

She cringed. "Look, it's possible I showed poor judgment, but—"

"*It's possible* you showed poor judgment? Are you joking right now?"

At last, she thought, *some real emotion.*

He practically had righteous indignation billowing out of his ears now, and while its companion was anger, that was at least something she could work with. Better than the cold stone wall he'd presented her at first.

"Okay, you're right. I absolutely showed poor judgment. But let me explain. Just look at it from my point of view, Dante. It was an easy five-hundred dollars from Vince, another hundred from the crowd, a sure win, and only thirty seconds of—" She bit off her words and gulped when the muscle in his jaw tightened and his eyes, already angry, darkened to black ice. "Look, it's not like I cheated on you, or like it will ever happen again." Maybe she'd screwed up, but he could at least show a willingness to straighten things out, couldn't he? She was making an effort to apologize here. "I made a mistake, and I'm truly sorry. I won't do anything like that again." She implored him with her eyes. "Will you please forgive me? *Please*."

He glanced away, and when he looked back at her the stone wall had reassembled itself. "I apologize for not being clear before. We're done now, Brenna."

Brenna huffed out a long breath and threw her hands up. "Fine. We'll talk more after you get home tonight."

"No, we won't. You don't understand. When I said we're done, I meant—" He cut himself off. His eyes stared into hers and the cold hardness gave way to regret and then to resolve. "This relationship is over, Brenna."

His words washed over her in an icy wave of realization. Her insides shriveled, and it was a moment before she found air.

"You—you're breaking up with me over this? This stupid, *stupid* challenge and the idiotic thing I did to win?" The burn of unshed tears crept into Brenna's throat. Nausea swirled again and she swallowed it back. Full understanding settled over her, and her hand shook when she clutched his arm. "Dante, please don't do this."

"You basically sold yourself for five hundred dollars to someone you know I detest, someone whose single goal in life is to hurt me any way he can, and you did it just to win a contest." He softened his tone. "I'm sorry, but we're not coming back from this."

Heat and shame burned the skin of her neck and cheeks from the inside out. "I'm sorry. I'm so, so sorry. I just got caught up in the contest, Dante. I didn't think. My customers were excited and involved, and it seemed like a harmless way to up the kitty. So I agreed to do it. I shouldn't have, but I did. And maybe it was wrong—" Dante dropped his head back and emitted an exasperated laugh, and Brenna scrambled to amend her words. "Not maybe, not maybe. It *was* wrong. I know it was." Desperate to explain herself she added, "But now we have another six hundred dollars going toward the sheriff's fund. Six hundred bucks for a stupid thirty-second kiss that didn't mean anything anyway."

"Can you hear yourself? You still don't think you did anything wrong."

"I know I shouldn't have done it. But given the circumstances, don't you think you're overreacting?"

"How would you feel if I kissed another woman like that? Are you saying you'd be okay with it as long as it was for a good cause?"

"No, of course not. I'm just asking for a little grace here, Dante. I screwed up. It isn't the first time I've done something stupid, and it won't be the last."

"Well, you're a woman who likes to win."

"Bet your ass." She crossed her arms over her chest. "At least admit you're the same way. I understand you performed a striptease this morning." Indignation, and the need to climb out of the hole she had dug for herself, battled for precedence over her growing mountain of regret.

"Yeah, I pulled off my jacket and tie, and shook my ass a little. So I need to quit being a dick, right? I mean, the L&G won the challenge, and the town upped their sheriff's fund. And it was just a kiss. No big deal. And that's easy money, isn't it? Six hundred bucks for a thirty-second kiss."

She ignored his sarcasm, and in an effort to alleviate the mounting shame for her actions, she sniffed and said, "Yes, actually, when you break it down like that, it wasn't a bad trade."

"Six hundred for a kiss." Dante's gaze stayed steady and hard on hers. "What's he get for a thousand, Brenna? Blow job, or a quick lay?"

Brenna shrank back from his words. The blade of his sharp insult stabbed into her and twisted. The pain flooded through her heart and veins in a hot gush of vicious internal bleeding, some kind of black poison that sapped her strength and her breath.

The tears she held back earlier bubbled up, and she blinked to send them back, but in spite of her effort to stay her weeping, Dante dissolved into a faceless blur.

She squeezed her hands into aching fists to avoid slapping his face. Her fingernails dug into her skin with painful pressure. He deserved a blistering slap which her hands throbbed to deliver, but she held herself in check. In spite of what he'd just said to her, he was gentleman enough to regret his words later, and she knew him well enough to be certain he'd punish himself far more than she ever could—more, probably, if she didn't do it for him now with a strike across his cheek.

Blinded by tears and throbbing hurt, she pushed past him, stopping only long enough to say, "Well, you're right about one thing. We're done."

e⁄ɔe⁄ɔ

Dante nodded to Roxanne, the bartender. She poured another shot of Glenlivet, looked beyond him with wide eyes, and a moment later Chloe slid onto the barstool beside him. She nudged his shoulder with hers. He glanced at her, picked up the shot glass, and downed the contents. "Relax, I'm not driving. I'm sleeping in my office tonight." He looked from Chloe to Roxanne. "Just bring me the whole damn bottle." He took a wad of cash from his wallet and threw it on the bar. "Ring it up like a regular sale so our inventory isn't screwed." He glanced back at Chloe. "What?"

Chloe sighed. "You're being an idiot. Just call her."

"I don't want to call her." He opened the bottle Roxanne set before him and poured another shot. "You want some?"

"No thanks. That stuff ruins me." She watched him pound down another one and shook her head. "Look, I know what Brenna did was stupid, but she didn't do it to hurt you. She just got caught up in the moment and didn't think first. Haven't you ever done anything stupid without thinking? You know, maybe something completely idiotic and black-hearted, like...oh, I don't know...telling the woman you love, and who loves you back, that she's a dirty rotten whore?"

"I didn't say that."

Chloe pursed her lips and gave him a scalding look. "Didn't you?"

Dante scowled at her and poured another shot, which he opted to nurse this time around. He might be an idiot Neanderthal, but he wasn't one hundred percent senseless. It only felt that way at the moment. He sipped and stared at the glass, which was getting blurrier by the minute. "Do you women tell each other every damn thing?"

"Maybe." She grabbed the bottle, sniffed the contents, and wrinkled her nose. "Nasty."

Dante grabbed the bottle away from her and set it out of her reach. "You're talking about a hundred-and-fifty dollar bottle of scotch. Show some respect."

"I don't care how much it costs. It's still nasty."

"Why are you busting my ass?"

"Because you're being stupid in the extreme. Call. Brenna. Now. Apologize for what you said, let her apologize for what she did, and you two can fix this. The longer you wait, the harder it will be."

Dante considered his words. It wasn't a stretch that whatever he told Chloe would make its way through the great and fearsome female grapevine. Best to take advantage of that, he decided, and save all of their mutual and well-meaning friends a lot of trouble.

"Yeah, here's the thing, Chloe." He looked at her, made direct eye contact. "You're making the assumption that I want her back. I don't." He waited while that sank in, knew that it had when Chloe's expression registered surprised understanding.

The young woman gulped and lowered her gaze, nodded, and murmured, "Okay." She slid off the barstool and gave him a quick hug, patted his back. "I think you're an idiot, but I love you anyway. See you tomorrow, boss."

Dante sat at the bar until the last of his crew left for the night. He grabbed his bottle, set the alarm, and turned out lights as he made his way to his office. Once there he attempted to crash, but the last time he'd slept here Brenna had been with him, naked, warm, and supple in his arms, and the memory twisted in his gut and sent him shooting up from the couch like the cushions had caught fire. He capped the Glenlivet, stowed it in his desk drawer, and returned to the front of the house where he sprawled in one of the booths and made himself more miserable by replaying the day, from the moment he stepped into the Lump & Grind, to his nasty scene with Brenna outside the Bistro.

He stared at the ceiling, seeing nothing in the relative dark until his eyes adjusted, and for the first time since his grandmother died, he wished he could cry. Tears might ease the constriction in his chest, the ache of loss that ate a man from the inside out. Women—some, at least—found weeping cathartic, but he'd been unable to muster tears since he was eight and his aunt had beat the shit out of him with a broom for crying over a broken toy.

Not just any toy, he mused, and closed his eyes, squeezed them tight for a moment to dispel the tired sting. A Transformer action figure. Optimus Prime, a birthday gift to Dante from his grandmother. He had been so excited that he didn't want to play with it, didn't want to risk anything happening to his personal treasure, so he'd hidden it under his bed to keep it safe. But nothing was safe from Vince, who whined to his mother, and Aunt Esther insisted Dante share.

Even the great and powerful Optimus Prime couldn't survive Vincent Caravicci. Vince threw it from the window of the family sedan while driving down the highway to Sunday church. Uncle Stan stopped for it on the way home two hours later, but by then it had been smashed by other traffic, tossed like trash across the blacktop. Even so, Dante spent days trying to fix it. Aunt Esther found him crying on the front stoop with the broken toy in his hands, and she'd taken the broom to him to "give him something to cry about." Vince watched his beating from around the corner of the house, his lips curved in the same smile he'd shown Dante earlier at the L&G. *I win*, said that smile, and damned if it wasn't true more often than not.

It took Dante weeks to jerry-rig Optimus Prime into a toy worth keeping. But by then, the only way to protect it from Vince was to give it away. It drove Vince to the edge of crazy, watching Dante give that refurbished toy to a neighbor kid, like it meant nothing. Optimus Prime preceded an endless parade of things and relationships that Vince ruined only to hurt Dante, and Vince was ever frustrated by Dante's easy release of ownership. Letting go was, in a very real sense, Dante's only sure win.

Vince never understood that Dante gave away the things he cared about most in order to protect them, and to protect himself, from further loss.

And also, if Dante was being honest, once Vince put his hands on something, it lost its shine and never quite regained its former worth. It was as if the touch of Vince's hands on a thing had the power to eliminate any desire Dante had to possess it. Letting go had always been easy.

Until now.

Brenna wasn't a thing, of course. She was his heart, she was *everything*, and she was supposed to be his. But she had been disloyal to him with that kiss in ways she couldn't comprehend, and he was incapable of explaining it to her. He wasn't sure he fully understood the dynamics himself, only knew that the betrayal went too deep, and because of that, the best solution for both of them was letting go.

He made a fist and rubbed it over the pain in his chest, massaged the Celtic cross as if it had the power to heal him. He hurt in places he couldn't reach, and his misery redoubled as Brenna's face floated into his mind. In spite of everything that happened that day, despite his need to let loose of things he cared about too much to keep, the woman would forever and always own him in a million different ways.

Dante covered his eyes with his arm and prayed for sleep that he knew wouldn't come.

❧❧❧

Brenna snatched a tissue from the box and tried to blow her nose, but the problem was sinuses swollen from hours of weeping. She balled up the tissue and breathed through her mouth. More tears welled, and she blinked, tumbling them onto her cheeks. Maddie tried to console her by rubbing her back.

"What was I thinking, kissing that idiot Vince?" Brenna shuddered a breath in and then out again. "I knew better, and I did it anyway."

"Was it at least worth it? I mean, he's a great looking guy if you're into bad boys, right? Pretty good kisser?" Rebecca said. Maddie glared at Rebecca, and Brenna choked out a sob. Rebecca wrinkled her nose and drew Brenna into a hug. "I'm sorry. I'm just trying to lighten things up a little. Epic fail."

"He's an awful kisser," Brenna stammered. "Like, a two, maybe. Why did I do it? Why? I knew it had to be a full-on kiss, and I agreed to it anyway. What kind of idiot does that?"

"The kind who likes to win," Rebecca replied. "Look, if it had been anyone but Vince, Dante would still be pissed off about it, but I don't think he would've broken up with you, or said what he said. Which was a total dick move on his part, by the way."

Brenna shredded the tissue and nodded then shrugged. "Good to know what he really thinks of me, I guess."

"You know better than that. That was just his anger talking," Maddie said.

"Still a dick move," Rebecca insisted, "and I can say that with impunity because he's like my second brother. He shouldn't have said something like that. But I agree that it was just his anger talking."

"No, it wasn't." Brenna wiped her eyes for the hundredth time. "I believe he meant it. Y'all didn't see his face, the look in his eyes. He was—" She sighed and blinked back more tears. "—done. Just—just done. With me." Her shoulders slumped and she pressed the heels of her hands against her eyes. A pitiful laugh escaped her lips and tears trickled out, a fresh flow. *How could anyone have so many tears?* "Oh, honey, look at me. I'm a mess, and all because of the damned Neanderthal. If you had told me six weeks ago I'd be crying a river over that man, I wouldn't have believed it."

"A lot can happen in six weeks," Rebecca said.

"Sweet Lord, can it ever," Maddie agreed. "And you need to remember that, Brenna, because six weeks from now things could be different again. Things could be better with you and Dante."

Brenna forced a smile through the blur and patted Maddie's leg. "Thanks for trying to cheer me up, but this is broken, and I don't think it will be fixed anytime soon."

The doorbell rang and Brenna sprang off the couch. Her eyes widened and she stared at Maddie and Rebecca, unmoving.

"I'll get it." Rebecca squeezed Brenna's arm on her way to the door. "False alarm," she called out a moment later. "It's only Chloe."

"Hey." Chloe walked into Brenna's living room and held up a bottle of wine. "Sorry to come by so late, but I figured you'd be up, and I thought you could use this. It's a lot less lethal than what my boss is pounding down."

"Oh, yeah?" Rebecca encouraged her with a nudge.

"He put down half a bottle of scotch before eleven-thirty, and he hadn't fallen off the barstool yet, so he might still be sitting there." Chloe put the wine down and hugged Brenna. "He's miserable as hell. Does that help at all?"

Brenna nodded. "A little. Did he—did he say anything? About maybe calling me or something?"

Chloe's eyes widened and she gulped. "Uh, well, you know, he's still pretty pissed off."

"What did he say, Chloe?" Brenna held the other woman by the shoulders. "Please. If he said something, you have to tell me."

Chloe's expression fell and she shook her head. "He's not going to call you."

"What did he say? Exactly."

Brenna caught Chloe's gaze in a chokehold, and for the first time in hours her tears had dried up. That was something, anyway.

"Look, I don't think—"

"What did he say, Chloe? Please."

Chloe sighed and her shoulders drooped. Her voice came through her lips in a miserable whisper. "He said he doesn't want you back."

Brenna nodded, and apparently the tears hadn't dried up, because her chest constricted and the salty bastards bubbled up and out again. "Okay. Well." Brenna wiped her eyes and straightened her shoulders. "He's going to have to rethink that position, because I don't aim to give up without a fight."

"Even after what he said to you?" Chloe asked.

"He said that to piss me off," Brenna replied, her brain engaging in something other than self-flagellation for the first time in hours. "Because he wanted to be sure I wouldn't do what I'm going to do."

"What is that?" Maddie asked.

"Oh, honey," Brenna said, determination burning through her tears. "I'm going to win him back."

Chapter 15

It was the longest three weeks of Brenna's life, during which her strategy was simple: show the man what he'd thrown away and make him want it back.

Success had eluded her so far, but she had no intention of giving up yet.

She had enjoyed lunch at the Bistro with Maddie and Rebecca multiple times over the last few weeks, and dinner as well, once with her parents, and once with Sean and Rebecca. To his credit, Dante had not practiced avoidance. He had visited their table every time, had been so damned polite and oozing charm from every pore, that Brenna wanted to kick him in the shins.

Direct eye contact with her didn't bother the man either, damn it. He looked at her like he looked at everyone else, and the simplicity of *that*, that she was no longer special in his eyes, no different than the Marilyn Monroe-a-like sitting at the bar right now—and watching him with the same kind of focus as a red-tailed hawk tracking a bunny—hurt more than anything else he might have done. She wanted to see desire, anger, regret—*something, for the love of god, anything*—but he continued to maintain a cool distance, as if they had never been lovers, had never said harsh words, had never parted in anger.

Brenna perused the menu and checked the time on her

phone. Where was Maddie? She was supposed to be here ten minutes ago.

The blonde, who Brenna remembered from the day she had come to the Bistro for lunch with Sean and Mrs. M, slid off her barstool when Dante approached. They spoke for a few seconds, and then the woman cried, "That's *perfect!*" and threw herself into his arms. Dante laughed and accepted her hug with easy grace.

"I can't tell you how excited I am," the woman said, all smiles. She grabbed her Ann Klein clutch from the top of the bar and drew Dante into another hug. "Call me the minute you're out of here, handsome, and I'll have everything ready for you."

Dante agreed with a nod, and accepted another quick hug from the woman when they reached the door.

Brenna's heart sank to her toes. This was bad. He'd replaced her fast, and with a woman who looked like she belonged in a clingy evening gown while on stage singing, "Happy birthday, Mr. President." The woman's boobs preceded her to the door, and Brenna shifted in her seat with discomfort. The man certainly had a type.

The door opened up. The sexy blonde breezed out, and Maddie flew in. Dante himself led her to Brenna's table and held the chair for her.

"Ladies, Gemma will be with you in a moment. Can I get you something while you wait? The rosemary focaccia is fresh from the oven, and if you're drinking wine this afternoon, we have a new pinot grigio I think you'll enjoy."

"I prefer red, if you don't mind." Brenna worked to keep her tone even.

"Merlot. I remember." His dark gaze held hers for a second and his jaw tensed before he smiled and turned to Maddie. "Mrs. Walker?"

"Oh, I do like the sound of that name," Maddie said. Her lips curved in a happy smile. "I'll try the pinot grigio. And the focaccia."

"Coming right up," Dante said. With his smile back in place, he left them and strode toward the bar.

"You okay?" Maddie laid her hand over Brenna's.

"Well, he grimaced at me for a second. That's progress." Brenna's lips curved in a little half smile. She plucked at the linen napkin lying over her lap and then gave her attention to the rim of her water glass before meeting Maddie's sympathetic gaze. "Do you think I'm wasting my time, Mads? It's been three weeks, and the man won't look sideways at me."

Maddie shrugged. "I don't know. I've tried to pry information out of Caleb, but he told me Dante isn't even talking to him about it. I nagged him to broach the subject when they did their basketball thing Saturday morning, but Dante shut him down. Men just aren't that chatty, you know?"

"I need to stop playing games. I've eaten more meals here at the Bistro in the last three weeks than I did in the last three months. He's not an idiot. He has to know why I keep showing up."

Brenna plucked at her napkin again and stole a glance around the room, lighting her gaze on Dante where he stood chatting with a man and woman near the patio door.

He looked so handsome in his dark suit, with the jacket tapering from his broad shoulders down to narrow hips. His hair needed a trim, and she folded her hands in her lap to stop the annoying itch that made her consider jumping up to comb her fingers through the curling ends. The woman said something, and her companion guffawed.

Dante dropped his head back and laughed with them, and the sound of his laughter made Brenna's chest ache.

"He doesn't know it yet, but we're having a conversation tonight whether he likes it or not," Brenna told Maddie.

"How are you going to manage that?"

"I'll wait until he gets home and I'll bang on his door until he lets me in. And if that doesn't work, I'll press the damned doorbell nonstop. Pavarotti hates the doorbell, and he'll howl." Brenna lifted her napkin, turned it over, and smoothed it over her lap. "Enough is enough. It's time to fix this thing."

❧❦❧

Dante stood with his back to the wall, ostensibly scanning the dining room for guests who might need attention. His gaze returned again and again to Brenna, who toyed with her napkin nonstop. He recognized that nervous tell, and he imagined giving her something else to be nervous about, other than whatever had started her worrying the edges of the linen napkin with her fingertips.

Looking at her was always a pleasure. She was gorgeous, with those Kinkaid blues, flashing with her special inner light, peeking out from her bangs, grown just the slightest bit longer then the last time he'd smoothed them from her face. When she came into the restaurant with her sundress and heels showing off her tanned legs to their best advantage, every man in the room had rubbernecked to watch her walk to her table. *She used to be mine*, he had thought in the moment, and he thought it again now, watching her smile at Maddie and fiddle with the napkin. What would she do, he wondered, if he went over to the table right now, dragged her out of that chair, pulled her up against him, and—

"*Boss!*"

Dante shot from his reverie. His head snapped around toward Chloe who stood next to him holding an empty tray against her hip.

"Jesus, Chloe. What?"

"I've been trying to get your attention, but your mind is obviously elsewhere." Chloe looked from Dante to Brenna, and back to Dante with a meaningful lift of her brows. "Why don't you just go talk to her?"

"Do you want something, or are you just being a pain in the ass?"

"The garden club ladies are on the patio. They're requesting your presence."

"Great." He glanced back at Brenna and reminded himself that he had ended it for a reason. The loop in his brain replayed the image of her pressed against Vince, and he peeled his gaze away from her, feeling like a fool. He knew his imagination embellished the scene, made that kiss and her involvement in it far more engaged than it had been, but he was unable to control the bent of his mind. He knew, for instance, that her hands had been pressed flat against Vince's chest—*holding him back?*—but when Dante saw the image in his head, her hands curled into Vince's shirt to pull him closer. *No, that's what she did with you, idiot.* He sighed, told himself it didn't matter. The end result was still the same.

"Ask Gemma to comp Maddie and Brenna's meal. Bar tab too," he instructed.

His eyes refocused on Brenna. He forced his gaze away again and looked at Chloe to await her affirmative nod. He turned his back on the dining room, and Brenna. By the time he slowed down enough to watch her again, she and Maddie were gone.

He pushed through the rest of his day and left the restaurant after the dinner rush, leaving Chloe to handle closing. He called Monica as promised and arranged to meet her at his townhouse a few minutes later.

Dante slowed before he reached his driveway and sighed. Monica stood on his lawn with a hammer in one hand and a "for sale" sign in the other. Her spiked heels disappeared into the grass, and he wondered if they had sunk into the soil, soft from recent rain. She smiled when she spotted him and then returned to her chore.

"Let me help you with that." Dante strode to meet her and took over the task. "How's that?" He stepped back from the sign and waited for her approval.

She clasped her hands in front of her. "*Perfect!*"

"Why the sign? I thought you had buyers already."

"Oh, well, you know." Monica waved her hand and then tucked it into the crook of his arm to walk across the lawn. "The agency still wants the sign up, for advertisement. As soon as we get everything signed and a down payment, we'll add an 'under contract' notice on it." She released him when he opened the door and motioned her in ahead of him. She paused to lift the briefcase she had left by the front door.

"I really love this place, Dante. It's *perfect* for two people. Just *perfect*."

"Uh-huh." He showed her into the kitchen, where she took a seat at the table, declined his offer of refreshments, and withdrew documents from her briefcase.

"So, I understand you already talked to Sean Kinkaid about buying his place. I didn't realize you were friends."

"He's married to my best friend's sister," Dante said.

"Oh! So you know Rebecca, then." Monica beamed at him as if his knowledge of Rebecca was some special skill. "She's delightful. And just *glowing*, isn't she? I do wish you had waited for me to intervene for you, though. I'm certain I could have got them to come down on their price."

"I did my market research, and we're friends. I'm sure the price we agreed on is more than fair."

Monica opened her mouth and closed it again, perked up and said, "*Perfect*. And thank you so much for bringing me in to handle the sale."

Dante acknowledged her statement with a nod. "So what's the timeline going forward?"

"I've got some documents for you to sign, and I'm meeting with your potential buyers later this evening. I expect everything to move right along once we get the ball rolling."

"Well, then," Dante said. "By all means, let's roll."

ᏭᏒᏭ

Brenna saw the "for sale" sign as she drove toward her

townhouse. She idled the Audi in the street to stare with renewed misery at the sign in Dante's yard. Was the man really so eager to be away from her that he planned to move? Was next door just too close proximity given his distaste for her now?

The sick twisting in her gut that developed upon sight of the sign grew worse as she fixed her hair and makeup in preparation for a conversation that she hoped would be a precursor to reconciliation. That seemed less likely now.

Brenna stared at herself in the bathroom mirror and trepidation had her pulse points thrumming. She pushed at her hair with her fingers, for a moment wished it long again, and then strode to her closet for a change of clothes.

Here we are again, Jack, she thought. *A closet full of clothes I can't fit my fat ass into.*

She ran her fingertips over a few favorite items of clothing she knew would be too small since she'd put on weight—a pair of Ralph Lauren jeans that used to make her butt look great, capris the color of the Caribbean, and a matching top that brought out the indigo in her eyes. She paused at the new black dress from the Blueberry Boutique, still hanging in the protective plastic wrap. Dante had surprised her with it a few days after the demise of the original one that had given its all for the fulfillment of their lusty satisfaction.

Brenna closed her eyes and replayed the moment she opened the door in that dress and heels, the look in Dante's eyes, and the swiftness with which he had ripped the garment off of her, eager to caress bare skin. Her body responded to the memory and she opened her eyes and emitted a tremulous sigh. That night seemed an eternity ago.

In the end, she stayed in the sundress and heeled sandals she had worn to the Bistro. She had turned enough male heads on her walk through the restaurant at lunchtime to be assured the garment complimented the curves she yearned to get under control.

She smoothed her hands over the front of the dress and

blew out a long breath of air. "It's now or never, Jack," she said aloud and took the first steps toward Dante's. She gave herself a pep talk about knocking on his door with confidence, but the opportunity eluded her. He was on his way out as she trod up the few steps to his door.

They avoided a collision by mere inches, and stared at each other in surprise. Brenna snapped her mouth shut when her voice evaporated. She hadn't been this close to him in forever, so near she could see the dark depths of his eyes, and the details of the slim scar Vince had laid into his face. The thought of Vince brought everything about that awful day in the L&G flooding back into her mind, and her face heated with renewed shame that she had done something so awful that Dante had made the decision that he didn't want her anymore.

Dante's expression shifted from surprise to cool regard, and Brenna felt the immediate chill.

"What can I do for you, Brenna?"

The distant tone of his voice brought quick moisture to her eyes and she glanced away toward the "for sale" sign and blinked back the threat of tears.

"So, you're moving. Have you found a new place?" She turned back to him with her emotions under control.

"I guess you haven't talked to Sean or Rebecca. I'm buying their house in town."

"Oh." Brenna nodded, forced a smile. "I knew you had discussed it. I didn't realize it was a done deal. That'll be an easy walk to work for you. Sean walks to his office almost every day. And it's a great house. Since he and Rebecca got married, they've made some nice upgrades."

"Yeah, I know." Dante cleared his throat and looked into the mid distance for a moment before looking back at Brenna. He jangled the keys in his hand. "Is there something else? I've got somewhere to be."

"Oh, um, no." She shook her head, and Jack's voice whispered in her ear, '*Quit being such a coward, meatball.*' "I mean, yes." She straightened her shoulders and lifted her chin. "We need to talk, Dante. We can't just leave things hanging like this."

His dark gaze bore into hers, and she swallowed back the hovering waterworks, squeezed her hands into painful fists, her fingernails slicing into her palms. She would not cry standing here with him, she would not. She willed herself to stare back at him with dry eyes.

"Nothing is hanging, Brenna," Dante said, and certain sorrow seeped into her because his voice was firm, but not unkind. "We were together, and now we're not. It doesn't have to be more complicated than that." He drew a deep breath, and his eyes softened to the warmth she loved, tinged now with infinite sadness. "Please, Brenna. Please don't make it more complicated than that."

If he had yelled at her, called her names, repeated the nasty accusation he had made on the sidewalk in front of the Bistro, she might have found the inner strength and fire to argue until words powerful enough to change his mind poured out of her. Instead, she knew only sorrowful emptiness in the face of his quiet resolve.

Brenna stood rooted in painful silence as he stepped past her and walked to his car. She continued to stand motionless and aching long after his taillights disappeared from view. She didn't force her legs to move until the easy mountain breeze brought goosebumps to her skin, and fireflies dotted the yard, beaming for their mates in the early twilight.

∽∾∽

"Hard to believe the old bitch is dead. You leaving in the morning?" Trina leaned back in her chair and regarded Dante from across the desk in the office of Caravicci's Pizzeria. At his answering nod, she added, "How long will you be gone?"

"A couple of days. I'll leave for home right after the funeral." He drummed his fingers on the arms of the guest chair. It always felt odd for him to come in here and not be the one sitting behind the desk, but Trina looked right at home.

"Vince will be coming into some money, right? So maybe he'll stay in Asheville and leave you alone for a while."

"He's on probation for that stupid party stunt he pulled, so he's not supposed to leave Georgia, but it's Vince, so who knows what he'll do?" Dante shrugged. "Not my circus, not my monkeys."

"He can at least go home for his mother's funeral though, right?"

Dante shrugged again. "I haven't talked to Vince since that day at the L&G. Everything I know I learned from Aunt Esther's sister, Olive. I'm guessing he'll go for the funeral and stay in Asheville to avoid probation. That's good for me, because it means he can't come back to Georgia without running the risk of jail time for skipping out. I'm traveling to Asheville alone, going to the funeral alone, and leaving alone. I don't know where Vince is or what he's doing, and I don't care."

"Right." Trina bit her lip and nodded. She scooted her chair closer to the desk, rested her arms on it, and leaned forward. "Listen, Dante. I know it's none of my business, but—"

"You're right, it's not. Stay out of it."

Trina straightened her posture and gave him a look. "You don't even know what I'm going to say."

"If it has anything to do with Brenna, I don't want to hear it."

"You're being a stubborn ass." Trina tucked her hair behind her ears and leaned back in her chair again. She shifted her gaze, and when she returned her focus to Dante, she lowered her voice and spoke her words with slow care. "I can only imagine how you felt, like maybe it was a déjà vu moment or something. But it wasn't. The circumstances were completely different than with—than before. Brenna didn't do it to hurt you. You know that. So punishing her this way doesn't make any sense."

"Is that what you think I'm doing?" Dante laughed without mirth. "The last thing I want to do is hurt Brenna. But what am I supposed to do when I can't close my goddamned eyes without seeing—" He pushed his hands through his hair, stood, and walked to the door. "This sounds crazy and possessive, but she was supposed to be mine. *Only mine.* What she did made a bold statement to the contrary, pretty damned loud and clear. She had a choice to make in the moment, Trina, and she made it."

Trina winced and swallowed hard. "But the circumstances matter, can't you see that? You're letting your history with Vince color your present with Brenna. That's a stupid thing to do. My god, Dante, the way you feel about Brenna is like a lightning strike. That doesn't just happen, and for some of us it won't ever happen at all. You're so damn lucky, and you're throwing it away."

Dante stared at Trina. He recognized those words. He had said something similar to Caleb once about Maddie.

"Thanks for taking care of Pav while I'm gone. I appreciate it," he said and headed out the door. When he glanced over his shoulder at Trina, she sat slouched in her chair, frowning at his back and shaking her head.

৩৩৩

Brenna opened the rear door of the L&G and peered out into the alley, relieved that the booming thunderstorm had passed. She waved goodbye to Shaniqua, who had offered to close up shop for the night, and locked up the L&G before walking to her car.

She paused with her hand on the driver's door of her Audi to cast a glance down the alley. Chloe's car sat at an angle among several others near the rear door of Dante's Bistro, but Dante's parking space was empty. She had heard through the grapevine that he was out of town for a funeral and wouldn't return to work until tomorrow.

Not that his schedule was any of her business anymore, but she had left her folder pertaining to the L&G at his house, and as she had made the decision to move forward with the expansion before summer's end, she needed to get it back.

God knew she needed to focus on something other than Dante Caravicci, and the Lump & Grind was the recipient of her time and energy.

After their encounter at his front door the other day, Brenna had come to the conclusion that further pursuit of Dante was pointless. Not forever, she reasoned, but for now. She told herself that they both needed distance and perspective, time to heal, and to think things through with more thoroughness than his kneejerk reaction to her idiotic decision to kiss Vince had allowed.

And, she reminded herself, he had insulted her with words that should never flow through the lips of a man who claims to love you.

Except, maybe he doesn't anymore. Maybe he never did.

The words hurt, but Brenna rolled them over and over in her mind as she drove the miles toward home. She didn't shut them out until the sky began spitting rain again. She clicked on her windshield wipers and slowed her speed to go around a curve in the road as the precipitation increased.

Headlights from an oncoming vehicle appeared the second Brenna turned into the curve. Fear slammed into her. She stomped her foot on the brakes and swerved onto the road's shoulder. The Audi jolted to a stop. The other vehicle zoomed around the bend and disappeared.

Heart pounding, body shaking, Brenna clutched the top of the steering wheel. She rested her forehead against it to steady herself and catch her breath. The windshield wipers slap-slap-slapped across the glass, and the sound reminded her of her recurring dream of Jack.

Her eyes welled with tears, and she didn't know now if she was crying over Dante or Jack, or both. "What do I do, Jack?" she whispered aloud, blinded by the rain and her own hot tears. "Please tell me, what do I do?"

She stayed unmoving on the gravel shoulder until her tears abated, and then she eased her car back onto the road and drove the rest of the way home.

Dante's car was not in his driveway, but Trina's Corolla was. It wasn't quite nine o'clock, so Brenna marched across the way to knock on the door. Best for her to collect what she needed while Dante wasn't home.

The door swung open and Brenna gave herself a mental head slap for rushing over without first freshening up and grabbing an umbrella. She suspected her eyes and nose were swollen from her crying jag, and the now sprinkling rain had dampened her hair and clothes. Trina, on the other hand, looked like her adorable elfin self, all perfect slenderness and wispy blonde hair, and her hazel eyes widened with surprise at the sight of Brenna.

"Hi." Trina offered a warm smile. "Come on in and get out of the rain." She stepped back to allow Brenna entry. "Dante's not going to be home for a few hours yet. He just called a little while ago to let me know he's stuck in some serious traffic due to an accident," Trina said while Brenna toed off her wet shoes by the door. "You know he went to Asheville for his aunt's funeral, right?"

Brenna followed Trina down the hall and into the kitchen. "I'm not actually here for Dante. I left a folder with some important papers in it, and I need it back. It was—" Brenna shifted her position and pointed to the breakfast bar. "—right there, under the basket. It's not there now, though." Uncomfortable being alone with Dante's too-cute ex-wife, she backed up a few steps, half turning to leave. "Would you mind asking Dante to return it to me? He'll know what it is I'm looking for."

"Wait." Trina touched her hand to Brenna's arm. "Please wait. I know what's going on with you and Dante isn't any of my business, but I think there are some things you should know."

Brenna steeled herself. The last thing she needed right

now was advice from the little elf. "You're right. It isn't any of your business. Thanks for letting me in, but I should go before Dante gets home."

Trina tightened her hold on Brenna's arm. "Please. I'm on your side here. I've known Dante since we were kids, and I can tell you unequivocally that the happiest I've ever seen him, ever, is when the two of you were together. Please, just sit with me for a few minutes."

Brenna stared into Trina's eyes, looking for a sign of insincerity, but instead saw genuine concern. She nodded and accepted Trina's offer for a cup of hot tea. While Trina brewed the tea, Brenna sat at the kitchen table and loved on Pavarotti who had positioned himself in her lap like the Sphinx. His purrs rent the air, and by the time the two women were situated for conversation, the cat had curled himself into a rumbling ball.

"Dante shipped Pav home from Afghanistan. Did you know that?" Trina asked, stirring a spoonful of honey into her tea.

Brenna nodded. "He told me the circumstances, about the little boy."

Trina's hand stilled. After a moment, she continued stirring, finally setting the spoon on a napkin and lifting the mug to sip the steaming brew. "That's interesting, because he never told me the details. In fact, he never told me anything about his time over there. He just wouldn't talk about it."

"He still doesn't, not really."

Trina set the mug down and met Brenna's gaze. "Did he ever tell you why we got divorced?"

"No, just that you were friends before you got married and stayed friends after your divorce. He made it sound uncomplicated."

"Typical Dante." Trina sighed and dropped her gaze, stared into the tea while her finger traced the edge of the mug.

Brenna said nothing, waited while the other woman put

her thoughts together. When Trina raised her eyes, Brenna saw misery in them.

"I kissed Vince."

Brenna sucked in a breath. The puzzle pieces began to shift.

"Totally different circumstance than with you, but to Dante, seeing you with Vince probably felt like history repeating itself." Trina blew out a long sigh and tucked her hair behind her ears. "Okay, let me go back so you understand how everything happened. We were friends from the time we were about ten—me, Dante, and Vince. I moved in across the street. Dante and I were best friends, right from the get-go, but I had a thing for Vince back then. Started big when I was about fifteen, I guess. Typical stupid girl, going for the bad boy, right? And he knew it, Vince did. He took advantage of me in a million different ways, and Dante was forever picking up the pieces and trying to smarten me up." Her lips twisted into a wry smile. "Always fixing things." She sipped her tea. "Did Dante ever explain what his home life was like?"

"No, but I got the impression it wasn't very happy."

"You're right about that. Dante and I had similar home situations. He was stuck living with his aunt and uncle, and his grandmother. His grandmother was great, but it wasn't her house either, you know? She had some health problems, so she was living on his aunt and uncle's good graces just like Dante was. His Uncle Stan was okay, and Dante worked with him at the pizza place all the time. But his aunt—the one who just died, whose funeral he's at—was a serious bitch. She thought Vince could do no wrong, and she'd beat the crap out of Dante every chance she got, until he got too big, and then she backed off.

"My situation wasn't any better. My mom remarried when I was little, and my stepfather was a religious nut. No matter what I did, it was bad in his eyes, so of course I was bad just to prove the point. Not very bright, because I got my ass beat on a regular basis, but there you have it. Anyway—" She shifted in the chair and fiddled with her mug. "—we muddled through, right? After high school, Vince went to work at his dad's pizza place, and I went to the community college. Dante got a full ride to Auburn—football scholarship—and that's where he met Caleb Walker. They were roommates. Did you know that?"

Brenna nodded and gave her an encouraging smile.

"While Dante was away at Auburn, Vince and I sort of got together. I say sort of, because even though we started sleeping together, it wasn't really a relationship. Dante was pissed off when he found out—not because he was jealous or anything, it wasn't like that with us—but because he couldn't believe my endless stupidity where Vince was concerned, and he knew Vince would only hurt me. Which of course he did, because he's Vince. It was a rough time for me.

"By that point, Dante had graduated from college and joined the army. His grandmother died, and that sent him into a tailspin. She was the only person in his world—and I mean the *only* one, except the Walkers—who never let him down. She was his rock, and losing her ripped his heart out.

"So, Dante came home for his grandmother's funeral, emotionally ruined, and I was a mess over damn Vince, so we got together to cry in our beer, got absolutely shit-faced, and ended up having sex. Talk about an awkward morning after." Trina blew out a little laugh. "I mean, we were best friends, you know? Not lover material. But shit happens, and a few weeks later I found out I was pregnant." Trina paused for a breath and gave Brenna a look. "You still with me?"

"Keep going."

"Okay. Well." Trina drew a deep breath and continued. "Because of the way I was raised, abortion was off the table. I told my mom and stepfather, hoping for support, but I should have known better. My stepfather threw me out of the house. I didn't have anywhere to go, so I called Dante with the news, and Dante, being Dante, stepped up to the plate. We got married right before he was deployed to Afghanistan the first time."

Trina stopped talking, and Brenna filled in the gap when the silence grew.

"That must have been hard for you, to be pregnant and alone with your new husband a whole world away."

Trina looked up from the mug and her hazel eyes glittered with emotion. "I was such an idiot. You want some more tea?"

"No thanks."

"I miscarried at five-and-a-half months. It was the worst experience of my life, and I wish I could say I handled it well, but I didn't. I couldn't go home—my mother stopped talking to me after my stepdad kicked me out—and I didn't want to be alone. It was unfair and childish, but I was angry with Dante for being away. For the first time since I'd known him, he wasn't there for me, and I blamed him. I was angry and stupid. In my mind, I knew it wasn't his fault. But in here—" She tapped her chest. "—all I knew was that I needed him, and he wasn't there. I wanted to punish him somehow, make him hurt too, and I knew how to do it.

"I invited Vince over to our apartment, and he showed up with a twelve-pack of beer and a smile. We got hammered which, after what happened with Dante, you'd think I would have learned my lesson. But no, not me. I remember sitting there in the living room thinking that I could kiss Vince, just one kiss, and Dante would never know. But it would be some kind of payback for him being gone." Trina's lips curled in a rueful half-smile. "I know that doesn't make any sense, but that's what went through my brain. So I let Vince pull me onto his lap, and—I let him kiss me. And I kissed him back." She pushed her mug away, crossed her arms. Her foot tap-tapped the leg of the table.

"I look back, and I realize that I should have known Dante would find a way to be there for me. That's who he was, who he is. He moved heaven and earth to get leave back to the States. I still don't know how he managed to convince—but it doesn't matter. I heard his duffle bag hit the floor. That's how I knew he was home. I looked up and he was standing there in his army fatigues, looking exhausted as hell—thirty-six hours on god knows how many airplanes—and there I am making out with the one guy Dante had spent half his life trying to protect me from.

"And just like that, it was done. We were done. He presented me with divorce papers before his leave was over."

Silence ensued. Stunned by Trina's recounting, Brenna could only sit and stare at the other woman. Brenna cleared her throat and found her voice. "You couldn't convince him to try and work things out?"

Trina shook her head. "There was nothing to work out. We had only gotten married because of the baby, and the baby was gone. And at the first test of faith I—I betrayed him. He put me in a box marked *fix this later,* and, when he was ready to take me out of the box, he did, and we resumed our friendship. That's the thing we were always best at." Trina cleared her throat. "The ironic thing is that the second I lost Dante I didn't want Vince anymore. Losing Dante—even though I never really had him, you know, not really—cured me of that particular stupidity, thank god."

"Were Dante and Vince always at odds?"

"Pretty much, yes. Vince's mother, Esther, thought Vince could do no wrong, and I think she resented that Dante bested Vince at everything. Dante was smarter, faster, better looking, more successful, and Esther would do whatever she could to give Vince a leg up.

"You have to understand, no matter what Dante had, Vince wanted it, and his mother made sure he got it. When I say everything, I mean everything. There wasn't a single thing Dante ever had that was really his, because he always had to give it up to Vince.

"When Dante was about fourteen he got into BMX racing. He worked his ass off all summer long at Stan's Pizza to save enough money for the bike he wanted. He didn't have it a week and Esther told him he had to let Vince ride

it, too. Vince totaled it his first time out. Dante put it in that
old box marked *fix this later*—you see the pattern?—and
when he was ready he pulled it out and took care of it. He
spent months putting the damn bike back together, buying
parts for it, restoring it. And as soon as he had it perfect, he
gave it away."

"So Vince couldn't have it."

"The only way he could protect it, he said, was to give it
away. He's been doing that with things his whole life. He
makes something better than it was, and then he lets it go,
like his restored cars." Trina leaned forward. "Do you understand what I'm trying to tell you? He's putting you in a
box, Brenna, called *fix this later*. For god's sake, don't let
him do it. Do you want to be me a year from now, irrevoca-
bly *friended*?"

"How do you propose I stop him? He doesn't want anything to do with me. I came over the other day and he—he
was kind, but very clear. He doesn't want me."

Trina threw her hands up. "But he does! I promise you,
he does. Do you love him?"

"More than anything."

"Then keep fighting." Trina leaned forward and laid her
hand over Brenna's. "He's worth it."

ᴄ⁄ᴐᴄ⁄ᴐ

Brenna followed Trina from the kitchen, almost bumping
into her when she stopped in front of the stairs and looked
up. "You know, the folder you want might be in Dante's
office. He cleaned everything up for the real estate lady—
have you met her? She looks like Marilyn Monroe."

"That's his real estate agent? Are they, uh, seeing each
other?"

Trina gave her a look. "Please. He's so hung up on you
he can't see straight. She's nice enough, but a little bit
much, you know? Anyway, take a look upstairs. I did some

laundry since I was here anyway, hanging with Pav, and I have to get it out of the dryer, so I'll be here for a few more minutes if you want to go check."

"Okay, thanks."

Brenna reached the upstairs landing, and it occurred to her that she had never visited Dante's upstairs before. She peeked into the bedroom off to the right. In her home that bedroom was a guest room, but Dante had his full of exercise equipment, none of it dusty, she noted. As in her townhome, the bathroom was straight ahead of the stairs, with a second bedroom off to the left. She flipped on the light switch and stood for a moment, taking in Dante's home office.

She perused it with a glance, ignoring the furnishings, which were scant, in favor of the framed photos covering space on bookshelves behind the desk. She took her time with these, most of which were of his grandmother and great-grandmother, she guessed. There was one of a woman with dark eyes and a smile so much like Dante's that Brenna was certain this had to be his mother. *You'd be proud of him,* Brenna thought, and set the photo back in its place.

She lifted a photo of Dante and Caleb from college, both looking cocky and victorious, decked out in their football uniforms, and another of the whole Walker clan. She smiled at the young Rebecca with her wild curls popping out from beneath a baseball cap. Dante must have taken the photo, she mused, because he wasn't in it. But there was another photo that Dante was in, looking handsome and confident in his army dress blues. He stood between Sada and Big Will, and the Walkers had their arms around him, glowing with pride, as if he were their own son. Brenna blinked back quick tears for the young Dante who never knew the love or pride of his own mother and father.

A loud thump caused her to gasp and jump backward. She spun toward the noise, only to see that Pavarotti had hurdled onto the desk. His furry body slid and he flew off with a howl, legs and tail extended like a flying squirrel.

Brenna might have laughed at the picture he made if she didn't feel so guilty for looking at Dante's personal things without his permission. The cat landed with a tumble and sprang to his feet, trotted back to the desk, and tried again. This time he leapt first into the chair, and then onto the desk, where he began head butting the desk lamp.

Brenna set the photo back where it belonged. She turned toward the desk and saw several manila folders forming a messy stack, thanks to Pavarotti.

She recovered the papers Pav had knocked to the floor and turned them into a neat pile which she set on the desk. She sat in the chair and flipped through the folders hoping to find the one containing information for the expansion of the Lump & Grind. And—*yes!*—she recognized her own looping script on the tab of the bottom folder and withdrew it from the pile.

Pavarotti head butted her hand, and she cooed at him and scratched behind his ears. Purring, he sprawled over the contents of the desk and reached his paw toward something covered by one of the papers his bulk had shifted. He batted at it with leisure, and then howled and batted it again.

"What is that, Pav?" Brenna asked and laughed at the cat. "Do you have a toy hidden under there, mister?"

She moved the paper and reached toward the item, and the smile froze on her face before melting away. Her hand recoiled as if the item blasted burning heat. She blinked, considering the possibility that it wasn't what she thought it was—*it couldn't be*—but then Pav howled again and batted at it with both paws. He turned his luminous eyes to her as if to say, "Well, I found it for you. Aren't you going to pick it up?"

Brenna tried to swallow, but the act was almost painful as her mouth and throat had gone dry. She lifted the item and stared at it, touching her fingers to the lettering etched onto the bauble: *Jack Kinkaid, CPA.* She gave the snow globe a shake and watched the glittery snow float around the jolly snowman.

Jack's voice echoed from the distance. '*You've always loved the snow!*'

Pavarotti meowed and batted at something else.

Brenna recognized the gray card stock with navy lettering, knew before she read the words that it was her brother Jack's.

Her hands trembled as she set the snow globe on the desk. She picked up the business card and stared at it, read the contact information that had ceased to be relevant the moment Jack died. She gnawed the inside of her cheek, a sure knowledge of what she would find making her slow to flip the card over. Her heart tripped in her chest and she caught her breath.

There, on the back of Jack's business card, was Brenna's name and phone number in black ink, written for Dante Caravicci in Jack's neat accountant's script.

∞∞∞

"More pesto on that sandwich, and don't forget the fresh basil," Dante said to the sous chef, and waited for the man's nod before he headed from the kitchen toward the dining room. He wished to hell he could go crash in his office and take a power nap—ten minutes with his eyes closed, even if sleep didn't come, would set him—but they had an early dinner rush going on and rest wasn't on the menu.

He'd arrived home after midnight the night before, after a hellish five hour ride from Asheville that should have taken no more than two-and-a-half. A serious accident had forced traffic to a miles-long crawl, and the heavy rain exacerbated the slowdown.

By the time he pulled into his driveway, exhaustion from the drive and emotional stress from the funeral should have been enough to drop him, but instead he'd lain in bed staring into the dark, wishing down to his marrow that Brenna was curled up beside him, and praying for sleep that didn't find him until dawn. Pavarotti woke him two hours later howling for breakfast.

"Hey, boss." Gemma appeared at Dante's side, her eyes wide. "Head's up. Brenna Kinkaid just came in."

As it always did, the mention of Brenna's name stabbed an ache into his heart. He forced a shrug and nonchalance. "Okay. So, seat her and take her order. What's the big deal?"

"The big deal is that she's not here to eat. She said she's talking to you right this second come hell or high water. And, boss—" Gemma lifted her brows and stared at him for a beat. "She looks like a hot volcano that's ready to blow."

e∽e∽

Brenna stood in front of the Bistro bar, trembling from head to toe. Whether the physical manifestation was derived from anger, trepidation, or sheer emotional distress, she didn't know. Probably all three, as she'd spent the night both weeping for, and cursing against, the damned Neanderthal and his self-righteous dismissal of their relationship. He wanted to be done with her? Fine. But she had some things to say first, and he was, by god, going to listen.

Her fiery anger lessened the moment he strode from the kitchen. He looked tired, as anyone would after returning home from a family member's funeral, and when he turned his gaze on her she was struck by the tension around his eyes and mouth. He came to stand before her and regarded her through weary and wary eyes. "What's this all about, Brenna?"

"We need to talk, and I'm not waiting anymore."

Dante glanced around them and motioned to the busy dining room. "I'm in the middle of a dinner rush, and this is hardly the time or place."

"It's never the time or place," Brenna said.

He stared at her, and she forced herself to stare back

without crying. The tears were there, damn them, burning the back of her throat and eyes, but she'd die before giving in to them now.

"This conversation is not happening here."

If he had used a different tone, she might have capitulated, but she recognized the tenor in his voice, watched his eyes slide to that black onyx that she knew must terrify many a subordinate. The last time he'd used it on her, she'd pushed back and won the battle, so she stiffened her backbone and returned his stony gaze.

Without breaking eye contact, Brenna lifted her hands and opened her fists. The snow globe lay in one hand and Jack's business card in the other.

"How the hell did you—"

"It doesn't matter how." She held her hands out and waited until he took the items from her. "Why didn't you tell me?" Her shaking voice rang out with more volume than she intended, enough that a few diners turned their heads to look.

"Brenna." His voice softened, as did his eyes. "I didn't know how to tell you."

"How about, *I'm your blind date, the guy your brother Jack said was perfect for you,* how about *that,* Dante? That would have been true, at least, instead of the lies of omission over the last five years."

"I never lied to you," Dante said, his own voice matching hers for volume.

"You knew it mattered to me! You knew it was important. That night at my house we talked about the snow globe, and Jack, and the damned blind date. You could have told me then. You *should* have told me then. But instead, you pretended to know nothing about it. You never even admitted to knowing my brother."

"I couldn't tell you."

"For the love of god, Dante, why not?" Her voice reverberated through the dining room.

"Because you didn't want it to be me!" he shouted back.

Silence reigned throughout the restaurant.

Someone lowered an eating utensil and it clicked against the plate.

Dante and Brenna stared at each other for an eternity before Dante sighed, dropped his head back, and closed his eyes. He opened them a moment later and returned his gaze to Brenna.

"Jack was my accountant," he said, his voice low and controlled, "and we were becoming good friends. We occasionally met at the Boot & Spur to watch a game and share a pitcher of beer. He talked about you. He was proud of you, Brenna."

Brenna blinked, and the tears she had held back brimmed and overflowed. Her hands shook as she wiped them from her cheeks.

"Vince was at the bar with me the night Jack wrote your number on that card. That's how he knew about the blind date." Dante cleared his throat. "My uncle had a heart attack later that night, and I brought Vince back to Asheville, stayed for about two weeks. I didn't find out about Jack's accident until I got back to Bright Hills, and by then the funeral was over. That's why I didn't attend, why we didn't meet then.

"I didn't call you at that point because the timing was obviously wrong. And then you moved in next door, and you hated me. I could have shown you the card, explained, but it seemed like an unfair advantage. And the longer I didn't tell you, the harder it became, because—" His eyes implored hers for understanding. "—I couldn't bear to see the look of disappointment on your face when you found out I was the one. I convinced myself it was kinder to let you imagine who it might be. You didn't want it to be me, Brenna."

Brenna sucked in a shaky breath that turned into a quivering sigh. "I never wanted it to be anyone *but* you."

"I could argue that, but there's no point. Nothing's changed."

"Everything's changed."

"No, it hasn't. Look, in the world I come from, when you belong to one man, say you love him, you don't let another man touch you, not the way you did. And I'm sorry, but I don't want to be in a relationship with a woman who doesn't understand that."

His words brought quick tears to her eyes.

Dante glanced out over the dining room and Brenna followed his gaze. All the Bistro diners sat in rapt attention watching the drama unfold.

"If you'll excuse me, please, I've got a restaurant full of guests to tend to," he said and began to walk away.

Brenna gulped back frustration when presented with his retreating back. "Sorry folks," she said. "But this isn't over yet."

At her words, Dante spun on his heels to regard her with a dark look. The muscle in his jaw tightened and flexed.

Good, she thought, *I'm not pissed off alone.* "You said you loved me. Was that a lie?"

"Jesus Christ, Brenna." He glared at her. "No, it wasn't a lie."

She strode forward until she was close enough to touch him, but kept her hands balled into fists at her sides. "Well, it feels like a lie. You know why? Because in the world *I* come from, when you belong to a woman, say you love her, you don't throw her away when she makes one stupid mistake!" Brenna's chest heaved with emotion and her arms gesticulated. "You get mad! You yell and scream and cry if you need to, and you fight it out, and then you talk, and maybe argue some more, and then you talk some more, and then you make up, and make love, and you forgive." She blinked her eyes to stop the tears, and blew out a quivering breath. "I did an idiotic thing that hurt you, and I'm sorry for it. I'd do anything to take it back. But I never lied to you, and I never cheated on you. I never would. Never. I made a stupid error in judgment. And if you love me, then you can't just throw me away. Love forgives, Dante. Love forgives." She wiped her tears away for the last time so that when she spoke her next words he'd see the truth of them in her eyes. "And you know what? Maybe I don't want to be in a relationship with a man who doesn't understand *that*."

She held his gaze for a few seconds, sadness rolling through her. She turned toward the door and took a few steps then stopped to look back at him. "I never belonged to you because you said I did. I belonged to you because I said I did. The choice was never yours to make, Dante. It still isn't."

ↄ/ↄↄↄ

Dante stared as Brenna walked away. Time slowed. He noted the gentle sway of her hips and the strength of her stride, the way a ray of late afternoon sunlight beamed through the Bistro's beveled front window and gleamed off her dark hair like firelight on black ice. His heart stopped when the hushed group of garden club ladies waiting at the hostess stand parted to allow her clear access to the door.

The snow globe lay heavy in his hand, and he set it on the bar top. But his fingertips touched the indentation on the business card where Jack had written Brenna's name and number, and he remembered the moment Jack handed it to him…

"Don't lose this. You're going to need it later," Jack had said with a smile. "And when you finally get around to using it, remember—she's not perfect, but then neither are you. But you know, for some reason, I think you're perfect for each other."

Dante had responded with a smart-ass comment, and Jack had replied in kind. They'd laughed, then, and Dante had stuffed the card in his pocket. By the time he found it again, Jack Kinkaid was dead.

'...*you're perfect for each other*...'

From the first moment Dante had met Brenna Kinkaid,

and every second of each day since, he'd known it was true. So why the hell was he letting her walk away?

"Brenna, wait," Dante said, unmoving, stuck in place by something unseen. "Please."

She paused with her hand on the door but didn't turn around. Her stillness shot relief blasting through him. He forced his legs to move, feeling slow and bogged down like a man battling quicksand. It took forever to reach her, and he stopped just shy of touching her.

"Jack thought we were perfect for each other. He was right."

She turned, a slow pivot. Her eyes, indigo in this light and shimmering with new tears, lifted to his. He was close enough to catch her subtle scent, the expensive stuff that reminded him of Edie's summer garden, and the underlying hint of something that was sweet and clean, and all Brenna.

Words died in his throat. He had, all at once, none and too many. At his continued silence, her eyes grew wary, and he was reminded of the day in the storeroom when he'd thrown caution to the wind and followed his instincts. And his heart.

He took her face in his hands and his mouth captured hers. A collective cheer went up throughout the restaurant when she rose to her toes, grabbed the lapels of his suit jacket to bring him closer, and kissed him back, no holds barred.

"Hey, keep it G-rated," someone hollered amid the clapping and laughter, and Dante responded by deepening the kiss for an instant, before ending it and drawing Brenna as close into his embrace as he could manage without absorbing her into his skin.

Her arms wrapped around him and she pressed her cheek against his chest. He smoothed his hand over her short cap of hair and held her head against him, knew she could feel his heart beating, beating for her.

"I love you," he said against her ear. "I know I've hurt you with the things I've said and done. I'm sorry, Brenna.

Will you forgive me for being an idiot Neanderthal?" He felt her nod against his chest, and he drew her back to look into her eyes. "Will you belong to me again?"

Brenna lifted her face up to his, her eyes luminous, and returned the words he had given to her weeks before. "I have always been yours," she said and slid her hand behind his head to draw him down for another kiss.

"See, Bertha? What'd I tell you," one of the garden club ladies said to another. "This is the best place to come for a meal. There's always some kind of a show!"

Epilogue

Brenna snuggled closer to Dante on the gazebo bench and held her left hand in front of her. She wriggled her fingers.

"What's missing from this picture?" she said.

He kissed her forehead. "You'll get your ring back on Wednesday. I know you didn't want to give it up, but it had to be sized."

Brenna sighed. "True, but I miss it. I look at it all the time."

"Be tough not to. The damn thing is huge."

"It is. And you did such a great job choosing it. Emerald cut is my favorite. I suppose my mother told you that." She drew away to look into his face. "Did you know that Rebecca doesn't even wear her diamond? She said she loves Sean, not the stuff he can buy her. Now, I love you passionately, but I'm not Rebecca. I like the bling." Dimpling, she batted her lashes and made him laugh.

He laced their hands together and smiled. "I'm aware. In fact, I'm so aware, that as it happens, Miss Kinkaid, I might have a present for you. A little something to tide you over until Wednesday."

"Is that so? Well, Mr. Caravicci, you're such a fast learner that I might just keep you around." She disengaged their hands and gave him a look. "Ready when you are."

Dante grinned and dug around in his pocket, coming up with a small box.

She smoothed her hand over the velvet lid. "It's too big for earrings, and you already bought me a spectacular ring."

Dante smiled and shrugged.

Brenna took her time lifting the lid and made the most of it, shooting looks at Dante to keep him smiling. She loved the way he watched her, more eager than she. When at last she opened the box, she gasped with delight. "My Celtic cross!"

Dante removed the necklace from the box, and Brenna bowed her head for him to secure it around her neck. "The diamonds were loose, so I had them reset. And the chain is new, stronger than the original—but I saved the old one for you, of course, if you'd rather use it. I had them replace the clasp, just in case. There," he said. "All done."

Brenna lifted her head and smiled. "The chain is perfect. I love it. This is the most thoughtful gift, Dante. Thank you."

"I'm still surprised by how much it resembles my tattoo."

"You know, the first time we met I thought you were ogling my boobs. That's why I didn't like you," she admitted, her tone rueful. "I had no idea you were just admiring my necklace. If I had known—"

"You're giving me a little too much credit," Dante said.

"So, you really were being a Neanderthal?"

"Maybe," he said, and his tone made her laugh.

Brenna stood and tugged Dante's hand. He followed her lead, and they walked down the gazebo steps to meander along the narrow pathways, enjoying the beauty of Maddie's faerie glen. The aroma of honeysuckle and roses mingled with the scents of pine pitch and loamy soil emanating from the surrounding forest. Recent rains had caused the creek to crest its banks, and the rush of water added to the peaceful ambience of the gazebo hideaway.

"It's getting dark," Dante said. "Shall we go back to the

house? We're missing our own engagement party."

As if on cue, muffled sounds of laughter filtered through the trees from Maddie and Caleb's house where Dante and Brenna's family and friends had gathered to help them celebrate. Belle's bark followed, a playful sound. A moment later, Pirate's answering '*woof*' echoed in the distance.

A tiny light flashed at the edge of the forest, and then another, and Brenna smiled. "Not yet. I want to watch the fireflies."

"Speaking of fireflies, I'm glad our wedding will be the first one to kick off Maddie's new venture," Dante said.

"Getting married here kind of feels like we're getting Jack's blessing on the whole thing, doesn't it?"

"We had Jack's blessing a long time ago," Dante reminded her.

"Hmmm." Brenna sighed and turned to press a kiss against his lips. "Thanks for making me a firefly."

"I have no idea what that means." He tugged her into his embrace. "I'm guessing it's a good thing."

"It means I love you, forever and ever. Why do you think Maddie chose that name for her new business? This whole place was built on love. Fireflies."

"I'm still not sure what bugs have to do with love, but okay."

"You're such a man." Brenna shook her head, but she smiled at him, and her voice brimmed with mischief. "You know what else it means? It means I win."

"Excuse me, what?"

"I. Win." She poked his chest with each word.

Dante scooped Brenna off her feet and spun her around. She squealed in surprise and laughed with him. Dizzy, she implored, "Put me down, you big Neanderthal. We both win."

When he set her back on her feet, she smiled up at him, lifted to her tip-toes, and spoke against his lips. "It's a win-win, Mr. Caravicci."

"Yes, Miss Kinkaid, it certainly is," he said, his face

lighting with the smile that never failed to fill Brenna's heart to overflowing.

They sealed their mutual victory with a kiss amid the luminescent glow of fireflies in the gloaming.

The End

Did you enjoy this book?
An author's success depends on
readers like you!

Please take a minute to post a review on
Amazon and Goodreads.
Your opinion will make all the difference.

Lisa loves to connect with her readers!
For the latest news, release dates, contests,
newsletter sign up, and to chat with Lisa
via her weekly blog, *Writing in the Buff,*
visit http://www.LisaRicardClaro.com.

Thanks for reading!